Circle of Animals

Circle of Animals

a novel

SADIE HOAGLAND

Red Hen Press | Pasadena, CA

Book design by Mark E. Cull.

Library of Congress Cataloging-in-Publication Data

Names: Hoagland, Sadie, author.
Title: Circle of animals / by Sadie Hoagland.
Description: Pasadena, California: Red Hen Press, 2024.
Identifiers: LCCN 2024001683 (print) | LCCN 2024001684 (ebook) | ISBN
    9781636281582 (paperback) | ISBN 9781636281599 (ebook)
Subjects: LCSH: Missing persons—Fiction. | Family secrets—Fiction. | Rape
    victims—Fiction. | Self-realization in women—Fiction. | LCGFT: Novels.
Classification: LCC PS3608.O157 C57 2024 (print) | LCC PS3608.O157
    (ebook) | DDC 813/.6—dc23/eng/20240117
LC record available at https://lccn.loc.gov/2024001683
LC ebook record available at https://lccn.loc.gov/2024001684

The National Endowment for the Arts, the Los Angeles County Arts Commission,
the Ahmanson Foundation, the Dwight Stuart Youth Fund, the Max Factor Family
Foundation, the Pasadena Tournament of Roses Foundation, the Pasadena Arts &
Culture Commission and the City of Pasadena Cultural Affairs Division, the City of
Los Angeles Department of Cultural Affairs, the Audrey & Sydney Irmas Charita-
ble Foundation, the Meta & George Rosenberg Foundation, the Albert and Elaine
Borchard Foundation, the Adams Family Foundation, Amazon Literary Partner-
ship, the Sam Francis Foundation, and the Mara W. Breech Foundation partially
support Red Hen Press.

First Edition
Published by Red Hen Press
www.redhen.org

Printed in Canada

To my mother and to my daughter,
I'm so lucky to be yours.

PART I

Marin County, California, 2005.

Sky didn't want to get out of her car. She was parked in the little lot adjacent to her office, a white stucco building that looked, Sky often thought, like a tooth. She ran her tongue on the back of her own right front tooth. Up. Down. Up. Down. A nervous habit. She had her hand on the door handle but couldn't quite muster the momentum to pull it open. After a minute of this, she let her forehead fall onto her steering wheel and her dark blond hair curtain her face. She took a deep breath.

She remembered her first few weeks at this job, when she'd show up early and practically leap out of the car. She'd been looking for a permanent job for two years that was in her expertise: landscape architecture, stonework, and patio design, really, a field so male-dominated that most of her interviews had been the result of managers assuming her name was short for Skylar, and that she was a man. They certainly were not expecting a blond woman to come into the room, with wideset green eyes, tiny freckles (like distant stars, one boyfriend had told her, to her disgust), an upturned nose, and olive skin that often made people ask her if she'd just returned from vacation. She'd often wished for a plainer, more earnest appearance.

She raised her head and watched as the owner of the company, Jerry, sweet old Jerry, pulled up and parked. He got out of his pickup truck and headed empty-handed into the office. He was short, bow-legged. A trim gray beard and forever in a faded blue ball cap, a walk like he was always in a hurry. He'd raised his eyebrows when she'd walked into the interview but had stood to shake her hand, a determined look of fairness in his eyes.

But her direct boss, Ned, had a different reaction when she first walked into the office. He tilted his head at her as if he was curious and smiled the whole time she talked. He told her about the job, that she would be helping draw up plans and visiting sites to check on progress, and suggested she drive around to look at some of their recent projects to see if it was a good fit for *her*. If it was, he said, the job was hers. She had told her best friend Liz over drinks that night that Ned seemed excited about having a woman around. She'd said, "He just seemed really progressive, you know?"

To think of that now made her stomach turn. A week into the job, Ned's motives for hiring her became clear, first in his overt leering, literally craning his neck to see her ass as she walked by, then progressing to comments of the "harmless" kind: "you look nice today, Sky," or "great shirt" when she was wearing a plain brown fitted turtleneck.

A week ago, after three months of harassment which she'd tried her best to ignore, he'd asked her out. She had been dreading that moment, had convinced herself it wouldn't come, but he had caught her at the coffee machine in the break room—a room the size of a closet that always smelled like popcorn and had flickering fluorescent lights. He didn't stutter or hesitate but spoke as if he was telling her that *he* was ready now, and that they would go out on a date. He was tall and well-built, maybe to some women he would have been handsome with his dark wave of Superman hair, but he was a little too clean-cut for Sky. He'd put his hand on the warped gray Formica counter and leaned into her space. She could smell his gum, an artificial cinnamon.

"What are you doing Friday?"

She cringed at this memory. Then undid her seat belt and pulled her phone out of her purse to check to see if she had any new messages. She thought about trying her mother again, whose advice on this subject she had not asked yet. At first because she didn't want to, but ever since he'd asked her out, she'd been ready to hear the completely off base and outdated solution her mother would deliver if only so she would know what she would *not* do. But her mother hadn't picked up.

She had told him she was busy, and he had immediately countered with, "Okay, then Saturday." She shook her head and turned to walk out of the break room. He reached out and grabbed her thin arm just above the elbow. "Well, then," he said, turning her to face him so that her coffee splashed onto her black silk blouse, "tell me when works for you." He still had a smile on his face but there was a tightness to him, a tremble of rage to one lip. A switch went off in Sky, it was an old safety switch her mother had programmed into her (*when dealing with potentially violent men . . .*). Sky relaxed, imagined a bowl of sugar, something her mother had also taught her, and smiled. She even leaned in. "Well," she said, "unfortunately for both of us, I don't date coworkers." She pronounced each and every syllable of "coworker" like it was a dirty and sultry word. Ned immediately relaxed. He let go of her arm and rubbed his chin, smiling. She turned to leave as he said under his breath, "Well, I guess I'll have to fire you then."

Now in her car she hit the call button on her flip phone and listened to it ring. Maybe her mother knew more than Sky gave her credit for, but she hadn't answered or called Sky back in a week. Though that was not unusual. Even though Sky had called her right after Ned had asked her out, saying on her voicemail she wanted to talk to her about something. Her mother was a true hippie—a "free spirit," as she liked to say—and prided herself on being liberated from the chains of the "human progress machine," including sometimes her phone, and her voicemail. Sky wasn't so sure that liberation had done much for her. Sky didn't have a father that was known to her, for one definite lack, and Edi's advice in a situation like this might just as likely be "slash that motherfucker's tires" as "why don't you just sleep with him once, and then he'll leave you alone."

She hung up on her mother's sing-songy voicemail greeting and groaned. She put her head against the window. The fog had not yet evaporated out of the bay, but there were wisps of blue peeking through. She couldn't stay in her car much longer—the windows were steaming up in the wet morning—but she couldn't take Ned's increasingly hostile advances much longer either. Ned had called her last night at 1:00 a.m. He'd clearly been drinking. He said almost nothing intelligible and when it became clear he was trying to have phone sex with Sky, she'd hung up.

Now the sky's promise of later-blue, and the whitening strength of the sun above, felt like an offense since she hadn't been able to fall back asleep. She had lain awake wondering if Ned knew where she lived, if he would drive over, if she should call the police. Quit her job. Or get a large dog. A German Shepherd, maybe.

A knock came at her car window, and she jumped. Lorenzo. Waving at her to unroll her window. She cranked it down. "Hey," she said.

"Hey, you okay?" He leaned back. "I've seen you out here for like, ten minutes." He looked around and laughed. "I thought maybe you were smoking up."

She smiled. He smiled back, his teeth brilliant white against his walnut skin. He wasn't that much older than her, but his time in the sun shone in deep, friendly creases around his eyes. Always clean shaven, and short black hair close to his head. He was, without a doubt, a handsome man.

Lorenzo had avoided her when she first started there. He'd been polite, but distant. She'd assumed he was another one offended at her gender. She'd worked around mostly Latino crews before and knew enough about *machismo*. But then a few weeks in, he quietly knocked on her office wall next to the open door and asked if she wanted to come to his house that weekend. "My wife is making lasagna." She'd happily accepted, and his house had been a warm and friendly place. His wife, Dora, looked her up and down once when she walked in and threw open her arms. The food had been delicious, and Lorenzo's three small children had kept her entertained the whole night showing her every trick they knew, every toy they had. She'd watched him around his family and knew she'd misjudged him. The Monday after that he was joking and friendly to her and when he could see she was a little surprised at the change, he said,

"Thanks for coming for dinner. My wife, she gets jealous, see, and she was worried about who is this new mujer in the office. But it's all good now, she's seen you, she knows you're way too flaca for me." He laughed, and for some reason, so did she.

Now she looked up at him and said, "No, no weed, but hey, wait up, we'll walk in together." She rolled her window up, put her phone in her bag, grabbed the extra-large latte she'd picked up so she wouldn't need to go to the break room and chance running into Ned, and stepped out.

She and Lorenzo would walk into the building together, and he'd walk with her all the way to her office, past the first door on the left—Ned's open door, and so past the most immediate problem.

When Sky was a little girl, Edi every so often used to dress her in a pretty dress and take her to Golden Gate Park and tell her: I want you to get as dirty as you can. She would push Sky toward the playground or sometimes take her to the edge of Stow Lake and nod with a huge grin on her face, her long wavy hair swinging like a pendulum.

Sky always hated it. She loved playing in the tall grass on the lip of the lake, which she imagined as a deep cup, throwing in stones, watching the ducks and the pedal boats, but on these days she never wanted to ruin the dress. It was always something her grandmother had sent, with tulle or lace and bows. Something her mother never would have bought for her. She always wanted to keep it nice, to wear it maybe someday to a restaurant, or to picture day at school, not to the park.

One day she sat toeing the dry dirt on the grassy slope by the lake, hoping her golden mother would attract some man walking by and be too distracted to notice that she was not following her instructions. The dress that day was a pale pink with lace overlay on the skirt and poufy shoulders with bows on each arm. Sky secretly loved it. So much so that she'd tried to hide it so that her mother wouldn't remember that it still needed to be grass-stained, torn, and dirtied if her daughter was ever going to be "free from the trappings of consumerism."

She fingered the lace of her sleeve, raking the damp earth of the pond bank with her bare toes and had just looked up to see a duck land a few feet from her when she felt a hard push from behind. She tried to keep her footing but stumbled forward into the lake where she landed on all fours in the mud and sand. She tried to stand up quickly, but it was too late. The dress was covered in mud and duck scum and her chin began to quiver.

Her mother was laughing, but when she saw Sky was crying, she picked her up and carried her back to their Mexican blanket. She wrapped her up in it and put her in her lap.

"Now, now, my little Sky," she said, "it's just a dress, and if there's one thing not worth crying over in this world, it's a dress. Or a man. But especially a dress."

Sky wanted to tell her that it wasn't just the dress. It was the push. It was that that had been a mean thing to do. But she just cried harder and harder and knew that she liked the way her mother was holding her, wrapped tight, rocking her a little, and humming a song Sky didn't know to remember except as something in her bones.

Sky got through the morning without much of a Ned encounter. There was the hum of a new client, and things were busy. Ned had winked at her from across the room, but she managed to duck him in the hall by detouring to the bathroom. She'd sat on the closed toilet with her pants on, briefly chanting to herself, "I hate my life, I hate my life, I hate my life."

Jerry came to get her after lunch to go on a site visit. He wanted to take her up to the new client's house and walk around the yard "as is" so she could get a feel for his overall vision—a Japanese tea garden feel, he said, but not exactly.

She climbed into his truck, and they started the drive up to San Anselmo, not too far north of Sausalito, where the office was based. Sausalito was also where Sky had found an apartment and signed a lease when Jerry had called to offer the job.

Jerry's truck always smelled leathery sweet, like old pipe smoke, but the sun was out now and Sky was relieved to be out of the office. While Jerry was a pretty quiet guy, they had a good conversation about possible stone choices for the patio. He told her a little about the clients. "He's a retired orthopedist, one of those real bigheaded guys that thinks he needs a fucking koi pond and a putting green, which I talked him out of—she's nice though."

Sky nodded. Jerry would never say anything bad about another woman in front of her. Sky didn't know if this made him progressive, but it certainly was preferable to anything she'd seen before in this business. At her first job, an internship set up by her grad program, she'd been teased in every way. It was either about her body, or some sort of statement that connoted that she must be a man or a lesbian to be in this field. During one terrible month she spent in a masonry outside Vacaville, one of her coworkers put Tabasco in her coffee. She'd felt like she was at a nightmare summer camp and quit not because one coworker was an idiot, but because when she thought of it, she realized it could have been any one of the five guys she worked with who did it. And at each job there had been some unwanted flirting—one guy who constantly and painfully referred to her as "Juliet" and himself as "Romeo," which made her gag—but nothing as directed and prolonged as Ned.

When they arrived at the house, Sky saw it was one of those lovely Spanish-style homes, with a red tile roof and tan stucco sides. Lapis blue tile lined the walkway to the door. The wife opened the huge old oak door and seemed pretty disinterested in the whole project, but promised to keep her two beagles inside while they walked around and studied the grounds.

Jerry pointed to a corner, currently a patch of dry grass and a broken fence. "I was thinking here we'd do a small water feature. Thinking limestone. Not a koi pond, since that would feel too big back here"—Jerry winked—"but a little gurgle."

Sky nodded. "Yes, limestone would be good. You said he wanted a Japanese look? So clean square lines here rather than a more natural stone stack?"

"Yes, and I think we will put a Japanese maple here . . ." Jerry pointed to the ground adjacent to the future "gurgle."

"What would you say to something like a ledgestone in ash? It'd be cleaner and darker. Might compliment the wood fencing better? We could even incorporate some blue tile to speak to the front of the house."

Jerry nodded and smiled. "I knew I hired you for a reason." He turned back to the house. "I think a path of the same stone from the porch to the water feature, with grass on the left, she wants some for the dogs, and mulch landscaping on the right. Some succulents."

Plants weren't her specialty, but Sky nodded. Jerry, Sky had noticed, liked to run his plans by her before he drew them up. She wondered if he had done this with anyone else before she arrived. His wife had died a few years earlier; maybe she was the one before Sky to ask questions, give him ideas, to be the listener. Either way, it felt good to have her opinion valued.

Afterward they drove back to the office listening to the radio—country music and ads for carpet sales—without saying much. But as they got off the freeway, Jerry turned down the radio and he cleared his throat. "Sky, I wasn't sure when you came on how it would all work out." Sky turned toward him to see he was trying not to redden. "But you've been great to have around." He squinted at her briefly. "You've got a good eye and a good head. I sure hope you stick it out."

Sky looked at him and nodded. She waited, but he didn't say anything more. She'd hoped that he would continue. Tell her he was going to do something about Ned. There was no way he didn't know, right? He, and definitely Lorenzo, had to have heard his comments, noticed his leers. Sky chewed her lip, but Jerry didn't continue, just nodded at the road, and neither of them said anything after that.

When Sky got off work there were three voicemails from her mother's neighbor, Janet. She groaned. The last time Janet had called, it was to tell her that her mother was sunbathing nude on the back stoop again (*for even Jesus to see*, as Janet had put it) and that if Sky couldn't come over and talk a shirt on her, then she'd just have to call the police.

Sky pulled out of the work parking lot and put the voicemails on speaker.

11:32 a.m.: "Sky, honey, it's me, Janet. Why don't you give me a call?"

1:00 p.m.: "Sky, dear, it's Janet again, listen, it's about your mother, that's why I'm calling, so call me just as soon as you get this."

4:00 p.m.: "Sky, it's Janet. Something very strange is happening at your mother's. For one, she's not there. And hasn't been. I don't want to worry you, but maybe you should head over here and check it out."

Sky groaned as she hung up and dialed her mother. This time straight to voicemail, like the phone was off or dead.

"Mom, it's me. Call me. Janet is on one again." She paused. "And I've been wanting to talk to you about something." She added this last part because it was true, but also because it was an extra incentive for her mother to call her back. Also, when she did finally talk to her, her mother wouldn't accuse her of "not having tried hard enough" to tell her.

In the meantime, she'd have to go over there. She sighed and switched lanes so she could head across the Golden Gate Bridge to her mother's house in Balboa Terrace. At least she'd be going against traffic and the fog remained out in the bay, waiting until dark to let down its breathy hair and spread its tendrils over the bridge, through the city.

As she drove, she was irritated but not surprised. Her mother was probably just on another one of her whims, though it had been years since she called Sky from Reno or Oregon to say she'd hitched a ride, or met a biker, or just really had to "get away from the repression of the city." Sky had assumed that phase was over, that she was settling into something like her age. But now she wasn't so sure.

Her mother's neighborhood, Balboa Terrace, was eclectic. The hills were not quite as steep as in other parts of the city, and the streets were lined tightly with mostly stucco block houses in pastel colors, some with splotches of black mold and dead lawns revealing the long-standing drought. But on every street, there were a few small Victorian houses, and her mother's was one of these. Painted a Kelly green with white trim that was now chipping away in small, ragged horizons, it stood out. The porch was covered in potted plants, some alive, some dead. The bay breeze batted at a faded turquoise dream catcher. When Sky pulled up in front of it, Janet came out of her own perfectly white stucco hacienda-style house to meet her. She had a tight pale face and wore a pink silk button-down with slacks. Her hair was white and coifed flawlessly.

When Sky was little, she used to sometimes want Janet for a mother. Janet, who was so nice and normal and who made cookies without pot in them that kids could eat and who seemed to pity Sky. It wasn't until she was older that she realized why her mother called Janet a bitch—when she realized that that pity was really condescension. But she looked tired today and was wringing her hands as she approached Sky with what seemed like real concern.

"Sky, honey, I called," she said.

"I know." Sky got out of the car. "That's why I'm here." She gave Janet a half-hug out of habit.

Janet hooked her arm and led her up the steps to her mother's door as she started talking. "Well, honey, let's see, it was almost a week ago, late in the night, and I noticed that your mother's lights were on. Like every single one of them. I thought it was strange but thought maybe she was up cleaning or something, I know she said she was having sleeping problems lately, so I didn't think too much of it. I left to go see the grandkids in Santa Clara the next morning but then I didn't get back until last night, five days later, and all the same lights are on. And they stayed on all night, and all day today. I knocked and rang too but no answer. I've tried her cell like a hundred times, but no answer. So, I just really want to make sure she's all right, so I called you."

Sky listened as they walked up the steps to her mother's house. Janet was right, she could see that a strange number of lights were on considering it wasn't yet dark, and considering her mother only ever had one on at a time. She tried the door as Janet said, "It's locked."

Then she rang the bell.

As she sat there waiting for a respectful minute before getting her key out, she noticed a stir inside her—a strange and unsettling feeling. It reminded her of the feeling of sitting in the dark of a theater right before the show begins. The anticipation she got when her mother cooked up some new and wild plan. She hadn't felt this way in years, but still she recognized the way in which the excitement was short-lived—and was immediately followed by dread.

When Sky was in the fifth grade, a secretary came to get her out of class. She was a sweet older woman that kept a bowl of butterscotch candies on her desk, and she crouched down to Sky's eye level and said, "Honey, your mama is on the way. Your grandmother . . . well, it's about your grandmother, so you get your things and come on down to the office and wait with me."

Sky went and got her backpack and headed down the hall. She had only one memory of her grandmother; she and her mother had had a falling out and didn't speak to each other. Sky had met her once when she was about four, she thought. Her memory was of a thin woman in silk and pearls, hair perfectly done like Janet's, with a slight Southern accent. She remembered her grandmother bringing her a doll. She remembered her mother telling her to say thank you and hug her. Every one of her birthdays a package came for her from her grandmother, one of the nice dresses and sometimes a toy, and her mother let her open them but there was never a card, or never one that she saw.

Still, she hoped the woman was all right as she sat on a chair too big for her in the front office and waited for her mother to arrive. The secretary kept looking up and smiling sadly at her. When her mother finally appeared, they both jumped up. Sky watched as her mother walked right in with purpose, looking unusually kempt wearing a black turtleneck sweater over a long floral skirt, and large black sunglasses. She didn't take the glasses off as she came in the office. Not even when she signed Sky out.

The secretary stood up. "Ma'am," she said, "I'm so sorry for your loss."

Her mother nodded and said, "Sky will be out for a few days."

"Of course, dear, of course. I'll let her homeroom know." And with that, her mother reached out to grab Sky in a tight embrace before leading her out of the office. Her mother's body was taut and shaking as they walked down a hall the pale pink color of dental molds, with the same hyper-sanitized smell. They left the building, and it wasn't until they were outside in the winter sun that Sky realized that Edi was not crying. She was laughing. Or trying not to.

Sky looked at her in horror as they got in the car. "What's wrong with Marguerite?" she asked.

Her mother pushed her sunglasses up to reveal a clear face, shining eyes. "What?" Edi looked at herself in the rearview mirror, ran a finger reflexively under her right eye. "Oh god, nothing," she said and looked at Sky, whose lip was starting to quiver. "Oh Jesus, honey, nothing's happened, at least not that I know of." She turned toward Sky and brushed a piece of hair from her face. "I just said she died so I could get you for a few days." Her mother's face lit up again as she gestured to the back of the old Saab hatchback. There were two suitcases.

"You and I are going to have some fun!"

Sky bit the inside of her cheeks hard so she wouldn't actually cry as her mother started the car and began talking. "I woke up this morning with the blahs, and I couldn't shake 'em. Everything just feels so routine and boring lately, you know? So, I called Deb, and of course Deb always has something cooking, and there's this music festival going on outside Humboldt, up in the redwoods, so it seemed like just what we needed. You and I are going to have a blast: we will sleep under the stars and meet new people and hear some great music and dance, dance, dance!"

Sky heard Edi as if from afar, a white noise inside her head mirrored in the brightness of the day outside her school building. She turned away from her mother, still trying not to cry as they turned onto the road. She was glad her grandmother was okay, even if she didn't know her. She had fantasies sometimes that her grandmother had to move in with them and that she was like Maria from *The Sound of Music*, and she cleaned their house and made them meals and helped Sky with her homework and made Sky go to bed early and made her mother quit smoking pot. She had always known it would never happen, but now it seemed especially impossible. Now that her mother had lied to her school and told them her grandmother was dead, it became apparent to Sky that she might as well be dead, packages or no.

Her mother squeezed Sky's knee with excitement and turned the radio on. "Hurdy Gurdy Man" was on, and her mother turned the volume up. Singing and slapping the steering wheel with her palms, her long-fingered hands elegant-looking even in this gesture.

Sky knew that most of her classmates would envy her. But Sky envied them. She didn't even bother mentioning to her mother that she had a math test tomorrow, or that she didn't really like camping or dancing in front of other people. She knew she'd spend the next few days trying not to be noticed, reading her book in the tent, and trying to sleep.

Her mother looked at her one more time, her beautiful smile bright and sharp, and whispered, "This is going to be so great."

Sky hoped Edi had remembered to bring Juju, the little bear Sky slept with every night, but she was willing to bet she hadn't.

Sky opened her mother's door and instantly felt the same rush of home she always felt—the smell of citrus and stale incense, of old wood and her mother's vinegar-based cleaning routine. She stood there for a moment listening and knew right away the house was empty. She knew it like she knew her own body. But from behind her Janet called out, "Hello, Edi?" and Sky felt her reach around her to push open her mother's door. Her jaw tightened with a tug of impatience. She thought about telling Janet to go home, that her mother was her own personal disaster, and not a new one. She wanted to be alone to discover whatever it was her mother was up to.

But it turned out there was little to discover. Janet, Sky could tell, had been expecting to find her mother with a broken hip in the bathtub, or worse. But all they found was nothing new—her mother's mess and all the lights on. They walked through the house, and everything was as usual. Clothes on the floor, bed unmade. Sky called her mother's name once but again already knew it was useless. She could still feel the house's emptiness.

They ended their search in the kitchen, where the dishes piled in the sink were dirty with what looked like tomato sauce. They were bone dry. Sky opened the fridge and pulled out a bottle of iced tea. She didn't offer one to Janet, who stood in the small kitchen with her arms crossed.

"Well, this *is* odd," Janet said, clearly peeved. Annoyed at Edi for making her worry. Or maybe annoyed that nothing exciting was happening, after all.

"Listen, Janet, thanks for calling me," Sky said. "I'm going to hang out for a bit and make some calls and find out where she is and I'll let you know as soon as I do, but she's probably just gone on a little jaunt." Sky made an effort to soften her tone and added, "You know how she is."

"All right, Sky, you know what's best." Janet threw up her hands. "But hon, I do think I should mention this in case it's important." She crossed her arms again and stepped closer to Sky. "Things haven't been quite as usual for a few months around here."

Sky waited for her to continue and took a sip of her iced tea.

"There's been some strangers, especially this one, coming around." Sky hadn't thought of it before, but she supposed that Janet did "know" all of Edi's friends and boyfriends after all these years, knew which cars on the street belonged to whom.

Sky nodded at her to keep going.

"He's got long brown hair he wears in a bun and a beard with a little gray in it. And, and this is odd, he wears white a lot. At first, I thought he was a house painter, but I think it's more new age than that. Like one of these Middle Eastern long shirt things."

Suddenly and involuntarily every muscle in Sky's body tensed. Sky could picture the man Janet described perfectly, almost as if from memory. *The man, a grassy hill, her mother screaming for Sky to get in the car.* She shivered.

Janet noticed. "Are you all right, dear?"

Sky nodded. "Tea's cold." And she took another big gulp.

"So that seems right up your mother's alley—but then there's this other guy, real clean-cut. Not really your mother's type. And young, real young, like your age. Maybe a bit older. Real businessman type. Looks like maybe a lawyer?"

Sky didn't know who either person could be, but she cleared her throat and said, "Okay, thanks, Janet, for letting me know." She wanted Janet out now. She moved toward the front door so that Janet would follow.

"Please let me know as soon as you hear anything, or find out where she is." Janet threw up her hands. "Just drives me crazy, this behavior." She trailed off at the end and gave Sky an apologetic look before reaching out to squeeze her hand. "Bye, sweetie."

"Bye, Janet." Sky closed the door and waited a beat, listening to the quiet behind her. Half expecting her mother to pop out and say, "Is that goddamn woman gone?" Sky chuckled briefly at a recent memory of her mother calling Janet a "narc" one day. Her mother was smoking a joint out the kitchen window, and Janet had knocked "to say hi to Sky, I saw her car out front."

Sky walked through the old house one more time, turning off lights as she went. If she was honest, the only thing strange about this "disappearance" was the fact that the lights were on. Edi was a staunch conservationist and usually had only one light in the house on at a time, whichever one was above her head. Suddenly it occurred to her that if her mother had left, there was a good chance she'd have left the door unlocked. Perhaps someone had gone through the house after she'd left? Sky headed up the narrow stairs, the wood worn smooth and curved with decades of footprints. She walked first into her mother's bedroom. There was her mother's wrought-iron bed, faded tribal pattern sheets, unmade. Which was normal. *Nothing* seemed to be out of order, or out of the disorder which suited her mother, she thought as she walked toward Edi's mother-of-pearl jewelry box on the table. It was still spilling over with large chunky necklaces. Lots of turquoise. Sky let her finger reach out to touch the giant jade Buddha at the end of one necklace. It was a happy, fat Buddha who looked a little cartoony. She remembered sitting on her mother's lap and rubbing Buddha's belly "for luck" when she was little. She rubbed his tummy now, just a stroke or two with her thumb, then tucked his beads back into the box and turned to the bed. There was a small piece of paper on the bedside table.

Sky walked over to it, and as she did, she kicked her mother's glass bong that sat on the floor by the bed.

"Shit." She leaned down to pick up the green and pink swirled glass and shook her head. It reeked of resin. She felt an ancient irritation.

The bong water had spilled onto the hardwood floor and Sky went into the hall bathroom to grab a frayed pink hand towel. Everything looked right there, too. Her mother's toothbrush sat at the edge of the sink. The claw-foot tub was dry. She went back to towel the floor, which brought her eye level with the small note on the bedside table. Before she had thought about it, she had picked it up and read it. "Love you. R." Sky immediately put the note back where it was. R. Roger. The closest thing her mother had to a real life partner. She would call him when she got back to the kitchen, and she'd get back there as quick as possible. Reading the note, being in Edi's bedroom made her feel now that she was invading her mother's privacy. And again, a wave of irritation came over her. If her mother communicated like a normal person, Sky wouldn't be wandering through her house in the first place.

There were only a few more lights to turn off upstairs. She turned off the light in her mother's study, the guest room—why was *that* light on? And then paused in the door of her old bedroom. There were still some of her things on the shelves of the bookcase, her soccer and softball trophies, a track medal. A bent school photo from freshman year, when her hairstyle was a regrettable bob cut, tucked into a glassless frame. Her bed was a mess. Then Sky felt the breeze and turned to the window in the corner.

It was open. The window sat above a postage-stamp patch of lawn but directly faced a steep, almost vertical uphill in the back that some former owner had once terraced, but that had long been overgrown. Looking out the window was like looking at a green wall. Sky stared at the darkening palms and ferns of the terrace that gaped through the frame for a moment before she felt her spine tense and straighten. Why would that window be open? What if someone *was* in the house?

She stood absolutely still. Listening. Her heart beat faster. She glanced toward her closet. It was open and not big enough to hide someone if the door was open. She wished now she hadn't sent Janet away.

"Sky," she said aloud. Both a reprimand and a reassurance. She didn't *really* think there was anyone in the house, but also thought perhaps she'd make those calls from her own house later tonight. She walked across the room, leaned over the bed, and closed the window. Looked out through the dirty glass, shivered once, and turned around.

She wasn't entirely surprised that the bed was mussed. When she was younger, she had often caught her mother napping in her room when she came home from school. The afternoon sun from her tall window bathed her bed in buttery light and made it the warmest spot in the house.

It was getting dark outside, and Sky was getting hungry. After turning all the lights off upstairs, she headed down to the kitchen and opened the fridge, grabbed a piece of vegan cheese that tasted like paper. She held it in her mouth while she gathered her purse and her keys. Then she walked out of the house, pushing the button in on the doorknob so it would lock behind her. Wondering if her mother would be locked out when she came back. Feeling an ever-so-brief moment of satisfaction at the fantasy of her mother calling her to come over here with the key. Her telling her mother, "Well, sorry I locked it. I had no idea where in the hell you were."

Once in her car, Sky drummed her fingers on the wheel for a minute. She'd go home and call Deb first, then Rog. If they didn't know where her mother was, then she might worry. No, before she'd worry, she'd call her Liz. Liz was a level-headed lawyer and as frank as they come. She'd help Sky figure things out and probably make her laugh while doing it.

She briefly thought about work tomorrow and felt her stomach turn. Maybe she'd call in sick. Tell them her mother was missing. No, she didn't want to explain this to them. Give Ned anything personal on her.

She sighed and started the car, noticing as she pulled out that Janet was sitting in her front window, turned toward her. She held her hand up but was sure that Janet couldn't see her now that it was fully dark.

⁂

When Sky was a child, she had a reoccurring dream. In the dream she woke up, got out of her bed, made cereal, and was sitting in the kitchen when she suddenly realized, one way or another, that her mother wasn't sleeping in her bedroom. Sky would then wander the house, room to room, looking for her. She knew she wouldn't find her—she recognized the dream once she was in it—but still wandered room to room over and over again. She never left the house in the dream, which was one of the reasons the dream was frustrating. A small, waking part of her would be willing herself to go outside, check for her mother on the porch, go to Janet's, but her body seemed destined to follow the same path each time, up and down the stairs, like a mouse trained to repeat the same maze. The dream varied in that sometimes she'd find something else.

Once, a lioness lay on her mother's bed, licking her paws calmly. Another time, a giant snake had come in through the top of the kitchen window, and another time her second-grade teacher, Ms. May, was getting out of the shower, and slammed the door in Sky's humiliated face when she peeked in.

Whenever she woke up from this dream, she'd tiptoe down the hall and open her mother's door. She'd watch the lump in her mother's bed and make sure it was breathing, and then she'd go back to her room and lie in bed, a strange sense of dread heavy on her skin.

The last time she'd had the dream, she was in college and sleeping next to a psych major named Colin. She woke up sweating in a poorly ventilated dorm room and had made the mistake of trying to explain the dream to him.

Colin had a small dark goatee and gray eyes, and was sweet, but Sky knew it wouldn't last past summer break. She'd gotten pretty annoyed as he explained to her that she probably was really afraid of abandonment. Probably to do with her absent father.

She resisted the urge to punch him, nodded silently, and moved to get dressed. She had finals to study for, she said. But when she walked home across campus, the early morning fog dripping off the trees, she'd wondered if he'd been right. If her deepest insecurities were that obvious.

The next morning Sky once again sat in her car listening to the engine click and creak as it cooled. The fog was thick in the bay that morning and she watched as water droplets on her windshield swelled and then rolled down the glass in tears. Sky had been on a run in the hills above her apartment building that morning, her favorite part about living in Sausalito, and now, after a quick breakfast and a shower, her body was beginning to chill. She shivered.

She sighed and pulled her phone out of her purse to check it one more time.

No messages, no texts, no missed calls.

She had called Deb on her drive home the night before and had gotten some woman she didn't know who said she was watching Deb's dogs. Deb was in South America, she said. Left about a month ago. Sky had told the woman she was looking for her mother, Edi Richard. She'd asked her if Deb was traveling with anyone.

"Nah," the woman had said, "she's on a spiritual journey so she definitely went alone far as I know." The woman had coughed and said something to one of Deb's dogs before she added, "And it wouldn't have been Edi she took, I know that." Sky had felt suddenly disoriented by this comment. What did she mean that she wouldn't have taken Edi? Who was this woman, and did she know her mother? Or where her mother was? Before she could ask anything, the woman said, "But good luck to you," and hung up the phone.

Roger, on the other hand, had answered. His voice was warm when she said, "Hey, Roger, it's Sky." She'd always liked Roger and had wished for a long time that he and her mother would get more serious. She didn't ever imagine it would happen, but she had hoped Roger would move into the old house with her mother, help her take care of it. Perhaps also to help Sky take care of her mother. To prevent the exact situation she was now calling about.

"What's up, sweetheart? Is your mom okay?" Roger's voice went higher with concern. Again, she felt a wave of tenderness.

"I don't know, I was hoping you could tell me where she is?"

Roger listened as she told him about Janet's call, the house, the phone being dead. She tried to keep her tone light, but felt this lightness more and more as a performance as it sunk in that neither Deb nor Roger had the answers she'd assumed they would.

The image of the open bedroom window, the thin curtain waving, came into her head.

"Shit, that's kind of weird," Roger said. "But Sky, I gotta be honest with you, your mom and I haven't talked in a bit. A couple of months ago she said, well, she wanted . . ." He trailed off and didn't finish the sentence even when Sky waited a minute.

"Oh," Sky said, "I'm sorry, Roger." She felt like she'd been slapped. Why hadn't her mother told her?

"Me too, love, me too. Call if you need anything."

She pictured him in his treehouse. A geodesic dome in Sonoma County he'd built in the '70s that now would go for a fortune. The last time she'd been there, it was for her mother's fiftieth birthday party. Roger had made pot brownies and served matcha tea and had a friend playing live sitar. Sky had brought Liz and Liz could barely contain her giggles. "It's just *too* much," she'd whispered. But then Liz had ended up making out with a woman she met, almost twice their age, which Sky would give her shit about later.

So her last call was to Liz, who talked to her for an hour, cheered her up, and told her to light Ned's car on fire.

She'd said, "Sky, this is your mother. This is *what* she does. Jupiter is probably in retrograde, or whatever. In two days, she'll knock on your door with a sunburn, a new cat or, at worst, a new boyfriend, and tell you where the hell she's been. Don't spend another second of your life trying to take care of this woman who doesn't need taking care of, okay?"

Sky thought of those words now as she once again hit her mother's number on her phone. Straight to voicemail again, but this time her mother's cheery voice had been replaced by a computerized voice telling her that the voice mailbox of the customer she had reached was full. A new tug of irritation replaced any worry—her mother *never* cleared her voicemail box—and she used that momentum to throw her phone in her old leather purse, get out of her car, and walk into work.

The office was quiet when she came in. She could hear the buzz from the refrigerator in the break room but not much else. She stopped to listen and could make out faint typing coming from the back office where Jerry's assistant Beverly sat.

Beverly was mostly retired and worked just three mornings a week now, spending time with her grandkids the other days and always bringing photos to show Sky. Sky liked her, but Beverly would always say things like "It's so nice to have another girl to talk to" as she handed her a stack of photos of messy toddlers. As if Sky's gender immediately made her interested in kids. What it did make her, she knew, was too polite to show her disinterest.

Sky walked past Ned's open office door without turning to check, his truck hadn't been in the parking lot. She put her things on her desk and went to check in with Beverly.

"Where is everybody?" she asked and leaned on the faux wood-paneled wall just inside Jerry's office suite.

Beverly started a little, "Oh, Sky, hon, it's just you. Didn't Ned call you?" Sky shook her head.

"There was an accident on the Henderson site, of course Lorenzo is beside himself and so everyone is out there helping. Young man fell off the pergola they were building out there, think he'll be all right but maybe a broken leg."

"Shit. No, no one called. I'll call Jerry's cell and make sure they don't need me to do anything."

"'Kay, doll." Beverly went back to her typing.

When Sky tried Jerry, he answered and ranted about OSHA for one minute, then told her to get going on those plans for the orthopedist and hold down the fort. Then he hung up.

Sky doodled some sketches of the property for an hour but had just sat down at the drafting table to draw in earnest when she heard the door and heavy footsteps. A whistle. Ned. She listened as he went into his office. She'd managed to avoid being alone with him since he'd asked her out, she'd said no, he'd gotten aggressive, and she had the stupidest survival tactic ever of flirting with someone who already didn't get the hint. She felt a turn in her stomach as she listened to him shuffle papers, and felt sicker when Beverly poked her head in.

"Have a good day, doll." She had her red wool coat on and was ready for the damp cool outside.

Sky heard the bells jingle on the front door and just as she'd feared, he was behind her a minute later.

"Hey, sexy." She turned but he was already too close for her to turn her body around to face him. She was pinned between him and her drafting table and could feel his breath on her ear. She cleared her throat and squirmed as his hands came up to her waist.

"What's up, ticklish?"

"Ned, no, Ned, I know I probably confused you the other day . . ." She tried again to turn around. "But really, this isn't what I want . . ." She tried to push his hands off her waist again and thought she'd succeeded when one hand released her but then he turned her around and grabbed her chin.

His mouth was sour and hard, he grabbed her breast even harder. She felt like she was choking. She started shaking her head back and forth, trying to purse her lips against his, against his tongue.

Finally, she twisted enough to get her mouth free. "Stop," she said, but his hands stayed on her so the second time she yelled it.

"Stop!"

He pushed her back against the table and she could see his face was beet red. He wiped his mouth as she regained her balance.

"What's your fucking problem, bitch?"

He took a step toward her and grabbed her wrist. He went to kiss her again and she turned her head away. Squirming with her whole body against him, she knocked over the lamp swung above the drafting table. He had his hands on her pants now, was trying to undo them. She couldn't breathe.

She knew she had to scream, to fight harder, but her brain was a step behind everything happening. He kissed her again and she bit his lip.

A flare of anger lit up his eyes and Sky knew that she was looking at something damaged. Something animal. She turned to run, but Ned grabbed her blouse and then they heard the bells of the door. A homey jingle.

He let her go, two of the buttons from her blouse were gone, and his sudden release made her fall to her knees.

Sky didn't bother to stand up or straighten her shirt. Both of them were breathing hard when Lorenzo stopped in the door.

"Hey," he said, and Ned looked to him, but he was looking at Sky. "Everything okay?"

Ned glared at Sky and walked out of the room, pushing Lorenzo a little with his shoulder.

"Sky, you okay? What the fuck just happened?" Lorenzo bent down to help her up. He was whispering but pointed to her shirt, picking up the pearl-colored buttons off the thin carpet.

Her whole body was frozen. She wanted to speak, but she couldn't.

The bells on the door rang again and they both listened as Jerry said something to Ned down the hall. Sky looked at her hands, they were shaking, she looked back up at Lorenzo.

"Why is your shirt . . . Ned's lip was bleeding . . ."

When Jerry poked his head in, she had straightened her shirt, but she knew she was still shaking. Speechless.

"Goddamn, we got to get that claim filed today. That kid's hospital bills are going to come back on us, 'cause there's an ice cube's chance in hell that he's got insurance."

Lorenzo cleared his throat and looked to Jerry, then looked back to Sky. He knows, Sky thought, Lorenzo has always known. Suddenly she wondered if she was the first woman to work there. Why didn't they replace Beverly with someone full-time? Had they tried before? She wanted to melt with a combination of humiliation and anger.

"What the fuck are you two doing? Sky, did you get those plans going? I'm thinking . . ." but Jerry trailed off when Lorenzo stepped between her and Jerry as he walked to look over Sky's shoulder.

"She hasn't had time, boss," Lorenzo said. "Someone's been bothering her. Maybe she'll tell you about it." He gave Sky one last look, a closed-lipped frown, and left the room.

"Sky?" Jerry asked, rubbing his eyes. She managed to find her stool and sit down but he stayed standing there. Looking at her like, she imagined, like, *please don't make my day any harder.* Sky heard the bells again, Lorenzo was getting out of there, and next thing Ned was in the doorway. Hands on hips and plain-faced, lip fat but clear of blood, like nothing had happened. Looking at her like, *I dare you.*

Jerry turned to Ned, frowning when Sky heard herself starting to speak. Her voice was hoarse. The fluorescent lights above her felt like heat lamps. She leaned her torso on the drafting table for support. "I . . ." was all she managed.

"Sky, are you okay?" Jerry looked again from her to Ned, and back. Tell him, she said to herself, say, Ned won't leave me alone. He just . . . he just . . . what did he do? Her face burned with it; her mouth was dry. Her skin felt like an itchy foreignness, like it belonged to someone else. She started to speak.

"I . . . He . . ." Ned looked at her with thinned eyes, his rage pulsing scarlet in his cheeks.

She thought about his call in the night.

Her fear that he'd show up at her house. And then her mouth was moving, and she was saying, "My mother is missing."

It sounded completely constructed, but as soon as she said it, she knew it was true. But she also felt a hard pit form within, a hatred of herself for saying it. For being once again sugar for Ned. Making it easy. She was afraid. She was weak. She pictured a peach, soft and bruised with this wrinkled, ugly, sharp pit deep inside sticking to the strings of sweet fruit. She felt its rough ridges turn her stomach.

"What?" Jerry asked and she could tell he was torn between disbelief and his relief that she'd hadn't accused Ned of anything. She could feel him wanting to mutter another offhanded "goddammit." But he bit his lip, lifted off his blue cap just enough to wipe his forehead.

"What?" Ned seemed thrown. Eyes wild in a different way. This made Sky straighten up.

"She's missing." Sky turned and started rolling up the drafting paper she'd been working on. "I . . ." But she couldn't say anything else. Her face felt rigid. Her skin was hers again now, but prickling all over and she was acutely aware of how much she was sweating under her arms. She had to get out of there. Get away.

Jerry stepped forward and put his hand on Sky's arm lightly. "Sky, you okay? What do you mean, *missing?*"

"That's all I know. Her house was open, lights all on, no one knows where she is. She's not answering her phone and I can't leave a message . . ." Sky turned to Jerry, thinking she might cry but then she caught Ned's stare behind her. Nothing came from him, no sympathy, no anger.

"I have to get out of here." She blindly shoved the drafting paper in her bag, grabbed her phone, a few pens for some reason, and pushed past Jerry to the door.

"Take a few days," Ned called out behind her.

She couldn't tell if it was an offer or a threat.

"What the hell is going on . . ." she heard Jerry start as she pushed out the door. Gulping in the faint sea smell, the cold fog, she practically ran to her car and for once didn't sit in it when she got in, but pulled out of the parking lot as fast as she could.

When they had pulled into EarthFest, the Humboldt music festival her mother had pulled her out of school for, they were greeted by a man with no shirt or pants on, only dirty white briefs, wandering through the parking lot selling rainbow necklaces he had braided out of embroidery thread.

"No thanks, love." Her mother had waved him on while Sky hid her head in the car, pretending to go through her bag, embarrassed by his nudity. "Sky, let's leave our stuff here and go find Deb's camp and then we will come back and get it, okay?"

As they walked into the grounds, Edi squeezed her hand. "There'll be other kids here, I'm sure."

But as they wandered through the market tents, people selling goat milk soap and essential oils and handmade flutes, Sky saw only sunburned teenagers and half-naked older people. She saw her first bellybutton piercing on a girl about four years older than her. The girl was freckled with two dusty braids and was skinny and hipless; she wore wide leg jeans that hung low. A red bandana-patterned crop halter top over tiny breasts. She saw Sky and smiled, patted her head as she walked by her, like Sky was a puppy.

Behind the market was a sea of tents you had to wander through, and beyond that a crowd scattered about on blankets and on the grass, and beyond that an empty stage. It took them about fifteen minutes to find Deb.

"CHICAS!" she'd yelled. Deb was short and had black curly hair, she stood waving both arms at them and as they picked their way over blankets and chairs and napping bodies, she kept talking. "THOUGHT YOU'D NEVER GET HERE!"

Then her arms were around both of them, Sky's face shoved against her large breasts. Sky smelled patchouli and pot and body odor but still was a little relieved. She did like Deb. When her mother got down—or got the blahs, as she called them—Deb seemed to take up the slack and pay extra attention to Sky. One week the year before, when her mother was especially quiet and moody, Deb came and picked up Sky and took her for a chocolate milkshake. Then she let Sky pick a movie up from the video rental store to take home and watch at her place. She and her mother didn't have a video rental membership anymore, because her mother couldn't ever seem to remember to take the movies back and it had gotten too expensive. She'd picked *E.T.* and Deb had said, *Perfect*, making Sky glow.

"How are my girls? I'm so glad you came; this is going to be so fun. It'll be just what the doctor ordered." Deb kissed the top of Sky's head and winked at her mother. Then she showed them the old red teepee she'd brought. The floor was lined with dreaded sheepskin rugs and bits of carpet scraps and wool blankets. There was an incense burner in the middle and the air was too warm. Worst of all for Sky, it was too dark to read in. The daylight diminished in the thick red canvas, as if they were inside a heart, Sky thought, or some other, less glamorous organ.

But within hours Sky found that if she lay near the flap with a corner of it gathered open, she could read. She'd wished her mother had brought her one of her own books, but instead she'd read the rest of what they were reading for school, a YA novel about the Great Depression. She didn't want to wander around much; she didn't like being pet and was too shy to go try to find the other kids her mother had talked about. So she committed herself to staying inside the teepee and to only talking to her mother, Deb, or anyone else that they brought back for their picnics of stale saltines, apple slices, and cheese wrapped in bright red wax.

But by the beginning of the second afternoon, she was getting bored. She'd even read three chapters ahead in her social studies textbook. After she'd combed through the tangled fringe on the rug she was lying on, pulling each string straight, she decided to go outside and walk the market.

She opened the flap of the teepee and squinted in the bright sun. The music was loud, but not as deafening back where the tents were. This area was quiet midday, people there were mostly napping, some just lying in the sun. She could hear a didgeridoo and see a cloud of smoke hanging over the crowd near the stage. Most people in the camp were young, half-clothed, with bare, dirty feet. One man sat nearby with a giant cut on his shin and was cleaning it with small bottle of vodka. He nodded his head and smiled at Sky and said, "It's all good." But really it didn't seem like it was to Sky. It seemed like he should get to a hospital. She frowned at him.

Sky wandered into the market area, which was busy. There were stalls selling handmade jewelry, much of it made from twine and beads and shells; pottery, dark nondescript ceramic mugs that looked like they were melting; wooden bowls, which reminded Sky of the tops of the acorns she used to find in Golden Gate Park. She'd break them off and pretend they were little fairy cups.

She looked at all this but tried not to spend too long or look too close at any one stall because she didn't want anyone to start a conversation with her, to think she had money to buy their things. She was eyeing a stall with earth-toned knit scarves and hats and vaguely wondering where her mother and Deb were, when she felt a tap on her shoulder.

"Hey."

Sky turned around to see the older freckled girl with the bellybutton ring. Today the ring was mostly hidden by shredded yellow cotton fringe that hung down from another crop top, and the girl wore shorts so small they looked more like denim underwear. Sky herself was in knee-length cut-offs, a baseball tee too big for her. Something in Sky felt a twinge of envy; she wanted those clothes, and she wanted what it would take to wear them. Maybe in a few years, when she was this girl's age, she'd get that.

"Hi," she said, blushing.

"Whatcha doing?"

"Nothing, just looking."

"Want to come to my tent? Meet my rabbit?"

Sky shook her head automatically, but the girl grabbed her hand. "Come on," she said, "he's really cute."

So Sky let herself be led by this girl, who seemed to her a bit too at home in this world. She looked behind her as they walked, making sure she could find her way back to the market, to Deb's teepee. She half-wished she had breadcrumbs.

A few minutes later, they were inside a large army-green canvas tent big enough to stand up in. It was humid and smelled like a locker room. There were green canvas cots taking up most of the inside, but a small path lay between them lined with rubber welcome mats, the letters mostly faded. On one of these mats sat a small cage with a ball of brown and white fur leaning into one corner.

"Isn't he the sweetest? He's a lop."

Sky leaned over politely to look at the rabbit. It was cute, she had to admit. It had fur that looked like a stuffed animal, all puffed out, and short ears almost like a teddy bear. Like Juju, she thought, with a small pang in her heart for the bear her mother had forgotten. She put her fingers flat up against the cage and let the rabbit touch its little pink nose to her.

"If you actually put your finger in the cage, he might give you a little nibble. Doesn't hurt though." The girl sat down on the cot and motioned for Sky to sit on the cot across from her. "What's your name?"

"Sky."

"Cool. I'm Daphne."

Sky kept her attention on the rabbit but watched in her periphery as Daphne took a small blue swirled glass pipe out from under the pillow and a baggie with a little bit of weed. Sky's cheeks immediately felt flushed. She watched her mother pack and smoke a pipe at least once a week, and she wondered if Daphne somehow knew that about her. That her mother did drugs. Maybe it was written all over her. Sky concentrated harder on the rabbit and wished anyone in the world would believe her if she said she had to go because her mother would be looking for her.

Earlier that year, they'd had a Just Say No anti-drug campaign at school. There had been a poster contest in her class, so Sky had sat in earnest at the kitchen table one night and made a poster by drawing a beer bottle, cigarettes, a marijuana leaf, and a syringe, with big red X's over each. She'd written Just Say No at the top using sparkly silver glitter glue. Her mother came in just as she was signing her name on the bottom. She'd laughed at the poster, said, "Is this what they are teaching you? Really?"

Sky's face had burned then as it did now, when Daphne put her hand on her shoulder and offered her the pipe. She was holding smoke in, and her blue eyes were starting to water. Sky just shook her head, knowing this probably made her uncool to Daphne, to her mother. She wanted to stand up and leave but didn't want to look like a total wimp, a goody two-shoes. She had no idea why she cared what this girl thought.

The girl finally exhaled, coughed and smiled. "Suit yourself."

Sky smiled back, and even briefly made eye contact with Daphne, relieved that was the end of it. "What's your rabbit's name?"

"Prince."

Sky nodded.

"I just love his music, don't you?"

Sky blushed again. She didn't know who Prince was. Her mother mostly listened to older stuff and folk stuff. She liked Billie Holiday and Joan Baez.

"Umm . . . yeah." Sky wished she could disappear. "So . . . How long have you had the rabbit?"

"A month. We found him in our yard. I caught him so my dad said I could keep him."

"Neat." Sky nodded, wondering if it would be rude for her to leave now.

"Hey, you know, you are really pretty." Daphne had a small smile on and reached out to touch Sky's hair. Sky wondered if she was already a little high.

Sky was about to say thanks when suddenly Daphne leaned forward over the rabbit cage and kissed her.

Her breath was strong and ashy, and her lips overly wet as they closed over Sky's. Sky felt just the tip of Daphne's tongue on her bottom lip when she pulled away, instinctively covering her mouth, even wiping it a little.

"Whoa, sorry, I thought you seemed into me." Daphne, still smiling, adjusted her top. Still somehow happy, confident.

"No!" Sky stood up, wanting to burst into tears.

"Hey, no need to run off. I'm not gonna, like, do it again."

Sky nodded but couldn't find any words. Her skin felt like she was on fire, and she could imagine how red she was. She stood for a moment paralyzed—trying to decide if it was more embarrassing to stay or run like she wanted to—before she sat slowly back down on the cot and looked at her hands. She didn't even bother to look again at the rabbit.

"So, you do like girls, though, right? I got that right?"

"I . . . I . . ." Now her skin felt tight with the heat. Sky had always been called a "tomboy," but only because her mother dressed her like one. Suddenly Sky's humiliation turned to rage. This was her mother's fault.

"Maybe you don't know yet?" Daphne looked like she was trying to help. "How old are you, anyway?"

"Eleven."

"Oh yeah, you'd probably know. Me, I like boys and girls. I'm bi."

"Bi?"

"Bisexual. Means I like both. So's my mom. It's an awesome way to be, you know, 'cause then it's all about the person . . . not the gender . . ."

Sky nodded as if she knew all this. As Daphne continued to tell her about her first time kissing a girl, how she knew, etc., Sky looked down and played with her pinkie finger. Daphne had lain back on the cot and occasionally reached out to touch Sky's long hair. The metal bar of the cot stuck into the back of her knees like a reminder she didn't belong here, but she felt powerless to move. She wanted out, but didn't want to be rude, didn't want to seem like she was against Daphne. Maybe part of her wanted to learn the stuff that Daphne was telling her, too. But even as she listened, she wondered what she could do to be more girly. She did have lots of friends that were boys. She was athletic, and mostly played out on the fields at recess while the girly girls leaned against the school wall, sometimes trying to get the boys to chase them.

By the time Sky felt like she could leave, it was late afternoon and she felt frayed. She hated her mother for bringing her here and hoped no one would see her when she got back to the tent. She didn't want them to guess what had happened.

When she got back to the teepee, it was empty—so really like a heart, she thought, and she lay down in the red glow waiting for the dark, listening to a reggae band sing about freedom, and catching bits of conversations going on around her. She heard a woman say, "Come on, baby, she'll never know," and a man's high-pitched voice screaming in the distance. The air outside was thick with smoke now and the teepee's incense stick smelled like weak soap. Sky sighed—she was more than ready to go home but knew it would be a few more days. She was humiliated, though not really, she realized, because Daphne had misread her sexuality, but because she'd imagined Sky as mature enough for a kiss. Daphne had been wrong. Sky knew now she was still just a child. She hadn't even been able to "be cool about it." Her shame felt much bigger than her skin and she burrowed in her sleeping bag and pressed her palms into her eyes, trying not to cry like the baby she clearly was.

She didn't know how long she did this before she played a game in her head, an old game for when she couldn't sleep, where she imagined "the perfect day." Usually in this fantasy, she met a father, and was dressed up and taken to a play in the city. In this one, she met a boy at the play too. She let herself imagine these sweet impossibilities until she finally fell asleep.

She didn't know how long she'd been sleeping when Edi shook her awake. It was dark and the music had stopped.

"Sky, Sky, wake up. We're leaving, honey, come on." Sky groaned and turned away from the flashlight her mother was shining.

She could hear faint conversations outside the tent.

Her mother's mouth came to her ear in a whisper-shout. "Sky, baby, I'm serious, we got to get out of here. NOW."

Electricity ran through Sky's body. Fear. Her mother was afraid. Her mother was never afraid. She opened her eyes. Deb was nowhere to be seen.

"Where's Deb?"

"Sky, now."

She slid up out of her sleeping bag as her mother handed her her canvas slip-ons. As she wedged on the second Ked, her mother threw her sweat-shirt into her lap. Sky pulled it on and started rolling up her sleeping bag.

"Leave it. Sky, leave it. Deb will get it for us."

"But . . ." Sky started to protest but just then caught her mother's face in the flashlight beam, her eyes big and searching. She threw her books in her backpack and put her pillow under her arm and stood up.

Her mother held her body to her briefly and Sky wondered if this was all a dream. Edi turned to lift the flap but stopped. She took a tie-dye scarf out of her bag and wrapped it around her head, partially covering her face. Then she found a thin muslin blanket on the ground of the tee-pee and did the same to Sky. It wasn't that cold, but Sky let her mother do it before she once again grabbed Sky's hand and led her out of the teepee, not through the sea of tents where Sky could see many of them now glowing, silhouetting the bodies inside, but back toward the towering redwoods.

Sky kept her eyes on the bouncing circle of light from the flashlight that her mother kept at their feet as they snuck out through the forest floor, padding between redwoods as black and thick as water silos. Like the legs of giants, Sky thought.

Quiet and tiny, they made their way back to the field that was the parking lot while Sky tried to remember what she'd been dreaming, waking up enough to wonder if she was glad they were leaving.

Once they were in the car and on the highway, Sky stared at Edi, her hands gripping the wheel and her body leaning forward, as if this posture would make them go faster. After several minutes, Edi's body began to calm and finally she caught Sky's stare and started to speak.

"There was a man," she said. She stopped and Sky could see she was trying not to cry. Edi reached over and squeezed Sky's knee as if Sky was the one whose whole body was trembling.

"A bad man," she said and wiped a tear away. "A bad man."

Sky thought about her own shame from the afternoon and wondered if her mother felt something like it, but worse.

Several miles later, her mother added, "We are safe now." And she sporadically repeated that phrase until they pulled onto their street, just as the sun was coming up. Their house square against the cold gray light of dawn, its neat symmetry a welcome sight.

Back in her apartment, Sky stared at her hands on the white subway tile countertop. She lifted them up, watched them shake, and set them back down, pressing her palms into the cold tile. Her fingers were tanned from site work in the valley, but white in the dip between each finger. A glass of water sat next to her, as if that would help.

It was a ridiculously early time to be home from work on a Thursday. She sat down at the kitchen table and didn't realize how much time had passed until there was a soft knock at the door, and she heard Liz's voice say, "Sky, it's me, hon."

Sky still felt on autopilot when she unbolted the door, but when Liz embraced her, she felt something snap, and she started to cry. Liz was five inches shorter but held her and rubbed her back. Guided her to the couch. Stroked her hair. Pulling the long blond strands straight with her fingers.

"Is it your mother? On your message you just said something happened. Did you find out where she is? I came as soon as I could."

Sky sat up and Liz handed her a tissue. She still didn't know if she could say anything. She suddenly wanted a shower. To get him off of her, to get it off of her.

"Ned . . ." she started. She didn't know how to articulate the way she felt to blame, the guilt, the shame, the anger, but Liz heard that one syllable and saved her.

"That fucking asshole, what did he do? Did he touch you? I'm going to fucking kill him. Or chop his fucking dick off."

"He . . . kissed me. Hard. And grabbed me. I told him no. I don't know what would have happened, but Lorenzo walked in." Sky realized she couldn't breathe and broke in heaving sobs, her chest stuttering up and down.

"Oh, sweetie." Liz pulled her close. Sky let her rub her back while she muttered, "He's a fucking asshole," then, "We are going to sue his ass for so much money," and then, "When you are ready, of course."

Liz kept going as Sky calmed down. "I fucking love Lorenzo," she said. And then, "He'll testify, right?" and then, "You can't be the first," and then, "You know it's not your fault, right? Seriously, Sky . . ." and here she made Sky turn and look her in the face.

"I'm seriously castrating that asshole."

Sky sat up then and wiped her face and laughed a little. "Thank you."

"Well, that's what friends are for, right?" Liz laughed; her laugh was always loud and at the ready. Sky had been jealous of how easily it came to her, but right now she needed to hear it.

"Wine or water or both?" Liz asked. Sky nodded and blew her nose as Liz crossed the room to the kitchen and pulled a bottle of red from the vintage wire wine rack above the fridge. They were all screw caps. Sky didn't own a corkscrew. She imagined when she got older, she'd buy a fancy automatic corkscrew that did the work for her but for now she just bought bottles with screw caps. Edi loved this about Sky when she figured it out, but only because she didn't know the part about waiting to own nice things later, only the part about not owning now.

Edi. Sky sighed a shaky exhale.

When Liz sat back down, she told her about telling them her mother was missing. Ned telling her to take time off.

"He told you to take a few days? He literally came into the room and told you take a few days? Oh my god!" Liz laughed. "This is going to be so easy! And Jerry heard him say it? God, I love it when people make my job so easy. He might as well have testified against himself!" Liz took a hearty sip of wine.

Sky didn't say anything.

"Wait, Sky, you don't really think your mother is missing? Don't, I mean, we've been over this . . ."

"I don't know. It's just weird. The lights on. The window open. Her best friends not knowing where she is, and implying a falling out of sorts, but what's really weird . . ."

Sky stopped, realizing that she had yet to articulate what she was about to say.

"What?" Liz drank from her glass again.

"Well, last week, in a moment of weakness, I called my mother for advice. It was after Ned asked me out, and I called and left a message that I needed to talk to her about something. And she never called me back."

"But it's your mother . . ." Liz started.

"I know, but when I need her, like really need her, she always knows somehow. I think it's really strange she never called me back. For a few days I thought she probably just hadn't listened to the message yet, but then Janet called."

"Shit." Liz slumped back on the couch and Sky took her first sip of wine. It tasted like jammy vinegar.

"This is really bad." She looked at the glass like it had betrayed her.

"I know."

"Why didn't you say anything?" Sky got up to pour it out and pulled another bottle down. Maybe one that cost seven dollars, instead of five.

"What are you going to do?"

Sky sighed as she poured a new glass. She had no idea. "What do you do when someone's missing?"

"Call the police."

Sky sat back on the couch and sighed. Liz put her head on her shoulder.

"Tomorrow, if you want, I'll take you in. I've got time in the morning between depositions. And I know a cute detective, she'll help us."

Sky let herself drink the rest of the bottle, with Liz's help. She didn't know when Liz let herself out, but when she woke up in the middle of the night, she had a blanket over her and the light was still on. She stood up to turn the light off but as soon as it was off she felt wide awake, plagued by a sense of dread and anxiety as she remembered the events of yesterday. Ned's mouth. His hands. Lorenzo's look. Her inability to say to Jerry what she had told Liz. Her stupid little trick when he'd asked her out. Her stupid mother's voice in her head that had told her to *be sugar*. Her mother.

Her skin felt hot and prickly. She got up to shower at 3:00 a.m. and lay in bed thinking about her mother. Her mother, probably off on some jaunt. But perhaps that wasn't an entirely fair assumption. This was an old tendency she had, always assuming the worst of her mother. Remembering the worst. When she played back over the memory of the EarthFest in her head, she rarely thought of the first night there. When her mother came to ostensibly tuck her in, but instead nudged her outside the red teepee to lie on a scratchy wool blanket and look up at the stars. There were a few people around, speaking in quiet voices, but most of them were listening to music across the grounds. Her mother pulled her close, and Sky smelled her. A mix of weed and her own sweet smell, like lemon and lavender. Sky, despite her anger at her mother, gave in and let her head rest in the crook between her mother's breast and arm as the two lay on their backs and looked up at the stars. In the background some kind of electric funk was playing, but Sky forgot all about it once she looked up at the sky. Far away from any city, the night had broken out in a rash that was new to her. She was used to being able to count the stars, but this was like an explosion. It was almost overwhelming until her mother's voice, soft with wine, began talking.

"Of course," she said, "you recognize the dipper. Ursa Major. A mother bear." Edi's fingertip swept Sky's hair off her forehead, Sky did know that one. "But now," her mother said, "if you follow the cup, the last star straight, you get to the North Star, that bright one there. Straight over from there you see what looks like a wonky 'w'? See it?"

Sky nodded.

"That's Cassiopeia. A queen sitting in her throne. But she's upside down, see? She's being punished for all of eternity."

Sky could see the stick figure queen, seated. "Yes," she whispered. "What'd she do?"

"Well." Edi turned away from the sky to her daughter so that her face was just up against Sky's. She touched her nose briefly to Sky's, rubbing it with hers. Then she started. "Cassiopeia had been bragging about her daughter, Andromeda's, beauty. She'd said that she was more beautiful than some sea nymph. Of course she was, more beautiful. But this really pissed off old Poseidon, the sea god, who then destroyed the land with angry waves, storms so violent it had to be his wrath. The people were suffering and so to get Poseidon to stop, the King tied Andromeda to a rock near the shore so that she'd drown when the high tide came in. An offering.

"But Hercules saved her and wed her. I think it was Hercules. Maybe Orion? But Cassiopeia was punished by the gods, then, who hung her up in the sky upside for eternity."

Sky traced the angles of the queen with her finger as her mother kissed her softly on the forehead. It was late, and she was tired. She let her mother guide her back in the teepee and tuck her into her too-hot sleeping bag.

She fell asleep dreaming of angry water, and woke up thirsty and alone in the teepee, a sense of longing as thick as the air around her.

Sky felt this longing again now, and even though she'd later learned that her mother had not gotten that particular myth exactly right, or at least that there was more than one version, she vowed to her dark apartment that she'd remember that moment as much as the others from that weekend—the humiliation of Daphne, or the fleeing into the night that followed. She didn't fall back asleep until the sky had turned the gray blue of morning in the bay. Friday morning. Her mother hadn't been home, according to Janet, for at least a week. And Sky hadn't talked to her for almost two weeks.

It was ten o'clock when Sky and Liz arrived at the police station; it smelled like metal and bleach. The waiting room was packed with people waiting to talk to someone, to file reports, get information, ask for restraining orders. Sky let Liz do the talking but felt she still might collapse under some unforeseen weight when the gum-chewing receptionist said, "Right, missing persons case. Have a seat. While you wait be sure to think of a good physical description. You wouldn't believe how many people can't tell you their spouses' weight and eye color. Did you bring a photo?" She handed them a clipboard with a chewed-up pen chained to it. "And what did you say the name of the person missing was?"

"Edi Richard."

The woman stopped and frowned, tilting her head. For a moment Sky wondered if she recognized the name, if she somehow knew Edi. They were about the same age. But then she just said, "All right, then," and shooed them away before turning from them and picking up her desk phone.

Liz turned to Sky and raised her eyebrows, but they took their clipboard and sat down. The woman sitting next to Sky was bleeding from the mouth. She was holding what looked like a thick sock up to her lip and leaning to one side. When Sky gave her a close-lipped smile, the woman turned to reveal a swollen eye that looked more like an overripe and bruised apple. Sky tried not to openly wince and looked down at her hands. Briefly she wondered if she'd be here if everything was fine at work, or if she'd still be waiting for her mother to just show up.

Sky had dreamt in that hot and fitful early morning sleep that she was swimming in a lake and her mother's figure had appeared as a ghost, transparent and unseeing. Sky had tried to swim to her, but it was like the light was playing tricks on the water. She kept disappearing. Then the dream shifted, and she was at the office and her mother was calling her name, but she couldn't find where in the little building the voice was coming from. She wanted to call back to her mother but was afraid Ned would hear her voice. Finally, she got up the courage to say "Edi" aloud. Then, almost as if her mother was speaking into her ear as she lay in her bed, she heard her voice.

"I'm right here," Edi had said, loud and clear.

Sky had started awake.

Liz texted her detective friend as Sky leaned over the clipboard and filled out the questions. Why hadn't she thought to bring a photo? She didn't have many; her mother didn't like her picture taken.

Her mother had long wavy dark blond hair, with a few strands of gray coming in.

Her skin was olive, like Sky's. Her eyes were green, like Sky's too.

She was petite in every way, maybe five foot four. Beautiful. Still beautiful, at fifty-one. Always beautiful.

The dream had made her sweat through her sheets. She had lain there in her still dark room, the colors of her things just stains of themselves. She lay listening to cars on the 101, the freeway that went by the hill her apartment complex sat on, waiting for the anxiety to quell. But instead, she had involuntarily pictured her mother at the bottom of a mossy ravine, with a twisted ankle, trying to survive until someone found her. She pictured her lost in the redwoods, drinking water droplets off fern leaves to survive. She pictured her mother captive in some basement, scratching at a barred window. So far, she hadn't allowed herself to imagine the worst but that morning in bed she had let these scenarios play through her head and in each one her mother was pleading for Sky to find her.

A shadow fell over the clipboard and Sky looked up. A young man, about the same age as Sky, in a gray blazer and white button-down (but no tie), stood over her.

"You the missing persons case?"

"Yes, we are." Liz stood up. "Hi, I'm Liz. A friend of Sky's. It's her mother . . ."

"You're Sky?" he asked as Sky stood up. He had bright blue eyes with thick lashes, light brown hair cropped so close to his head it was practically shaved. He was disarmingly good-looking but in a very familiar way. Sky briefly wondered if she'd come across him somewhere. Before she started her job, she'd broken up with a long-term boyfriend and then had been active on a dating site and she wondered if she'd looked at his profile there. She inwardly cringed at the thought of him making this connection, if it was indeed true.

"You both can follow me," he said and he led them through a set of double doors and down a linoleum hall into a large room of cubicles. Phones rang, and a hum of conversations made the place feel buoyant. At the end of the room was a fishbowl room with a table and chairs.

"We can go in here," he said. "Less noise."

"Just to be clear," Liz said as they pulled the folding chairs away from the table, "since we are in this room: we are just here to make a report. Not to be interviewed. I am acting as Sky's friend but if needs be, I am also her counsel."

The detective looked taken aback, and glanced briefly at Sky as if disappointed in her.

"I'm Ryan, by the way. And yes, this is just for you to make a report." He said this looking at Sky. "Tell me about your mother."

He leaned back with a little notebook and Sky thought, this is just like the movies, before she began the story with Janet's message.

The house. The lights. She spoke in an even tone all the while watching his pen move. The open window. He stopped her there.

"Wait, I thought you said this was just a missing persons case?"

"It is, well . . ."

"That sounds like possible breaking and entering now? And now we have a reason to suspect foul play . . ."

"Maybe."

"What do you mean, maybe?" He said this a little harshly but then immediately softened his features.

"I . . . it's just that . . . I don't think you understand how weird my mother is. She really could be, actually is most likely, on some unplanned escapade."

"It's true," Liz said.

"Okay." Ryan asked, "When was the last time you had contact with your mother?"

Sky counted back in her head. She wanted to be exact. The Sunday before last, her mother had called to ask her how to fix her browser window in her old desktop so Google didn't always come up. Her mother had been very chatty, and they'd talked for about a half hour.

"Two Sundays ago."

"Twelve days ago? What about anyone else that may have talked to her more recently?"

"I called her two closest friends, and they hadn't spoken to her in a while. Janet says she hasn't seen her in the flesh since before last Friday."

"Who is Janet again?"

"The neighbor."

"Well, we should definitely talk to her."

"We?" Liz leaned forward. "You mean you are going to take this case and actually do something?" She looked genuinely surprised as she said this.

"Yes." He looked again at Sky. "I'll help you." He slid across a piece of paper. "Write your mother's address on here, and I'll meet you there tomorrow morning at ten." He also wrote his name and phone number on a piece of paper and slid it across the table to both of them.

"In the meantime," he said, "is there anyone else you can call? Really, you should call anyone who knows her at all well. Does she have any siblings, cousins, long-lost exes . . . ?"

"No siblings or cousins that I've met. She has lots of exes, but not any she still talks to that I know of, or any that I think would have any information. If she didn't tell me where she was going, I don't think she'd tell them . . ."

Ryan nodded and Sky thought his face was unbelievably hopeful. "What about her parents? Are they still alive?"

"Oh," Sky said suddenly. Liz and Ryan looked at her. Sky turned to Liz. "Marguerite." She said it so quietly she practically mouthed it.

"What?" Ryan leaned forward.

"She has an estranged grandmother," Liz said to Ryan.

"Well, we should . . ."

"She's *really* estranged," Sky piped in, "like I've haven't seen her since I was four and am not entirely sure she is still alive."

"Where does she live?"

"San Francisco, as far as I know."

"Do you know her full name?"

Sky nodded and he slid her another piece of paper. She wrote Marguerite Jeanne Richard. Such a plain sounding name if you didn't know to pronounce all three names in Louisiana's version of French.

"I'll be right back." Ryan pushed back his chair and stood up for a moment. Sky let herself notice that he was in really good shape as he left the stuffy little room.

"Ha!" Liz said, she was reading a text. "My detective friend, Amy, can't believe we got back here that fast. She went looking for us in the waiting room. I'm going to write her back, *that's what happens when you're two smoking hot girls* . . . is it okay if I don't mention you're straight? I'd like to make her a little jealous . . ."

Sky stuck her tongue out at Liz, an old gesture between them, and picked up the paper. Orion James. She smiled; he was a product of hippie culture too, or at least his name let her imagine that. That explains his need for rules, order, Sky thought, but also his hopefulness. Or was she just projecting her own personality traits that resulted from growing up with a hippie onto this stranger?

A few minutes later, he was back with another piece of paper. This one with Marguerite's phone number and address.

"How'd you?" Sky looked at him.

"Phone book. Anything else you need to tell me before you leave?" This question had a tone not of accusation, but not completely devoid of it either.

He's a cop, after all, thought Sky, shaking her head. "No."

"All right, make those calls, call your grandmother, call me if anything else comes up and I'll see you tomorrow at ten."

They all stood and shook hands and Sky felt like she was in some movie version of her life. As he walked them back out to the waiting area, down a yellowed corridor this time, he let Liz lead the way. He dropped back next to Sky and said quietly, "Sky, I am sorry," and she looked at him and his youthful expression, those blue eyes, and wondered so many things at once. If she did know him from somewhere, if he was single, if she should tell him anything else, what he would say about Ned, if he was helping because it was his job or because he cared about people, or both, and if he and she would find her mother or if her mother would show up that very afternoon and make a fool of her in front·of him. Finally, and with a pinch of guilt, she wondered if he'd really help her if he knew her mother the way she did.

Sky had her first date at sixteen. She was shy and lanky, but even still Tommy Wain asked her to go to the Winter Formal with him, and she did, and his palms sweated through the red velvet gown she'd borrowed from a neighbor girl and afterward he'd kissed her lightly on the cheek and asked her to go to a movie the next weekend.

Sky must have changed outfits twenty times. Standing on a stool to see her full body in the mirror above the bathroom sink, she looked at her headless torso and wondered if she'd ever grow to have her mother's body, her perfect figure. Before that, she'd washed her hair and asked Edi to give her two French braids and wrap them around head. Her "Princess Leia" they called it, even though it wasn't quite the same. As she sat in the small yellow kitchen in the early dark of winter, her mother tugged her damp hair extra tight. She hadn't said a word since Sky had reminded her that she had a date a few hours before. Edi had wanted her to come sleep at Deb's with her. A not-too-rare event where Sky watched movies and Deb and Edi drank jug wine on Deb's back porch late into the night.

She finally pulled a strand so hard Sky's eyes watered. "Mom!"
"Sorry," Edi mumbled.
The silence seemed to get tenser as Edi neared the end of the second braid. Sky wondered if she should apologize for making her mom miss a night at Deb's. Her mouth felt heavy with words she might say, making it hard to swallow.
She said nothing, and when Edi had clipped up the second braid, she went to get dressed with a quiet, "Thanks."

When she heard the doorbell ring, she was pinching her cheeks. She'd just put Vaseline on her lips. No makeup was one of Edi's firm rules ("for every possible reason. Feminism, environmentalism, to name a few"). She looked at her face in the one clearing of the old mirror without black spots or scratches and gave herself a little smile.

She ran downstairs, skipping the second to last step out of a habit—she'd fallen on it as a kid and hadn't stepped on it since.

Edi had opened her own bottle of wine and was eyeing Tommy, who stood sagging in the kitchen like an overwatered house plant.

"Ready?" Sky asked and Tommy turned to her and smiled. He looked back at Edi with some hesitation and then said, "Right, let's go."

As they walked out the door Edi yelled, "Remember what I told you—see if you can't loosen her up a bit."

Sky turned bright red and closed the front door fast behind her, but not before Edi yelled, "But use protection!"

She cringed at this, but Tommy didn't say anything, and she let herself forget as they walked down the block to Tommy's car.

The two didn't say much as they drove to the theater. Sky asked Tommy if he liked the actor in the movie they were about to see. He said, "Yes," but didn't ask her if she did as well. When they got there, Tommy parked in the back of the lot, even though there were plenty of spaces up front. He turned off the car and Sky reached for the door handle, but he said, "Wait," and put his hand on her leg. The outfit she'd settled on was a jean skirt with red tights and a fitted navy cable sweater.

"You look really pretty tonight."

"Thanks." Sky reached again for the door handle, but Tommy grabbed her face and pressed it to his own. He smelled like cologne and mouthwash.

Sky tried to gently kiss him back, but he was already jamming his tongue in her mouth so much she wanted to gag. She pulled back and they both looked at each other.

"I really like you, Sky." He put his fingers just underneath the edge of her skirt. The way he pressed them into her thigh, she imagined that when he lifted them his fingerprints would stick to her tights in black swirls.

Sky reddened, coughed a little. "I like you too," she finally said, "but I also like movies?"

Tommy laughed. "Yeah." And he gave her one more little kiss on the cheek before they got out of the car. As the crossed the parking lot, he slid his hand into the back pocket of her skirt, and she went stiff for a few steps before she decided she'd allow herself to like it. Maybe this is what it was like to have a boyfriend. And she had been wanting one for at least three years.

During the movie, *The Pelican Brief* with Julia Roberts, Tommy kept creeping his hand higher on her thigh. Sky gave him a closed lip smile each time and grabbed his hand to hold it. But a few minutes later, he'd wriggle free and try it again. He leaned over and sucked her ear during an Oval Office scene. By the end, she couldn't wait for the lights to come on. She liked Tommy, but she'd thought he was shyer. More like her. They had been friends for two years before he asked her to the dance. He had only barely been brave enough to flirt, usually by telling her he liked her hair. Her hair in braids piled on her head.

Once they were back in the car, Tommy kissed her again, this time leaning into her. She kissed him back, all the while wishing it was a more pleasant experience. She had fantasized about this moment, but not like this. He tucked his hand into her sweater, and she pushed it back down. It was as if his desire was so strong it didn't give her any space to feel hers. To remember the fantasy. He tried up her skirt again, and she again pushed him away. She was too busy playing defense. After a half hour of this, she finally pulled away from their too wet kiss.

"'Tommy," she said, "I like you, but . . ." she sunk at the thought of saying the words "take it slow." What if he didn't like her anymore? What would that say about her? Did she still like him?

He sat waiting for her to continue. His hand hadn't left her knee, where she'd last relegated it.

"I just, you didn't seem like . . ." Sky was glad it was dark inside the car. She could feel her ears burning.

Tommy sighed and coughed. "Sorry, it's just your mom said some weird stuff, so I thought . . ." He took his hand away now. "I thought maybe you were more . . . experienced."

Sky flashed back to the overwatered plant in the kitchen. The awkward goodbye and her mother's completely embarrassing parting words. She wished the bottom of the car would open up and reveal a hole in the earth. One she could crawl into and stay in forever.

"My mother," was all she replied. Tommy coughed and laughed a little. "It's okay," he said, and started the car.

They said almost nothing on the way home, he gave her only a small peck on the cheek and said, "I still like you," but Sky was too angry to rekindle the infatuation. She barely registered saying "See you Monday" as she got out on the street in front of her house and focused her gaze on her mother's bedroom window, a lone yellow eye open in the dark face of the house.

That night was one the biggest fights in Sky's memory. But it was also so much more. It was the night her mother stopped being "Mom," and became "Edi."

The paper in her hand was crumpled from her pocket and she stared at the digits of Marguerite's phone number as if they were a message she could decode. She stood in her kitchen tapping her thumb on the counter making a sound like a fast drip of a faucet. She had been trying to find excuses not to call since Liz had dropped her off at her apartment after the station. She kept thinking maybe things were not really all that serious. Or not really happening. Ned. Work. Her mother. If her mother was dead, then she'd have to call Marguerite, but truthfully, she hadn't imagined any scenario in which she'd contact Marguerite since her teenage years.

So this was the one. Should she give it another day? But if something was really wrong, Sky would feel terrible later if she did nothing now. As Sky moved the phone onto her lap, it briefly occurred to her that perhaps this was part of Edi's plan. That she'd contact Marguerite and learn something more about her mother, that Marguerite was a clue after all. Edi had been slowly revealing herself to Sky her whole life. What if this disappearance was one more reveal of who she really was? What if Marguerite and her were together, right this very moment, drinking white wine?

No, no, Edi hated Marguerite. Sky needn't doubt that, and it made every push of the glowing numbers of her phone feel like that much more of a betrayal.

She willed herself not to hang up after the first ring. Practicing in her head the message she'd leave. Very neutral. Her name, and that she was calling about Edi Richard. Don't forget to leave her your number, she told herself.

But then someone picked up. A woman, younger than her grandmother would be. With an accent. Maybe Russian.

"Hello?"

Sky fumbled.

"Hello?"

"Hi." She recovered and cleared her throat. Maybe Ryan had gotten the number wrong. "I'm looking for Marguerite Richard."

"Yes, may I ask who is calling? "

"It's"—Sky paused and gathered her breath—"It's her granddaughter."

"O, moy." There was a pause, and she could hear the woman thinking. It was like a faint clicking on the phone. SOS, thought Sky.

"Moy, moy. How do I know you are really her? What is your name?"

"Sky, Sky Richard." It sounded odd to her now, felt strange on her tongue. While she usually went by the anglicized pronunciation of Richard, she knew how to pronounce it REE-shahrd in this moment, when it would matter to get it right. She wondered briefly if this woman would think she was lying. Wondered briefly if she was lying. "I'm Edi's daughter," she added.

"Okay. At least you know how to say her name. Give me your number. She's resting and she's going to need her rest more when she hears this. Her health is . . . well, she's not so young anymore."

Sky gave it to her and the woman, Ilana, said she would call her back when Marguerite was ready, maybe later today, maybe tomorrow.

Sky hung up and for the next two hours felt like she had as a teenager when she was waiting for a boy to call her back. She kept looking at the phone as if it was some foreign object that had landed in her home, pulsing with electricity. She wondered if her grandmother was doing the same, trying to figure out who this person was who had called her, claiming to be Edi's daughter. Vaguely she wondered if Marguerite had been scammed before, if that was the reason for Ilana's reaction, or if she was just a genuinely paranoid person. The opposite of Edi, but not the opposite of Sky. While Edi would take a ride from a stranger, Sky wouldn't even have a conversation with one. She was untrusting to a fault, always worried about people's intentions. So maybe she'd do the same thing if someone called, claiming to be Marguerite. Though she doubted it.

When the phone finally rang, it was Ilana again. "Sky, it's better you come here. See her in person. She's worried it's a prank. Maybe someone after her money. Better you come here. Can you come tomorrow, two o'clock?" This time Sky could hear someone else talking in the background. Was that her grandmother's voice?

Sky nodded reflexively before she said, "Yes," and took down an address. She wondered if she should tell Ilana it was about Edi but was a little afraid that if she did, she'd never meet her grandmother.

And ever since she'd heard her grandmother was *resting*, that her name had a body, and a body getting old, with a voice in the background, Sky wanted to meet Marguerite in spite of everything she had done.

After Tommy dropped her off from her first real date, Sky walked into the kitchen from the back door and poured a glass of water from an orange plastic pitcher she pulled from the fridge. She wanted to run up the stairs and shake her mother, scream at her, and she would, but first she wanted to think of the words that would hurt Edi most.

You are a horrible mother. *She'd laugh at that.*

What kind of a mother whores out her daughter? *Better.*

You *ruined* my life. *Accurate.*

I wish Deb, no, Janet was my mother. *That would infuriate her.*

Ten minutes later she'd said them all to her half-asleep mother who was quickly waking.

A half-finished coffee mug of wine was resting on a book next to her and it sloshed onto the faded bedspread when Sky got to the part about Janet.

When her mother saw the red stain, she was suddenly very much awake. She laughed a little and Sky was perturbed she wasn't angrier.

"Janet, huh? You want to wear tight panties and go to church twice a week? Be my guest, sister." She grabbed a black T-shirt off the floor to wipe the wine stain.

"At least Janet is normal."

"Yes, she's normal if you count having six locks on your front door as normal."

"I wouldn't mind being safe."

Edi looked up at her. The room was small now, and Sky was chewing up the inside of her cheeks.

"Jesus, Sky . . ."

"It'd be better than my mom treating me like I'm trash."

Something about this one seemed to make Edi snap up straight. "Damn it, Sky." She raised her voice. "I made a joke. A fucking joke. You are SUCH a Capricorn." Edi dabbed at the wine stain, letting her long hair fall into her face.

"Nobody else's mom would do that! It's not normal!"

"It was a joke," Edi said again, her voice lower. "You've never been able to take one, not since you were little, always too sensitive." Sky watched her calmly blotting the quilt and wanted to scream.

"Well, maybe I got that from my father, but WE'LL NEVER KNOW, will we?"

Sky had her fists balled and the second this came out of her mouth she knew she'd crossed a line. All that silence, that heat building up in her mouth over months, years. Out now.

"You little . . ." Edi jumped out of bed and looked as if she would hit Sky. Her face, always a weedy calm, was now like a wild sea. She charged at Sky but caught herself, turned back to her bed.

In her rage she threw the pillows from the bed onto the floor where they landed with harmless thwomps. Sky watched in awe then as Edi threw a paperback book against the wall behind Sky. The rest of the wine and the mug were on the rug now.

Sky tried to keep from smiling. This is what she had wanted, her mother as mad as her. Not dismissing her. Finally. There was a euphoria in what Sky perceived was their mutual and total lack of control, and Sky looked around for something to throw too.

But then Edi caught her breath and began a tirade that would change Sky's relationship with her forever.

She brushed her hair from her face, took a breath, and then, "You are so fucking serious. *Lighten up*. I mean, come on, Sky, it was a joke."

This was nothing Sky had not heard before—her mother's inappropriate sense of humor always an excuse—but now her mother's face had turned a shade darker, and she kept going, her voice now less of a yell and more of a hurried whisper. She took a step toward Sky and went on.

"For Christ's sake, quit holding your virginity like it's some delicate flower! Sex feels good, Sky! It's natural! You are not better than anyone

because you don't give it out! Have I fucking taught you NOTHING?"
Her mother yelled this last word and seemed to get angrier with her own
volume.

Sky took a step backward as Edi turned and picked up a glass of water
by her bed and threw it at the wall where the book had hit. Somehow it
didn't break, rolling instead to the rug. A spray of water landed on the
faded wallpaper, staining their own two shadows.

Sky stared at the stain, thought of the childishness of throwing things,
and her own rage was rekindled. She looked at her mother and could feel
the anger between them like a magnetic pull. The kind of mad that only
exists between mothers and daughters.

"Why are *you* so mad?" Sky yelled, "I'm the one whose date went
bad . . ."

"You want to know how I lost my virginity? My fucking *piano teacher*!
When I was fourteen! What do you think my mother said when I first
told her? She told me, 'Edi, you get used to this.'" Edi was panting and
pacing now.

Sky's anger froze. She shook her head at Edi, but Edi kept going.

"She said, 'Edi, men take whatever they want.' Do you think she did
anything for me when it turned out I was pregnant? Pregnant by this
fucking rapist piano teacher? She made me go through with the pregnancy; she didn't even ask me what I wanted!" Edi's rage quivered into
something else, and she leaned up against the water-stained wall.

The room seemed to have tilted and Sky put her hands to her cheeks,
stopping herself from covering her ears despite her desire to.

"But did you ever have to fucking deal with any of that?" Edi's voice
trembled now. "Did I make you carry a child at fifteen, take you out of
school, keep you in hiding, then take that child as soon as it was born and
give it to some goddamn couple from Sacramento?"

Sky pressed her ears now and knelt to the floor. She closed her eyes
and could hear her mother's heavy breathing. She could smell the wine
on the rug, its acrid warmth. She wished she could disappear from the
conversation, walk backward out of the room, rewind the evening all the
way to her mother braiding her hair.

She would say, in the revised version of the night, she would say, "Mom, I'll just go to Deb's with you. It'll be fun."

"You are just so naive, Sky," her mother said with a sudden softness, and a moment later she was kneeling next to her as Sky began to cry. She felt her mother's thin, shaking body covering hers. Felt her mother start also to sob into her back. Felt the hard floor on her knees, the rug too thin under them. She imagined her mother covering her like an exoskeleton she could curl up in, this mother-daughter creature for the first time becoming the heart of the home they lived in.

Huddled on the floor in the one lit room of the house.

"I'm sorry," Edi whispered.

That night the two slept in Edi's bed together, Sky crying for her mother and for herself, and Edi stroking her hair, shushing her until she finally fell asleep.

The next morning when Sky pulled up to her mother's house, an un-marked police car was already there. Liz had called her an hour before, asking her if she wanted her to tag along for moral support. Sky had said it was okay, that she'd call her later, but now as she watched a detective get out of his car in front of her mother's house, she wished Liz was there. At least for this part of the day. She knew she wanted to meet Marguerite on her own. She knew that even though she didn't know the woman, they had secrets together.

Right after she'd gotten off the phone with Liz, the doorbell had rung, and a small woman peeked through a bouquet of pale pink peonies at Sky. "These are for you," she said. Sky felt a brief panic. *Ned.* She'd barely thought of him yesterday but now it all came sinking back. Ned. Her job. His smell. Lorenzo's look. She didn't breathe as she fumbled with the tiny white envelope sticking out of the flowers.

To Sky, we are thinking of you. Jerry, Lorenzo, Ned, and Beverly. The mes-sage was typed. Jerry must have called Beverly. This was her kind of thing. Sky breathed a sigh of relief and tried to simply read the gesture as nice. Not as any kind of gag order. She knew Beverly wouldn't know anything about what had happened.

She hadn't thought about her mother at all since the flowers, had been thinking only of her job and what she would do as she showered and drove, but now she was standing in front of the house back in the version of life in which her mother was "missing." And she thought of it this way still, the word in scare quotes.

"Hey there." Ryan met her at the bottom step and smiled and again Sky felt a twinge of warmth toward him. If only he knew, she thought, knew everything.

"Hey."

"Do you have a key?"

"Yeah," Sky said.

"Are you ready?" Ryan seemed to be watching her closely.

"Yes," she said and turned to walk up the front steps. She pointed at the house next door. "That's Janet's house. The neighbor I told you about. I know she hadn't seen her for a few days, which is why she called. It doesn't look like her car is here though."

Ryan nodded and stood back as Sky unlocked the door.

As they walked into the house, he seemed to take a deep breath in. Sky turned around just in time to catch what she thought was a brief frown on his face. She briefly wished for the millionth time in her life that Edi was cleaner.

He saw that she was looking at him and said, "Well, we'll just take a look around. You can let me know what is out of order, show me that window, and if we see any evidence of breaking and entering or anything else, I'll get a crime scene unit down here."

Sky nodded and let him pass by her in the hall.

As he entered the kitchen, he turned and said to her, "Probably best not to touch too much, though." She took off her blue canvas slip-ons in the hall, an old habit, and wondered if she should tell him about the piece of cheese she'd eaten the other night. The toilet she'd used.

She followed his back through the hallway. "I told you I turned all the lights off and closed that window—those were the only strange things I saw."

Ryan stopped in the entrance to the living room, so quickly that Sky almost ran into him. She stepped around him and looked at his face. He was staring into the corner. There, a straight-back chair had been knocked over, and it lay on the floor with her mother's large and bright rainbow-colored crocheted purse beside it, as if the purse had been sitting on the chair and they had both decided to just lie down together. Sky looked at it like a picture. Some distant scene. A few items had spilled out of the purse and dotted the faded Persian like a constellation. Cassiopeia, Sky thought. The old queen hanging upside down in a chair down in the sky. A ChapStick. A pen. A Ralph Nader button. A tin of beeswax. Her wallet.

Sky turned her head as if to right the queen, as if to better see the picture. It was almost too disorienting to absorb it as it was. Her memory flared: her mother tilting her own head to look at tea leaves in the bottom of a white china cup from Goodwill, a book on fortune telling spread out in front of her.

Ryan walked to the purse and chair and crouched down, walking around and looking carefully at the wall, at the chair, at the floor.

Sky felt her body rush to get her mind going again. How had she not seen this before?

"I don't think," she started to speak, "I don't think this was here the other night . . ." She replayed walking through the house, glancing through at each room before turning off the light. She couldn't have missed this, right?

Ryan had stopped mid-crouch over the purse contents and was looking up at her.

"I mean, I couldn't have missed this, right?" She had turned off the lights in the living room before going upstairs. When her irritation had been building, when she in no way thought her mother had done anything but run away, maybe with Roger. Maybe she wasn't looking the way she was now. But still, a turned over chair?

"Did you come into the room, or just stand in the doorway to turn off the light?" Ryan asked. He stood up now but kept looking at the purse items.

"Just the doorway." Sky stared down at a tube of hand cream that had edged under the coffee table covered in faded rings, water marks. She saw her mother rubbing her hands together, her long fingers circling the palms. She wanted to pick it up but stopped herself. "But still . . ."

Ryan stood up and walked back to the doorway. "The couch." He pointed. "Since the chair's in the corner the couch might have blocked your view, or at least made it less obvious than it seems right now, in the full daylight."

Sky just nodded. "I'm going to get a glass of water." She felt a little dizzy.

"Go sit down, I'll finish looking around down here." Sky nodded and watched as he pulled latex gloves out of his pocket. Like he owned the place. And indeed, Sky had never felt less at home.

Sky sat in her mother's seat, the sunny seat, in the kitchen. She felt a wave of something, maybe grief? She wished her mother would walk in the front door. Laugh at her. Embarrass her in front of Ryan. Tell them that she'd just been at the beach for a think, and why was Sky causing all this ruckus? She put her head in her hands, pushing the heels of her palms into her eye sockets until the image of the purse and Cassiopeia became a thousand fragments of tiny light. She stayed that way until she heard Ryan's footsteps. Felt him standing over her.

"Hey," she said, but didn't move.

"Are you okay?" He sat down in what had always been her seat at the kitchen table, the one close enough to reach back to get the butter if it had been on the counter. Or ghee. There were many years when her mother only kept the lemon-yellow Indian butter in the house.

The light hurt as soon as she lifted her face. She pictured the red marks around each eye, the puffiness, and measured it against Ryan's calm, symmetrical, and pretty face. "I don't know," she answered.

"Listen." Ryan took off the gloves and put them in his pocket. Then he began to pick at his cuticles on one hand. "Listen, this obviously seems weird, this purse thing." He caught himself and lay his hands flat on the table. "What I'd like to do is get a unit in here as soon as we can, probably it will be Monday morning. We won't cause a neighborhood fuss, I promise, no white coats or even cop cars out front. No yellow tape. Just get a good look, photograph the purse and bring it into evidence. How does that sound?" He watched Sky and she wondered if he was newer to this job than she'd imagined. This careful compassion, it had to fade over the years, right? Or was the hardened detective just a trope she'd seen one too many times on television?

"What I'd like to do now," he continued, "is have you show me that window that was open. Do one more walk through with you in case you see anything else that seems odd. Are you up for that?"

Sky nodded and thought maybe she'd get the water she came in for after all. She started to stand.

"One more thing," Ryan added. "The purse is, well, like it seems like your mother would have taken it if she's just gone away for a bit, as you thought might have happened the other day, but I have to ask. If your mother *did* leave the house voluntarily, like if she had to evacuate, is there something she would absolutely not leave behind?"

Sky's mind flashed first to a silver necklace with a small charm. It was a silver disk with a blue sun in the middle, its rays stretching out to form twelve lines like a clock, but instead of numbers on the edges there were the twelve symbols of the zodiac, which she had learned by heart to recognize when she was little, sitting in her mother's lap, playing with the necklace. She described it to Ryan, ending with, "but she wears it every day, even sleeps in it." The second item she thought of was a smoky photograph of Edi as a little girl with her father in his Navy uniform, holding his toddler so high that their noses are touching. She kept it tucked in the bottom corner of her bedroom mirror. Ryan nodded when she told him this, and she thought she saw that frown again. As if he could see her mother's sadness through these tiny details.

"Do you want some water? Is it okay if I get a glass out?" Sky asked.

"Go ahead, I won't check it for prints." He smiled like he was trying to joke but it didn't quite come out that way. His voice too high a pitch. He cleared his throat.

Sky filled the water at the sink so as not to touch the fridge and drank it down in a few gulps. She blinked at the brightness of the kitchen window. Then the two walked through the rest of the downstairs. There were no more surprises. Nothing out of the ordinary. Ryan looked at each window to see if it was locked. Upstairs, Sky led him first to her old room, showed him the window that had been open. As she pointed, she said aloud, but mostly to herself, "That *was* odd."

Ryan peered closely at the wood frame around the old paned glass window. He looked on the glass and Sky could see all the fingerprints smudged around the two handles used to lift and shut the window. Most of them probably her mother's. Or hers. Maybe from years back. "What I'd like to do," he said, "is get a good look from the outside, see if it was pried open. Not obvious from condition of the paint and the trim. Lots of wear and tear. But we need to clear the prints first."

Sky just nodded in response. Caught the eye of the high school photo of herself and suddenly hoped Ryan wouldn't notice it. She looked at him and saw that he was looking at her trophies. He walked closer to the bookcase that held them all.

"Those yours? Soccer, huh? And softball?" Again, he tried to shift into a lighter tone, but again it fell flat.

"Yep," Sky said, "we were pretty good." She walked toward her bedroom door as he asked her what position she played.

"Defense, and short stop." Always defense. She was much too shy for goal scoring.

She watched from the hall as Ryan tilted his head and reached forward to touch one of the trophies. He ran his finger along the gold plate on the bottom. Almost nostalgically, Sky thought.

Next Sky led them to her mother's bedroom door. In the doorway, she suddenly felt uncomfortable showing this strange man her mother's room. The room had a quietness to it and the light filtered in through a muslin curtain. The watermark still on the wallpaper. More than one wine stain now on the rug. Ryan was waiting just behind her, close to her, waiting for her to keep walking. She thought about turning around, pushing him quietly backward, down the hall, tiptoeing down the stairs as if her mother was sleeping in her bed all this time, and they shouldn't wake her.

Sky blinked and saw her mother's disheveled bed. Empty. She sighed and stepped in so Ryan could step around her. She glanced toward the mirror and made a sound like a surprised animal, grabbing her hand to her mouth.

The photograph was gone. For the first time in her life, the mirror was without it. Though you could see the square of clean glass where it had been. A ghost shape.

Sky pointed so Ryan could see and walked to the dresser below the mirror, checking to see if maybe the photo had slipped, was wedged behind the jewelry box. But she also felt herself start to smile, to breathe—this had to mean her mother left on purpose—and was about to pull the dresser out to make sure it hadn't slipped behind it when Ryan spoke from right behind her.

"Hey, is this . . ." Swinging from his thumb and index finger was her mother's zodiac necklace. The twelve symbols. The one Sky had only seen her take off once, when she drove her to get a mammogram last year. Edi had made Sky put it in on her own neck while she sat in the waiting room so it wouldn't somehow get lost.

Her mother wouldn't have left that behind. Not on any jaunt.

"It was on the floor by the bed," Ryan said softly, head down.

She reached for the necklace and took it from Ryan. It looked so childish in her hand. Something a teenager would wear.

She was not usually a crier, so it took her a moment to realize she was crying for the second time this week. She felt her face buckle and quiver and Ryan reached for her shoulders, turned her toward the door, and led her downstairs, back into the kitchen where he poured her another glass of water from the pitcher in the fridge.

She watched him pour and willed herself to stop crying. To steady her breath. She wiped her eyes with her fingers. When she had the cold glass in her hand she asked, "Do you think she's dead or that she ran away or what?" She was surprised at how flat her tone came out.

Ryan looked at her, his eyes widening. "I don't know," he said. "I don't know. The photograph gone is like she left on purpose. But the necklace, and the purse, is like she didn't. We need, you need . . . Sky, you need to talk to everyone again. Starting with your grandmother. I'll help you with everyone else. But her, you should talk to her alone first."

Sky nodded and pressed the cold glass into her cheek. Mom, she thought, Mom, Edi. Mom, Edi. What are you up to?

When she was in college, Sky had taken a psychology course in grief and trauma. She remembered reading that trauma can put its victims on autopilot so as to allow them to function like normal human beings. In some cases, superhuman beings. Like when distressed mothers lift up cars to free their babies trapped within. The victim "compartmentalizes" in order to survive. The victim focuses intensely on the present moment, what needs to be done, and keeps moving. The dull moments are when the grief returns, so the victim avoids dull moments.

Sky thought of that as she stopped to fill her car with gas on the way to the city. On the way to her grandmother's house. Sky thought of the wolf in the story of Red Riding Hood. The wolf in grandmother's clothing. The venom with which her mother described Marguerite made Sky think of an older woman with carnivorous fangs, but she let that image move through her, resumed autopilot. Washed her buggy windshield. She would call Liz later, think about this later, decode it later, feel it later. Now, she had to get to Marguerite's.

But as she got on the freeway and fidgeted with the radio, she knew compartmentalizing wouldn't work for her. She'd never been good at shutting off the screaming part of the brain. And all throughout that college course in trauma, she had thought only of her mother. Of her mother's other child. Of the shape of that loss for a fifteen-year-old. How her mother had run away shortly thereafter and was at times homeless. How good her mother was at this particular survival skill. That of unfeeling.

Her professor had stressed that this repression of emotions led to long-term damage, ranging from severe health problems to sociopathy. Fear of abandonment led to attachment issues for the victims, making forming true connections and healthy relationships difficult for some victims. When Sky had sat in that class, she felt for the first time like she was understanding her mother. Her intense mood swings, her distance at times and her complete and utter love at other times.

She had come home the Christmas after she took this class. Driving up the coast in her old gray Volvo from UC Santa Cruz even though it took much longer than driving through the Central Valley. She'd given a ride to her boyfriend at the time, dropped him off in Half Moon Bay, before heading to the city. When she got home her mother was out, the house empty and dark. When Sky heard the quiet when she walked in with her bags, she felt an old hurt. Like her mother had forgotten she was coming. Wasn't excited to see her. But then she saw a plate of snickerdoodles on the kitchen table. Still a little warm under two folded and worn dishtowels. Her favorite. And literally the only thing her mother baked besides pot brownies.

From Half Moon Bay on, Sky had practiced two conversations with her mother. One was simple, about how she was going to intern for an advertising firm in the city this summer and sleep on a friend's couch. She was anticipating resistance to this—consumer culture lectures, capitalism lectures, but she knew she could handle all that.

The other was a response to the trauma class, and Sky fantasized this conversation happening a million different ways.

In one version, she simply asked her mother to talk more about what had happened. The rape, the child, the years of vagrancy after. In another, she talked abstractly about the class, the effects of trauma and repression. The need for the survivors to produce a narrative about the event. She would say this, and then her mother would put it together on her own. Talk about how she never thought about it that way. In another fantasy, the ultimate one, the conversation ended with them both in her mother's bed, crying to catharsis and then secretless and sleeping in each other's arms.

She knew the space she wanted to get back to. The day after the bad date. The day after her mother revealed her secret to Sky. They had stayed in Edi's bed almost all day. When she had woken, her mother brought her toast and a book, but really, they had talked quietly. Both had swollen eyes. Her mother kept saying, I'm so sorry, that was an awful thing for me to say, and Sky kept saying, I'm so sad that happened to you. They talked about the child. It hadn't lived, Edi said. It would be twenty-two by then, and Edi didn't know if it was a boy or a girl. Marguerite had insisted on heavy sedatives during the birth, so she didn't remember much. Marguerite wrote her a few years later to tell her the adopted parents had let her know it had died of influenza. Edi cried as she said this and held Sky to her chest. Thank god I have you, she said, pulling her pinkie finger through Sky's tangled hair, and it was the most loved Sky had ever felt.

They stayed like that all day, dozed until it was dark again, and then finally got up and ate sandwiches at the kitchen table. It was a day of grief, that stood out like magic from all of Sky's other memories of her mother. It was a day that she could ask her mother anything, that each of their defenses were down.

But even by the time they were cleaning their dinner dishes, sweeping crusts into the garbage, Sky could feel that space closing. Her mother had become quieter, and she looked exhausted. She wanted to sleep alone that night.

In the days that followed that one, Edi seemed to be withdrawn, to stare more. Sky walked into her room more than once to see her just looking out the window. She seemed to Sky to have aged since the week before, when she had mocked Sky for getting ready for her date.

When Sky brought it up after that night, and she did several times in the following months, her mother had said either nothing if she was in a bad mood, or if she was in a good mood, something like, "Hush, now, let's not talk about that, it's too sad."

So her mother's past became again a territory of silence, for which there was no language.

Sky had hoped that over that college break she could bring her mother back to her the way she'd been that night. She wanted to cry with her, hold her, not out of a desire to see her mother in pain but out of a desire to see her mother as human. To be able to talk to her about anything. To be closer.

But now, six or so years later, as she drove into the city to meet the woman who'd put Edi through that hell, she thought of how naive she'd been. A child with a hooded sweatshirt with her college mascot, the banana slug, wanting to baby her mother like a doll.

And that wasn't what happened when she brought it up with Edi, in fact she'd made things worse in regard to that particular space in their relationship, and now she felt hot with the possibility that maybe this story was over. She felt a distant panic, and she knew she probably looked horrified to the young woman who walked in front of her car, peering in at her with big eyes, as she sat stopped at a light at the intersection of Market and Dolores. Yet still she couldn't quite connect that panic to a belief that they'd never get back to that place where they were open and honest and safe with each other, where they each wanted to give and receive the same amount of love, of trust, where neither was a disappointment to the other.

Edi, are you really gone?

When Sky pulled up to her grandmother's, she was astonished to see how close it was to Golden Gate Park. The street down to it was a steep hill, but Sky could see the lush trees of the park where she and her mother often went from the parking spot she'd found a few blocks down from her grandmother's address. All those times playing there, her grandmother had been only a few minutes away. She wondered that her mother hadn't been bothered by that. She wondered if part of Edi had hoped they'd run into her mother.

The bell sounded more like a buzzer, the old and European kind, and Sky realized she could very well throw up. Ilana, she assumed, answered the door and looked Sky up and down before she stepped aside and waved her in. She was an older woman herself, maybe sixty, with black and gray hair and a kind face. She ushered Sky in, looking behind her, like Sky was some kind of secret. In a way, maybe she was.

"It gave her quite a shock yesterday when I told her you called, but now she's very happy, come in, come in." She led Sky through a dark and narrow entryway crowded with a coat rack and into a sunnier parlor. The house smelled like an old library. The furniture in the parlor was antique and ornate, and the loveseat Ilana led her to was framed in oak-carved roses and upholstered in a rich blue damask pattern. A glass-topped coffee table with a wooden rose base that matched the loveseat sat on a gold and blue Persian rug. Sky could hear an old clock ticking one room over, probably the dining room. In the corner was a tiny woman with white hair, red lipstick, and a blue silk pantsuit. Sky wondered if she dressed like this every day, or only special occasions. She wondered if she had been the occasion. She wondered if she should have dressed up more. She was wearing black jeans and a gray sweater, her blond hair down and barely combed. She probably looked like a time traveler in this old beautiful room.

"Hello," she said.

The woman, her grandmother, put her hand to her mouth and then beckoned Sky to her. "Come, dear, I can't stand up as well as I used to, come."

Sky moved toward her and recognized Chanel no. 5. She remembered the smell of the dresses Marguerite had sent; they lingered with what Sky learned was the iconic perfume. It was Deb who had told her. When she held up one of the last dresses she'd received, maybe at age nine, Deb had said, "Well, geez, your grandmother definitely wears Chanel." After that, Sky had tried all the Chanel perfume samples at the department store when she went to the mall with her friend and her friend's mom. She came home reeking, Edi had said, like a funeral home.

Marguerite reached for Sky's hands and pulled her in until Sky leaned over for a hug. Marguerite kissed her on the cheek and when they pulled away Sky could see her green eyes were watering.

"You are so beautiful, just like your mother."

Sky opened her mouth slightly at the word "mother." Marguerite noticed.

"Does she know you are here, dear?"

Sky sat in the chair nearest Marguerite. "No." She watched a cringe pass over Marguerite's face. Sky realized that perhaps her grandmother had thought she'd been sent to offer peace, perhaps even that when she walked in the door, Edi would be with her. She would have to tell her right away.

"Actually, my mother is why I'm here."

"Oh?" Marguerite frowned and Sky could tell this was a habitual expression.

"You see—" Sky hesitated as Ilana came in with a tea tray. She set it down lightly on the table and began to pour steaming water into two thin and delicate cups.

Marguerite signaled for her to go on. Sky looked from Ilana to her.

"I can't find her."

Marguerite's eyebrows rose. Ilana looked up from her tea pouring.

"I can't find her, and I'm getting a little worried." Sky suddenly realized that she was about to cry for the second time in a day. But she took a deep breath in and imagined her face as stone. She couldn't cry in front of this woman. Edi would be horrified.

Marguerite scoffed a little, as if this angered her, but she looked at Sky expectantly.

"It's been about over a week since anyone's heard from her. At first, I thought she'd gone on one of her jaunts, but her phone is dead, none of her friends are with her or know anything, and there's, there's . . ." Sky tried to find the words to describe all the bizarre details, Ryan's involvement, how strange it was she realized now, what he had suspected, what he'd found out at the house. So much had happened, even since she woke up this morning, not to mention since the week before. Her life was almost unrecognizable.

Marguerite seemed to sense her distress. "She is probably on, as you said, one of her jaunts, dear. Edi's always been a runner . . ."

"Her purse," Sky interrupted. "We, this detective and I, found her purse spilled in the house . . . a window was open . . . all the lights were on." Sky stopped because she knew she sounded like a crazy person to anyone who knew Edi. Edi's life was chaos, so these weren't so much clues as they were symptoms.

Marguerite signaled to Ilana to hand her the tea and said, "Have some tea, dear, this is stressful for you."

Sky was afraid to pick up the dainty china, afraid her hand would shake too much, but Ilana handed her the cup and placed it and its saucer in her lap and then faded from the room. She could feel the heat of it through her jeans. She took a deep breath and dared a sip. Mint.

"The detective, he thought, he thought I should talk to you."

"Me?" Marguerite blew softly onto her tea.

"Yes," Sky said and felt herself reddening. Ryan had probably thought there was a chance Edi was here, maybe in hiding. Or had been here, on her way out of town. Because Ryan didn't know what Sky did know, and probably should have told him more emphatically instead of coming here: they are strangers to each other. Marguerite is *dead* to Edi.

"I think, he thought . . . I mean I told him you were estranged but I guess he thought maybe . . ." Sky stared into her tea. She felt embarrassed. She felt exhausted, too.

"No, she hasn't been here. I haven't spoken to Edi since, well since . . . you were young." A look of confusion passed over Marguerite's face and Ilana seemed to sense it, she poked her head back in the doorway and raised her eyebrows at them both. "For a while, I sent you things . . ."

"I got them," Sky interrupted. The dresses, once a teddy bear with a maroon bow, she suddenly wanted to tell her that these things had meant something to her, especially in her fatherless and siblingless world. "Thank you."

Marguerite nodded and the two sat in silence for a moment. The clock in the other room ticked faithfully.

"You look like your grandfather—well, really, you look like your great-aunt. Jack's sister. Adelaide was her name."

Sky nodded. She wanted to ask Marguerite why she had done what she had done, given up Edi's child, but she could feel her mother's imposed silence on that subject, even here.

Again the two sat for a moment in silence. Marguerite cleared her throat.

"I want to ask you so much. About you, your life, but I can tell you are upset, dear. What can I do to help?" Marguerite placed her teacup down on the small table beside her.

Sky tried not to let her face display the emotion she felt: suspicion. Marguerite seemed delicate, caring, and somehow not the woman she had been expecting. She looked down at her own teacup and spoke into it.

"Is there anywhere you think she might be? Any place I wouldn't know about?" As she said it, Sky pictured some family cabin in the mountains, her mother reading under a ratty afghan.

"Oh, dear, you'd know better than I would at this point." She stopped there, and a look of distress passed over Marguerite's face. "Unless."

Sky looked up.

Marguerite, now, spoke into her lap. "I'm sure she wouldn't go back there, though." Then she looked up at Sky. "I was thinking of the Ashram, of course."

"The Ashram?" Sky saw an image of her mother cross-legged and meditating in the morning sun on Sky's bedroom floor.

"Yes, you know, the cult."

Sky stared blankly at her.

"Down outside Carmel."

"The cult? What cult?"

"Yes, dear, the Ashram. Where you were born?" Marguerite gave another slight wince as Sky waited for her to go on. "She never told you?"

Sky shook her head. Her mother had told her she'd been born at San Francisco General. That it had been a rainy day after a dry, warm summer.

"Oh, dear. Oh lord." Marguerite looked toward the doorway, as if waiting for Ilana to come in and rescue her from this situation.

Sky reached forward and set her own teacup and saucer down on the coffee table, careful to place it over one of the lace doily coasters.

"Tell me about it, please." Sky's voice was inexplicably hoarse all the sudden.

"I'm not sure I should . . . if Edi didn't want you to know."

Sky nodded; she understood this but also felt something like hope for the first time all day. "Yes, but she's gone, and I want to find her."

Marguerite sighed. Sky leaned toward her again.

"It's hard not knowing anything, really, about where I came from." She looked down at her feet, aware of the way she must be playing her grandmother's heartstrings. Emotional manipulation was something she'd learned from her mother, but she felt that pit of self-loathing harden whenever she actually used the tactic herself. And she was surprised she was using it now, that she wanted to know her mother's past *that* much. She felt once again, out of her own body, as she stared at the ornate pattern of her grandmother's rug.

"I'm really not sure, Sky, it's just, we just met and . . ."

"Please, I think it would help. Me and her." Sky looked up but resisted giving her some kind of pleading look. Her grandmother was already nodding.

"Your mother left here." Marguerite opened her mouth and closed it. "Well, you know your mother left here at sixteen?" Sky nodded. "For a few years, I got postcards from various places in the West. I think the farthest she made it was Montana. Missoula. They were usually blank with just a stamp, but once in a while she wrote her initials. This was, after everything, a kindness of her. Letting me know she was alive. But after three years or so, when she would have been about nineteen, I didn't hear anything more.

"There was a lot of vagrancy among youth then, in the early '70s, you must understand. The streets were full of young kids who had left home, especially here, in this city. I saw them every day, laughing on the street, playing music, asking for money. Skinny. Dirty. I always thought of their mothers back home. The ones who had raised them, only to be forgotten. Punished with worry.

"When I didn't hear from her for a year, I contacted the police. We'd had the Zodiac Killer, and the hitchhiker murders, so I needed them to know who I was, and that I had a missing child. Of course, they did nothing more than take my name.

"Not long after that, a letter came. From Edi. In it she told me she forgave me for all, that she'd found light and happiness and a spiritual father. She was in a place called the Ashram, she said. She gave me the address and invited me to write her, even.

"After that, I heard from her every few months. Long, rambling letters in which she talked about vegetarianism and yoga and spiritual enlightenment and mythic stories of transformation. And forgiveness, which meant something to me. But I worried about the other things. It seemed she was speaking someone else's language and very little of *her* came through. A year into these letters, I notified the police that she had been found, and of the cult. But they already knew about it, they said. Had a list of cults a mile long at that time. That one, they told me, was pretty harmless. Worst comes to worst, I remember the officer telling me, your daughter will get pregnant."

Marguerite paused and looked at Sky. A sad smile curved her tight lips.

Sky waited for her to continue. She could feel her brain, her body, wanting to catch up to what Marguerite was saying but not quite able to. She tucked her palms inside her sweater sleeves, a nervous habit and a relic of her childhood.

"She spent four or five years there. She sent one photograph, which I still have, and I'll find . . . Ilana can get it. His name, the guru leader, was Bridger. Jake Bridger. Went by some other name, of course, as did Edi at that time. They all wore white. There were many more women than men, all long-haired and beautiful, like your mother.

"She left when you were almost three."

Sky put her head in her hands and closed her eyes. She saw flecks of light again. Cassiopeia, too. Then she pictured the man in white that Janet had described. The flash of memory, the dry grassy hilltop, her mother running toward her, telling her to get into the car. She wished this all didn't make so much sense, but it did. She wished she didn't have to ask the next question, but she raised her face and said it.

"So, my father was this guru guy? Jake?"

"I . . . I think so. I must say I'm surprised Edi never did tell you all this, if only for your own protection."

Sky's mouth felt dry and again she put her face in her hands. She heard Marguerite calling for Ilana and briefly wondered if this really was all perhaps a lie. She thought of the wolf. Of her mother. Where is Riding Hood's mother in that story? Who sends a child alone into wolf-infested woods? What would Edi say for herself if she were here? Would she call this all lies?

In her gut, Sky knew she wouldn't. It had never seemed right to Sky that her mother claimed she didn't know who her father was. She'd said when Sky was younger, "it was a crazy time in my life, sweetie," but now Sky saw the other meaning to that. She knew that her mother was spontaneous and had espoused free love but had actually never been anything but faithful to Roger, and the few boyfriends before that. It was one of Edi's many paradoxes.

Sky sighed. Of all the fantasies she'd had about a father, if this was the truth then she almost didn't want to know it.

Ilana tapped her. She was handing her a glass of water. Marguerite was telling her to bring a box of photos next.

Sky tried to get back to autopilot. Why she was there.

"You said she wouldn't go back there? Does this place still exist?"

"Oh very much so, it's gotten weirder and more extreme over the years. Edi got you out because she saw signs it was getting that way, it's still up inland from Carmel, far up the valley. I see news articles about it still once in a while, though I guess it's been years since the last one of those. But as far as I know, Jake is still alive, and they are still in the same spot."

"You really don't think she could be there?"

"I doubt it." Marguerite paused. "They did not take kindly to her leaving, especially not with one of 'their' children. I got the impression she could never go back."

"So you talked to her after? You were still speaking at that point?"

"Yes, she came here and brought you. You both stayed for a few months until your mother found a job. I helped her buy your house."

Sky stared into Marguerite's face. Was this true? Hadn't they stopped speaking mostly because of the child, years before she was born? That's what Sky had assumed, but why would Marguerite lie to her? If she thought Edi was gone for good, would she remake the story to gain Sky's trust? Why didn't she remember any of this? She had only that one memory of when Marguerite gave her the doll and the air between her mother and grandmother already felt like thick ice, opaque and soundless.

"It was a turbulent time. Jake sent people more than once to try to get her back, to get you back. We even had the police here a few times."

Ilana came into the room with an old round hat box, painted with poodles in different kinds of hats. She pulled a chair next to Marguerite so she could open the box and hold it while Marguerite looked through it. Sky could tell they'd known each other for a while, their two bodies worked in a rhythm together.

"Here." Marguerite handed her an old color photograph, slightly overexposed. In it was a picture of a young man in white with a long beard, and several people stood around him, also in white. Right by his side, Sky recognized her mother's face. Smiling broadly, tanned skin, her hands resting on her belly. Her very pregnant belly.

"That photo is how I found out you were on your way into the world," Marguerite said. "I was so happy, and I was so sad, but then so happy again when your mother left them. I had prayed and prayed that she would bring you home, and she did. Thank god. Thank god, especially where that man ended up taking things . . ."

Marguerite trailed off. Sky had so many questions but also knew she'd heard about all she could take for right now. Her ability to focus was rapidly diminishing. She wondered if she should even drive home.

"Well," Marguerite said, "I'm sorry to be the one to tell you this. And sorry your mother is missing. But she will turn up." Marguerite reached her hand out to Sky and Sky felt she had to take it. "When she does, I hope you'll both come back, or at least you . . ." Marguerite squeezed her hand. "There is so much I'd like to tell you, to tell someone before I go . . . your grandfather. Your great grandparents, all these stories. Someone should know them. I've written some of them down of course, with Ilana's help. She'll get them to you if I . . ."

Sky felt the urge to squeeze Marguerite's hand and she did. She couldn't feel guilty for betraying Edi, not just then. Not when Edi's silence had led Sky to this moment. This moment where she had to rely on someone she barely knew to learn the truth. This moment when because she knew nothing, Marguerite could tell her anything and she wouldn't know what was real.

"I'll come back," she said and knew it was true as soon as she said it. "May I take this?" She held up the photograph. "The detective might want it . . ."

Marguerite smiled and nodded. "Of course, dear." Marguerite wiped a tear from her cheek. Her skin was deeply creased with age, but Sky noticed now how clear her eyes were. The same shade of fern green as her mother's. As hers. "Thank you, for coming."

"Thanks to you too." Sky got up to leave, and Ilana rose to show her out.

"I'll let you know what happens. I'm sure you are right, I'm sure we will find her."

"Yes. But . . ." Marguerite paused, and Sky waited in the doorway. "Yes, but Sky, my dear, I think you should know that in my experience when Edi disappears, she does not want to be found."

Sky looked at Marguerite. What she said struck a chord within her—this woman, she realized, knew Edi just as well as she did. But from the other side of a chasm.

She was the before, and Sky was the after.

One of Sky's earliest memories was of her mother crouched beside her, showing her how to rub her flat hands together to make heat. There was a dry sunlight around them, and they both wore white. Though now Sky couldn't be sure she wasn't inventing the white. Or the hills around them.

Her mother was telling her to imagine fire. Imagine fire *into* her hands. Your skin is fire, your skin is fire. This memory was linked to one of her mother singing "Puff the Magic Dragon" to her because, she imagined, of this fire.

"If you do this right," her mother said, "if you let your mind control your body, you will never be cold."

Sky rubbed her hands together and they didn't make the dry leaf sound her mother's made, they were damp and chubby but still she tried. "Rub until it burns," her mother said, rub until it burns, and imagine fire, good. Rub, rub, rub, keep rubbing. Faster. Faster. Now *stop*. Put your hands on my arm so I can feel."

Sky placed her hands on her mother's forearm.

"Good," her mother said, gifting Sky her beautiful smile.

"Good, Sky. But one day, I expect you to burn me."

After the terrible first date with Tommy, but before the serial monog-
amist she became in college, Sky had tried for a while to be more like
Edi. She watched Edi's carefree way when she talked to men. Watched
her play with her hair absentmindedly when a cyclist stopped to talk to
them in the park, or an old "friend" asked if he could join them when
they were wandering the farmer's market. She watched the easy way Edi
opened herself up like Venus in her shell, her whole body seeming to become receptive. It wasn't always an obvious gesture, a hand on the arm or
anything as clichéd as that, but more something inside of her mother, on
the cellular level, that shifted and transformed her within her own skin.

At sixteen, Sky began to think it was something like magic. And she
began to practice it. Though it didn't come naturally to her, she found
she could turn it on. The sugar. A long gaze, small smile, a real flirting
technique that seemed to work for her. She liked male interest, the power it made one feel. She even began to understand the way her mother's
moodiness served her, though Sky faked hers. One day flirting shamelessly with a classmate and the next day pretending to barely notice him.
While she was pretty sure Edi actually did forget people like that and did
get easily annoyed when they fell too easily, Sky had to force this behavior. To be conscious of it. Patient. But she saw the power it gave her, or at
least at that age she thought it was power. It wasn't until much later that
she realized not talking to someone when you are dying to talk to them
isn't power, it's weakness.

She remembered when she made this realization senior year. She had
been flirting with a couple of different guys, but one she really liked. She
wanted him to ask her to prom. Prom, Edi was already disgusted but by

now she'd become complacent about Sky's insistence on a normal teen-age life. His name was Diego, and he was beautiful. On the soccer team. They'd met in art class. He could draw too, and Sky found it unbelievably sexy to watch his strong forearms delicately posed over a page, carefully penciling a portrait of his mother with her eyes closed. Sky was prac-ticing her normal hot/cold routine, and when she was warm to Diego, he was warm right back. Leaning over her back to look at what she was drawing, already a building, a scene, a design. But when she turned cold, acted disinterested, he wasn't more interested. He was hurt, maybe, but mostly annoyed. Like he thought she was better than that. One day she hadn't even looked at him, even though her attention was fully on him. Finally, toward the end of class, he went to borrow one of her pencils and she'd snapped, "Hey I'm using that."

He'd stood there for a moment, mouth slightly open, before putting the pencil back.

"Shit, you don't have to be a bitch about it," he'd said. She'd turned bright red. She'd gone too far. The next day he didn't look at her. She tried to apologize at the end of class, but his interest had flown.

Like any teenager, Sky blamed her mother and sulked for three days. Went to prom with another boy who she liked okay, but Diego became the person she obsessed over until graduation. The one who represented what she'd have if she'd just been herself, if she'd been better. More mature.

And that's when Sky began to see Edi's coldness, her wishy-washiness, the way she seemed to pull men into her life and push them out not as a capricious, sexy, and "free" aspect of her being, but rather as insecurity.

Her mother, Sky understood, was deathly afraid of being hurt. Of be-ing left, maybe. Of letting anyone else into the life she had made for her-self and for Sky.

❧

Sunday morning, Sky woke early. A sense of dread blanketed her body, and she was sweating despite the cold damp air in her apartment. Last night before bed, she had been resolved to go see Roger. But now she felt weighed down by the prospect of movement. She took a breath in, and a breath out, and replayed once again the events of the past few days in her head. Finally, she willed herself to sit up, put one foot out of bed, then another. Her feet hot on the beady carpet. Moving with a heaviness to the kitchen. She'd just started a pot of coffee when there was a knock at the door.

When Sky opened it, Liz stood there, two large lattes and a bag of pastries in hand. Sky wanted to both cry and laugh as soon as she saw her. She was relieved, maybe, but also knew she'd have to say aloud to Liz everything that had happened yesterday, and saying it would make it real.

The night before, Sky had gone to bed with a pounding headache. The events of yesterday seemed to have taken place over months. Ryan and her mother's house. The purse. The photograph. The necklace. Marguerite's revelations. There was no one narrative, in Sky's mind, that could connect all of this without gaping holes and yet there had to be an answer. Her mother was somewhere, alive or dead, because no one really just disappears.

Sky tried to explain the events to Liz like a reporter, leaving out the moments of crying. The oddness of Ryan, of a detective, in her house. The surprising tenderness of Marguerite. But when she got to the cult, god, *the fucking cult*, she broke.

The drive home from Marguerite's had been a blur. She'd gotten back in the early evening and had gotten into bed with her laptop and a glass of wine. She'd listened to three voicemails from Liz, who was both concerned and curious, one from Janet checking in, and one from Lorenzo's wife, Dora, who had heard about her mother, she said, and wanted to see if they could help. Sky thought, though, from the tone of her voice, that Lorenzo had also told her about Ned.

"A cult?" Liz pulled her cup quickly away from her mouth as if it had burned her lips. "Are you serious? Was she telling the truth?"

Sky'd spent three hours the night before googling the Ashram and Jake Bridger. There was not much recent activity, but she found some old articles, a weak Wikipedia entry, and—most disturbing—a blog entry from a woman who had escaped the cult in the early eighties, a few years after Edi would have left with Sky. She remembered one section of the woman's testimony clearly: *Jake Bridger controlled everything, what we ate, when we slept, woke, who we slept with, and even who was allowed to have children by whom. He was like an intermediary between my body and me, and since I was a drug addict, at first this was a good thing. It wasn't until later that I realized to stay under that kind of tyranny would be to die.*

Liz picked pastry crumbs off her jeans as Sky told her what little she'd been able to find out. Jake had been a graduate of Yale. Spent a few years in India in a huge ashram, got really into yoga, meditating, natural healing. Came back to the states and ended up in California where he bought some land with family money and started a "yoga center." Recruited followers through yoga classes in the city. By 1977, the year Sky was born, he had over fifty followers, mostly women, at the Ashram.

"I feel like Edi would have told you about a five-year stint in a cult. She *loved* shocking you with shit like this," Liz said.

Sky nodded. "Maybe. But if she was afraid or didn't want me to know I came from there . . . Maybe she thought I'd try to find my father. I probably would have. I still might. Last night when I was reading about this place, I felt a sense of disbelief but something else, too." Sky paused and tried to name the feeling she'd felt—familiarity, perhaps? A little like finding something you've been missing for a while. She also remembered the chilling account of the woman who escaped and thought about her mother's difficulty in talking about certain parts of her past. "Maybe she didn't want to talk about it because it was a really bad experience."

"On the other hand," Liz said, "it is *very* Edi to have been in a cult. I've never met someone so susceptible to New Age fads. Every time I came over in high school, she was onto something new. Remember the mushroom diet?"

Sky did. She remembered all the diets, because she'd had to inadvertently be on most of them. Diets that her mother claimed rejuvenated you or gave you brain power or lifted moods. Weight loss was never the primary goal—her mother was already small, but Sky always thought that part of the reason Edi liked these diets was because they did keep her rail thin. The mushroom one involved eating mushrooms with almost every meal, similar to the legume diet that followed. Goji and acai were old news to her by the time those foods started showing up on half the city's menus.

"And then there was the time . . ."

Sky inwardly cringed. She knew what Liz was going to say next, and she hated this story.

"Edi the UFO hunter. Oh my god, remember your house was like a sea of newspaper clippings of people that were missing that she thought may have been abducted . . ."

"It's ironic now, isn't it?" Sky could not hide the bitterness in her voice.

"Oh god, I'm sorry Sky, I didn't . . ." Liz trailed off, picking at the edge of her coffee cup's lid.

Sky didn't jump in to tell her it was okay, instead she stared at the cinnamon bun sitting on top of a paper bag on the coffee table, knowing she should eat. Feeling so tired. She didn't know why that story made her defensive, but it was a button for her and always had been. Her mother had met a man at her salsa dance class whom she dated briefly. He claimed he had been abducted, and Edi became intrigued. He was friendly enough and handsome with curly hair but, retrospectively, Sky could see that he was probably mentally ill. He'd also had once told Sky that she should never pay her taxes because the money went straight to human medical experimentation. They were making super soldiers, he told her. The abduction obsession had led to several weekends of driving to small towns to meet people who also claimed to have been abducted, her mother pay-ing for everything while this man, Mick, tagged along. It was just another phase for Edi. And yet, something about that relationship with Mick had shown Sky again how vulnerable Edi was, how quickly she could get swept up either because she cared too much, or not enough. Sky had never been able to figure out which with Mick. Maybe that's why she didn't like talking about it.

But now she looked at Liz and sighed. "I'm sorry, I'm just really tired. And confused."

"You don't have to apologize—we don't need to be talking about Edi, and all that past, there's plenty to focus on now just to get you through today."

Sky nodded. "I think I should go see Roger. Deb is out of town."

Liz's face brightened briefly. "Can I come? Or drive you? Or help in some way? You know how I love Rog."

"Yes, yes to all of that." Sky reached for the cinnamon bun. Maybe she could shower, she could eat, she could do this. Get through today.

The sweetness of the bun seemed to wake her up, and she licked her fingers as she ate. As she did, Liz cleared her throat.

"Sky, I know you have a lot going on, to say the least, but I am going to talk to you as a lawyer for moment, is that okay?"

Sky nodded, mouth full.

"If you want to file a claim with the Department of Fair Employment and Housing, or with your work, or both, then the sooner the better. For lots of reasons. Tomorrow, ideally."

Sky put down the half bun in her hand and attempted to wipe her fingers with a flimsy paper napkin. She did not meet Liz's eyes. This was the last thing she wanted to think about, but that wasn't Liz's fault. It took her forever, it seemed, to swallow the bite in her mouth.

"I'm sorry . . ." Liz said as Sky gulped her latte to clear her throat. The milk was a little too sweet, for some reason.

"It's . . . God, I don't know. I know I don't want to hurt Jerry, he had no idea . . ."

"Really?" Liz had her eyebrows raised.

Sky opened her mouth but closed it. It did seem likely that Jerry knew what kind of guy Ned was, but still, he'd built that business from the ground up. She couldn't do anything to ruin that. But she couldn't do nothing. She certainly couldn't go back to work with Ned there. And they'd expect her to at least check in by midweek, if not return.

"I just want to leave Jerry out of it, I think he was in over his head with Ned."

"All right, what I need from you is an official statement—again, ideally, I'd take that later today or tomorrow morning and would you trust Ryan, or my friend Amy, if we have to get the police involved? I mean I know you want to leave Jerry out of it, but in the end, it may hurt him more not to give him the opportunity to take action."

Sky didn't answer because she couldn't, she knew her voice would quiver; her face was already hot, her trademark blush rising. She put her coffee down and pressed her forehead into her hands. The idea of talking to Jerry, or anyone for that matter, in a deposition about what had happened was just a further humiliation to her. She imagined the faces there, the way they'd look at her, the ways they'd wonder what she'd done to bring it on herself. Was this deep sense of shame, she wondered, so retrogressive, connected to what had happened to Edi? She felt like a child again. Nothing was right.

But then again, the idea of doing nothing—of quitting and letting Ned off the hook so that he could go on working there, while she'd have to leave and again look for a job when it had taken her over a year to find that one—was appalling. And it would probably take him five seconds to find a new job where he'd make more than her.

Liz scooted a little closer to Sky and cleared her throat. "Oh, Sky, I'm so sorry, I tore myself up on the drive over here about whether I should bring it up like that, but in the end, I thought you'd be mad later if I didn't give you the best possible advice for the situation."

"It's okay," Sky managed. "I know." Sky grabbed a pillow from the sofa and buried her head into it. It took her a few minutes to steady herself and when she did, she raised her face, took a deep breath. Liz was there with some water which Sky took from her but didn't drink. She thought of Ryan handing her the water yesterday. The glass she'd poured herself Thursday when she got home after Ned had tried to rape her.

"Do you know I've cried more this week than I've cried in the last five years put together?" She tried to smile. "I'll make a statement, even though it sucks. And probably won't go anywhere."

Liz bit her lip.

"Right?"

"Legally, no. Less than one percent of reported rapes lead to conviction, even less for attempted rapes."

"See? It all sucks."

"It is," Liz countered, "worth pursuing the workplace harassment report. We'll get somewhere with that."

"Ugh, maybe I don't want to go through this. I don't want to do this to Jerry . . ."

"Sky! You didn't do this to Jerry, *Ned* did this to Jerry." Liz stood up.

Sky nodded. "Okay," she said, "okay."

Liz leaned down again and hugged her, and Sky hugged back. She had never really been a hugger. Cold fish, Edi had said, but she didn't squirm now. She needed it, and she let herself lean a little into Liz's shoulder. "This is just really hard."

"I know. Well, I don't know because *my* mother is the most boring person alive who if she was missing would definitely be at the scrapbooking store."

Sky laughed. She pulled away and wiped her face even though she'd kept it dry. She was getting better. Not like the leaky faucet she'd been yesterday.

Someday I expect you to burn me, Sky.

"I think I might take a shower—would you call Rog for me and see if we can come by?"

"Of course, hon, just give me his number."

Sky nodded and stood up. "Do you think you could fill him in a little? I just don't know if I can say it all aloud again . . ."

"Of course, yes."

A few minutes later, Sky stepped into the shower while listening to Liz's muffled voice on the phone. Liz telling her mother's boyfriend, or ex-boyfriend, that her mother was missing, maybe kidnapped, maybe run away, maybe dead, and that she'd also been in a cult. Sky wondered how much of this story Roger knew already. If she'd been inhabiting her adult life as the child, the one that didn't know anything. The one everyone protects.

She turned the water as hot as she could stand and tried to think of nothing for a moment. But still she found herself absentmindedly saying Edi. Edi. Edi.

Where are you?

When Sky was in school, she'd had to take a course in theory of landscape design. It was a small group of almost all men. There was only one other woman in the class. A woman only slightly older than Sky, with curly brown hair, a nose ring, and a tattoo up her forearm of Japanese characters. Her name was Brittney, and Sky found her endlessly annoying. She was annoying because she came in late and opened diet soda cans in class with long purple nails, but most of all because she flirted shamelessly with every male in the class and by extension completely ignored Sky's presence.

Sky was surprised when Brittney asked her to look over her final plans at the end of the year. They had each been given a design challenge. Sky had been given an outdoor wedding venue which left her feeling less than inspired but she made what she felt was good effort, complete with a stone ceremony stage. But Brittney's project, a historic churchyard restoration, was beautiful, with each gradient careful shaded. Sky felt that she could sense Brittney's anxiety through the piece and was slightly less annoyed.

The next year, Sky heard that she had accused one of the instructors in the program of some sort of sexual assault, and she was ashamed that her first thought was, "Could have seen that coming."

She thought of Brittney now, as she turned off the shower, and wondered what had really happened. If that was why Brittney quit before finishing the program. If she felt how Sky did now: sullied and somehow to blame. Sky sickened at the thought that she had not even considered reaching out to her. They weren't friends, she'd reasoned at the time, not seeing that there were more important things than friendship when you work in a world dominated by men.

She thought of Ned and held a towel to her face. She knew she had to do something.

She wondered what it would be like to work in a field with more women, if it would be easier. Edi would say no, of course. Her mother believed firmly that the patriarchy was fully entrenched in everything, and impenetrable. They'd had an argument about it once when Sky was in college, the kind of fight that left Sky shaking in frustration.

Edi, the progressive free-spirited feminist, had argued that almost every movement purporting to liberate women was just another performance by the patriarchy. She pointed out that yes, while women are "allowed" to do many of the same jobs now, they do them for a lower wage and increased workload.

Sky, standing in her mother's kitchen, had countered with *Roe v. Wade.* Her mother had snorted. "That," she said, "is *always* under threat. It will be overturned someday. Women's bodies are the main currency of the patriarchy; they will chip away at those rights until they take them away completely. The performance of progress," she said, "is a distraction from the fact that we are still consistently marginalized in every sphere of life."

Sky had said to her, "How can you say that? You are literally the poster child for every women's lib cause. You can't really believe there's no possibility for change."

Edi had sighed like she was talking to an idiot. "Sky," she had said wearily, "oppression is the most innovative force known to man. It's easy to see from the top down when you are at the top. And it's not just men: women constantly turn against each other, so as not to be identified as not-the-patriarchy. Women deny other women rights just as freely and vehemently as men. I wish it wasn't so, but it is. Why do you think they allowed women to vote? So they'd double their husbands' votes. Sure, there may be little steps toward progress, won in small, personal victories, but most of these policies are smoke and mirrors, I'm telling you."

Sky wrapped the towel around her wet hair and sighed. Maybe Edi was right, she hadn't wanted to be associated with Brittany, so feminine in that masculine space. But to be honest, she probably wouldn't have acted differently in another field or situation, either. And now here she was, not wanting to ruin the party, and everything she'd worked for, by being the "tattletale."

Her own cowardice stung her damp skin as a wave of nausea came over her. Maybe there was no winning now that she'd already lost to Ned.

It took an hour and a half to get to Roger's place in Sonoma County, just outside the town of Occidental. When people think of Sonoma, they think of wine country, but Roger's place was in the forested hills near the rocky and ragged coast. In fact, you could wander from his place down to the steep bluffs overlooking the ocean. Roger had even scrambled down the rocky drop-off from time to time when Sky had visited to go abalone diving. Various inky, silver shells shimmered their scalloped edges out of the dirt near Roger's front door, brought from the sea and planted among his wildflowers.

The light was golden and the early spring hills were in their brief phase of glowing green before everything would turn brown and dry. Under different circumstances, the drive might have had that lazy carefree Sunday feel. Liz drove, so Sky could close her eyes and think.

Edi was always big on intuition, going with your gut. Sky had never been sure what this meant and now she felt that failure larger than ever. She felt she should know in her bones where Edi was. What she was doing. While Sky didn't usually subscribe to any of this, preferring knowledge over feeling twice over, she kept telling herself that *if* she did have confidence in her "gut-feelings," she would say that Edi wasn't dead. But then again, isn't that how grief works? The first stage always denial.

And she'd imagined this scenario the night before: someone had taken Edi, had come into her home, come in through Sky's window maybe just as Edi was leaving, just as she was reaching for her purse. They'd knocked her out. (Did that really happen? Or only in movies?) Then searched the house, turning on all the lights. They'd taken the photo. Then taken Edi away.

But that story didn't sit right with Sky. She couldn't imagine anyone besides her mother leaving that necklace, taking that photo. Unless it was someone who knew her as well as Sky? But who would take her mother?

"None of this makes sense," she said aloud. They were passing pastures, just out of sight of the ocean, cows grazing on the gentle hills like a painting.

"I still think your mother is up to something . . ." Liz said, "but you know I have my issues with Edi."

"I know," Sky said, "I do too. The weirdest part is that I think she's alive, and so part of me is furious with her for being so irresponsible, so inconsiderate, and yet another part me feels guilty for feeling this way because what if something bad really has happened to her?"

"It's shitty, Sky, that's for sure." Liz reached to turn the air slightly up, the sun coming in warmer through the windshield now.

"The weirdest thing is that purse—why didn't Janet or I see it when we first walked through? Do you think that happened after?"

"What do you mean?"

"I mean, do you think Edi came back to the house?"

"In order to leave her purse in such a way that implied a struggle? Your mom's weird, but . . ."

"I know, I know, that doesn't really make sense either. But what if she was in a hurry? What if the purse was an accident?"

"What did Ryan think?"

"He didn't really say. He said it could still be that she's just run away but he's getting some CSI people there today or tomorrow."

"It's lucky you've got someone invested in the case. A lot of my clients have a hard time getting detectives to call them back. I thought we'd have to get Amy involved to get any movement on it." Liz paused and looked over at Sky. "But do you think it's weird?"

"What?"

"Like, do you think Ryan is interested in you?"

Sky blushed. "He hasn't really flirted . . ." Sky remembered the pained look in his face when he told her he was sorry all this was happening. "Either way, that'd be a super weird way to get a date."

"Yeah, it's just . . ." Liz changed lanes to avoid a tractor on the road. The highway was getting narrower as they drove north of Petaluma, a town traditionally known as an "egg basket" because of its poultry industry but that Sky always associated with those picturesque cows grazing land that had to be worth a fortune. Sky looked out the window instead of at Liz.

"What?" Sky sighed.

"Well, I was filling Amy in, and she did think it was a little strange. Normally, she said, you'd have made a report with an officer and only later would a detective be involved. Her advice was to proceed with caution, just in case he does have ulterior motives."

"Good lord, not all men are like Ned . . ."

"Sky, I know that. Jesus. I'm just being protective."

Sky's phone rang. "Speak of the devil."

Ryan sounded breathless on the phone. "Sky?"

"Hi, Ryan."

"Listen, we are just wrapping up at your mother's house. Where are you?"

"Sonoma."

"Why?"

"I'm going to talk to my mom's longtime boyfriend, well, maybe ex-boyfriend. Roger."

"Are you alone?"

"No, I've got Liz with me. The friend you met at the station." Sky paused and Ryan didn't jump in. "Why?"

"Listen, Sky, I don't know how to tell you this but, well, the CSI team found traces of blood in your mother's house."

Sky felt her heart drop deeper into her body. "What? What do you mean? Where? We didn't see any of that."

"No, it'd been cleaned, but there was a weird stain so they tested it. It was in your room. Near that window."

"Jesus." Sky watched as Liz pulled over. They were about to head up into the hills and lose cell reception. She felt like the car was still moving. Motion sick.

Liz clicked on the emergency flashers as a pickup truck slowed and gave them a small honk. Liz waved them on.

"Sky, we don't know yet if it was your mother's blood but from here on out, we need to treat this like a possible criminal investigation."

Sky didn't respond. She couldn't. She could hear the hum of the engine, could feel Liz watching her.

"You need to be careful. Roger, as an ex-boyfriend, could be involved. You should come back home. It'd be better to let us interview him first."

Sky felt a hot salty swell from the back of her throat.

"Sky? Are you there?"

"Roger . . ." Her voice sounded hoarse. "I know him. He wouldn't hurt a fly."

"You don't really know that. No one ever does."

"He's a fucking pacifist, Ryan."

"Still . . . I'd prefer . . ." Someone else's voice in the background. "Hang on . . ."

Sky looked at Liz and shook her head. She felt a sudden irritation be-yond any grief; she wanted to hang up the phone.

"Sky, I have to go but please consider what I said. Or at least, be careful."

"Bye, Ryan."

"I'll call you later," he said and Sky noted how casual it sounded, like he had been her friend for years. It was both uncanny and comforting. She should have told him about the Ashram, she realized, after she hung up.

Liz was turned toward her, her brown eyes wide. Sky, again, couldn't find any tears. Just a dry heat where emotion should be.

"I heard most of that."

"They don't really know anything, yet."

Liz nodded. "Do you want me to turn around?"

"No." Sky sighed. If she had it in her to laugh, it would be at the idea of Roger hurting anyone. Roger, who once nursed a baby fox back to health after it got hit on the road by his house. Roger, who didn't buy shampoo because he thought companies lied about animal testing. He used bar soap in his long curly hair.

She couldn't believe it was her mother's blood. She'd sooner believe her mother had killed an intruder and was on the run. Her mother was not, despite everything that had happened to her, a victim. Never one to bleed. Or at least not yet.

They reached Roger's house forty-five minutes later. Sky couldn't help but feel a small relief when she saw him climb down the stairs of his dome-shaped house. Sky had thought, since she first saw it in her teens, that it looked like a wooden golf ball. Triangular panels, some of them wood, some glass, some solar panels, making what looked like a perfectly round tree house.

"Oh, the nipple house," Liz said as they pulled up.

Roger was waiting in the dirt driveway by the time they parked. He opened Sky's door and wrapped her in a big hug. She leaned against his tall frame and fought the urge to cry. Letting the aroma of the pines around them, and the faintly sour smell of Roger, envelop her.

"How ya holding up, kiddo?"

"Okay."

He took her hand and led them both up the stairs into the wooden cocoon of his house. It was warm and sunny, and smelled like sage. Plants hung potted in macramé nets by every window and faded Persian rugs overlapped each other to cover the whole floor. Stacks of books lined most of the outer walls in the open room. There were no other walls in the house save for the bathroom: everything else was visible, including the loft bedroom. There was a cast-iron kettle blowing steam on the small stove in the kitchenette. Sky exhaled—it was nice to be here, but also weird to be here without her mom.

"Sit down, you two, I'll get us some tea."

Liz squeezed Sky's shoulder and then took a seat by a window, giving Roger and Sky a little distance.

Roger spoke from the kitchen as he poured tea into handmade ceramic mugs. "Liz filled me in on everything, I think, Sky, and it's very strange. Frankly, it's got me pretty worried."

Sky's stomach turned; this was not what she wanted to hear.

"But I'll be honest," he continued, "I'm not sure I can be of much help. I'll try, but as I told you on the phone, your mother ended it with me a couple of months back and was pretty clear she didn't want to stay friends." He looked away from Sky.

Sky nodded. "I'm sorry, Roger, she didn't tell me that." She knew she didn't need to apologize to Roger on her mother's behalf, but she felt she could understand rejection from Edi better than anyone.

Liz cleared her throat from the corner.

Sky thought about the blood. She took a sip from her tea and burned her tongue.

"Roger." Sky lowered her mug to rest on her knee. "Did you know that my mother was in a cult, the Ashram?"

Roger looked up, alarmed. "How did you find out about that?"

"Marguerite."

"Fuck." The word surprised Sky out of Roger's mouth. "You talked to her?"

"Yes, I went to her house."

He laughed and sat back. "Well, wherever Edi's at, if she finds out that you saw your grandmother, she'll come back just to let you have it."

Sky reddened. She didn't like to think about her mother being upset with her, but Roger was right. She'd broken family law with that visit. She had wanted to.

"She wasn't that bad."

Roger snorted a laugh. "Not what I heard, but"—he threw his big hands up—"I am a big believer that families shouldn't forsake each other over past hurts, so I'm glad you went and saw her. I was worried you wouldn't meet her before she died. I used to tell Edi that."

"Was she telling the truth about the Ashram? That Jake Bridger guy? That I was born there?"

"I don't know what exactly she told you, but yes, it's true your mother was involved with them for some tough years in her life."

"Why did she leave?"

Roger rubbed his chin and sighed. "Listen, Sky, I really wish I could help . . ."

Sky could feel Liz lean forward from her chair.

"I don't know all the details, but I do know she left because she didn't want you growing up there."

"And is it true when we left, we lived with Marguerite for a while?"

"I believe so, yes."

"So why did she and my mother stop speaking, if that was after the adoption incident?" Sky reddened again. She and Roger had never spoken of her mother's rape, of the first child, and she was just assuming Roger knew about it. But what if he didn't?

Roger, too, looked pained and embarrassed. He folded his arms. "Look, Sky, that's a question for your grandmother, or your mother when you find her."

Sky let out a shaky breath she'd been holding and held her head in her arms.

Liz moved to sit on the couch next to her.

"Roger," Liz said, "a detective called us on the way here. They found blood in Edi's house. "

"Jesus." Roger put his hand to his mouth.

"We don't know anything yet," Sky chimed in, annoyed at Liz for saying anything about it. Though also vaguely wondering again if she sounded like the child in denial.

"But if there's anything odd . . ." Liz continued, "Janet mentioned that some new people had been around Edi's house. If there's anything that you could tell us . . ."

"Could she have gone back to the Ashram?" Sky interrupted. Roger shook his head, so she continued, "Janet said a bearded man in white clothes had been by the house."

"I do not think your mother would ever go back there of her own free will." Roger rubbed his forehead. "But I will tell you something strange." He paused again, as if unsure of how to phrase this. Sky tried her tea again, this time blowing on it before she raised it to her lips.

"When your mother broke up with me, we'd just spent this beautiful weekend together. We'd slept under the stars on the porch and stayed up talking half the night. She seemed a little sad, but I thought our relationship was stronger than ever. Then before she heads back to the city, she sits me down and is sobbing. Telling me she has to end it. That it doesn't work for her anymore. That we've grown apart. I was shocked." Roger's face showed his anguish even now. "So shocked, I ended up comforting her, she was so upset, and then she went on this long thing about how grateful she was for having me in her life, and how she didn't want to be in touch but that if you reached out to me, I should remain your friend . . ."

"She mentioned me in her breakup terms?" Sky put her tea down on a table made from a polished cross section of a tree trunk, its rings like a golden ripple frozen in time.

"Yes, and when you called me last week my first thought was honestly that, oh my god, Edi knew. She knew she was leaving, or whatever happened to her, she knew it was going to happen."

"For the record," Liz chimed in, "I do think Edi's up to something."

"But then again," Roger added, not seeming to have heard Liz, "maybe I just want to believe that because she broke my heart. I want to believe she did it for a reason."

Sky knew how he felt and reached over to hug Roger. She knew what it was like to have Edi break your heart. Had been wondering for days if this was just another occasion where Edi showed how little she could care about her loved ones. She'd given up her mother, she'd given up Roger, and now Sky wondered, would she give up her daughter too? But for what? Sky couldn't imagine a cause or an adventure that would push Edi to that extreme.

Liz interrupted their hug. "Were you angry with Edi?"

Sky turned and gave Liz a look, a *He's not a suspect* look. "Liz . . . Roger, sorry . . ."

"No, Sky, it's okay, it's a fair question. To be honest, I was more confused than anything at first. What had happened? Why was she breaking it off if she was so sad about it? But a few days after she left, yeah, I got a bit angry. I felt after all these years, and especially given the pretty, well, the pretty lax terms of our relationship, I felt I deserved more of an explanation. So I drove down there a couple of weeks later."

"To her house?" Liz asked.

"Yeah, to her house. I didn't call ahead of time because I wanted, well, I wanted to confront her. Catch her off guard the way she did me. But I should have called because when I arrived, well, it wasn't a good time."

"What do you mean?" Sky leaned forward.

"She had people over. There were two or three cars I didn't recognize parked out front, and I could hear a little get-together going on from the porch. So I didn't knock. Drove all the way there, walked up to the door, and then didn't knock."

Roger bit his lip and Sky could see the memory made him upset. "Felt like I was sixteen again, the guy who got dumped."

Sky had never heard him sound that bitter. She was starting to feel a little uncomfortable, like she should once again apologize for her mother's behavior, when he added, "There was something weird though. I didn't think much of it until you were filling me in on everything, Liz—but you know your mother, Sky, your mother the conservationist had every light on in the house that night."

"What?" Sky asked.

"Yeah, all the upstairs lights, even the porch light, which I don't think I'd ever seen on in my life. The lights made it seem like a much bigger party than I think it actually was based on the cars and the noise, but I think, retrospectively, it's another reason I didn't knock. Just kind of threw me off."

"Yeah, that is weird." Sky wondered if whoever had taken her mother had been with her in the house that night. She pictured her mother sitting on her sofa surrounded by white-clothed figures convincing her to join them again.

They all sat in silence for a moment, the steam from the mugs rising.

Liz cleared her throat. "Did Edi leave anything here?"

"She left everything of hers here. I was going to box it up for you to take and give back to her, but I didn't want to burden you with anything else. When she's back, you can ask her if she wants it."

"You think she'll be back?" Sky met Roger's gaze.

Roger paused. "I just don't see your mom up and running out on you, Sky. Not at this point in her life, anyway."

"You always saw the best in her, Roger." Sky felt a pulse of grief for their relationship.

"Can we see her things?" Liz asked.

"Sure," said Roger. He directed them up to the loft where he pointed to a built-in wood dresser. "I gave her a drawer years ago. Bottom right."

In the drawer, Sky found only clothes, and the overwhelming smell of her mother. She wanted to press the clothes to her face but was aware of the others watching. Edi was an embarrassing figure to need. If the others saw any hint of raw, daughterly dependence, then they could probably guess at how continually hurt she'd been by Edi's carelessness. At the bottom of the clothes was a small toilet kit with a nail file, toothbrush, and the only makeup Edi ever allowed herself, a tinted lip balm. There was also a dog-eared Agatha Christie novel. Sky briefly flipped through the pages, as if hoping to find a note inside, but it was empty.

A half hour later, Liz backed out of the driveway while Sky waved at a sad-faced Roger in his doorway. They drove most the way back in silence.

Sky was remembering their last drive home from Roger's together, the night of her mother's birthday party. She'd been driving, as Liz had had too much wine. Liz had fallen asleep and Sky had watched the halo of headlights in front of the car carefully, sure a deer would run across the road at any minute.

She'd felt guilty on that drive. Roger had asked her at the last minute to give a toast to her mother, and she'd flailed a bit. She didn't love speaking to a crowd, and not off the top of her head. She'd said her mother was "an adventurous spirit," and that "there was never a dull moment having her for a mother. My childhood was never boring." This had gotten a laugh from the crowd and while it was true, Sky had glanced at Edi's face across the warm glow of the room as she said it and could have sworn she'd seen her wince. Edi wasn't one to show any weakness, but Sky knew she had soft spots—had discovered them more and more as she grew older—and she wondered if she'd accidentally hit below the belt with those words. And perhaps, she thought, as she drove back into Sausalito that night, it hadn't been entirely fair. True, yes, but it was an old wound between them: everything that Edi was not when it came to the word *mother*.

Now as she drove back from Roger's, completely at a loss as to where her mother might be, she thought about what she would have said if Roger had asked her ahead of time to write a toast. She would have come up with something more, she knew. Perhaps sharing some of her best memories of having Edi as a mother. These were quiet memories. Maybe all nice ones are, as people seem to remember the trauma so clearly. Trauma, after all, has such cultural cachet these days. But those good memories, hushed though they were, were there. Moments when Edi really *saw* Sky.

Like one day in sixth grade, there was a mandatory talent show. Every student in the grade had to get on stage in front of the entire school and show some talent. This was Sky's nightmare, and she'd been dreading it for weeks. She hadn't learned to play any musical instruments, for what were now obvious reasons, and singing sounded mortifying. Her mother and her came up with the idea that she'd learn to juggle. Sky agreed, as she wouldn't have to talk—or even look—at the audience. Edi had a male friend who'd worked as a clown for many years (of course she did, Sky thought now), and he came over for several evenings in a row to teach her how to juggle. She was up to three oranges, but still dropped one or all of them more than half the time. The night before the talent show, Sky had fought to hold back tears as she fell asleep, not wanting Edi to see her cry. Edi had told her many times over the past few weeks, "It's time to get over this stage fright thing. You can't be *that* shy," she'd said to her. Sky finally fell asleep while imagining that there was a big earthquake and her school was reduced to a pile of bricks, thereby canceling the show. But the next morning was sunny, and Sky didn't say a word as Edi shook her awake. She'd slept through her alarm. She couldn't eat breakfast and stayed silent as Edi placed three oranges in front of her. One. Two. Three. On the table.

"Want to practice one more time?" Edi had asked.

Sky shook her head, staring down at the piece of toast that she'd torn in two.

Edi put the oranges in Sky's bag. Her whole body was worn with defeat. She fought back tears as Edi handed her her backpack at the door.

"Hey, why don't I drive you over there?"

Sky shrugged. It was only a ten-minute walk, but she was a little late.

"That way you won't be late." Edi was trying and Sky nodded; she did usually hate to be late but today it didn't matter.

"Let me grab my purse." Edi ran and put on a sweater and grabbed her purse and the two walked up the block to her car.

"You are going to do great, Sky, and who cares if you drop all the oranges the first toss, it really doesn't matter . . ."

Sky didn't say anything but just got in the car. Edi drove her to school and the two were quiet. Two minutes later they were there already, the street crowded with kids, Edi slowed as if she were looking for a place to stop.

But she didn't. She drove slowly past the school and up the next block.

"Mom?" Sky asked, turning to her. Edi had a huge grin on her face.

"Screw it, Sky, let's call the school and say you are sick today."

"Really?" Sky asked.

"Really," her mother responded and kept driving. Sky almost shrieked with happiness. She took off her seatbelt and threw her arms around her mother's neck. "Oh, thank you, thank you, thank you." She wanted to cry with the relief she felt.

Edi laughed. "Okay, okay, you're welcome. Now, what should we do?"

They both glowed the rest of the morning. Sky wasn't sure if Edi was just happy because she liked things like playing hooky, or if she was happy that Sky was lighter than she'd felt in weeks. They spent the sunny spring morning down at the Wharf. Watching the seals and the tourists, and eating pulled taffy.

She wished now she'd summarized that story for her mother's toast, for her mother. Let her know she'd done some things exactly right.

She bit her lip hard as she briefly wondered if she'd have to say things like this at a funeral someday soon. She remembered once that a high school teacher of hers, when teaching Camus' *The Stranger*, had told them all it was completely normal to imagine the death of your very closest loved ones. It was a sign of attachment. But she'd never imagined her mother's funeral, only her mother disappearing, leaving her to her grandmother, to Janet. In other words, Sky fantasized not about her mother's loss, but about having someone who knew how to conform, to perform "normal," something that suited her shy personality just fine. There were no words for the kind of guilt this thought produced for Sky on that drive—just a heavy rock in her throat.

When they pulled up to Sky's apartment complex, Liz asked if she could get Sky some food, but Sky told her she just wanted quiet. And she did. Especially if Liz was coming back in the morning to help her complain to her place of employment.

Liz nodded and reached over to give her a hug.

What, Sky wondered, as she walked into her messy apartment, had happened to her life?

ॐ

Sky heated up a microwave dinner for herself that night, something she usually only allowed herself to do once a month but had already done three times this week. As she sat watching the white cardboard container rotate sadly in the microwave like some terrible game show prize, her phone vibrated on the counter.

It was the call she'd been waiting for: Ryan.

Sky stepped away from the microwave and into her living room and answered. "Hello?"

"Hey, Sky, got a minute?"

"Yes, of course."

"Okay, what we found today was"—Ryan seemed to be searching for the right word—"concerning."

"The blood?" Sky heard the microwave beeping in the other room.

"Yes, but we don't want to draw any immediate conclusions. I should have the lab results tomorrow so at least we will know if there's a decent DNA sample. Then we can swab you too, so we know if it's related DNA, and rule out that it was yours."

"Okay," Sky responded. She'd seen a thing about DNA and crime on the news, the science getting better every day.

"Other than that, we didn't find anything else that we thought of particular significance, she had all her affairs in order . . ."

"What?"

"All her files, with like her birth certificate and financial statements, and her will, were all really well organized."

"That does *not* sound like my mother."

"Well, it was there. Her will was very clear and signed two months ago."

Two months ago, when she broke up with Roger. Maybe broke with Deb?

"That's weird," Sky said, more to herself.

"We don't think the window was forced. Given that it's an upstairs window, it would be odd if someone came in that way. But going out . . . it's not a big jump from there to the back porch roof but really, we don't know. Prints will be processed too."

Sky nodded, forgetting that Ryan couldn't see her.

"But how are you doing?"

"Umm . . ." Sky put her hand to her head. She heard the microwave beep again. It would do that periodically until she opened the door.

"Stupid question, sorry."

"It's okay, I'm a little overwhelmed . . ." Sky felt her voice pinch. She knew he was trying to be nice, but she didn't want to cry to him.

"Of course you are, it's a lot to take in. And look, nothing we found means anything certain today. Your mother could show up tomorrow. How was Roger's?"

"Fine." Sky took a breath. "He hasn't talked to my mother lately. She broke it off with him a couple of months ago. He did confirm some strange things Marguerite told me about my mother's past, and it seems like their breakup was out of nowhere. In fact, Ryan, the more I think about it, the more I think she planned this exit. Or knew something was going to happen to her. Ryan, I've been meaning to tell you, she was in this cult when she was young . . ."

"Sky," he interrupted, "I can understand how it can be tempting to look at every little detail as meaningful here. And to some extent we should. But before you get too invested in an outcome like, well, like she planned this, we really need to find out more about the evidence we do have. Okay?"

Sky was a little taken aback. She picked at the skin on her nail, an old habit. Tried to remember, *This is his job.* She wondered how many cases like this he'd worked. How many families he'd watched get worked up over some theory about where their loved one was, only to have to knock on their door and tell them the worst-case scenario.

"Yeah, okay." She still wanted to keep talking to him, but she wasn't sure why.

"Are you going to be working tomorrow?"

"No, I'm . . . it's complicated."

"Fair enough. What do you do?"

Sky felt a little flush of something as the microwave beeped again. He wanted to keep talking, too.

"I work in landscape architecture. I mostly design layouts for patios, decks; I specialize in stonework."

"That's cool. I've never met someone who does that."

"Never met someone who does that, or never met a woman who does that?" Sky laughed a little too loudly so that he'd know she was teasing despite not seeing her face.

"No, really, never met someone who does that."

Sky felt another little flush. Pride, maybe? "You haven't hung out in Marin County enough, then."

"Probably not, I'm mostly a city guy."

"Hmm." Sky wanted to ask him another question about himself, but she didn't know if it was appropriate. She didn't want to be unprofessional.

"So, you are free tomorrow?"

Sky thought about Liz coming over in the morning, but still she said, "Yes."

"Maybe I could come over and ask you some more questions?"

"Yes, of course."

"All right, I'll call you in the morning."

"Okay."

"Have a good night, try to get some sleep."

"Thanks, good night."

And she hung up the phone, feeling an odd tingling of happiness. The microwave beeped again, and she frowned at the sound, at herself. It was something Edi would do—in the midst of a crisis develop a little crush on the detective working the case. She smiled at this thought and walked to the kitchen, where she knew the food would be lukewarm, but at least she wouldn't burn her tongue.

That night, or rather, in the early hours of Monday morning, Sky's phone rang. She fumbled for her phone in the dark and felt a crazy sense of anticipation. Edi, it had to be Edi.

"Sky?" His voice was drunken and slurred but unmistakable. Ned.

"Sky, I can't stop . . ."

She hung up the phone and stared at it in disbelief. Then she threw it across the room. She heard it thud against the wall and possibly break.

"Motherfucker." She said it aloud before turning on the light. Her phone's back battery had popped out. She rubbed her head, wondering if all that had really just happened. Getting out of bed, she picked up the phone and then the black square battery.

She wanted to leave it off, but what if Edi did call?

She decided to wait fifteen minutes, so Ned would think it was disconnected for the night, and then put the battery back in. She sat half-dazed, half-angry in the lit room and watched the clock—finally putting the battery back in and turning off the light. The lamp already warm to the touch.

But then instead of falling back into the sleep she knew she needed, she sat awake in the dark the rest of the night, replaying her own life, her mother's life, and trying to imagine the scenes she didn't know.

Trying to remember everything that mattered.

That college break when Sky had tried to talk to her mother about the rape and about the effects of trauma, it had not gone well.

Sky had made them both a spaghetti dinner with a homemade sauce recipe that her Italian American boyfriend, the one she'd dropped off in Half Moon Bay, had taught her. The two had been pronouncing the names of pasta shapes in cartoonish Italian accents.

Her mother, she remembered, had brought the frivolity into a space of slight discomfort when she asked Sky in this accent, "Now, your boyfriend, is he a penne, or a macaroni?"

"Jesus, Mom." Sky blushed as she poured the noodles into a strainer in the sink, hiding briefly in the cloud of steam. She thought immediately of her professor, of a "lack of appropriate sexual boundaries exhibited by victims who have had their own realities and boundaries distorted by abuse."

"Mom," Sky said after they'd cleared their plates from the kitchen table and Edi was pouring them each a third glass of cheap red wine.

"Sky," Edi said, mock frowning at Sky's serious tone. Edi's face shone with youth, and wine, and Sky marveled at her mother's ability to look and act sixteen.

"I wanted to talk to you about this class I took. That psych class I told you I liked, it had a lot about trauma." Sky spoke into her wine glass, an old mason jar.

"Oh?" Edi played with a drop of wax left on the tablecloth from some long-ago candlelight dinner.

"Yes, a lot about sexual abuse, rape victims, and lasting effects." Sky could feel the shift immediately as Edi put down her wine and leaned back in her chair.

It was like there were tectonic plates beneath them, Sky thought. With her mother she lived on an emotional fault line.

Edi folded her arms and looked at Sky. But Sky had lived through the '89 earthquake, so had her mother, and so had this house. So she ignored this warning signal and kept going. She wanted, *needed* Edi to see the way she kept herself out of relationships, the way she hurt people. The way she hurt Sky. The way though, too, that it wasn't her fault.

The wine made her feel flushed, ready. So buoyed by the confidence of what she'd learned in class, the terminology ready on her tongue—she told her mother about victim behaviors and the long-lasting effects of rape and trauma. She just told it exactly how she'd learned it in school, using the term "the victim" and not mentioning Edi's particular life at all. But when she finished talking after about ten minutes, she said quietly, "The class made me think of everything you went through as a teenager. I thought of you a lot, Mom."

"What happened to Edi?" Edi's voice was cold. She pushed her chair back from the table.

"What?"

"You usually call me Edi but since you've been home it's been Mom, Mom, Mom."

"I guess . . ." Sky was flustered. She had decided, though hadn't quite articulated this to herself before this moment, that the purpose of this whole mission was that she wanted to be closer to Edi.

"It's fucking annoying." Edi stood up.

"That's exactly the kind of defensive behavior Professor Collins . . ."

"Oh, fuck you, and fuck Professor Collins." Her mother picked up her glass and then set it back down. "Really, Sky, I mean, how dare you? I wanted you to go to college so you could avoid my life's path, not study it, for Christ's sake! The people that write those theories are full of shit— they haven't been through what I've been through."

"I know, but Mom—" Sky stopped. "Edi, you have to admit, there are patterns . . ."

"Sky, I'm done with this conversation! I don't want to hear anymore." Edi put her hands up in the air.

"I just want you to talk about it sometimes!"

"Sky, it's a shitty thing that happened to me. I don't want to talk about it. I don't want to think about it. You think I don't know how it fucked my life up? Every decision I made after that was affected by that one afternoon where he . . ."

Edi stopped herself. Her hands were shaking, Sky saw, and she suddenly felt so, so stupid. She watched her mother walk out of the room and heard her climb the stairs up to her bedroom.

She'd learned nothing. Fixed nothing. Had appeared arrogant and now felt ignorant. She gathered up the rest of the dishes and filled the sink with scalding hot water. She briefly raged at Professor Collins, at all her college friends with perfect, intact mothers and fathers, brothers and sisters—but she knew the more she blamed them, the more she herself was to blame for this humiliation.

She knew her mother, she knew Edi. She should have known better.

What she didn't know until now was how terrible it felt to have anything like that happen to you. She hadn't known, until Ned pushed against her, how disgusting it felt. How shameful, how criminal it felt to have a body. How it was the first thing you thought of in the morning and the last thing before you went to bed. How you sure as hell didn't want to talk about it. And how no matter what your brain thought, your body felt it was your fault.

And Sky, as she lay awake in bed that night in the wake of Ned's drunk dial, *missed* her mother for the first time. Missed her and felt that she'd been robbed of the moment when she could finally look at her mother and understand her.

ॐ

When the blue glow of dawn started swelling from Sky's window, a hollow was growing in her stomach. Liz would be there in a few hours to help her write an official complaint. She'd brought it up again on the way home from Roger's, telling her she or Sky could call Jerry and then file a complaint, or they could report it to the police together. When Sky had asked her which she should do, Liz had said, "It just depends, do you want Ned just fired or do you want the bastard in jail? Not that he'll go to jail, because again courts rarely convict on cases like these, but the charge would haunt him."

Sky didn't know then and still didn't know this morning. She knew she didn't want to deal with it. Wanted it to go away. She thought perhaps the easiest and yet hardest thing to do was for her to call Jerry and tell him what happened.

And then there was everything else. Ryan. Marguerite. The Ashram. Roger. Edi.

Edi, Edi, Edi. *Where are you? Where are you?* She chanted to herself in a tired delirium while the room slowly lightened. Her exhaustion in the light felt like radio static behind her eyes.

She got out of bed as the blue turned into the blushy bruise of dawn. She felt dizzy from lack of sleep. Her phone was chipped on one side from throwing it across the room. She fingered the new sharp edge and briefly wondered if Ned was planning to apologize last night, and if that mattered. She wondered if it was too early to call Jerry; she wanted to get it over with. She decided on a shower and an attempt to eat before calling him. She'd call Liz one more time to go over exactly what she should say.

An hour later, Jerry answered after one ring. Sky's mouth was dry.

"Sky, how are you? Did you find your mother? I've been thinking about you all weekend, worrying for you."

"Hi, Jerry, no, not yet. There's a helpful detective involved, and I've learned a lot, but not where she is, unfortunately."

"Well, listen, Beverly wanted me to let you know that she has some newspaper articles for you. About older folk going missing. She had a cousin I guess get a kind of Alzheimer's and one day she just suddenly wandered off. And you take what time you need. I told the Ortho we might be delayed, and he huffed a bit, but I told him we were waiting to see a celebrity's house to model the plans after and that seemed to calm him down. Ned said he could drop the specs off to you if want to work on the plans at home, too . . ."

Sky's stomach churned, and she briefly wondered if it had been a mistake to eat before making this call.

"Listen, Jerry, my mom's not why I called." Or why I left on Thursday, she wanted to add, but now that she knew what she knew, it seemed ridiculous that she would have kept on working.

"Huh?"

"Jerry." Sky reddened, she imagined this was how it felt to disappoint a father. "Jerry, Ned has been . . . bothering me."

There was a silence on the other end. Sky put her palm to her forehead and cringed, her face hot, as she continued.

"On Thursday, he forcibly kissed me, and . . ." She stopped. This was too humiliating. Liz had gone over the phrasing with her "forcibly kissed me . . ." She skipped the next part and went straight to last night. "He called me last night, at two a.m., and that's not the first time . . ."

"Jesus. God damn it."

"Jerry, I'm sorry." Liz had specifically told her not to apologize but she couldn't stop herself.

"How long has this been going on?"

Since I started, she wanted to say, but Liz had advised her to include only concrete events, so the leering that had been going on since day one would not be included in her account.

"He asked me out the week before last, and I said no." Sky dug her own nails into her palms. The flirty no. The center of her shame. She released her clench before she drew blood, but tiny crescent moons imprinted her palms where her nails had been.

Silence again.

She thought about telling him Lorenzo would corroborate her story, but she didn't want to drag him into this. At least not yet.

"Jerry, I'm sorry, I know this is not what you want to hear. But I really like working for you, and I'd like to keep working for you." This is that part where Sky was supposed to add, "I have a friend that's a lawyer and she advised that because of that, I approach you first before filing any charges against Ned."

But she couldn't do it. She couldn't find those teeth in her. Sky could picture Jerry; she knew what he looked like when he was upset. Hand on back of neck, face sallow, pacing.

"Well, what the hell should I do?"

Sky knew he wasn't mad at her, but it was still hard not to wince at his tone.

"I don't know . . ." Sky stopped before her voice broke. Her chin was slightly quivering, and she was thankful Jerry couldn't see her.

"Ned's worked for me for fifteen years, I can't just . . . You are putting me in a hell of a position, Sky. Shit."

Sky could already hear Liz's ire when she told her this response. But Sky wasn't angry, she understood Jerry. He was soft-spoken, kind, and not really equipped to deal with a sexual harassment lawsuit. She knew this about him, and she was still tempted to play the boys' girl, the girl who was cool, who wouldn't make trouble, a girl she'd pretended at being before. But she resisted the urge to apologize again and wiped her tears, though she couldn't go back to the script Liz had outlined. The part where she told Jerry that a formal complaint in writing was coming to him.

So she stayed silent. She hated herself for it, but nothing would come out.

"Shit, Sky," Jerry said again in response to her silence, his tone a little softer, she thought. "Well, I gotta take a minute here."

Sky heard voices in the background. "I understand," she said, because she felt like that was what she was supposed to say. Her voice coming out almost as a whisper.

"And now I gotta run," Jerry said, and Sky heard Ned's laugh. She felt fear and hatred and jealousy all at once. He got to be there in the office, going about business as usual while her life was falling apart.

She didn't get another word in before she heard the dial tone, heavy and even.

She put her phone down on her bed and sat down. The sunlight coming into her room was disorienting. She was angry. Why hadn't she put her foot down more? Told him that it was Ned or her. That she could file charges against Ned, or even Jerry if he ignored this complaint.

"Fuck," she said aloud. Being assaulted was one thing, talking about it was another kind of violence.

She lay back down on her pillow. She was exhausted, she knew, but there was also a sense of bereavement. On a normal Monday morning, last Monday morning, for instance, she would get up at 5:30 a.m. and go for a trail run in the hills above Sausalito, or maybe do yoga. She'd come home, shower, eat her favorite yogurt in a little flowered bowl, dress. Then she'd sometimes stop at a drive-through coffee shop for a latte on her way to work, where the baristas knew her face and always drew pretty designs in the top of her cup, which she'd see fifteen minutes later when she sat down at her desk and took the lid off. A leaf, a flower, a fountain, and once, from the cute barista with a shaved head, a heart.

Now she could hardly breathe. She wondered what Edi would say to her right now. Edi could generally be counted on to tell Sky to relax, to trust the universe, but Sky wondered if that Taoist attitude would extend to Ned, or to her own disappearance. She wondered if she'd have time to go back to the house today, she wanted to see the invisible blood stain for herself. She'd tried to remember any past blood spilt, to be able to account for it with an anecdote. To say to Ryan, oh, don't worry about that, that's from when I cracked my head open. There'd been a few incidents, but decades ago and in other parts of the house. A split lip from running too fast on the stairs, getting that unlucky step. Stitches in her hand from falling with a glass of water when she'd tripped over a small stack of records that Edi had just picked up secondhand and had left on the hallway floor.

She sat up from her bed and walked to the living room, where she started to pace. She looked at her phone on the table and before she could talk herself out of it, she picked it up and called Ryan. She was going to make him listen to her about the Ashram. It seemed important to her, and she wouldn't let herself be interrupted this time.

He answered on the first ring. Sky felt her heart twist a little at that.

"Ryan, it's me, Sky.

"Hey."

"I know you want to talk today, so I thought I'd call . . ."

"Hey, yes, I'm just about to head in to work, but how about I come over this afternoon? One-ish?"

Sky opened and closed her mouth. She'd meant to demand he listen to her, but she realized she couldn't take out her conversation with Jerry on Ryan.

"Yeah, sure," she said. She let the adrenaline die down as she gave him her address. He left off with a cheery "see you soon," and she just hung up.

She was delirious, she thought, and lay down on the couch. She tried to calm her body, eventually drifting into a weird dreamless sleep until there was a loud knock on the door. She sat upright too fast, and her vision faded for a moment. Was it Ryan already? She glanced at her watch. 10:30. It'd be Liz.

So she stumbled to the door, groggy, and opened it.

"Holy hell, did you sleep?" Liz was dressed for work.

"Not really. Ned called . . ."

"He didn't!" Liz walked past Sky and into the apartment, setting down her black messenger bag and sitting on the couch.

Sky nodded. "He was drunk . . . I hung up on him."

"Well, let's add harassing phone calls to this complaint." Liz sat with legs spread wide, placing her laptop on the low coffee table between her knees. Sky stood watching her, feeling she should offer Liz coffee, or go wash her face—but her feet felt like dead weights, dragging her body down. If only she'd been more upfront with Jerry about all the action she *might* take, that Liz wanted her to take.

"Okay, how does this sound so far?" Liz was typing furiously. Sky knew Liz had to get back to work soon and was both appreciative she was here, but also somehow annoyed. Jealous perhaps. How easy she made it all look.

"Sky Richard hereby lodges a formal complaint against her place of employment, Scenic Scapes, requesting one Jerry Edwards to investigate her allegations against one Ned Hanson, and take the appropriate punitive action against the aggressor. Richard's allegations are as follows: 1) That Mr. Hanson engaged in inappropriate behavior, verbal comments, and coercion toward Ms. Richard. This harassment was not limited to the workplace but has included late night phone calls where Mr. Hanson made explicit sexual references to Ms. Richard and tried to engage her in a sexual relationship. This harassment culminated in an act more serious and criminal in nature . . ."

"Stop, Liz, just stop." Sky's voice was hoarse. Her feet were lead.

Liz looked up, surprised. "Look, I know all this legal speak is weird, but it's got to be . . ."

"No, it's not that." Sky willed herself to sit down on the couch next to Liz. "I just, I need to process things. Everything is happening so fast. Plus, I talked to Jerry this morning and . . ." She flushed red at the memory of the conversation. Of the words, the assertive words that had stuck in her throat. "I don't know why, but I couldn't say any of the things we talked about. I just felt like I was disappointing him . . ."

"Sky, seriously?" Liz turned to face her directly. She seemed irritated. Why was Sky so afraid of annoying her?

"You don't know what this industry is like. If you are a woman, you are expected to behave like a man. To be cool with the occasional dick joke, it's a weird insiders' club that I've worked really hard to get into, and now I don't want to throw that all away because some asshole . . ." She could hear how wrong she sounded but still it made her sick, to think of not being able to do this job anymore.

"But you know you can't ignore it. Right, you at least know that?" Liz raised her hand to her mouth and began biting her nails, something Sky didn't see her do very often. Only when she was really agitated.

"I know, I know. I just need a day; it's just been a lot. With my mom . . ." Sky let her voice do its wavering.

Liz opened her mouth and Sky thought she'd protest more but instead she nodded. "Okay, okay."

Sky put her head in her hands and spoke, her voice muffled, "Thank you."

"But I'm going to stay on you about this."

Liz left a few minutes later, after making Sky a cup of coffee and telling her she'd call her later. She closed the door and when Sky was alone, she felt worse than she had since it happened. Since any of it happened. Like it was sucking all the energy out of her to think about any of it, to have to take action.

She wondered what had happened to her mother's rapist. She didn't even know his name. Had he kept on teaching piano? Sitting in rooms with young girls, alone? Had there been more? Was he still alive? Still teaching? Did he sit in an armchair, surrounded by grandchildren, being served iced tea by a doting wife, unaware of the wake of pain he caused? Of his dead child? His missing victim?

It was just not likely her mother was the only one he touched.

Maybe she should ask Marguerite. Yes, when she felt like she could move, she'd go see Marguerite again. Maybe tomorrow. She felt an ache, wondered again what Edi would say. Wondered if Edi would have offered any comfort. Perhaps she would have, given that she'd been through something similar before. No, what happened to Edi was so much worse. She'd been a child, and she had actually been raped. So chances are she wouldn't have been sympathetic, but Sky realized her mother's "tough as nails" act in and of itself would have been a comfort right now.

Ryan, true to his word, rang her bell at 1:02 p.m., and Sky buzzed him in. He was wearing a black T-shirt inside out and a blazer. Jeans. She was a little surprised at how casual he looked compared to when she'd seen him on Friday, Saturday.

Sky's face must have been easy to read because he said, "Technically Monday is my weekend, but not today," as he walked in. "Nice place here." He walked into her living room. She had an okay view, mostly of the freeway below, but the complex sat on a hill above it, and you could see the water on a nice day from her picture window.

But today the fog had rolled in. Sky had been napping again, in and out of strange dreams she didn't really remember, each time waking up hot. Thirsty. But half an hour ago she'd gotten up, made herself eat a piece of toast with creamy peanut butter. Drank some water. She'd had time to brush her teeth before Ryan came over, but now as she stood looking at his tall frame silhouetted against the gray of her window, she could still taste peanut butter in her mouth.

She ran her fingers through her hair, an old habit, as Ryan turned around. His eyes once again struck her as the bluest she'd ever seen. His hair was a little messy, and he hadn't shaved this morning. He looked good. She suddenly wanted to laugh. Her mother would love that Sky was attracted to a man sent to help her find her mother. Her mother, who was forever wanting her to be more adventurous in her dating. Her mother, who called Sky's last boyfriend "a bit of yes-man, don't you think? He was a Pisces, right? Not my type, I'll tell you." As if Sky should, or wanted to, date Edi's type. She wondered Ryan's sign. That kind of detail was crucial to Edi. Inevitably, she knew which signs were supposedly good with her own, Capricorn.

"Do you want some water? Coffee?" she asked.

"No, I'm good—let's just get to it."

She nodded and offered him a chair across from the couch. The couch was low, and she didn't want him trying to interview her in it.

"Ryan, before we start, I've got to tell you something that Marguerite told me."

"What?"

"The Ashram, Jake Bridger, have you heard of it?"

Ryan glanced quickly up at her, but then focused on finding a pen in his pocket.

"No, I haven't. I'm not from California, so . . ."

"It's okay, I hadn't heard of them either. But my mom joined this cult, the one I mentioned on the phone, I was born in it, and then she left. I think she may have been seeing them the last few months. The leader matches Janet's guy-in-white description, and Roger said he saw a bunch of people at my mom's house after they broke up . . ."

"You didn't tell me *that*," Ryan interrupted. "About the guy being like someone Janet had seen."

"I tried, it's just—it's been a little crazy."

"Okay, well, when I get into the station tomorrow I'll look into any files we have on Jake. Anything else you want to tell me?" Ryan's tone was a little irritated as he got out his notepad and wrote Jake Bridger, underlined. Once again and for just a moment, Sky thought maybe he was capable of being the brash detective she'd pictured, but then he leaned back in his chair and gave Sky a tight-lipped smile. She watched him, looking at those blue eyes more carefully. Suddenly, his face visibly relaxed. "I know it's been difficult. But did Roger have any information?"

She told him about the breakup, the strange fact that Roger had seen people over, again with all lights on, but as she said it, she realized it probably didn't sound that weird to people who didn't know her mother. So, her mother had a get-together. And lights were on. She felt her cheeks burn a little. "Sorry," she offered when he didn't respond right away.

"No, this is good," he said. "Anything else?"

Sky shook her head, suddenly wishing she'd made them tea or something, so she'd at least have a prop.

"Okay." Ryan tapped his pen on his pad. "Can I ask you a few questions?"

"Sure."

"Can you think of anyone that would want to hurt your mother, anyone that might have been angry with her?" Sky could think of a dozen people irritated with her mother, some permanently irritated with her, like Janet and her mother's mailman who was always leaving her angry notes reminding her to get her mail so that the box wouldn't overflow. But no one that would be mad enough to hurt her.

"No, not really—my mother is pretty hard to fight with. She can be annoying but many of her convictions are hard to argue with, if that makes sense."

"What do you mean?" Ryan tilted his head.

"Like . . ." Sky chewed her lower lip and thought for a moment. "Like for a while last year she was convinced that a certain brand of veggie burger was actually not vegetarian. It was crazy why she thought that, some reaction she had to it, where she said she could feel 'animal energy.' But there was no real arguing with her because whatever you said, she'd say 'well, of course, that's what they want us to think.'"

Ryan was smiling at her.

"What?" she asked.

"It's just that, just now—you were smiling, telling that story. It's the first time I've seen you smile."

Sky put her hand to her mouth, instinctively hiding it. "There hasn't been a lot to smile about, I guess . . ."

Ryan nodded. After a moment he looked down at his pad and asked, "And you?"

"Me?"

"Yes, were you on good terms with her?"

"Are you kidding me right now?" Sky felt a rush of heat in her blood. "I'm the one who came to you because I was worried about her . . ."

"Sky, calm down," Ryan said. "In my mind you are not a suspect, but I wouldn't be much of a detective if I didn't ask. But what about Roger, you mentioned he was angry?"

"Again, Roger wouldn't hurt her . . ." Sky felt now how raw her nerves were. How tired. She liked Ryan, she did. Or she wanted to, but she was starting to realize she didn't know him. Not at all. To make her let down her guard like that and then ask her if she'd have a motive to hurt her mother? She looked at him with narrowed eyes.

"Are you sure? A disgruntled ex-boyfriend? Sometimes we don't know people as well as we think we do, Sky."

Sky opened her mouth to speak but immediately shut it. She'd certainly learned that about her mother, that she hadn't fully known her. But Roger? Was he really Ryan's only idea? She took a deep breath.

"Well, he seemed pretty concerned. And he doesn't seem to me to be the type, but I hear what you are saying. We never know each other as well as we think. Look at me, my mother." Sky looked at Ryan's bent head. "Look at you."

Ryan looked up from his notepad when she said this. His blue eyes had smears of shimmery green that reminded Sky of those abalone shells in Roger's front yard. He stared at her, and she stared back but felt her skin prickle under his gaze. As she rubbed the goosebumps off her forearms, she felt his eyes wander there too. He looked away, and Sky thought she saw the quietest hint of a blush. He flipped his notebook closed and leaned back.

"So," he asked, "do you like living here? In Sausalito?"

Sky exhaled. Whatever that moment was, it had passed.

"I do, it's nice to be out of the city but close enough to go in anytime. Mostly to see my mom. Do you live in the city?"

"Yes, in Sunset."

"Nice. I like that area."

"Not much landscape architecture there."

"Nope, not much landscape in the city in general."

They sat staring at each other for another few moments.

Ryan looked away first, put his pen in the spiral at the top of his little notebook, and put it in the pocket of his blazer. "Guess I better be going."

"No more questions?"

"Not without your lawyer here."

Sky winced.

"I'm kidding, kidding. Like I said, I don't think you have anything to do with this."

He stood up, looking suddenly embarrassed in his height. She wondered again if perhaps he was newer at his job than he'd let on. He seemed to go from too tender to too harsh. Her mother would like him, she thought.

She walked him to the door but let him pull it open himself.

"I'll check in tomorrow," he said.

"Okay," Sky nodded, a little disappointed, she realized, that he was leaving. Odd as he was.

"And Sky?" He turned to her in her doorway, his tall frame and broad shoulders taking up most of it. "Do you know your blood type, by chance?"

She looked at him, "O-negative."

"The stain is either pretty old or was cleaned really well, so getting DNA off of it might present a challenge. But if we can eliminate the possibility that it's your blood from something, then that'd be . . . helpful."

Sky nodded again. Then said, "Okay."

"Okay, bye." Ryan leaned toward her, and she thought for just a moment he might give her a hug, but he stuck out his hand. She shook it firmly, like she'd taught herself to do.

"Bye," Sky said, and closed the door behind him. Twisting the deadbolt quietly so that he wouldn't hear it as he made his way down the hall.

When he was gone Sky felt a little queasy, like she'd said something wrong to him. Why had he just asked her about her blood type? Made that lawyer joke? And he'd seemed to recognize Jake's name when she'd said it. She felt like a crazy woman talking to him. *My mother is missing. She broke up with her boyfriend. She left lights on.* These were behaviors that fell in the realm of normalcy for most people, but not her mother. Again, she wondered if this was a cruel joke her mother was playing on her: Just try to explain me to those suits, she would have said.

Or perhaps he didn't really believe her? And what was this chemistry between them? She should have told him about the photograph she had, the one from Marguerite. She wanted to talk more to Marguerite.

Should she wait? What if her mother came back today, would she be able to talk to Marguerite still? She was an adult, but if her mother asked her not to, she'd probably comply. Was this her only window to ask questions, to hear those stories Marguerite had to tell? Tomorrow, she thought.

In the meantime, she'd curl up on the couch with her laptop and google again the Ashram, Jake, how cults worked on their followers, jobs in landscape architecture, and when it got be almost midnight, other missing persons.

A few years ago, a fourteen-year-old girl in Salt Lake City, Utah—Elizabeth Smart—had been kidnapped from her bedroom in the night. If Sky remembered right, the man had cut the window screen open and threatened her little sister, with whom she shared a bedroom, to stay quiet with a knife. He was a deluded man who thought he was a prophet. He and his female partner kept Elizabeth for six months, raping her daily. But one of the most striking parts of the story, for Sky, was that while an entire city looked for her—she was everywhere. The assailant took her out with him, dressing her in a white head and face covering which his partner also wore. Photos were taken of them at a New Year's party, months before she was found. People later reported seeing them at gas stations, grocery stores—they were an open secret. Hiding in plain sight.

Sky had just moved back up to the Bay area when it happened and was staying with her mother while she looked for internships and jobs. When Elizabeth Smart was found and the truth came out, it was a foggy and cool spring day. Her mother came home from the store while she sat at the kitchen table on her laptop, job hunting. She silently put away the groceries, but Sky could tell by a certain punctuation to her actions, the sharpness with which she opened and closed a cupboard, that she was angry. She could feel her own body tighten up in response to her mother, and scanned the events of the morning, wondering if she could be the source.

Just as she was wondering if she should have offered to go to the store, or pay for some of the groceries, her mother said, "That sick fucker!"

Sky didn't say anything.

"I just heard on the radio in the car—they found Elizabeth. Some gardener took her from her room, had her for months, some religious fanatic.

Believing what he did was willed by God; he raped her every day. What the fuck is wrong with our society that people think they can do that, and that they are right? And he took her places—she was too scared to run away." Her mother slammed a cupboard closed just as Sky was realizing that she must be talking about the Elizabeth Smart case. Her mother's use of her first name was, well . . . Sky hadn't even realized she'd been following the case. She wondered how often her mother had thought of this girl. She resisted a twinge of jealousy.

"All I'm saying is that there's a special place in hell. And there was a woman involved. Her too. She watched the whole thing, went along with it. She's probably been so mentally fucked up by this guy . . ." Her mother stopped with the groceries and placed her hands on the counter as if to stop herself from some tirade. After a moment, she said, "At least she got out."

"That's good news, her parents must be so relieved."

Sky turned back to her laptop as her mother repeated, again, "At least she got away," as she put the soy milk in the fridge.

The next day, Tuesday, Sky stood in her grandmother's doorway, and Ilana didn't look surprised to see her. Her face revealed even a little relief.

"Your mother?" she asked as she swung the tall door open wide and ushered Sky in.

"Nothing. I . . ." Sky was about to tell her why she was there but realized she didn't really know. Driving into the city, she told herself that everything was about finding her mother, or what happened to her mother. She needed, she felt, to actually visit the Ashram. When she had googled it the night before, she had focused on images, and again felt a sense of déjà vu. Perhaps because the photos of women with long, swinging hair and sunned skin reminded her of her mother. Most of the images were of Jake, who she was sure she'd seen before. His eyes so striking as to look animal. She'd scanned every face for Edi's but didn't find it. One image that had stuck out to her was a photograph taken from afar, by an onlooker. A group of maybe twenty-five "followers" in white were lying supine on a beach. Lying still, hands outward and limp as if they had completely relinquished something. They actually looked dead, like fish washed up from the sea. Jake was standing over them, his hands grasped behind his back, his gaze down but distant, as if he was just walking on the beach, contemplating things elsewhere. The bodies around him invisible to him. A careless puppeteer, she'd thought, as she leaned into her computer and again looked at each face for Edi's. In this photo, she thought she had found her, only to look at another face and think perhaps no, that this one was her mother and not the other long-haired woman. The photo was gritty, the faces small but also similar: young, beautiful. And in this one there were just as many men as women. Sky looked at the bodies of the men, looked at Jake and wondered if she'd finally find a father if she went down there and talked to him. Like her conversation with Marguerite, Edi's disappearance seemed suddenly a doorway into a hidden past. One she had never had before and might never have again. A chance to have conversations, ask questions, and get answers that she'd always wanted. She needed to talk to Deb, too.

But first, she needed to know more from Marguerite. The missing pieces from the other day. So that was why she was here, but she couldn't quite say it, so she just said, "I just . . ." and Ilana smiled kindly.

"Come in, dear, she's just eating her lunch. Will you eat something?"

"I, no, you don't need to . . ."

"I'll make you a plate. You look like you could use a little something."

Ilana showed Sky into a small formal dining room at the end of the hall with a beautiful mahogany table and a china cabinet in the corner. One shelf full of ornate ashtrays. All of a different era. There was a faded gold wallpaper with faint bird etchings. A phoenix, perhaps, Sky thought. Marguerite sat at the one end of the table; a *Reader's Digest* crossword folded under a giant magnifying glass next to her. Chicken salad and rye crackers filled her plate. A small crystal glass of white wine beside her. There was something comforting about the scene to Sky.

Marguerite looked startled to have this private moment intruded upon. She quickly wiped her mouth with the paper napkin balled into one hand, already stained with her magenta lipstick.

"Oh dear, dear you, Edi? It's not Edi, is it?"

"She's fine," Sky said quickly when she realized Marguerite thought her unexpected visit was one to bring bad news. "Well, she's not fine. Or she might not be. I still don't know anything, I just . . . I just wanted to know a little more about—I thought it might help . . . I'm sorry. I should have called."

"Oh, thank god. No, I'm glad you're here." Marguerite visibly relaxed, unclenched her hand with the napkin and pushed her plate away from her a little. "Perhaps some coffee, dear? Please, sit." She turned to Ilana, who was already on her way to the kitchen.

Sky sat down at the chair closest to Marguerite.

"How can I help, dear? You look tired."

Sky nodded; she was beyond tired. There had been so much information to take in; her brain felt like it was wired to some high frequency that kept vibrating between her two temples, making a dry wind behind her eyes.

"I think I'd like to know more about what happened to Edi. The child, the running away. That part of her life. And if you know any more about the Ashram, I really think . . . somehow, I think it's important."

Marguerite nodded and pushed her chair back a little. Ilana came in and brought her a small plate of chicken salad and crackers.

She decided to take a bite to be polite and had just reached for the fork when Marguerite started to speak. She was looking down, talking to her hands.

"I didn't know what had happened to Edi right away. It was a couple of months later, when I took her to the doctor. She'd been throwing up, I thought she had some kind of stomach virus. The doctor pulled me aside and told me she was pregnant. Handed me a brochure for a home for unwed mothers. I was furious. In the car, I knew she already knew. Had already known. I was too angry to speak. When we got home she tried to go up to her room, but I stopped her. I asked her who in the hell she had been sleeping with. I told her her father was lucky he didn't live to see this. I threw a teacup at her, and oh, the things I said. And she just stood there, waiting for me to calm down so she could tell me, what he, what that vile man did to her . . ."

Marguerite bit her lip and turned to the corner of the room, as if the ghost of her former self was there, or maybe Sky's teenage mother.

"I had been out. Left them in the house alone. Trying to run to the bakery to pick up a cake for my bridge club. Something so little . . . so stupid. To trust him. I thought he was too old, in his thirties. I was stupid. Naive.

"That afternoon, and what I did in the months that followed, those are my biggest regrets in life. I couldn't do right by Edi, nor by that child. And when I tried to make it right, two times after, I made it worse."

She looked back at Sky, and then again into the hands in her lap.

"What do you mean?" Sky set down the fork quietly.

"Hiding the pregnancy, finding the child parents, I thought it was the right thing to do, and Edi certainly didn't fight it. I didn't think either of us could bear to look at *his* child every day, and I wanted to spare her . . . but then when we both saw that sweet babe when it was just new to the world. I think you forget, in times like that, how limitless love really is . . ." Marguerite looked again to the corner of the room. "But it was done. The adopting parents were waiting outside the delivery room. They seemed like good people. I just wanted Edi to have a normal life, the stigma was, then, well, it was strong. It would have affected even the child's life, I thought. But perhaps times had already changed, and I didn't know it. After all, you grew up fine without a father . . ."

Sky wanted to correct her, but she realized she was right. "Fine" wasn't the word she would have used, but in its essence, it was true. She was fine.

"Did you ever think of contacting the police? Telling other parents?" Sky leaned forward.

"I did contact the police. Right away. Edi was horrified. Humiliated. An officer came and sat in our living room and asked her the most personal questions. It was awful. He kept asking her if she had flirted with the piano teacher, what she had been wearing, trying to turn the story in his mouth. I finally asked him to leave, and he smirked. Said he didn't think the report had any 'clout.' Even today, I remember he used this word. I wanted to spit in his face, Sky, I did. I wish Edi knew how mad I was, but she was only mad at me. Telling me I should have asked her before I called them. Telling me I always made it worse. I've come to believe she was right about that."

Ilana arrived then with steaming hot coffee served again in those thin porcelain teacups, on saucers, with perfect squares of sugar nestled on small silver spoons. This world, this opulent domestic scene was, Sky realized, the opposite of the world her mother had cultivated in her own house. The perfect details, the matching china, the silver, the daughter who played piano, it was all something to be escaped. Spun together with rape and humiliation and loss. Sky felt such a swelling of compassion for her mother then that it almost made her throat close. She resisted rubbing her eyes. Took a sip of the coffee, welcomed the slight sting of its heat.

She had to find her mother. She turned again toward Marguerite.

"What was the second time you made it worse?" Her voice came out hoarse.

"Telling Edi the child was dead, that was a mistake."

Sky nodded, "You think you should have saved her the grief? I think it was good that you . . ."

"No, Sky dear, I lied." Marguerite looked to the ghost in the corner again. "She was in so much pain at the time, all of this hopping around, drugs, I thought it might close a chapter for her if she thought the child wasn't out there somewhere. So, I told her I'd heard he'd died of an illness."

Sky felt her mouth sucked dry of any words. She remembered her mother telling her that the child had died. She remembered crying for the little sick child. For her mother's double loss.

"It was an abhorrent thing to do. I'm sure you see now why your mother hated me. There's no way to excuse it, but it did help. She quit drugs, she found the Ashram, which was actually a safer and more stable place than she'd been for the couple of years before that. She began to write me, actually write me, not just blank postcards." Marguerite shook her head. "But it didn't last and when she found out . . ."

"How did she find out?"

"I told her. I thought I was dying, so I told her. It was when you two were living here, you were no bigger than three. After the Ashram. Everything was finally perfect; I had my girls here safe under my roof." Marguerite's voice started to shake a little and Sky could see she was resisting the urge to cry. "And then one morning I was toweling off after the shower, I could hear your mother singing to you down that hall and then suddenly there it was. Like a stone under my palm. This lump, this mass. The doctors thought it was . . ." Marguerite let out a shaky sigh. "They eventually did an operation and it turned out it was benign, but I didn't want to carry a lie like that into the next world. Ilana thinks the lie was what caused the tumor . . ."

"What happened when you told her?"

"She cried, she told me she could never forgive me all that had happened, that she had tried but this was too much, she said. She asked if I knew where he was."

"He?"

"The child. It was a boy."

Sky looked at this white-haired woman. This stranger. She looked at her and wondered if she was dreaming. Disorientation again. Dizziness. A hot ringing in her head. She knew Edi had told her that she didn't know the sex, hadn't she? Or was Sky misremembering everything?

"Did Edi know it was a boy?"

"Yes, of course. She held him after he was born, wanted to name him, some hippie name like yours."

Her mother had lied to her daughter the way she'd been lied to by her mother. Sky felt as if her vision of the past, previously a straight line of images leading back behind her was now split into two lines of competing images, like when you walk into an electronic store and there are a hundred TVs all on different channels. Different versions of now. Different versions of then.

"I'm sorry, Sky." Marguerite clenched her fists and leaned forward in her chair. "I do like your name."

Sky let out a small laugh, laughed that that's what Marguerite was apologizing for in this moment. An offhanded comment about names.

"It's okay, you're right, it's a hippie name. Perfect for the product of a cult, right?" Sky didn't expect the bitterness in her own voice.

"Oh dear. Perhaps I shouldn't have told you all that. I guess your mother can't do worse to me than she already does, but maybe *you* didn't want to know that. I'm sorry."

"No, I wanted to know. I want to know everything. I want to find my mother, or what happened to her . . ." An image of a ghostly bloodstain on her mother's floor, a faded Rorschach someone had tried to blot clean— that's how she imagined it—came to mind, but she had already decided she wouldn't tell Marguerite about it. Not yet.

Already, she thought, taking a sip of her cooling coffee, she had inherited this trait: lying to protect.

She cleared her throat. "About this cult, you said the other day that they'd gotten more extreme over the years—what did you mean?"

"Oh, dear, honestly one never knows what is true and what is rumor with these things."

"Do you think they would hurt my mother?"

"No, dear, I don't think so. Jake became more controlling, and I know that's one reason your mother left, and I imagine it's only gotten worse since then." Marguerite opened her mouth to continue, and then closed it again.

"Whatever you are going to say, you can tell me, I want to know."

"I also heard he was being investigated for bringing younger and younger women into the cult, underage girls, and to that I say it's about time. If you look at that photograph I gave you the other day, there is no way some of those women are more than sixteen. Edi herself was barely of age. This latest investigation was in an article maybe about a year ago, dear Ilana clipped it out for me. It's around here somewhere, if you'd like I can have her look for it."

Sky nodded, she wanted to tell her grandmother not to bother, but she felt too desperate to let go of any possible thread that might lead back to her mother. She felt she should think of more questions, about her mother's life before her, but also felt like she'd heard enough for now. She didn't know if she could take any more of Edi's life, it was already a lot: rape, running away, finding a cult, having a second child, leaving the cult, falling out with her mother over her first child. It was exhausting just to think about.

"Thanks," she said, "for everything. I should probably be going." Sky wiped her hands on her jeans, wondering if she should not be in a rush to leave.

"I'm glad you came again and let me know if I can help you in any way. I've made a lot of mistakes in my life . . . but, well, the past is the past."

"I'll let you know when I know anything." Sky stood up and extended a hand to her grandmother, a gesture that felt both too formal and too masculine.

"Thank you, Sky, I appreciate that." Her grandmother saved her by taking her hand in hers and squeezing her fingers. Sky walked out the door and couldn't believe how much cooler it was outside, how much brighter it was, as she walked the couple of blocks to her parking spot.

Sky had, like many only children, fantasized extensively about having a sibling. In one fantasy that she could remember clearly because it had played so often in her head, she was being picked on by some older kids, something that happened from time to time in her neighborhood. They were making fun of her: the reasons varied, maybe because she was learning to skateboard, or because she liked to play with the boys during recess. And behind her a shadow would appear. The kid adversaries would go pale and back away, and Sky would turn to see her adoring older sibling, coming to her defense. The older sibling would always have the perfect insult ready, and the other kids would be afraid but also jealous of her. Sometimes it was an older sister, but most of the time it was an older brother, someone who treated Sky both like a baby and like his true platonic love.

Sky had always gotten along better with boys, and now with men. There was an easiness to them, and she supposed that her mother was the same way. While Sky had Liz and Edi had Deb, the majority of the visitors to the house were male. Mostly friends. It was easy for Sky to see that most of these men were at least halfway in love with her mother, but now she wondered if that had also been true for herself in college and high school. As she'd finished school, she'd evened the scorecard a little, made more women friends, but the fact that she worked, and had worked, with all men was something she had sort of liked in spite of the difficulty, at least she had liked it until Ned. It had always seemed to her to be easier to get to know men. You knew pretty immediately if you were going to get along with a guy. But women, Sky had never been able to tell if they liked her. She'd always been a little intimidated by women she didn't know—she assumed they had all been told secrets about femininity that Sky didn't know and never would because Edi was her mother.

Now, she wondered if perhaps she'd been intuiting an older brother. Someone out there. Where was he? Could she find him? Was that legal? Ethical? Fair? What if he was another Ned? What if he looked exactly like his father? Her stomach sank at the thought of her sibling out there, maybe not knowing he was the product of rape, enjoying a perfect life until one day she showed up and let him in on his biological mess of a family.

She thought about all of this as she drove back across the bridge, never tiring of the way the russet orange contrasted with the dark teal of the bay. Today only a few sailboats dotted the water, braving the white caps. A sleepy line of gray fog waited out above the water. Sky knew that when the sun went down it would move in, shrouding the city.

When she got home, Sky dug her phone out of her bag to see that she had three voicemails. One from Deb, one from Ryan, and one from Janet. It was almost four o'clock but felt much later. She'd managed to pass another day down the rabbit hole. She walked into her house, grabbed a can of sparkling water from the fridge, and sat down on the couch to listen to the messages.

From Ryan: "Hello, Sky, it's Ryan, call me, I don't have any news but wanted to check in."

Next, Deb, and at Deb's voice Sky felt a sudden swell of hope: "Sky, it's Deb, listen, I just got home and heard Edi's missing? Call me as soon as you get this . . . love you, sweetie."

Sky skipped Janet's message; she knew it would just be Janet wanting to be updated on everything and she was preemptively annoyed. But she called Deb back right away. Deb had always been a maternal figure to Sky, and while the phone rang Sky felt both a flood of relief that Deb was home, and an urge to cry when Deb said hello, her voice sweet, loud, cheery as always.

"Deb, it's . . ."

"Sky, oh, thank goodness you called, I heard you called while I was gone, and then I called Roger when I didn't get you the first time and he filled me in on everything. Jesus, dear, how are you?"

"I don't know, tired. I . . . I've been finding out all sorts of things, I met Marguerite?"

"You did? She's still alive?"

"Yes, and she told me about the Ashram, and . . ."

"Oh, good *lord*. Listen, Sky, are you busy? I'm jetlagged as hell but how about I come over for a bit now and bring a pizza and then I'll be asleep probably by seven. Would that be good? Are you still in that same apartment in Sausalito?"

Sky nodded quickly with gratitude, ready for Deb to come and fix everything, feed her, before she remembered to say, "Yes, yes, come," aloud into the phone.

Sky called Ryan next—she'd been so excited to talk to him the past few days, hoping each time they talked would reveal something new about her mother's whereabouts—but now she was tired and felt a certain stagnation in their conversation. Yesterday had been weird. Maybe even awkward. But she wanted to move past that, and she did appreciate his involvement in the case even if she didn't fully understand it. Sky played with the top of her soda can, twisting the tab off as she held the phone up to her ear.

He answered after one ring. "Sky. How are you, what have you been doing?" He almost sounded as if he'd been concerned for her safety.

"I'm okay." Sky paused but Ryan was waiting for her to go on. "I went back to my grandmother's. I wanted to talk more about some of my mother's history."

"Anything helpful?"

"No, well, other than that I do think this Ashram thing is important."

"I put a request in for the files on Jake Bridger, I'm still waiting for them."

"Okay."

There was a silence on the line. Sky wanted to end it, so she said aloud what she'd been thinking on the way home from Marguerite's.

"I'm thinking I'm going to drive down to the Ashram tomorrow," and as soon as she said it she knew it was true. She had to see it. This was her chance. And this was an action she could take, instead of just waiting for her mother to show up. She wanted to go while she had this momentum of searching for things past. "When I was googling it, it looked like it's still where it's always been, back in the hills between Carmel Valley and Gonzales."

"Sky, that could be dangerous. Let me get that file, and we can talk more about it. But cults like that, they don't always take kindly to outsiders . . ."

"I'm not an outsider, remember?" Sky's voice was irritated, she was tired. Maybe she was a little mad. But not at Ryan. She just didn't want to sit around. She was ready for something to break. What if her mother was just . . . there. And this whole thing could be over. It was worth the drive to find out. Then one part of her messy life would be fixed.

"Which may make it more dangerous . . . Sky, just, look, let me get this file and I'll call you later. Maybe I can come with you. But I promise I won't leave here today without getting that file and calling you."

"Okay." Sky breathed and added another, softer, "Okay."

"Good, I'll call you in a bit."

Sky hung up the phone without saying goodbye, a habit she'd inherited from her mother. She remembered it used to bother her when she sat in the kitchen and watched her mother hang up on Deb with an "okay."

"What?" Edi would say. "The conversation was over, she knows that."

She put her phone and the soda can down on the scratched wood coffee table and sunk back into her worn but soft sofa. She had a headache, she realized, and had had it for many hours. She pressed her head back into the sofa cushion. She tried to let the pressure erase any thoughts, but she couldn't help but rethink the last real conversation she'd had with her mother.

They'd been sitting on her mother's front porch. Sky had brought dinner over for the both of them, Lebanese take-out. It was a nice evening in early March, and they'd pulled kitchen chairs out onto the porch to eat, the take-out boxes balanced awkwardly on their laps, a box of hummus and pita on the planks between them.

Sky had been talking about work, the newest project she was working on, but they'd fallen silent as they'd eaten.

Her mother wiped her mouth with a thin paper napkin from the take-out bag.

"Do you know why I named you Sky?"

Sky looked up. Edi wasn't usually one to reminisce. She was chewing so she just shrugged, she didn't know, and she knew Edi knew she didn't know.

"When I was pregnant with you, I used to lie on my back and look at the sky. Having you, it felt like I was doing something right. Doing something important for the world. Bringing you into it. And I wanted every possibility for you, the world open for you, easy for you. Easy as looking up into the sky." Her mother stared straight ahead for a moment before turning to Sky, smiling sadly. "I was naive, really, but now you know."

Sky had smiled back, but she'd honestly felt a little irritation at this story. She felt like her mother wanted her to say, "It *has* been easy, thank you." And she was tempted to give in to this, but also felt if she added to the sentimentality in the moment, Edi would automatically recoil. Later, on her drive home to Marin, she'd felt a sense of bitterness. Her life had been easier than her mother's maybe, but at the same time every difficulty she could think of had been created by her mother. Her mother's refusal to let Roger into their lives fully, to give Sky a father, to tell Sky the truth, to behave like a normal mother or what Sky imagined a normal mother would be.

Now as she sat on her couch and remembered this moment, it was cast in a whole other light. Before, she'd pictured her mother in Golden Gate Park, long-haired and big bellied, loose hippie dress. Now she pictured her in the dry foothills where the Ashram was, maybe under an oak. The sentence "doing something important for the world" was different now, too. It sounded like cult speak, propagating the chosen people.

But she also felt, as she drifted involuntarily out of consciousness, a stiff regret that she hadn't given her mother any affirmation in that moment. That she hadn't said, "You did it, Edi, it's been pretty easy." Especially given what she knew now about her mother's life, it would have only been a small sacrifice on Sky's part to say those words.

Though, of course, those small inches had always felt impossible to give someone like Edi, who almost always took the mile.

ॐ

The sound of her doorbell woke her from a heavy, black sleep. She walked to the door and buzzed Deb in. She cracked the door open and listened to her shuffling up the stairs.

A moment later, Deb swept into the apartment, put down the pizza and her purse on the hall floor before she tucked her petite stature under Sky's chin, wrapping her arms fully around her. She smelled like sandalwood and Sky breathed in this familiar presence. Deb had always been generous with her affection, and Sky had often thought she would have been a natural mother. Now she held Sky and muttered, "Oh sweetie, oh honey, don't worry, Deb's here." She paused and added in a muffled voice from Sky's shoulder, "And she brought pizza and Pinot."

Sky laughed and pulled away, wiping her face even though it was dry.

"You look like hell, dearie." Deb picked up what she'd brought from the floor and stepped behind her to put down the box of pizza on the subway tile of Sky's counter and pull a bottle of wine from her purse.

"Sorry, I just woke up, it's been . . . oh, Deb, it's been so weird." She suddenly wanted to tell Deb everything. "Things have been bad at work, too, this guy . . . and my mom, and all this crap I'm learning that she never told me."

Sky bit her lip, and Deb led her back to the couch. "Edi will be back, dear, I know it, and I have some ideas about it too, but you have a seat and I'll get us some food."

Sky let herself be wrapped in a gray wool throw that Deb found on the back of a chair and listened as Deb opened and closed cupboards in her kitchen, looking for plates. Wine glasses. Deb had only been to her apartment once before. She'd stopped by with Edi when Sky was moving in. They'd both stood in the sunlight and raved about the picture window as Sky had unpacked dishes. But now she was in Sky's kitchen. This, Sky thought, is what it would be like if Edi was dead. People in her space, taking care of her, the abnormality of grief. Sky let *that* thought, the thought *if Edi is dead* swim by like a dark fish under a current and quickly willed herself to wonder what Edi would think if she walked in right now. She briefly imagined a look of betrayal on Edi's face, a flash of jealousy that her daughter and best friend were having dinner together.

Deb spoke loudly from the kitchen, "So Peru, *wow*, a week in Machu Picchu and two weeks in the jungle with a shaman doing some ceremonies. Some real cosmic shit. It was mind-blowing. I feel so refreshed, in fact, I can't wait to talk to your mother about it. The stuff we were on about before I left, what stupid small shit in the face of the great universe, you know? Talk about perspective. I've got to take her next time."

Sky listened to Deb's certainty that her mother would return. She tried to let it buoy her up as Deb came in and set an overly full wine glass in her hand and a plate of veggie pizza on the table in front of her. She waited for Deb to sit down before she asked her.

"Deb, do you mind telling me what you were 'on about' with Edi?"

"Oh, silly stuff, really. It was about a long-ago past . . ." Deb looked at the pizza in her lap. "Actually, it was about the Ashram you mentioned on the phone."

"So you knew about it? You knew I was born there?"

"Ohfcourse I knew, dearie, I was there."

Sky once again felt a strange disorientation. The lines of the past dividing, shaded in different colors, playing on different screens. She set down her glass of wine in case her hands were as shaky as she felt, even though she watched them move fluidly to the table and back.

"What?"

"At the Ashram, we didn't have outside doctors, so we helped each other give birth, so I was there in the beautiful moment you came to earth." Deb reached over and grabbed her hand and Sky glimpsed a flash of deep sadness, a strange backdrop to the smile lines of her eyes.

"Deb, you were there? In the cult?"

"Yes, I joined about a year after your mother. In fact, she helped recruit me. And when it was time, she helped me get out. Actually, you both did—you were with her when she came to get me."

Sky remembered the dry hills, her mother yelling at her, or someone, to get in the car. The man in white. When Marguerite had told her that she had left at age two, she figured it must have been a dream. But now everything was too real.

"Jesus," Sky said, and let Deb put the plate of pizza in her lap. "Why did Edi keep everything from me? Why did you?"

"For our protection, and yours. At least at first. We were worried Jake would find us, of course, but also, well, not everything the cult did was legal, and there was an atmosphere of suppression around parenting then. You know, protect the children from everything. Especially the truth." Deb took a bite of her pizza. Sky watched her chew for a moment.

"Do you think she would have ever told me?"

"Yes, I do. In fact, that's what our fight was about, in part. She wanted to start digging up some of that past, to set some records straight, including your birth certificate. I wasn't ready for that . . ."

"My birth certificate?" Sky had never seen her birth certificate, she'd realized. Her mother had told her she'd lost it. She turned to Deb, who was taking a large swallow of wine. "Deb, Jake is my father, right?"

Deb took more wine in her mouth before setting down her glass. "Dearie, there are some things I'd really rather you talk to your mother about . . ."

"Deb." Sky suddenly felt feverish, she leaned forward into Deb. "I really think the Ashram might be a clue to where my mother is. Maybe she's there, or they know where she is. Did Roger tell you about the people he saw? And the man in white Janet saw? I really think we need to go up there . . ."

"Whoa, sister. Your mother wouldn't go back there if they paid her a million bucks. Neither would I, and neither should you. That place got. Well, it got weird. In a bad way."

"What do you mean? Why did you leave?" Sky felt the pizza plate warm in her lap but didn't register any hunger, so she moved it to the coffee table.

"When the cult started, well, when we joined, it was all about love and freedom and living sustainably away from a capitalist society, like so much of what was happening then. But as the cult got bigger and as Jake got more and more power, he . . . changed." Deb dabbed her mouth with a paper towel she'd grabbed as a napkin. One for each of them.

"Changed?"

"Or maybe he'd been that way all along. He became more controlling, things became less democratic and more about being an absolute blind follower, and he took the cult into some territory that made Edi and I increasingly uncomfortable. Thank goodness for you, really. It wasn't easy to leave, but Edi knew she didn't want you growing up there, so it gave her the courage to leave. And her leaving gave me the courage to leave. I don't know if you can imagine what it's like to be in a group like that, to be young, and homeless, and . . ."

Deb's voice broke a little, and she concentrated on her wine glass again, raising it to her lips.

"Sorry . . . jetlag. And all this old shit . . ."

"It's okay. Thanks, Deb, really, for coming." Sky put her hand out to touch Deb's knee.

"Would you eat already? Because the reason I came was to tell you something you need to tell your detective friend in case it's important."

"What?" Sky leaned forward.

"I'm not telling you until you take a bite of pizza."

Sky smiled slightly, it felt good to be mothered. She reached for her plate and took a bite of the lukewarm pizza. She let her hunger take over and was surprised to find herself taking another bite before she'd even swallowed the first.

"You need to look into Phil Hayes. The piano teacher."

"Phil?" Sky remembered watching her grandmother's mouth, placing this phrase "the piano teacher" in her grandmother's house, her there, her there imagining her mother there as a teenager.

But the pizza was bright in her mouth, and she let her brain fail to make a connection.

Deb helped her. "You know what happened to your mother? The piano teacher?"

"Yes."

"His name was Phil Hayes, and if anyone has harmed your mother, it was him." She swallowed what she had in her mouth, already like a lump of wet paper. Her appetite once again gone.

"But that was decades ago, why would he . . . how would he even find her?"

Deb shook her head. "She found him." She took another small bite.

"What? Why?" Sky waited for Deb to finish chewing.

"When your mother decided to leave your grandmother's with you, she had no money. She decided it was time for Phil to pay. So, she contacted him and told him she'd press charges, and tell the newspapers what he'd done, and about the child, if he didn't send her a monthly check."

"Jesus." Sky's stomach turned at the thought of her mother, calling her rapist, inviting him back into her life, feeding her child off money from a man that had ruined her life. She knew Edi would be comfortable with that, would feel the justice. Her mother, perpetually sixteen. Her emotional maturity frozen by the trauma he'd caused her. She moved her plate from her lap back to the table and held her hand to her forehead. "Edi, Jesus."

"I know, sweetie. But it was the only thing she could think of. You know Edi, proud. And she tried applying for other jobs, but she had you to take care of and not even a high school degree and it was a year or so before Marguerite sent any money."

"She sent us money?"

"Yes, she did, all through your school years. There was always an envelope for your mother with those awful dresses she sent you."

Sky felt a renewed sting. Not just because she had loved those dresses, but because once again she felt that every fact of her life was now up in the air.

"How long did she blackmail him?"

"It was years. He paid monthly for a long time and then he'd started to once in a while refuse, and so she'd scare him, and he'd pay again for a while, and it was off and on like that. They formed an odd relationship. Eventually your mother found a lawyer to advise her and a few months ago they settled on something, and your mom walked away with a good amount of money and Phil was *not* happy . . ."

"Who was the lawyer?" Even though Sky already knew the answer and felt it like a stone underneath her tongue, she needed Deb to say it aloud.

Deb spoke into her wine glass. "Liz," she said and took a large sip.

Sky folded her arms in front of her and looked at her own wine glass untouched on the table. "Why didn't she tell me?" Her voice was too tired to express the anger she felt.

"I'm sure lawyer-client confidentiality is what she'd tell you, Sky. None of this was kept from you to hurt you, the opposite really . . ."

"I know, to protect me . . ."

"I'm sorry, I know it's a lot to take in all at once." Deb got up to get another piece of pizza from the kitchen.

Sky stared at her hands as Deb yelled from the kitchen. "I'm going to eat one last piece and then let us both get some sleep."

Sky sighed and finally reached for her wine. She took a sip and was surprised at how strong it tasted. She needed to eat more. She needed to sleep. Deb came back in, chewing as she sat, folding her legs under her.

"It's okay, Deb, thanks for coming over, really, and for being honest with me. I'll call Ryan, the detective, and let him know about Phil. It just makes me sick . . . the whole thing. It's so much more fucked up than I ever could have imagined."

"Edi hasn't had an easy go of it, that's for sure. But she wanted you to. She really did. She wanted you to have a life that wasn't a part of this mess."

"But you think she will be back?" Sky put her head on Deb's shoulder. Letting the sip of wine she'd had swim in her head.

"I do."

"Where do you think she is?"

"I think she's probably sowing some wild oats, like she's done before. You know Edi, and me, we've been going through the Change . . ."

Sky raised her eyebrows.

"Menopause, dearie." Deb patted Sky's knee. "And it's a bitch. And it's not just physical. It's like a wake-up call. A reckoning. A sweaty, irritating nudge to get you to take inventory. That's why I went to Peru. To get some perspective. Maybe the people in white were a group Edi found consolation in. God knows there's plenty of spiritual groups around here."

"But all the weird things . . . the lights, her purse, did Roger tell you about the purse? Her zodiac necklace, that one she always has on, was left in my room, a photo taken . . . and blood. Deb, they found blood by an open window. I mean, the detective is already asking questions about suspects."

"Sky." Deb put her hand on Sky's cheek and leaned closer in. "I know this sounds weird. But I was in deep liminal spaces in Peru, between life and death, and I swear to god I think I'd know if Edi had gone over to the other side. I know that's not much to go on, and I still think you need to look into Phil and make sure, but really, I feel her alive"—Deb closed her eyes and held her other hand over her chest—"in here."

Deb kept her eyes closed and took a deep breath. There was a silence that might have been awkward, but Sky had to smile a little. That was so Deb, in the face of all logic, to favor cosmic intuition. She felt a small ache for her mother.

"And at that"—Deb stood up—"I'm out." She straightened her sweater and began clearing her plate.

Sky followed her into the kitchen as she found space in the fridge for the leftover pizza. "Do I need to put a sign on the box that says 'eat me,' or will you please remember to eat it?"

"I will, Deb, thanks."

Deb quickly gulped the last of her wine and set the glass in the sink. She stood on tiptoes to kiss Sky on the top of the head.

"Love you, dear, call me tomorrow, and for goodness' sake stay the hell away from the Ashram. It's a can of worms you don't want to open . . . think of it like letting missionaries into your living room. You'll never get rid of them."

"Love you too, Deb."

Sky closed and locked the door behind Deb. Wishing she'd had time to tell Deb about the Ned situation, to hear Deb tell her she'd done the right thing by just talking to Jerry and waiting to file a formal complaint despite Liz's advice. Liz's advice. Jesus, Liz. Sky let out a bitter sigh. It seemed everyone knew more about her life than she did.

She returned to the couch and tried to finish her pizza slice, now cold, and wine. She did better on the wine than the pizza, sitting back into the couch and trying to process, to even begin to process, what she'd learned. She closed her eyes and for once she didn't try to stop any dark thoughts; she let them all swim under the black water of her headache, her heartache.

Sky and her mother were back in that redwood forest, the silent giants towering above them. The earth beneath their feet was dark and wet and again they were trying to get away from someone, back to the car. Edi started to run, and Sky rushed to catch up, but her foot got stuck. A root had grabbed her ankle like a gnarled hand and suddenly it was Marguerite there, in the forest, holding her back and she wanted to run but she couldn't move. She tried to call out to Edi but couldn't speak, either.

Then her mother, her beautiful golden mother, stopped, turned around, and walked back through the trees to her. She smiled at Sky, calm now, and reached out to Sky and handed her a pink mess of something. A pomegranate. Broken open to reveal a nest of bloody eggs inside. Sky took it, and her mother's mouth suddenly turned black. A patch of tar swallowing her face just as Sky was finally able to speak.

To yell *Mom*.

Sky woke up in the early dawn unsure of whether she had been yelling in her sleep. Unsure if she was really yelling "Mom," or if it would have been "Edi" that came out.

She was still on the couch, cold. Her whole body ached. *Wednesday.*

She sat up and looked around. The empty wine glass had fallen out of her hand onto her straw rug and had left a few drops of red beside it. The plate of pizza sat undisturbed on the coffee table, and it occurred to Sky that maybe she should at least have a cat. Another sentient being who would have nudged her awake, reminded her of routines, of teeth brushing, bed.

She rubbed her face, pulling blond tangled strands behind her ears, and reached for her phone on the table. It needed charging, but she could see she'd missed three calls after Deb left. Another one from Janet, one from Liz, and one from Ryan.

She didn't want to fill Janet in; she pictured the woman secretly thriving on all the dirt Sky had learned about her mother over the past four days.

She moaned as she remembered what Deb had told her about Liz. Liz helping her mother blackmail Phil, or stop blackmailing Phil, or doing something that involved her mother behind her back. She became more awake with a flare of anger and part of her wanted to call Liz, wake her up, confront her immediately. But a larger part of her didn't have the energy for that right now.

Ryan. She skipped right to his message, heard his voice telling her to call him right away. She kicked herself for missing his call, what if he had found something, or needed some piece of information? She hung up on her voicemail and wondered how it was that a detective who she had barely just met, who seemed odd in his own right, was the person she wanted to talk to most right now. *Chemistry*, she briefly thought. She was her mother's daughter, after all, even if she rarely felt it.

She looked at her watch, just before 6:00 a.m. Too early to call, though she felt like he was probably the type to be up at five, or earlier. She lay back against the couch and squeezed her palms into her cheeks. She didn't feel better after sleeping for ten hours, but worse. Like she'd just taken a red-eye flight. Her blood coursing with an edge to it, hot against her skin. She was anxious. The small turquoise ring she wore on her right hand was tight and she twisted it off but held it in her hand. Liz had gotten it for her in Santa Fe a few years ago, for her birthday. Edi had noticed it on her hand immediately and when Sky told her that it was a birthday gift from Liz, Edi had raised her eyebrows.

Edi had always seemed mistrustful of Liz, since she and Sky had met at the end of high school playing on the same competitive soccer team together. In college, a couple of years into their friendship—Sky's closest friendship ever—Edi had told Sky one Sunday dinner, after a couple of glasses of wine, that it was only a matter of time until her friendship with Liz "blew up."

"Sky," Edi had said, "think about it. She's a lesbian. You are gorgeous."

Sky had blushed, they were eating on her mother's cramped sofa, plates of vegetarian spaghetti on their laps. "Edi, not everything is about sex . . ."

"Yes, it is, Sky." Edi took a gulp of wine, her green eyes twinkling with a pleasure that made Sky uncomfortable. "But you've never gotten that."

"Maybe for you . . ." Sky ventured, even though it was the kind of comment that might send Edi into a pouting fit.

"No, it's that way for everyone. Every guy 'friend' I've had has, in the end, made it clear he wants one thing. Some are more romantic and are happy to be in love from a distance, but they all at some point reveal their feelings. Eventually Liz will make a pass at you, I'd bet my life on it."

"No."

"Sky." Edi took another sip of wine. "If she did, let's just say. Would that make you happy?"

Sky turned bright red. She'd wanted to barge out of the room—her mother was such an idiot at times, and it was worse when she was slightly drunk. But she took a breath, controlled herself ("oppressed" herself, as Edi would have put it during this phase of their lives), and set her wine glass down gently on the coffee table. Edi continued, "I just want you to know I absolutely respect all sexualities . . ."

"I know you do, Mom. I do too, but I'm not gay."

"Are you sure though? Maybe your friendship with Liz is a subconscious desire. I mean she's a Virgo, right, that's a good match . . ."

"Jesus Christ, Edi, I'm twenty years old. I think I would know my own sexuality. I know people think I'm boyish. Masculine. I don't know why. Probably because you never let me wear what I wanted to wear. Probably because it's mostly men around here. Maybe because . . ."

"Oh, so it's my fault? Don't blame me for who you are. Don't you dare. And while you are at, don't apologize for it either—you're fine how you are. It might mean that Liz thinks she has a shot, but . . ."

"If you think that, then you don't know Liz." Sky spoke defensively but also confidently. Liz had a very clear type, and Sky was the opposite of that type. Liz also wasn't an idiot. She thought her mother was being particularly old-fashioned, for someone who prided herself on being progressive. Sky wanted to ask Edi if she thought everyone had a crush on her, gay or straight. But she stayed quiet. She knew Liz, that's what mattered.

Now she squeezed the ring and wished Liz had told her about Edi's continuing relationship with her rapist. She knew lawyer-client confidentiality was serious, but still, couldn't she have breached that once she'd watched Sky in agony the past few days, looking for her missing mother? She already knew the answer and knew Liz had done what she felt she needed to, but it didn't keep her from feeling hurt.

And why, of all lawyers, had Edi gone to Liz and risked Sky finding out? Was she really that desperate? Sky felt her skin buzz with electricity, the desire to move, to go somewhere. Whereas two days ago she'd felt that she couldn't handle any more, didn't want to know any more secrets, now she wanted to know everything. Her body had been lead, but now as she thought about everything, her anger felt like an electric charge running through her. With a short laugh out loud, she thought how she should take advantage of this adrenaline. How she should call Ned and tell him off. Threaten to press charges. Bully him into quitting. She wished she could call her mother, yell into the phone. Tell her to grow up already.

Sky watched the room become lighter as the morning fully opened. Carmel was only two hours away, give or take. The valley a little further, probably an hour further if it was as far back in the hills as Marguerite had made it sound. She leaned forward, placed the ring on the coffee table, and got up to start her day.

Not much more than an hour later, it was only 7:00 a.m. and Sky had just gotten out of the shower when the buzzer rang. Ryan was at her door with two gas station coffees in hand. For once he wasn't wearing a blazer. Just the black T-shirt and gray denim pants. Sky poked her head out the door, the rest of her covered only in a towel.

"Sorry," was the first thing he said. "You didn't answer last night, and I was worried you were going to head down to Carmel before I had a chance to warn you. Coffee?"

Sky frowned a little. "Umm . . . yeah, can you—?" She bit her lip. "Maybe just wait in the hall a sec until I get into my room to dress and then come in, I'll leave the door cracked."

"Yeah, okay. Sorry, again. I really should have called . . ."

Sky walked into her room and listened from her bedroom as he closed the door to her apartment, listened as he cleared his throat. She could almost feel how awkward he looked standing in her kitchen. She wondered if he'd even allowed himself to put the coffees down on her breakfast table. She tried to hurry as she glanced out the window and saw the sun peeking out through the morning fog. She pulled on jeans and a T-shirt. Shook her wet waves over the T-shirt and took a quick glance in the mirror. An old part of herself wanted to pinch her cheeks, but she reached for some lip gloss on her dresser instead, applying the sticky apricot hue lightly to top lip, then bottom lip. Finally, she put on a cream-colored lightweight sweater. Carmel, on the coast, would probably be cool, but the valley and hills to the east of it would be plenty warm already in early spring. Besides, the sweater was cuter than a T-shirt and if he was here at 7:00 a.m. with coffees, Liz was probably right. He probably did have an interest in her. And Sky didn't entirely mind. That would explain a lot, actually.

She walked out of her room, toweling off her hair. Ryan looked up and smiled a close-lipped smile.

"Morning," he said and held out a coffee to her. "It's just black, I wasn't sure what you'd like in it . . ."

"That's great, thank you, I'll be ready to go in about ten—you are coming, right, that's why you're here?" She put the coffee down and went to the kitchen table to check her purse for her wallet and her keys. She should fill a water bottle.

"We need to talk first, Sky. I found out some things. Jake Bridger is no flowers in his hair peacenik; he's a serious criminal. I think we need to rethink our approach . . . can we sit down for a minute?"

"Yeah, okay," Sky sighed. She really wanted to go, to move, to feel like she was running against the machine that was her life right now. But she liked the way he said "our approach." She wanted to tell him how she believed she'd find something there, at the Ashram, but also mostly she wanted to see the place where she was born. As if seeing it would suddenly make everything in the past few days make sense.

She motioned Ryan to the couch she'd slept on, wondering if he could tell from its rumpled look. She was glad she'd at least picked up the wine glass from the floor, though four red drops still dotted the rug like a rash. "Do you want breakfast?"

"Um . . . no. But you should eat . . ." Ryan eyed the uneaten pizza sitting on the table.

"Why does everyone keep saying that?"

"It's important for the brain under stress, and you look . . . under stress."

"Shit, thanks."

"No, I mean, I work with people under stress a lot. They often forget to eat, to sleep, it makes it hard for them to think. They get tunnel vision, they decide they know the answer, often they focus on one suspect and can't see the whole picture . . ."

"The Ashram."

"What?"

"That's my tunnel vision. At least today it is."

"Is it? Well, we need to talk." Ryan put his coffee down on the table.

"Well, let me grab a banana so that I can *not* be the crazy person in the Hitchcock film that is my life. Want one?"

"No, thanks."

When Sky returned with the banana, Ryan had moved to the chair across from the couch, his elbows on his knees. It was a professional man pose she'd seen again and again. When women did it, or rather when Sky sat like that, she felt she was posing, or that she looked overly aggressive. Definitely manly. She'd read once that it was an actual thing—power poses. Taking up space in your chair marked you as assertive, made you more likely to get a job. Man or woman, though men more often did it naturally. So as a result, she'd sat like that for all of her job interviews.

Ryan began to speak as soon as she sat down on the couch, breaking the top off of the banana.

"Jake Bridger is under investigation for kidnapping, rape, statutory rape, theft, child abuse, and manslaughter. There are also unsubstantiated reports that he may have murdered a young male follower at one point. Under no circumstances should you just drive into the Ashram and introduce yourself as one of his own. Sky, I'm serious. You may not come out alive."

Sky chewed a piece of banana which suddenly felt dry and unswallowable in her mouth. She put it down next to the uneaten pizza.

"Well, I guess nothing surprises me at this point. Why hasn't he been arrested?" She regretted the question as soon as she asked it. It probably made her seem naive.

"It's hard to get witnesses to testify against him, or evidence, seeing as most of his victims or their parents believe he is a living god."

"Oh."

Ryan nodded. "Perhaps we could try interviewing some more of your mother's friends . . ."

Sky shook her head. "I still want to just see it—maybe I'd remember something that would help. Do you think I could pretend I was a jour-nalist?" She looked defiantly at Ryan. She wanted to say to him *I am not afraid of Jake Bridger.* Jesus, she was beginning to act like Edi.

But he was shaking his head so adamantly that she wondered ever so briefly if maybe he had another lead he wasn't telling her about. Or an-other reason to keep her in town. She took a sip of the coffee. Her fatigue, and Liz, and her mother were all filling her with paranoia. No, she trust-ed him. She'd already decided that.

"I think that would make things worse, I've heard the cult has gotten more private, more aggressive toward outsiders and more insular as well. For example, it was noted in the file that the authorities believe that there are several teenagers born in the Ashram that have never been allowed to leave the property."

"Jesus." Sky heard her phone buzz from the kitchen table, a text, but she ignored it. Edi would never text her. Probably Liz.

"It's not your mother's cult anymore, Sky. Whatever it was when she was there, it's not that anymore."

"Huh. Both Marguerite and Deb mentioned that Edi left because things were changing, and that was twenty-six years ago. How old is Jake now?"

"In his early fifties. Sky, can I use a bathroom? Too much coffee . . ." Ryan sucked his lips in, a bashful gesture, Sky thought.

"Sure." Sky got up and pointed to the door in the hall. She hoped it wasn't a total disaster but knew it wasn't clean. Toothpaste on the sink, towels on the floor. She walked to the kitchen to check her phone.

It was a text from Liz. Sky felt a twinge of irritation. She knew it would be some affirmation, a word of encouragement for Sky to hang in there that would normally make her smile but today would feel insincere after she'd learned what Liz knew but had chosen not to tell her, the thing she needed to tell Ryan after he got out the bathroom—about Phil.

She was irritated, but she opened the text.

Left you message. call me. it's about Ryan.

Her phone vibrated. Another text.

Talked to Amy. HE'S NOT ON SFPD PAYROLL. her friend in HR doesn't know who he is. more. call me !!!

Sky read the last text three times.

She heard the toilet flush.

She remembered sitting with Liz in the police department waiting room, expecting to sit for an hour or more, and then suddenly, there he was. Like magic.

With all the time in the world for her.

She could hear the water running.

Who seemed not to have any cases more urgent than hers.

She looked at the door of her apartment, knowing perhaps she should go toward it, but not entirely sure why. Her body caught up to her brain and she took a step forward, wondering if she should just walk out of it before he got out of the bathroom. Or should she just show him the text and ask him to explain?

The sink handle squeaked as it was turned off.

She had to do something. He'd be out any second. Frantic, she tried to use the callback function to call Liz but when she raised the phone to her ear, she just heard the start of a voicemail. She'd hit the wrong button. *Shit.*

Ryan opened the door, shaking his hands dry, so she quickly held up a finger like she was on the phone and turned her face away but not her back. She wanted to buy time, hear Liz's message, maybe call her back but her brain was buzzing loudly, and she realized she was hearing Janet's voice on a message instead.

"Sky, it's Janet, I've been trying to get a hold of you, but I guess I'll just leave a message. Sky, the young man I told you about, the one visiting your mother the past little while. He was around here on Sunday, little older than you, cute. Brown hair. Wears blazers. Handsome. Came alone. He seemed to have keys. Very interesting things going on over there . . . we should talk. And should I water your mother's herb garden . . . it's getting . . . well, call me?"

Ryan. He wasn't a police officer. He had been seeing her mother before she died. He hadn't had a crime team there on Sunday, just himself. And now he was standing right behind her.

"Everything okay?"

Sky turned to him, and he tilted his head at her. Sky slammed her phone closed and shoved it into her back pocket.

"Yep, fine," she said. She bit her lip and watched him. She thought, suddenly, of the note on her mother's bedside table, *Love you, R.* No, that had to be Roger. It had to be. Right?

Ryan took a step toward her, and without thinking, she took a step back.

"Why are you acting weird, Sky? Who was that on the phone?" He gave a smile and took another step toward her. This time she resisted stepping back. She tried to channel that energy from earlier. The adrenaline. The *I am not afraid.* His blue, blue eyes met her challenge.

"Who are you? Who are you really?"

"What do you mean?" Ryan snorted, a bitter sound she hadn't heard him make, one she wouldn't have guessed he *could* make—the man just moments ago practically blushing at asking to use her bathroom. "You know who I am, Sky. Who was that? On the phone?"

"You are not a detective?" Sky took another step back. She could suddenly feel every pore on her body gape. Sweat.

"Of course I am . . ." Ryan held his hands up to her, a gesture that Sky couldn't quite interpret.

"No." Sky's voice was even, like she was talking to a growling dog. "I just learned that you don't work for SFPD, and . . ." Sky backed away more, closer to her apartment door. "You knew my mother."

"Sky, I don't know who told you that." Ryan's smooth expression twisted for the first time. He crossed his arms and snorted again. It was again an odd sound, like he was trying to make a casual laugh. It was a sound that told Sky she was right, and if he'd lied about all that, he could be lying about what happened to Edi, too. Maybe he'd found the blood because he knew right where to look for it. At this thought, she turned and made for the door just a few steps away.

She'd just caught the handle and pulled it open when Ryan caught her, pushing the door closed and pinning her left arm behind her back. He pushed his body against hers, so she was stuck between him and the door. She tried to stamp hard on his foot, but in a second he had her other arm and then she felt him handcuff one wrist, then the other, and then his hand was over her mouth.

They were both breathing hard.

"It's not what you think . . ." Ryan's voice was soft in her ear. "You have to let me explain."

She tried to speak but couldn't. His hand was firm over her entire mouth. She tried to remember how she'd escaped Ned, remembered Lorenzo standing in the doorway. She took a panicked breath through her nose. She wasn't getting enough air. She pushed back against him.

He still had her pinned, his palm now damp over her lips.

She couldn't breathe.

There was no Lorenzo here. If she could just scream, maybe a neighbor would hear her. His palm was flat, nothing there for her to bite.

She tried to take breaths from her nose, to shake him off her. Was he going to kill her? Had he killed Edi too?

She felt her lungs reaching, arching, for air.

"Sky, breathe." Ryan loosened her arm a little. "Sky, breathe . . ."

She couldn't. Could she? She felt air going in and out of her nose fast but like none of it was getting to her lungs.

"Breathe, seriously . . . breathe!" Ryan's voice sounded like it was much further away than in her ear. His hand dropped from her mouth.

And then there, there was Cassiopeia again. Hanging upside down in the sky for eternity. Punishment for doing something that would likely kill her own daughter once the tide came in.

PART II: EDI

I want to try to explain everything.

I was a girl and then I was an animal. He'd teased me gently before, placing his hands over mine on the keys, but I'd never been uncomfortable. I couldn't imagine what he wanted. Didn't know yet to recognize the smell of that *desire*. And then one day the door clicked closed. Mother was out. He waited while I finished playing "Für Elise." I could feel what I thought was irritation as he sat next to me. Impatience. I'd missed a note in the second bar. He shifted in his seat. Made me so nervous I missed another note, hit B instead of B sharp.

I remember that room like I just walked out of it.

I remember dust floating in the line of sunlight that entered between the two tall curtains.

I remember the night before my mother had cooked fish, and the scent still hung in the kitchen, faintly sour.

I remember wanting the lesson to end so I could go and meet a friend. Sneak cigarettes in the park. Flirt with boys.

I remember the cushion on the piano bench, crushed red velvet that reminded me of the stains raspberries leave on your fingers.

When I was almost finished with the song, I felt his long famous fingers squeeze my thigh. Again, I read this as frustration at my playing. His language of exasperation.

I remember he said, No. No good. He stood up dramatically and began pacing. You hit each note too long. Stand up.

I stood up slowly. I remember I was wearing a blue sleeveless shift dress with large bright daisies on it.

Come here, he said. His face was beginning to blush red. I hadn't thought I'd played the song *that* bad. He walked to the back of the grand piano, cracked open. See, he said. Look. You hit only long enough for the hammer to hit the string. To tap it. Look, look at it.

I bent over to pretend to look at the piano and was about to make a polite feign of interest but then I felt him behind me. His hands on my hips. Shoving up the back of my dress.

I remember moving, trying to move away, but he kept me pressed.

I remember him saying, But you, wearing this dress, I bet you're better at this than piano.

He shoved down my underwear and I felt a pain that was bright and shocking.

I remember making a protest. A weak one, as a child does to an adult twice her size.

Please. Please, don't. I said that to him.

I remember him saying, But this is your fault, yours. Between breaths. Between thrusts. Slut, he said. Slut.

Tears ran into my mouth before I knew I was crying.

It couldn't have lasted more than five minutes. That's all it takes to change your life.

He finished and cleared his throat. Went to the bathroom to wash his hands. I leaned too hard into the piano. My forearms later would be bruised from its ebony edge.

He came back into the room but didn't seem to see me, barely standing. Wetness leaking down my leg.

He sat down at the piano and played some symphony by heart. I could feel the piano vibrate under my leaning body, like an extension of him, and I stepped away as if the sound had burned to touch.

What song did he play? I can't name it, but I heard it once later, in a café downtown, when Sky was small. We left without ordering, and I threw up on the sidewalk outside, knowing I was embarrassing her even at that young age. She stood behind me with her arms crossed. "Mama," she said. "Mama! Stop!"

He finished the song and said, Practice Beethoven more. Next week I want it perfect.

I didn't look up at him. He got up to leave.

Tell your mother this one was free, he said.

I remember then the bloom of hot shame that opened inside me in that moment and would never fully leave me. I was too young and too stupid to feel angry. That would take years.

The door clicked closed, as it had not fifteen minutes before, and I ran into the bathroom to wash. Shoving a cold yellow washcloth between my legs, not realizing it would be pink with blood when I finally pulled it away.

I hate remembering all this, but it's one of the days I can return to most clearly in my memory.

I was too ashamed to tell my mother. Too sure it was my fault, too embarrassed to talk about anything bodily with her, a woman who used the word "private parts" all my life and who never told me about sex. That was Gina Russo, on the steps behind the school in sixth grade.

The secret would have stayed with me, too, had it not started to swell. My breasts first, too tight in my bra. I'd come home from school aching and go right to my room to unhook the clasp. My appetite gone. I didn't want to think about the possibility, didn't allow it to enter my head. Until I threw up one morning at the breakfast table. Didn't have time to sneak into the bathroom. My mother thought it was the flu and sent me to bed, and I was so relieved to be able to rest. When I threw up again the next day, she took me to the doctor.

When Jake later taught me about women's cycles, and that there are only a few days between when the egg comes out and when it dies, I felt like I'd been especially unlucky. That God had been especially cruel, if I still believed in God, which I was pretty sure by then I didn't, but I still *thought* of him. Still used his name in my head. In sayings my mother used to say. God didn't want it that way, God is watching over you. The good Lord provides.

She didn't have any of those phrases when we took the trolley home from the doctor's that afternoon. Her silence vibrated with rage. The doctor had told her first. Smug bastard. I could tell she was humiliated when they both stepped back into the room, I just didn't know why yet. Or didn't want to imagine I knew. She wouldn't look at me as the doctor asked me when my last cycle had been. While he used a small pocket calendar and counted aloud. Twelve weeks, he'd said.

We got home and the door clicked shut. My mother put down her purse, took off her gloves and I turned to go upstairs. "Wait," she said. I turned and saw she was now a shade of purple. Visibly shaking.

What followed gave me reasons to hate her for a lifetime. The things she called me, her own daughter, who had been raped. The things she said. For some reason she kept bringing up a boy who had brought me half-wilted roses two years before to school. A boy I never liked. I remember she kept smacking her lips between epithets and when she did this, I wished I could rip out the thing growing inside me and hurl its bloody mess at her.

I remember she said, "Your father would have killed you, taken you out like the trash you are . . ." and not long after she picked up a small Limoges porcelain box her mother had bought on her honeymoon, a rabbit nestled around a carrot, and hurled it at me. It hit my shoulder and fell to the rug. Somehow, strangely, not breaking, though I'd be bruised later. Then she threw a teacup from the breakfast table, the dredges spilling out onto the rug, and I ran up the stairs, finally crying. From the top step, blind and hot, I heard myself screaming, "He did it. Phil did it."

My mother held me in bed that night. I told her everything. She told me this is what men did: take. A few weeks later she called the police, stupidly, as it just brought more humiliation. She fired Phil and called the music school where he worked. I never knew if she was trying to help me or trying to save her reputation. Either way, it took me a long time to appreciate those actions for how progressive they were in the 1960s. She told me to get used to it. No one listens to women, she said.

For the next seven months she babied me, planned everything. Found the parents. We didn't refer to the baby as a he or a she or an it, we only talked about the pregnancy. "When it's over . . ." my mother would say, while she spooned chicken soup into our bowls at night, "we'll take a little trip." She had me excused from school for illness, but I knew everyone knew. Still, I was glad they couldn't see me, couldn't see the growing orb of shame.

I remember the day he was born so clearly. I woke up in pain, pain coming in rhythmic waves that seized my whole lower body. But still, I lay there as long as I could before calling to my mother. She came across the hall, and when she saw me, panting on my side, she was flush with excitement. She called a cab to drive us to the hospital, but I remember little of what followed. My mother asked them to take away my pain, and they did. But I do remember feeling as if I was cracking open, that an animal that lived inside me was taking over to do the work of birth. When I heard the cry, I was too weak even to lift my head to see him, so it was my mother that the nurse handed him to first.

The love on her face instantly replaced all the hatred, the weeping, the screaming she'd done at Phil on the telephone before he hung up on her. All of that was just gone as she looked at the little bundle that had just come out of me, that still had my blood in its hair.

It's a boy, she said.

Let's name him, I said, let's name him Sorrow.

Oh, Edi, she said, oh, Edi, and she brought him to my bed. His eyes were open, black small wells. His features were so tiny. I was afraid to hold him, but my mother placed him on my chest, and I felt I could cry for days.

He was mine, but never mine, and always mine, and about to be gone from me forever.

My mother took him back into her own arms and I could see that she wanted to keep him. The little creature, her husband's grandson.

And then he was gone. I saw him one more time the next day when the parents came in to thank me. The mother was shining with happiness, and she held him to her heart. She had mousy features and thin hair but to me she was a thousand times more beautiful than I. I couldn't say anything to her, just nodded. Thought to myself, Well, I get raped, and you get a child. But it wasn't a bitter thought. I was too removed, too exhausted. More like an observation.

And then they were gone, out the door forever.

As soon as I stopped bleeding, I was out the door myself. Gone on weekends, staying at Gina Russo's, whose parents gave us wine and didn't care what time we got in. I went back to school, but already I'd missed too much to not have to repeat the grade, so to finish the last three months of the year only to have to do it all again the next spring felt like a waste of time. My body lost the weight quickly, and I felt like a bird that had been let out of its wire cage. I flitted and flew and hardly came down to see my mother, who let me do what she thought I needed to do. Who had watched me give birth and seemed to have retired her authority.

When I came home, I often found her in the corner chair in the living room, a finger of scotch in a crystal tumbler, staring at the rug still stained from the tea.

It was years before I was a mother, a real mother, myself, and could imagine that she must have felt guilty for what happened. But at the time I thought she was mourning the child. The child that I had started to think of as a skin my body had shed, a scab that had finally fallen off from the wound that Phil had made. Leaving me pink and new and now with nothing to lose.

It was months before my mother thought to try to slow me down. Keep me in. Impose a curfew. When she did, our fights became frequent and loud, with us both screaming. I'd met a new group of friends in the park and was wearing borrowed bell bottoms and cropped shirts my mother hated. I don't remember the fight that had me pack a small overnight bag, and I don't remember thinking I wouldn't be back for years. But that's how it turned out.

I went to Gina's for a week, and then stayed with a boy I met in the park for a month or two. He introduced me to just about every drug there was. The few years that followed are mostly gone from my memory. Before Jake, it was all one long night. That sounds melodramatic, but it's what happens when you sleep days and wander the city until the light comes up like a slow glow growing between the buildings, like someone turning the sound up. By the time it was bright enough to make sharp geometric shadows on the city, I'd be already unconscious on some couch or floor and, a few harder times, outside somewhere. There was a lot of drinking, cheap beer and whiskey, out of shared bottles. A lot of pot and acid. It was all everywhere. Easy to get, especially for a young woman. Not that I had to do much. Just attention, pretend to like someone, to see them.

I do remember one night toward the end of that period, early in the evening, waking in a house I'd been staying in for a week with some guy and girl I'd met at a bar. They were from Scandinavia and were artists and said I could come stay and they'd draw me. All over the house were smudged drawings of me, naked. Naked on my belly, my back, one, from a night with lots of wine, with my legs wide open, the dark center of me, the wound from which a child had come, a too-large diamond rubbed vigorously in the center of the paper. There were two of every drawing, one of his, one of hers. You could tell which one did which—he always made my boobs cartoonish, cherries of his imagination while she drew them how they were, pinched from childbearing, one slightly larger than the other. Sometimes I liked his better.

They had kept me drunk most of the week. They were in their early thirties, and he taught classes somewhere and they had money for good wine. We'd wake at around five o'clock in the afternoon and eat cold cereal and then have vodka and orange juice. A while later she'd make spaghetti and open wine and the three of us would talk about people we'd met, the shit going on in the world, Vietnam, etc. It was getting time, I thought, to move on. I had people I knew who would be wondering where I was. Friends that were used to seeing me every few days. I said as much to the artists and they both frowned. They were both blond and tall, as if they could have been siblings. No, no, stay, she said. Yes, stay, he said. And he poured another large glass of wine for me, reaching behind him to get another bottle. Since I had no place to go really, or no need to be sober when I went, I drank the glass.

One more drawing, elskling, she said, calling me by a pet name she'd been calling me since the first night.

Yes, one more. You owe us, for dinner, he added playfully.

I hesitated, mostly to tease them, but I was flush with wine. All right, I said, but after, I must away into the night.

Undress, he said, we'll get our things. I went to the twilight corner of their apartment where they'd had me pose all week and which was always a little cold—she'd said it brought out my nipples. I took off my clothes as they came in with their pads, a charcoal pencil in her mouth.

Turn around, I think, tonight, she said. So I turned around, my back to them, and leaned into one hip, trying to imagine the drawing I was already. A little unsteady from the wine. We'd had more than usual, faster than usual. Especially me.

I waited for the sound of their pencils.

I stood there, drunk, naked. I was seventeen.

I heard them whispering instead and was going to turn around when I felt a large hand cover my mouth and two hands spread my butt cheeks.

It was her, her tongue on my anus. You want this, she cooed, as he reached the hand not on my mouth down and up toward the dark diamond they'd drawn. I was too surprised to scream when he took his hand off my mouth, slipping instead his fingers into my mouth.

I wondered briefly if I owed them this, too. Or if she was right, that I wanted this. But when she put her finger up my ass, I knew I didn't. I realized I'd felt like paper all week, a rough line drawing, ephemeral, but now I felt my body was a bottle that had just been sealed shut, his hand in my mouth, and her finger in my ass.

I swatted her, pushed away from him. No, no, no, no. They stepped back and I grabbed my clothes and ran out the door and down the stairs. It wasn't until I was out on the street, naked in the dark, that I realized they weren't chasing me. I stood on the corner and pulled on my shirt and bell bottoms—she'd washed them for me—and walked back up the street. I looked back from the top of the hill to see them in their window, watching me. She was naked and raised her hand to me. I realized all I'd had to say was no. But still, I felt that shame once again bloom hot and promised I'd be more careful.

Not long after that my friend Mitts—a redheaded girl from Davis who had a birthmark covering half her milky face like a coffee stain, one finger of it crossing over her chin like Florida—told me she'd met someone, this guy, and wanted me to meet him too. She said, "He's like . . . I don't know . . . it's like meeting the center of the universe. He's so *connected*. I swear, when I met him, I had this total out of body experience where everything else was gone, like the earth and the sky and the people around us and it was just him and me on some other universal plain." Mitts wasn't my most out-there friend, either, and so one rainy Wednesday I let her take me to his yoga class in a cramped apartment in Richmond. I remember the room exactly. The ratty furniture had all been piled in the corner. A bare-bulbed floor lamp balancing precariously on the top. A ceramic dog in the corner. A white cocker spaniel. The tall old windows fogged on the inside.

I remember I knew who he was immediately, even though the room was full of half-dressed men and women. He stood at the center; a good six inches taller than anyone else. He had wavy dark hair down to his shoulders. Biting blue eyes. And Mitts was right, there was something about him. When he first looked at me and smiled, a perfect and kind smile, I swear I lost my breath. But it didn't seem that it was *all* attraction, although he was very attractive, it was something else. He looked at you like he knew you, left and right, in and out. Like he knew all the shitty things that had happened to you, the crappy stuff you'd done, like he saw all that and loved you anyway. Maybe I just wanted to see that in him, but I did.

And it's not like I had anything else going on. At that point I hadn't been home in over two years. Had no stability. And Jake offered that, first through his classes. Sometimes I went twice a day. It was the only time, I came to realize, that I'd felt at home somewhere since before Phil. I noticed too that when I went, I didn't feel like I needed to get lit afterward. I could spend a night just sleeping. He talked about love, about love for the body, for the earth, for the whole self, for each other. He talked about how capitalism fed our ego, encouraged us to hate each other over petty things, made us forget what it meant to be human. To be free with our desires. It was so much better than what I'd heard growing up. My mother cared so much about keeping up appearances, at all costs. I didn't want that life.

I didn't want that life for you.

Lots of people came and went from those classes, but there was a group of us that were there at least once a day. Then more and more, we were there for both the morning and the evening class, and sometimes we wouldn't go home in between. We'd just sit around and talk, listen to what Jake had to say. Some days I'd barely eat and wouldn't remember my hunger until after I'd left the building to go stay wherever I'd stay that night.

One night, as I was leaving, a month or so after I started going regularly, Jake asked me where I lived. I shrugged and smiled. There were so many of us without permanent homes then, teens that had run away, folks that had come to California looking for something. The next day when I arrived before class, he beckoned for me to follow him. Whenever Jake gave you any attention that was all yours, you felt like you'd risen up above everyone. I imagined, as everyone in class watched us disappear into the kitchen, that this must be what it is like to be with someone famous. We walked through the small kitchen with the white chipped tiles, and he opened a door usually blocked by a small table. He flipped a light and showed me a small rectangular room with a tiny window near the ceiling. The glass was dirty and cracked. It might have been a pantry at one time—it was just big enough to lie down in. Yours, he said. I turned to him and thought I might kiss him. Or he might kiss me. But he motioned me out and as we headed back to the living room, he said gently: I don't like my family sleeping on the street.

I heard this and I didn't think I'd ever felt so loved.

I began to watch him even more carefully after that. Not only was there an attraction, a crush, but others had talked. One woman, Jeanine, swore she saw him levitate one afternoon when she opened her eyes during meditation. Like, literally floating, you guys, I swear to god, she said.

One of the other women, Star, who knows what her real name was, hung around him a lot. She seemed to have known him a long time, and I thought maybe she had come to California with him. It was her friend who owned the apartment we lived in. Her body moved like it was made of grass during yoga, bending whichever way she wanted. It was mesmerizing to watch. *She* was mesmerizing to watch.

One day someone new was there, a real cynical guy with a blond ponytail who had not been taken with Jake's charisma at first. He even scoffed aloud when Jake began the practice by asking us to give a releasing breath and release our life spirit into the room. I watched Jake not even flinch at this; he just continued the "breath," as he called it. Once you gave your releasing breath, you had to breathe continually in and out without pause. When I first did it, I felt light-headed. When I became used to it, it always unleashed some intense euphoria within me. Something about the relentless rhythm, the inability to think or hold anything in. Later, I'd learn this is a whole therapeutic thing, breathwork and releasing stored up energy and emotions and trauma. Jake's not the only one who teaches this, it turns out, but at the time it was revolutionary.

That day was colder out, and I remember the windows were dripping with our heat. How good the warm room felt. You could hear a light rain and the furnace clicking and smell the eucalyptus from the oil Jake rubbed on the tops of his feet. I wanted not to be distracted by the ponytail guy but a few breaths in he turned to the girl who had brought him, and I heard him whisper, "Is this guy for real?"

Jake tilted his head in smiling curiosity at the guy. Now that I look back on this moment, I realized he must have met so few people in his life who weren't taken with him right away.

Let's keep breathing today, he said. Seems like there is a lot to release. So we stood still, in mountain pose. Breathing in, breathing out, he walked among us, tall and mostly naked, save some small shorts. He'd touch you lightly if he caught you distracted, holding your breath, pausing, to remind you to keep going. The room sounded like the hissing and puffing machinations of some factory. *In, out,* like pistons, *up, down.* As we breathed, Jake talked about the ego.

He said, "The ego is the part of ourselves we seek to protect most—it's what tells us we are separate from the other. Sometimes it tells us we are worse, sometimes it tells us we are better. It looks to the outside world for validation, and it allows others—mothers, fathers, brothers, sisters, lovers—to wound us. And we protect it by keeping who we really are from ourselves, we protect this fragile little ego like it's an egg and we give so much care to it and keep it warm and safe, but the great irony is that it is this egg that wounds us most. After all we give it, all we feed it, it's what hurts us. Every negative thought we have comes from the ego. The ego tells us we are alone. *Deep breath in.* It tells us others are better. *Out.* It makes us want what is not ours. *In.* It makes us ache with yearning. *Out.* It keeps us from our animal purity, our ability to be present in our body. *In.* It keeps out the light . . ."

Jake continued with this litany as the room became warmer, until it seemed to me to almost glow with not the cold white light from the windows but one that was yellower. I felt myself shudder at times, my body releasing energy as I could no longer contain anything. I heard others laugh, cry. Jake's voice was smooth and even and as my ear became accustomed to it, it was as if the voice was the very surface of my skin, both outlining the end of my body and touching the pumping blood within.

Eventually everything went a sepia white, but I did not pass out. I stayed standing, anchored by Jake's voice, quieter now: within and without. I have no idea how long we did this, how long he spoke for. I was vaguely aware of people collapsing around me. I stood like a tree, a breathing tree on some barren white planet for what might have been minutes, or hours.

I remember little of what was said after a while, it was as if I'd moved beyond the language of Jake's words and into a space of light we shared. Where I did not begin or end.

I've never before or after had another experience like it.

When I came out of it, Jake touched my shoulder. My eyes flew open, and he guided my body to sitting. I blinked and slowly took in the room around me. Everyone was lying or sitting, and there was a communal catharsis, or rather its aftermath. Mitts' face was puffy from crying. Star wore a smile like she was on LSD. I was already completely a believer in Jake before that day, but here's what got me: my eyes found the blond ponytail guy. Jake had left me to sit next to him, and the man had his head in Jake's lap and was quietly sobbing. Jake's hand was on his back, rubbing it like you would comfort a child. Whispering words I couldn't hear.

Outside, it was getting dark, but no one thought to get up and turn on a light until much later. And no one left for hours. Everyone talking quietly about what they had seen, but me, keeping mine to myself. My antique white, empty plain.

It was about three months after we met that Jake asked me if I'd come with him to Carmel Valley. I didn't even blink before I said yes. I was honored. Mitts was going, and ten or so others that also came every day. More would come later. He'd bought a property high up Carmel Valley, somewhere beautiful and private and where people wouldn't mind a group of people living their own way.

Even though we were staying in the same apartment, along with five or six other people, I hadn't slept with Jake, and I know Mitts hadn't either. Both of us wanted to. Star was one of the most beautiful people I've ever seen, startling gray eyes and jet-black hair, and Mitts and I talked about whether she and Jake had fucked. We talked about it in whispered giggles, like they were our parents, and I always felt a little ashamed after these conversations. Like I was tainting the purity of Jake's vision. Of what we all did there together.

As we got ready to go, though, it became clear that Star was expecting a child. That part of the reason for going was so that they could start their "family," of which we were a part. We didn't talk openly about whether we'd be their children or lovers, but once we got to Carmel Valley, things became more familiar that way. Jake had made a no relationship rule, or as he put it, "all equal relationships." He said there would be no love triangles, no hierarchies, only family, only sisters and brothers. It was California in the seventies, and many of us were deeply invested in astrology. Did you know, he told us, that "zodiac" is an ancient Greek word that translates to "circle of little animals"? We are like a circle, he said, this circle of animals. Following our desires to love and nurture each other. Balanced by our astrological strengths, our weaknesses. He seemed so wise, with his knowledge. He preached that we should be friends with everyone, could be lovers with anyone. And since there were nearly as many men as women at first, there was a lot of sex happening. But it wasn't . . . there weren't fights. Once in a while, there would be a jealous type, usually a woman, but it wouldn't be long before Jake noticed and pulled her aside. I don't know what he would say, or do to her, but afterward she was always happy. Saw things differently. Or at least put on a good show of it. Envy, Jake always reminded us, was one of the ego's favorite ways to make us feel bad.

And so it did seem a utopia, or a hell of an effort at one. Carmel was beautiful, too. The coastline rocky, foggy, and wild-seeming, and the valley even less populated. The land Jake had bought folded into the warm hills which rose like mounds of dough around us. We were protected from winds, and you could hike for a beautiful view. The dry oaks were enough shade for us while we built, and a small creek ran through the property, and back then it actually had water in it. It was gorgeous.

It wasn't all easy, though. We moved up there in late winter, which was by no means cold, and built yurts with canvas tops that were perfect for the time. We had one well, no flushing toilets, and we weren't at all prepared for the summer heat. Even though the ocean and cool bay were only an hour away down the valley, in the hills we baked. The dry grasses made us fear fire, and Jake made a strict no smoking rule. In fact, that was the first real restriction, after exclusive relationships, he put on us. And it made sense, given the fire danger. If you wanted to smoke, you had to hitch a ride or walk down the road. That first summer there seemed like a dream. The oaks were like sentries, wrapping around us. At night I used to look at their stooped and twisted shapes in the moonlight, their long arms, and try to imagine what animals they were and if these creatures were part of the circle that Jake talked about.

We still did yoga every morning and evening, and we worked on trying to grow some hardier crops. We worked on building more permanent buildings, starting with a barebones house for Jake with a yoga patio. It was hard, but I loved it. I was happier than I'd ever been. I loved so many of the people there, and everyone was so positive. I felt half in love with three or four men at a time. And I know how that sounds, but it wasn't base. Not there. There it seemed only natural.

Star gave birth in late summer, and it was a beautiful event. So different than my experience. No doctors, no drugs besides a few hits of pot Jake gave her for the pain. We all sat on the edges of the yoga patio while she paced, naked, and moaned. She had skin browned from the sun, and her black hair was straight down to her butt. Her nipples were large and dark above her taut belly, but her limbs were thin still. I remember thinking she looked like some goddess. She caught my eye and smiled, beckoned me forward. For the next hour Jake dripped a cold washcloth over her back and I pushed on pressure points in her hands she showed me. Now, she'd say, and I'd press with my forefinger and thumb as hard as I could into the meat of her hand. When the contraction had passed, she'd kiss me on the forehead.

And then she began pushing and it seemed like it took hours, witnessing her pain like that, me pressing her palms right below her thumbs so hard that the next day my own hands would be cramped closed.

But then he was here. His brown head emerging just as the last of the light faded from the patio. Someone had gotten some lanterns and hung them on the edge of the patio. When he cried, everyone let out a breath, and the hot pulsing quiet of us was broken. Everyone clapped, and laughed, while Star and I both began crying as Jake held up the baby for us to see.

Later, he'd take him out into the night, just as the stars were coming out in full, and name him.

But before that, Star leaned her head back into my lap and reached out for him, and I cushioned her as she breastfed him, umbilical cord still attached, another woman helping her with the afterbirth. As I watched him fall asleep after just a few suckles, my tears dripped down onto Star's hair spread across my lap like a skirt. I watched them disappear into the thick rug of her hair and let myself mourn for the first time the one gone from me forever.

It wasn't long after that that Jake invited me to spend the night with him. We'd talked frequently about the birth, about how amazing Star had been. And then one evening after yoga, he asked me if I'd like to come stay with him that night. I almost couldn't answer, just nodded. I had wanted it for so long. His attention. Him.

That night I went to his wood house, which didn't have any glass on the windows yet. It was windy, which gave us privacy because it was loud. Hot air blew over us and through the room. We lay on rugs covered with thin and bright fabrics that Jake had bought in India. We drank water with lemons from a tree on the property, I still remember the tart dryness it left in my mouth. I was so thirsty I drank three glasses.

Then Jake bent down and kissed the tops of my feet, his long wavy hair hanging down and tickling my shins. Then his lips, wet from the water, kissed my knees, the rough skin part, and then he lifted my dress and kissed each hip bone rising out of my pelvis, the skin smooth and taut. His lips crossed my belly button, the faint stretch marks there, and every part of my torso, my neck, my ears so that by the time he climbed up to enter me I was practically quivering with desire. My body felt like a plucked string, singing for him.

I felt like an animal again that night, but in a different way. It was a mindlessness, a contentment to want one thing and one thing only with no thought for what was outside the room. The others, the past, the child, Star. It, *he*, was all consuming. I felt so present and so free of shame in that moment—this is exactly what Jake had been preaching to us. His circle. Equilibrium.

It wasn't until much later that I realized we hadn't used protection, that he'd come inside me all three times that night. When I realized that, it was the next day and I was washing a dress, a cream shift of raw cotton, in a tin washbasin in the midday heat, and it was as if I was waking from a dream. The dream of my body, of the place, of Jake. A wave of sickness washed through me, and I remember standing there in the sun wondering where I had been. What had I been thinking? What had been done to me was consensual, wanted, but why didn't I remember this one basic protection for myself?

I left the tunic in the water, floating like a drowned woman, and went to sit in the shade. What had I allowed? Where was I?

This was one of the few moments I remember having early on—when I'd wake from the fantasy briefly before reentering it—that I could see clearly. Those were incredibly uncomfortable times, and that is why I would always recede back into Jake's reality because having these doubts felt dangerous at first, and later they were what made me think about leaving. And I didn't want to leave. I didn't want to go back to the life I'd been living. And I certainly didn't want to go home. In my eighteen-year-old mind, those were the only two options.

I was quiet the rest of that day, but Jake had me come to him again that night. He was intuitive, and without asking he knew I wasn't as firmly enveloped in him as I'd been the night before. So, he ran his fingers through my hair and told me his secrets. He'd been wealthy growing up. But unhappy. His parents were miserable, cruel people. He was lonely. He got into Yale and went to please them, because it was "what I was supposed to do." But he hated it. He hated the entitled pricks that were his classmates. Was embarrassed by them. But then he took two classes, one on Indian culture and another on Marxism. Everyone was terrified of communists, but at Yale they were talking about it abstractly, the ideals of ideologies. Jake was transformed. His other passion, as I already knew, was Greek mythology and astrology. He studied both and finished school on one condition: that his parents would give him enough money to travel for five years. He went to India for two and had been in California for two. He was hoping the Ashram would be self-sustaining before his money ran out in a year. He told me all this while I lay on his chest, listening to his heart. He lightly stroked my back. Told me he saw me as one who could help him. Help him to achieve his vision. *You are smart,* he said, *and beautiful. People love you, they really do. I've seen the way you light up the room.*

That night I also told him all that had happened to me. Phil, the pregnancy, my mother. I teared up when I told him about the child, and how I thought my mother wanted it in the end, how I didn't, how the child had later died, and he listened without judgment. He told me I had to let go of my shame, and I cried so hard that I shook and then was emptied out and we laughed.

We were still talking when the sun began to glow blue from behind the earth, and when it arrived in the windows without glass, we were just drifting off to sleep.

We started spending at least three nights a week together. Sometimes two—Jake tried to keep it irregular so it wouldn't seem he was breaking his own rule, treating me special. We both still saw our other lovers. But I was distracted. I'd never met anyone that smart, that knew so much about things like philosophy. It was like I'd tuned into a higher frequency and was listening to that, rather than to the other people around me. I came to decide, after watching Star with her newborn, that a baby wouldn't be so bad here, but I wanted to make sure it was Jake's, so I used protection with other lovers. It wasn't until much later that I realized Jake tracked our cycles, that he only had me come to him when I wasn't likely to conceive. That Star helped him, that they had a yellow-papered ledger with dates and moon diagrams to indicate our periods. It was just one of the ways he controlled us more than he appeared to.

But at the time I thought I wanted another child. I'll be honest and say that as a few more children arrived, it became clear that a child did have a certain currency in the community; mothers had power. What I'd learn later, once I had one, was that I was a fraud. I liked children when I was in the mood, but I didn't like the relentlessness of parenting. The demands of an infant or a small child, the boredom of the routines. I was lucky, in some ways, to have had my daughter in a cult. For those first difficult months, there were a million open, loving arms I could hand her off to. Another woman who'd breastfeed if I was busy, or tired. I don't think I could have stood it alone, the postpartum, and at times I wonder if I had been alone if I would have been one of those women you read about that hurts her child. And for even having these thoughts, I felt sorry and inadequate. And while I never hurt my child, it was clear to me I wasn't cut from mothering cloth.

Too much had been taken from me by the time I had you, Sky, I think, to not involuntarily exact some revenge on your stubborn little practical being. And when you grew, you were tough. Your being like a string on a violin about to snap. Where I was soft and easy, you were stiff and rigid. Where I was flirty and feminine, you were curt and masculine. I was both proud and ashamed I had raised you to be this way. But mostly proud to have a daughter so genuine in her concern, so honest in her answers. For someone so smart, and so keyed up against the world, you are oddly naive. Sweet. My sweet Sky, who thrived in spite of me.

We'd been there about a year when Jake announced that we needed to grow our numbers. We owed it to the world. He asked me to come with him into the city again, to find young lost souls like I'd been. To show them our life. We started to go to San Francisco every other week to hold talks at yoga studios, coffee shops, sometimes in the park. We didn't wear white yet, and Jake always picked his most beautiful followers to come and help. It was amazing to watch a crowd be drawn to him, mostly women, but some men too.

On one of the trips, at a meditation circle at a local yoga room, a skeptical little dark-haired woman was standing in the corner with her arms crossed. She wasn't buying what Jake was saying about communal love. She'd come for yoga and wanted yoga. But I could see she was hungry in other ways. I don't know how, maybe Jake was rubbing off on me. Had taught me to smell a wounded animal. Or maybe I just recognized myself in her.

I approached her. The studio was hot that day because a radiator was overworking, hissing and crackling to keep the lower floors of the building warm. Jake had given his spiel, his invitation to come visit us in Carmel, and was surrounded by a small group who'd felt his pull, who wanted more. He met my eyes as I leaned back against the wall next to the woman. She was beautiful, of course he'd noticed her. I tried to suppress jealousy by thinking *Light, light, light,* which is what I'd learned to do when I knew Jake was with someone else, and instead tried to think of her as a prize, a gift I could give us all. I turned to face her and saw the perfect pout of her mouth.

"It sounds crazy, right?" I tried.

"Yep. I mean nice, but impossible."

"I'm Edi."

"Deborah."

"Want to grab a coffee? Get out of this hot room?"

She cocked her head at me and looked back at Jake. I think she was trying to figure out if I was trying to sleep with her.

"It's just coffee," I giggled, and put my arm in hers, walking her out of the hot room, knowing Jake's eyes were on us.

For the next hours, well past dark, Deb—as she told me to call her when we hugged goodbye—and I sat in a dark corner of a coffee shop with steamed windows and cigarette smoke clouding the room.

She didn't let me pretend I just wanted to talk but rather said as soon as I sat down, "So why is it you follow this guy, and why should I?"

I liked her right away. Jake had taught us a little spiel, all about the ideals, and I believed it but knew that someone like Deb (*you know Deb*), would smell it as propaganda from a mile away. So I told her the truth. All of it. More than I'd ever told anyone.

I realized later that maybe she had an effect on me like Jake. She held my gaze, with these big dark eyes, and barely even touched her coffee while I talked. She didn't offer any trifles of sympathy either, just listened as I told her about Phil, the pregnancy, the doctor, my mother, the police, the adoption, running away. I told her about a few times when I'd been scared, about a time that I'd even allowed myself to forget: when I was sleeping in an empty church and woke to a guy holding a knife on me and searching my clothes for money. I told her about the artists. And then I told her about Jake. What I'd seen, felt. How it was the first time I'd felt unconditionally loved in my life, and accepted.

When I got to this part, she got tears in her big doe eyes. She quickly wiped them and we both let out a nervous laugh, breaking the trance of telling I'd wound around us. I got up and got us two fresh coffees and asked her about herself.

"There's not much to tell, compared to all that," she said. But she told me that her mother had also raised her on her own, her father had just never been in the picture. When Deb was fifteen, her mother had remarried a man whom Deb hated. When she mentioned this man, her shoulders folded up to her ears, her hand went right to her neck, and she looked in almost physical pain. I'd learn later that his man routinely assaulted her, the kind of groping and touching himself in front of her stuff that women didn't know how to talk about then, and maybe still don't. But that day, I only knew this man had ruined her life. And that I really liked her. It wasn't about winning her anymore, but about wanting her to be my friend. I think she knew this, and maybe that's why she gave me her phone number when we finally said goodbye that night, giving each other a long hug.

I convinced Deb to come down to the Ashram for a weekend the next week. She moved up a month later—her lease was up, and she was working a shitty job and her stepfather still liked to come around when he was drunk. She was my first real recruit and closest friend and I felt like a mother to her. It was she who started calling me Mother. As a joke, but one that Jake found appropriate. The only one who didn't like it was Star, who chided, reminded us that there were no hierarchies, that we were a circle. It was clear I was becoming Jake's new favorite, and he was less careful about hiding it now that their child was toddling. It was me he took along when he went food shopping, and me he turned to for advice more and more. Or that's what I thought, anyway.

Another year passed and more yurts were built. Jake had recruited a few wealthier followers, and he got glass in the windows of his house. Fans, too. But money was something we constantly struggled with, and he and I would often stay up late to brainstorm ways to make money. I thought we could make something, keep bees and sell honey, make clothes, but all these ideas seemed to frustrate Jake with how slow that income would

be. I should have seen that frustration as a sign of what he'd later turn
to, but I didn't.

One trip up to San Jose, we went to the fabric store and bought a dozen
bolts of white cotton. A month later, on the summer solstice, we all burned
our "old" clothes from our "old" lives in a big bonfire on the Carmel beach.
The sleepy seaside town barely blinked if they noticed forty young and
shining people all dressed in white, dancing around flames streaked with
the colors of our past lives. It wasn't until a decade later that the locals
would start to resent the Ashram, but by then I was long gone.

That night at the fire, my arms around Jake and Deb as we all stood
in a circle and sang Cat Steven's "Moonshadow," I again felt so at home.
There were many of us then, beautiful young bodies dancing around a fire
like an ancient ritual. Everyone's skin glowed. Everyone moved with love.
I was certain this was my forever. That'd I'd found it, and that the world
would be a better place now that I had.

I lived for a while like a balloon, floating and gliding along, feeling happier than I'd ever felt. Only once in a while the vision I inhabited would
snag, and I'd catch a glimpse of the man behind the green curtain: his
plain shoes, his shabby con. But I don't know that I thought of those moments as revelatory at the time—in fact I know I didn't. It was only later
I was able to see them for what they were.

Like one night walking into Jake's house, finding Star naked, crying,
lying on her side and bleeding from her mouth, their small child playing
with a wooden stick whittled to a point in the corner. I walked over to
take it away from him and Star jumped up and screamed at me, her raven
hair a wild wing flapping about her, her face bloody, her yelling at me that
I'd never know the real Jake. Never.

Another time, in the city recruiting, someone stopping me and asking
me if I was part of the Ashram. It was a young guy, and I beamed at him
and told him yes, thinking he might be interested in joining us. But instead his smile went watery and he spit on my white tunic, telling me to
tell Jake to go to hell like the conning pimp he was.

And this: one morning I woke to Jake counting on his fingers and his lips moving silently. I smiled and asked him what he was doing. He turned to me, his face lit up, and said simply, "I'm just counting my concubines."

It was like a different person inhabited his body and I sat up on my elbows, wondering if I was still asleep, and when he saw my frown he laughed. Edi, he said, I'm just kidding, and then rolled on top of me.

Little things like this would happen that would bother me for a day or so, and then I'd shake them off. Fall back into the bliss. It wasn't until I'd been there three years that something really changed. And that something was named Mitch.

He was as attractive as Jake, and he showed up one day when Jake and I were planning who to send out to work the coming year. A few would have to and bring money back. And they'd have to be followers firmly entrenched, that could get day jobs housecleaning, or doing yardwork. We were talking it over in his house when Star came in, with a tall blond behind her. He had eyes the color of moss, and an army bag slung over his shoulder. Star had a slight smile on her face when she saw my mouth open a little at his presence.

"Look what I found," she said. Flirting with him and Jake at the same time. "He just walked up the road, said he hitched a ride from Big Sur. Joanna, down at Nepenthe, told him about this place and he wanted to check it out." Joanna was a tiny Latina who had a bright laugh and who came up sometimes to the Ashram to have sex. At least I think that's all she wanted. She worked at a bar at a restaurant, Nepenthe, that hung over the Pacific like a plate on the edge of a table.

Mitch gave a warm bright smile. He said, "Hope it's okay, wanted to see what you guys were all about, it sounded cool."

Of course, Jake stepped forward to embrace him and I felt an almost maternal cringe at how small Jake looked compared to this man, who stood a good three inches taller. And Jake so tall himself. He turned to me. "Edi, show him around, would you? I'm going to see if Star has any good ideas, money-wise." I nodded. Later I'd realize that the real money came in from sources he and Star contrived, sources much more illegal and unethical than housekeeping work. I'd realize that some of the young women we sent out to work were being victimized in ways I couldn't even imagine. That the peace and love was a veneer.

But that day I was naive and proud of the Ashram and thrilled to show Mitch around. I took him to my yurt to put his bag down and then decided I'd pretend that what Jake had really meant was to seduce him. Before anyone else could. I didn't like to acknowledge, even privately, that that kind of competition existed among us, but it did.

I pushed him down on my pallet. There were others who slept in my yurt, but in the day it was empty. Sitting, he was still tall. I told him I wanted to give him a real welcome to free love. Would that be all right? I asked as I stepped over him. His large hands found my hip bones and he was surprised and not surprised at the same time. I realized women probably did this to him all the time. He was that beautiful.

I was so taken in the moment, in the power I felt, the rush of confidence. It was one of the most intense sexual experiences I've ever had. When it was over, we lay back on my pallet, naked, and Mitch rolled us a joint. I ignored our no smoking rule, as Jake often did with new recruits, waiting until they were fully invested to give them any constraint. We smoked and talked for the rest of the afternoon. It was different than it was with Jake, there wasn't that feeling of a higher plane, but there also wasn't that pressure. We were just enjoying each other's company. Mitch asking how I got here, showing such concern when I told him the short version of what had happened to me that I had to laugh. It's okay now, I'm here and that's all in my past, I kissed his shoulder. I asked him to tell me his story.

He told me he'd been called up to be deployed. Was supposed to be in Monterey in two days. But he didn't want to be in the military anymore. Had been drafted in the first place. When he told me that, I knew he was in, that he'd stay, and that Jake and I would protect him.

I thought I knew everything that afternoon, as we lay there naked with our limbs entwined, our bodies already shaping to each other, the sound of a squirrel outside chattering away. I thought I knew I couldn't get pregnant again, since Jake and I hadn't used protection for two years. I thought I knew I was completely in charge as we made love one more time, this time him climbing on top of me, slow and sweet.

After, my skin felt swollen with him, with my own self-assuredness, with what I thought I knew, and I took him out to meet everyone as the sun finally slipped down past the Western ridge like it was a letter into an envelope.

Mostly, what I knew that night was that he'd stay and be my victory for all of us.

What I didn't know is that it might have been safer for him if he'd gone. That even though I thought I was one of the ones holding the strings, practically drunk with power when we walked to group mediation that night, that I never really knew who Jake was. Or what he was going to become.

I never knew that when he said circle of animals, he meant he believed that we *are* animals. That morality is a farce compared to instinct, desire, brutality.

When I think of it now, my naivety, my blindness, my stupidity, it is like remembering being really sick. The motion of the memory brings the sickness back again, the body tilting in space.

But I do try to remember Mitch, for your sake, I do. And when I do, I remember that he was handsome and kind. He was funny but quiet. Shy. He was a little shy. That's where you get it from.

Your father.

And after he died, things were very grim. I was not cut out to mother, and grief exasperated this lack. And Jake made me suffer for my betrayal. Treated me as he never had before.

I saw a whole other side to this man, a darkness unlike anything I'd ever seen, and I began to realize how wrong we all had been.

I've always suspected I'd pay more for what happened to him, your father. And for the ways I'd brought others there, to that place, to follow a man whose heart was black. One way or the other, I knew I'd have to take responsibility for the ways in which I was to blame. Not Jake, but me. This was my own circle: my own ending waiting in the wings.

I'm just so sorry it had to be this way. Because in the end I loved not being a mother, but being your mother. And I loved you, Sky, I did. I do.

You are, and always have been, my horizon.

PART III

Sky felt like she was falling and gasped for air. She opened her eyes. Not falling, moving. She was in a car. A sedan. Lying in the back seat, her face smooshed against gray upholstery. She was handcuffed. She wanted to groan but stopped herself. She could feel a seat belt around her, tight on her hip bones. Her head was on the seat behind the driver's seat, her legs folded, knees to stomach. A sweatshirt had been folded carefully under her head. The passenger seat was empty, she could see, and she already knew who was driving. Or at least, she knew what he looked like. But not who he really was. If his name was even Ryan.

She felt her back pocket for her phone. It was gone. *Shit*. She looked up at the window above her, all she could see was sky. No buildings. By the speed and noise, she'd guess they were on the freeway. The sun was hot on her shoulders, so assuming it was still morning, they were heading south. She told herself not to panic. If he wanted to kill me, he would have done it, she told herself. Though she wasn't at all sure that was true. His car smelled like a holiday candle, maybe a pine air freshener. Which seemed ridiculously dissonant with how she felt.

So it was true, there was a specific reason he was interested in her case. Janet had seen him. He knew Edi. He didn't work for the SFPD. He hadn't had a team of detectives there on Sunday. So, was the blood even real? Had he planted the purse? The necklace? Why hadn't she seen the necklace when she read the note on her mother's bedside table? Had it really been there on the floor or had he pulled it out of his pocket?

He'd looked familiar that first time she'd seen him, in the station. Did she know him from some long-ago time? Why would he be interested in her mother, in her?

Her head ached from the back of the neck forward. Her wrists felt tender where the metal of the cuffs had pressed into her skin. Briefly, she wondered when someone would notice she was gone. It would be hours. It would be Liz. She'd have to try to get out of the car when they stopped. Yell for help. Hope someone would see her. She thought about her mother—had she been in the back of this car? Handcuffed?

It had been over a week before Sky even noticed *she* was gone.

"You're awake." Ryan was glancing over his shoulder. No menacing smile or predatory tone. Just stating the fact.

Sky went to speak but her mouth was dry, her throat sandy.

"Are you okay?"

Sky almost laughed. Was he seriously asking if she was okay as he was abducting her? The edge of emotion welling up made her realize if she laughed, she'd cry, too. Instead she cleared her throat and steadied her voice. "Where are you taking me?"

"Where you wanted to go."

"The Ashram?"

"Yes."

"I thought you didn't want me . . ."

"I didn't. But you seemed pretty insistent. Short of arresting you as a suspect, there wasn't much I could do to stop you. So we are going, but we are going on my terms."

"Who are you?"

Ryan sighed; she could see him raise his hand to the back of his neck. She slowly, awkwardly tilted her body until she was sitting up.

"Who are you?"

"I can't tell you that. Where I am taking you, someone else will decide what they want you to know and what they don't want you to know."

Jake Bridger. Did Ryan work for him? Had she been right all along? The cult had somehow seduced her mother back. This was her answer to growing old, the reason to forsake the people she loved. Sky's desire to meet him, see him, flared again. *Father.*

"Jake Bridger? My father?"

"No, Sky. I don't work for Jake Bridger. I would think that would be obvious by now." Ryan's voice had a vibration of irritation. As if Sky was still supposed to remember their good and trusting relationship over the past week and still see it as a truth she could rely on. But for all she knew, every word could have been a lie. His tenderness a ruse.

"Is your name really Ryan?"

"Yes, Orion, officially. But I prefer Ryan."

Orion. Sky remembered reading it on his card. Her warmth at it, that he had a hippie name like hers. Then her brain flashed to Marguerite. How he told her to find her. How, in the last meeting, she'd told Sky about the baby boy. He was alive. Five or so years older than her. Ryan's age. *Edi wanted to name him some hippie name, like yours.*

Sky opened her mouth to speak but shut it. She wasn't sure she wanted to ask him that yet. It didn't quite fit, did it? Why would her mother's long-lost son be involved in her disappearance? Be taking Sky to the cult where she was born? If he was her brother, *brother*, she wasn't sure she wanted to know yet. And if he wasn't, she didn't want him to know that she had a brother out there.

She watched as they passed a sign for Silicon Valley. The dry grassy hills were almost too bright to look at. Scattered oaks. A somehow lush golf course alongside the freeway, even though Sky knew they had to import water here from the Sierras. The few jobs they'd done here, they'd had to do coastal xeriscaping: succulents, other plants that required no regular water. The land, she'd known from job sites, was parched to a crumble. Like the surface of her own tongue now.

He had seemed so familiar, she thought again. A chemistry there that maybe she'd misread. But they didn't look much alike.

Her mother had once told her the story of Orion. They were up at Roger's. On the patio. Years ago. The three of them ate homemade blackberry cobbler that Roger had made, and then got wrapped up in blankets to sit on his deck stargazing. A happy memory. She shut her eyes, trying to remember her mother's words. Orion, the hunter. Dawn's lover, son of Poseidon, and walker on waves. He wanted to rid the earth of wild animals. Gaia disapproved of this and sent a scorpion to kill him. Zeus placing him among the stars, with his dog Sirius. Not the most glamorous of Greek heroes. But a recognizable constellation, his belt sagging with the weight of his sword, making a smile in the night sky. Her mother hadn't remembered which stars exactly made up Sirius, and then Roger had started making up his own constellations, one after his mailman, making them all laugh.

She opened her eyes and watched the cars around them, wondering if she could make eye contact with another driver, mouth the word *Help*. But everyone was driving too fast, eyes elsewhere. She took a breath and resolved to keep taking them. To save her energy. In case she needed to run, to fight. She briefly thought about last Tuesday with an ache of nostalgia. Janet hadn't even called her yet. Ned was her biggest problem, and he hadn't even assaulted her yet. A week ago, she hadn't met Ryan, or Marguerite. She hadn't known who her father was.

She had been, in essence, a different person. A child, it seemed, kept safe from the secrets that ran invisible currents around her feet as she waded obliviously through her life. Naive enough to believe she'd been walking upstream, that she'd been struggling when, really, she'd been going the path of least resistance.

Sky had very few memories of being afraid as a child. Nervous, yes, but not that heart-pounding fear. She wasn't prone to nightmares and had little experience with terror. Ned's assault had made her heart beat in a way it hadn't before, her neck shrivel, and her breath catch. When she had thought about it since, she felt the same quickening of her heart, the same sickening shrinking at the base of her skull. It didn't work like her anxiety, which would build up slowly over hours or days to a peak of insomnia, shallow breathing, crankiness. Rather, it was just sheer and immediate terror, curtaining her whole body.

Liz had dated a woman once who had been attacked, a knife held to her throat while she was robbed. Liz used to tell Sky that this woman would wake up panting, clutching her throat like someone had strangled her in her sleep. She'd look accusatorially at Liz before she fully woke up, and when she did wake up, she'd sob. But that moment, Liz had told her, before she realized I was me and not her assailant, was always uncanny. The look in her eyes. Fear, but also hatred. Like she might murder me, Liz said.

Sky had nodded; she knew that look from her mother. Once her mother had shaken her awake in the night. It was a school night, and Sky had a book report due the next day. She was in second grade when she woke to her mother's bony hands shaking her shoulders. A wild look in her eye. Her skin damp with sweat. We have to go, Sky, we have to go. He's coming, she said, he's coming. She frantically pulled Sky's red rain boots out of her closet, even though it was dry outside, and tossed them one by one to Sky. When Sky didn't move from the bed, she leaned over then and pulled the boots on Sky and yanked her by the wrist down the stairs and to the front door where she opened it and stopped. The cold air rushed in, and her mother stood stock-still on the porch, her white nightgown silhouetted by the eerie orange glow of the streetlights in the fog. Sky stood behind her in the open door and started to cry.

Her mother turned slowly back around to her; her face changed. She looked tired, groggy. "What are you doing out of bed?" she asked.

Sky started crying harder, and her mother came in and shut the door, led them both back upstairs. She pulled off Sky's boots—each came loose with a little suck, the sounds ending the whole episode. She crawled into bed with Sky and shushed her until they both feel asleep.

The next morning, Edi didn't remember any of it.

She shook her head as Sky told her, pointing at the boots still on her floor, asking, "Who is he, Mom? Who was coming for us?"

Finally, Edi stopped shaking her head and got up. She put on a smile like one puts on a too-small hat. "Sleep walking, Sky, haven't done it since I was a kid. Must be the sleeping pill I took. Just a bad dream. How about I make us something special this morning? Pancakes?"

But that morning Sky had watched her mother closely as she poured the batter into the shape of a bear on the griddle—never plain circles for Edi—and decided that Edi knew more than she was saying about whatever had made her afraid. Even if she didn't remember the dream. Sky put too much syrup on her pancakes and chewed slowly, knowing then that there was a shadow in Edi's life, one she'd see again at EarthFest, and then continue to see glimpses of throughout her life. And she knew from her mother's look that night, in her sleep, that Sky'd never been afraid like that.

Until this week, until now. And now it felt more like a dream than being awake.

After an hour or so, Sky could see the Pacific Ocean over the sand dunes of Seaside. It was sunny but a line of thick fog hung low out over the bay like a gray streak of acrylic, a dark mistake in the painting of the bright day. They had been driving in silence, making eye contact in the rearview mirror every five minutes or so. Highway One turned hilly as they drove up into the tall pines, the forested area of Pacific Grove. Sky's mother had never taken her down here, but she'd been here with a college friend who lived in an opulent mansion off the famous Seventeen Mile Drive. She remembered reading *Rebecca* over the weekend so her friend could drive her down to the old stone castle-looking house on the rocky cliff where they'd made the film. They drove through iconic cypress trees in the perpetual coolness and past the romantic cottages of Carmel-by-the-Sea, some of them with storybook roofs and cross-hatched windows, looking as if a gnome might pop out of the door. Sky's friend had told her that Carmel had, over the course of her childhood, gone from kitschy to ritzy. The cheesy souvenir shops, the shop with glass animals in the window, had slowly been replaced by Tiffany's and upscale cosmetics and designer dog boutiques selling bedazzled collars. Much of its rustic charm, gone.

So they *were* going to the Ashram. While Sky was still keeping her breath even, reminding herself, *in, out, in, out,* her mind was all over the place. She went from thinking about how Ryan was bigger than her and that she didn't have much hope of physically overpowering him, to being absolutely sure he wouldn't hurt her. If she couldn't make an escape before the Ashram, it would still be okay. He didn't work for Jake, but they were going there. Jake was her father, and he wouldn't hurt her, she felt certain of that. At least not right away. She would tell him she wanted to get to know him. She could keep herself safe until she could either get away or until someone came looking for her. Both Liz and Deb knew she wanted to go the Ashram today, it would be the first place they'd look. She just had to get there and stall for time until they came. She'd tell the first person she saw there that she needed to talk to Jake. It would be okay.

The freeway ended and they passed the turn-off for Ocean Avenue, Carmel's main drag if she remembered right, before heading down toward the Carmel River. Sky could see the impressively green spring hills of the ragged coast just south of Carmel, a layer of fog still hanging just off coast. But they turned east before they reached those rocky enclaves, up Carmel Valley Road. Sky took a breath in. Past shopping centers and gas stations and into the green valley, past a golf-course resort, an organic farm so big it was a household name in Marin.

Sky remembered to exhale.

The road narrowed and became curvier, the hills still green but less so than those on the coast. Ryan slowed the car and pulled into an old gas station that might have been charming in another situation. There were a few wine tasting rooms lining the road, but it was much quieter here than it had been down valley. She knew he hadn't wanted to stop where it would have been easy for Sky to call for help. But still, she cleared her throat.

"I need to go to the bathroom."

"Can't you wait? We aren't that far. Maybe forty-five minutes."

"No."

"Okay, I'll go see if the bathroom is outside and has a key. If it is, you can go."

"You are honestly not going to let me go the bathroom? If you are really taking me where I wanted to go today anyway, then you don't need to keep me prisoner."

Ryan sighed, looked back over the seat at her. He looked tired. He stared at her for a minute before he said, "Okay. But I'm walking you to the door and waiting there for you. But let me get gas and find out where the bathroom is first."

Ryan popped open the gas valve and Sky tried to twist her hands out of the cuffs. She didn't care that he could probably see her squirming. Once the car was being filled, Ryan disappeared into the store and Sky looked out the window, willing a car to pull up next to them. If she could just get someone's attention, tell them Ryan wasn't a cop. Would anyone believe her? A woman in handcuffs in what looked exactly like an unmarked police car? A handsome guy like Ryan rolling his eyes at his crazy prisoner?

Ryan was back in a minute with a key attached to long piece of smooth wood that someone had written WOMEN on with black permanent marker in long, slanting letters. He opened the car door and bent over, his face almost touching hers as he reached over her to unbuckle her seat belt. "I told the owner you were in my custody so try not to do anything to scare him. He's probably the type that keeps a nine-millimeter under his counter."

Sky glared at him as he kept his hand around her bicep as she got out of the car, but he was gentle.

She didn't really have to go to the bathroom but now that she was out of the car, she wasn't sure what to do. She thought maybe she could push him and run into the store, ask the owner to call the real police. But Ryan had been smarter than that, and now she saw the owner standing behind the glass door of his shop. A balding man with a large stomach, his arms crossed, frowning at her, ready to protect his store if need be.

When they got to the door, Ryan opened it and held it for her.

Sky turned around and held her cuffed hands to him and waited.

He sighed, "Really?"

"Unless you want to undo my pants and pull them . . ."

"Fine."

Sky heard as he took his keys from his pocket and felt the handcuffs loosen. Her shoulders were sore as she pulled her hands in front of her, rubbing red marks on her wrist.

He closed the bathroom door behind her. She decided to use it. To put water over her face. To drink from a faucet she wouldn't normally dream of drinking from. She wanted to be ready for whatever she needed to be ready for. Taking in as much water from the faucet was the only possible way she had any control over her situation.

When she felt like she might throw up if she had more, she swung her head up and wiped her mouth on her sleeve, catching herself in the mirror. She looked tired, but certainly not like a convict. She silently told her reflection, "It will be okay." She wanted to walk out calm, quiet, to try to convince Ryan with her demeanor that he didn't need to put the cuffs back on her.

When she opened the door, he was standing up against the wall and turned to block her, cuffs in hand. He immediately slapped one on her.

"Do you have to . . ."

"We got to keep up the show." Ryan gestured to the owner now looking out the side window of his store. "Once we get there, I'll take them off."

But he let her keep her hands in front of her, led her to the car, and once again leaned close to her as he buckled her seatbelt over her waist. He smelled like lemon soap and Old Spice. He smelled good. Sky tried not to notice it, but once she did, she tried to use that information. He smelled like a cop, an upstanding citizen, not a criminal. A killer. Or so she told herself, as he closed the back door and got in the front seat.

As they pulled away, Sky caught the eye of the gas station owner, outside now, watching her with disgust in his face. She met his gaze and thought, *Help me*, even though she knew there's no way he'd read that from her.

Forty-five minutes later they turned off the main road. They had been winding through a canyon, the hills becoming blond and dry, the only green the oaks that dotted the hills. Now they turned onto a dirt road next to ten or so rusty mailboxes lined up against the highway. Along the road was a thicker spread of trees, but still the ground was bare, almost nothing growing but parched grasses. Sky imagined a fire would swallow this place whole, in one giant orange breath.

She wanted to ask how much farther but decided on silence. It was her only power. She'd stay quiet, pay attention, in case she had to find her way back. She watched as the road forked into three. Watched Ryan take the middle road. The left one had a metal horse gate chained with a padlock. At one point the gate had been painted red but now it was chipped almost bare to the metal. Once on the middle road, they passed three more dirt roads leading off the right that Sky realized were driveways. Some had numbers painted on boards and nailed to oaks. One said "The Lambournes." But they kept driving past all of these, until the hill became steep and the dust around the car thick. They wove up and around until they reached the end of the road, where a beautiful wooden house surrounded by wooden decks sat. It was smaller than Sky had pictured. She had pictured many houses, many people, a village of sorts. There's no way a whole cult lived in that house.

"I thought we were going to . . ."

"Not yet," Ryan said as he steered the car to the top of the drive, where he pulled it as far under the shade of an oak as he could. Sky felt a sickening wave of fear. There was not another car in sight, not another person.

He opened the car door and Sky could feel a hot wind. That shrinking at the base of her skull made her want to throw up.

In. Out. In. Out.

Ryan reached in to help her out, and as he did, she looked around her. Steep hills surrounded the property, with thin oaks. No good place to hide up here, no place to run.

As Ryan pulled her up, her face was right in front of his. Again, he looked tired. She was not.

Her heart was beating like a large drum. She felt sure he could hear it.

She looked again at the house. She did not want to go in there. What if she never came out?

Sky thought of her mother. What Sky would do to save her. The way adrenaline can take over the body, make possible the impossible. Just breathe and wait, she told herself. *In. Out.*

As Ryan took Sky by the arm and closed the car door behind her, he seemed more relaxed. More like he was helping her, not detaining her, his grip gentle. He feels safe here, she noticed. He, too, thought there was nowhere for her to run.

She let him help her, mimicking his relaxation. They stopped and Ryan gestured for her to take in the view—it was almost 360 degrees, save for the hillside which the driveway was carved into. Golden hills, and greener hillsides to the west.

"Come here, I want to show you something." Ryan led her back down the rocky drive to the edge of the grated driveway where there was a large circle for extra parking that perched above a steep downhill and looking out to the east, the rolling dry hills.

"There." He pointed down the folded hill where there was a small valley, an almost dry creek bed winding through. At first, Sky didn't see anything. Then slowly it came into focus. A series of low circular buildings between the oaks, all a cream stucco that blended them in with the earth. One larger house, she saw now, and between the houses now she saw some movement. Figures that looked tiny from where they were but that were all wearing one unmistakable color. White.

Sky opened her mouth and shut it. Ryan was watching her, smiling a little. "The Ashram," he said.

Sky nodded and turned to Ryan. She opened her mouth and closed it again. She had so many questions but thought it best to keep her mouth shut. She could feel the weight of the house behind her. The importance of staying out of it. The sun, too, felt suddenly searing even through the dry wind. She could hear some sort of insect buzzing in the air, as if the very land was vibrating. Or maybe that was her heartbeat, making her feel as if she was floating just above her own skin. She suddenly remembered the sour taste of Ned's mouth, her pearl buttons on the office floor like knocked out teeth. How much can happen in one minute.

Ryan reached into his pocket. "Now that I've brought you where you wanted to go, I suppose you don't need these anymore," and he took out his keys. Undid her handcuffs. She watched him. Felt how careful he was being, his fingertips grazing her wrists. It took all she had not to shiver at his touch.

Ryan cleared his throat. "But I should say that this is the closest you will ever see it. There's a much larger picture here I need you to start understanding."

Sky looked quickly at him. Was he making a threat, or trying to tell her something else? Sky listened to the drum of her heart, felt the heat of the day, their isolation. That buzzing, vibrating.

A plane flew somewhere overhead, and she wondered if time was passing, or if it had stopped up here on this hill.

Again, that feeling at the top of her neck, a sick wave. Was she that rotten peach, soft and easily bruised, the way she'd felt after she hadn't stood up to Ned?

That pit within she'd also felt, a hardness. A resolution, maybe.

She looked down below to the buildings, the figures. Her father was there. And what was a father, if not a protector? He would protect her, she knew. He would tell her about her mother. Once there she could leave, or Liz would come get her.

She took a breath. *In.* She bent down, pretending to adjust her boat shoe. *Out.* Glad she hadn't worn sandals. *In.* She picked up a handful of the baked earth, the color of ocher. *Out.* She stood up. *In.* And she threw the dust in Ryan's face.

And then she ran. Straight downhill.

She heard him swear, she heard him stumble behind her. She kept going.

She heard him call her name. Tell her to stop. She kept going.

She heard him yell that she didn't understand. That he'd explain it all. He heard him swear at her. But she launched each foot forward, practically falling downhill, and didn't stop until she was at the bottom of the steepest part of the hill, where the brush and oak were thicker. Once the ground became less steep, she dared look behind her. She didn't see him, but she didn't stop running. She knew if she just kept heading toward the bottom of the slope, she'd be at the creek bed that the Ashram was built around.

Dropping into a steady rhythm, she kept running. All in all, the distance from where she'd been to where she was going was at most a mile. Rough terrain, but not far. She ignored the rocks gathering in her shoes and thought of all her runs up and down the trails behind her house in the early morning, when the bay fog was like a companion, snaking around the hills with her. After a few minutes, she looked behind her again and caught her foot on a root. She flew forward.

"Shit." Her voice loud in the woods, she quickly picked herself up, the sting on her palms barely registering.

She looked around again. Oak trees spread out generous arms toward a floor of golden grass. The world still seemed to spin around her, but the buzzing was quieter down here.

There was no sign of him. Her breathing and her heartbeat were too loud, she thought, and would give her away. He wouldn't just give up, would he? Maybe if he was working for Jake, he would. What if she had just done exactly what he wanted her to do? No, she couldn't overthink it. She tried to quiet her breath, but it was coming in gasps—she realized she had run so hard she literally couldn't catch it.

She put her hand out against a gnarled oak trunk and gulped for air. She closed her eyes. It was still hot, but the dry breeze from the hilltop was gone and the plants smelled sweet. Sweat was drying almost as quickly as it hit her skin. She watched the twisted oaks behind her as she waited for her body to calm itself.

Her breaths started to slow a little. She could start to hear the quiet around her. The buzz now just a soft hum of the earth. She stopped her breath for a moment just to listen.

And that's when she heard it. First, a rustling behind her. Then another. Footsteps. Ryan. He must have circled around her.

She slowly turned around to face him.

But there was no Ryan.

She blinked.

There, before her, stood a child. Wearing a too-small white T-shirt and white cotton shorts smeared with yellow dust but still bright against his sun-darkened skin. He had long, shiny chestnut hair. His feet were bare and caked in dirt, there was a fresh cut on his knee that was bright with a line of blood, the skin around it a different shade than his dust-coated leg, like he'd licked his wound clean. He'd been playing hard too, his own chest moved quickly as he stood staring at her curiously.

She was about to venture a "hi" when she heard another sound behind her. She turned but saw only the maze of oak branches, their arms bending and crossing in layers across her vision. It was the same view in every direction. No Ryan.

When she turned back around to speak to him, the child was gone.

She let out the soft "hi" that had been on her lips and took a few steps toward where the child had been standing, looked around again. No sign of him. But where could he hide?

Her heartbeat was rapid and shallow; she realized she was dizzy.

The oaks were spaced such that she was sure she would see him if he was walking or running.

The air hummed again.

The scent of the grass was strong now, earthy and sweet. The heat seemed to pull the smell out of the oaks even, she could smell the vinegar of their bark. She rubbed her forehead.

The trees seemed to watch her as she did it. Maybe she needed food. Water. She would start walking in what she thought was the direction of the Ashram, she had to be close.

Again, a sound. A clearing of a throat.

She turned, thinking the boy was back, only to see a woman suddenly standing twenty feet from her. Sky took a step back, noticing how her own feet were noisy in the brush.

The woman, standing in a white tunic, gestured calmly for her to stop. Their gazes met, and Sky noticed the blue of her eyes.

This woman was younger than Sky, maybe early twenties, skinny, with long auburn hair that looked like it had just been brushed, its soft edges giving her head an ephemeral glow. Cleaner than the boy, but with the same look of dreamy curiosity on her face. Of play. And the same white fabric made up their clothes.

So she was here. Or close enough.

Sky took a breath and tried to smile. She didn't want them to think her a threat. She wanted their help, and she wanted them to know it. The woman saw her smile and stepped forward, closer to Sky until she was so close that Sky could see her lips were slightly chapped. Sky wondered briefly if this woman was real. If the boy had been.

The woman reached toward Sky's body. Sky stiffened when the woman's hands patted her front jean pockets, then the back ones. Moving her hands up her sweater, now sticking to Sky with sweat, the woman spoke.

"Sorry, security. First things first, we have to make sure you don't have a camera or a camera phone or any other recording device. You don't, do you?"

"No," Sky whispered. So this was real.

"Well then, come on." The woman turned and walked into the oaks.

Sky almost expected the woman to vanish into thin air like the boy, but she didn't. She walked evenly and straight, without looking back to check on Sky. Soon they were on a small dirt path under a thicker patch of trees. Out of sight from above, thought Sky, and she wondered briefly if anyone at the Ashram knew that someone from the house above could easily be watching them. Probably not. The way the house was set into the hill, it would be hard to see it from below. Maybe she could use that information later, but then again maybe it wasn't information. For all she knew, Jake owned that house.

Jake. She cleared her throat. "Jake."

The woman turned back and smiled a small, knowing smile. The heat and dust made her look like an old gritty photograph. But beautiful, and still somehow clean except her bare feet, which were clothed in dust. Sky wanted to ask her her name, but she had a feeling she wouldn't tell her.

So she followed the woman through the oaks for five minutes or so before they reached the first small yurt. There were several small round buildings, little houses like she'd imagined, clustered together. A few women, and one man, sat on the porch in the shade of one bigger structure that looked like a bunkhouse, talking quietly. The man sat up a little when he saw Sky. The women stiffened. It was as if she'd interrupted an intimate conversation, and she could see immediately that they viewed her with suspicion. She caught the man's gaze briefly before looking down. Or maybe it was desire.

Soon they came to a small round wooden house with no door, just an opening. The woman led her in. She saw an old claw-foot tub against one side, several sinks, and a few crude pipes sticking out of the wall higher up that she assumed acted as showers. There did not appear to be electricity in the room; a window had been cut into one wall to offer light, but not privacy. An older woman with graying curls who was washing her face at one sink looked up and scowled at the younger woman. Then she saw Sky and her face changed. The young woman who had led her here gave Sky a reassuring smile and nodded at the older woman.

"Look what I found," she said.

The older woman didn't seem impressed. She snorted a little and nodded at the young woman, who started running water into the old claw-foot bathtub. Then the older woman came over to check Sky's pockets, her clothing, even running her hands over her breasts.

"I'm here to see . . ." Sky started.

"Undress."

"I'm only here to see Jake, I don't want to bother . . ."

"Now. Undress. First you bathe." She looked at the young woman, who was running a finger under the pipe that spouted water into the bath. "You, bathe her and get her something to wear."

Sky hadn't moved. Immodesty was her mother's trait, not hers. She didn't want to surrender her will so easily.

The older woman turned back to her. "Undress, or I'll find someone to drive you back to town. Your choice."

She pictured a quiet ride back to Carmel, finding a phone to call Liz. Being back in her apartment by tonight. But without answers, without her mother. A retreat was exactly what Edi would expect from her; this was the same weakness Ned had counted on. She felt the hard pit within her again. *Fuck it,* she thought.

Sky turned away from the woman as she pulled her sweater off. The woman snorted again. She slowly pulled her T-shirt over her head. Stepped out of her boat shoes, sticky with sweat and dust-filled now, undid her jean's button and pulled them down over her hips. Briefly she was grateful she had shaved her legs this morning, trying to freshen up after sleeping on the couch. She thought of letting Ryan in when she was still in a towel. How trusting, even flirtatious that had been. She felt a wave of embarrassment, fatigue, as she stepped out of her jeans. The woman turned the pipe off and Sky turned to her. She raised an eyebrow, and

Sky slowly unhooked her white cotton bra. Pulled down her blue silk underwear. At least she'd worn nice ones, even if they didn't match.

She looked briefly over her shoulder and watched as the older woman's face twisted itself in scorn. She looked like someone who rarely smiled, her frown lines deep. Grouchy. Quickly, Sky stepped into the deep tub. The water was so cold it was shocking at first. Of course. There'd be no hot water here.

She wondered briefly where Ryan was. If he was still looking for her.

The young woman handed her a crudely cut bar of soap that looked homemade. It smelled like almond milk and had bits of sand in it and felt rough on her skin when she ran it over her shin. Her feet were filthy from her run down the hill. She washed her toes carefully and then looked at the younger woman.

But it was the older woman, Grouchy, who spoke from behind her. "Please wash yourself thoroughly. *All* of·yourself. Sunshine, see that she does it—I'm going to tell *Her* we have a guest. I'll be back in a moment."

The woman left them, and more light came into the small room. She'd been standing right in the doorway, blocking the light, Sky realized. Sunshine, still wearing her happy, peaceful expression, took a broken bit of sponge that looked like a chunk of yellow cake and squeezed it over Sky, as if it was the most natural thing in the world to help a stranger with her bath.

"Your name is Sunshine?"

"Yes."

"Always?"

"I was born here, if that's what you are asking." Sky was surprised at the quickness of this answer; Sunshine's expression had made her wonder if she was "all there."

She thought about saying, "So was I," but thought she'd better keep that to herself a little longer.

Sunshine held the sponge chunk out to Sky and she took it. Then Sunshine leaned into Sky and Sky could see what it was, the oddness about her: even though she looked about Sky's age, she acted like a teenager.

"Did you run away?" She spoke in a low voice to Sky. "Did someone hurt you?"

Sky turned to her in surprise.

She nodded. "Jake's told us all about how many women are assaulted out there, like one in four?"

It was true. She remembered that statistic from the news last year.

Sunshine put a slender hand on Sky's bare shoulder and whispered, "It's okay, you are safe here."

Sky opened her mouth to protest, she felt she should defend her world, "I . . . I don't know. It's a pretty safe place out there too, for most people . . ." but she trailed off. Was she really going to brush aside sexual assault rates, having just been assaulted at her own workplace? "But, yes, it's a problem."

Sunshine nodded happily, affirmed. Jake, she realized, was smart. Use real facts about the world, terrifying truths, to remind the followers why it was best to stay where they were.

"Well, we will protect you, don't worry," and with that Sunshine broke the sponge over Sky's head, and Sky gulped a breath in as the cold water ran over her face.

"We need to wash your hair too."

But Sky felt like she was getting baptized.

She kept her face tilted upward as Sunshine rubbed the soap over her scalp and tried not to think about how much her life had changed in the space of a week. If she thought about it, she might cry. And she did not want someone named Sunshine to see her cry. She did not want to be party to her indoctrination against the outside world. Sunshine poured water once again over her head, and Sky took another sharp breath in.

"That should do it." Sunshine handed Sky a faded thin white Turkish towel and Sky stood up. Wiping her face, then wrapping the towel around herself, she was squeezing water out of her hair when the older woman came back. She was carrying a plastic squeeze bottle labeled coconut oil in marker and when she came in, she looked at Sky and Sunshine suspiciously.

"Sunshine, go now, get her a clean robe." Sunshine nodded and met

Sky's eyes one more time and smiled. Sky admired how she was wasn't afraid of this cantankerous older woman, who was maybe in her fifties.

"You. Give me the towel."

Sky wanted to hesitate, but she didn't want to show any weakness. So she handed it over and pretended it didn't bother her at all to stand there naked. The woman tipped the oil bottle into her hand, and a clear oil ran into her palm. She stepped toward Sky, and it was all she could do not to step back.

The woman rubbed her hands together and then touched Sky's shoulders. Vigorously rubbing her shoulders, down her arms, across her collarbone. She got more oil and turned Sky around, rubbing it over her back, across her buttocks, down her legs, crouching to her heels, reaching then around front to get her shin, up her thighs, belly, and Sky sucked in as the woman's hands reached around her and roughly rubbed her breasts then down again to her ankles. The woman worked brusquely, like Sky was a child or an animal.

"There," she said, standing up. Then she turned to the door to wait for Sunshine in silence. Sky did not say anything. That was the second time in a week someone had touched her body without her permission. But it was nothing like when Ned had grabbed her, forced his mouth on hers. This woman's actions had been almost clinical. Completely void of desire.

Safety, Sky realized, was a relative term. She would tell Sunshine that if she got the chance.

After a minute or so of silence, during which Sky held her naked body rigid, Sunshine came back in the door carrying something white.

"Sunshine asked me to bring this." She handed a white cotton garment to the older woman. Sky did a double take. This was a different young woman, but one that looked almost exactly like Sunshine. The same long auburn hair, the same dreamy smile when she looked up at Sky.

"Arms up," said the older woman, taking the white tunic and pulling it over Sky's head. It was a soft, light material, an all but shapeless dress until the older woman pulled a white belt around her waist and tied it. Sky took a breath in when she cinched it tight. "All right, follow me."

Sky stepped outside. The dirt felt warm on her feet. The light of the day was bright, and she watched the tableau before her. The commune was more populated now, a few women sat on the step of the largest yurt. She saw three more young women, walking arm in arm and laughing, and a fourth woman sitting in the shade of a tree, playing with a young man's long hair. She saw one man carrying a child on his shoulders. They no longer stopped to stare at her. With her wet long hair drying in waves, her oiled skin, her white clothing, Sky realized that anyone that came to rescue her wouldn't be able to tell her apart from these others. The cult members. She realized that was, perhaps, the point. Hiding in plain sight.

The older woman walked quickly, and Sky tried to keep up with her even though she wanted to take small and careful steps to avoid small rocks. She was unaccustomed to walking barefoot outside. It's not like you leave an apartment building without shoes on. Ever.

She followed the woman as she wove around little outbuildings. Sky had seen a clearing which seemed to take the brunt of the foot traffic and now she wondered if the older woman, Grouchy, as Sky began to think of her, was keeping her out of sight. How did news travel here? What would news of her arrival mean to these people? They walked between patches of oak shade, and Sky's oiled feet and shins quickly became the same curry color as everyone else's feet.

In not much more than a minute, they'd reached a small house, nicer than the yurts but not as nice as the bigger house behind it. The house was a simple white stucco, its base stained yellow from rainstorms, its door a heavy oak. The corners of the house were rounded off. There were no windows on the front of the house, and while it was taller than a ranch house, Sky would be surprised if it had more than one story inside.

The woman gave three distinct knocks. Paced evenly. One. Two. Three. Then she looked back at Sky and nodded. The scorn seemed, for the first time, to have disappeared from her face and to be replaced by something else. Fear? She couldn't be sure and didn't have time to look at her again as Grouchy opened the door and led Sky into a dark room. Her eyes adjusted from the bright light outside and she saw what looked like a woman sitting with her back to them in front of a large plate glass window, its purple velvet curtains mainly drawn despite one small sliver which revealed a strip of sky, oak, earth. The woman's silhouette revealed long, wavy hair and a certain stillness, as if two people had not just entered the room. The house smelled like lavender, had old wood floors, and there was a small gurgling sound of water coming from what Sky would guess was a plug-in indoor water feature. The kind Jerry detested, and that she had also come to see as a bad combination between New Age and bourgeois, even though that exact mélange could be used to describe her own upbringing.

Jerry. Another life, and another world compared to where she was now. What would he say if he saw her? She felt a strange pang, a physical realization that she needed help. That she was in over her head. She swallowed hard and looked at Grouchy.

Grouchy kept her eyes on the sitting woman. There was small dining table between them and her, and on the table sat a stack of blank paper and a large feather. There was also a glossy gray box of condoms. Trojan brand. Sky looked at them for a moment before the box's strange presence fully sunk in. Her shoulders involuntarily stiffened and she did another quick glance around the room to see if there were other oddities, signs of orgies or anything else she should be wary of.

Grouchy wrung her hands and stepped forward just as the woman spoke, causing Grouchy to start.

"Leave her . . ."

"But . . ."

"Thank you."

Sky didn't turn her head to take pleasure in the flustered face of Grouchy. She could sense it, but her eyes were too riveted on the voice she'd just heard.

She kept her eyes on the woman even when she heard Grouchy snort, *Yes, Mother,* then turn and exit the room, pulling the heavy door behind her quietly closed.

When Sky was a child, her mother read to her from a thick book of fairy tales, the red cover faded and the corners softened. Sky's favorite story, which now came to her like a sudden rush of blood in her veins, was the one about the Snow Queen. A little boy, Kay, gets fragments of glass from an evil mirror in his heart, in his eye. He becomes cruel to his best friend Gerda and then disappears, taken by the Snow Queen in her sled. Gerda travels long and far, with bleeding feet, to find him in spite of his cruelty and when she does, he does not recognize her at first.

His heart is a raw lump of ice, his skin powder blue; he has become fully entrapped in the world of the Snow Queen.

Now Sky thought of that moment—when Kay is lost to Gerda, before he is regained, his hoar heart, his skin of death a note held—and she felt a chord strike in her own body as three simultaneous notes: the memory of that story; her eyes adjusting and bringing into focus that hair, same as her own; and that voice.

That voice that echoed in her head and then spoke once more.

"You shouldn't have . . ." The woman turned and stopped mid-sentence.

Sky had last seen her mother only two weeks before, but it felt like it had been years. Between them was a hard floor, a table, and five feet of empty space, but to Sky it was a chasm, a space where the air vibrated between life and death, between truth and lie, between every version of her life. She was afraid that if she blinked, or even took a breath in, the specter of her mother would flicker and fade.

The two stood looking at each other. A minute might have passed, or maybe ten. There was very little movement in Sky's body, at least that she was aware of, but as she watched her mother's face, held her gaze, she saw bewilderment, anger, and love pass quickly through it. There was a time in her life when that kind of emotional reaction from her mother would have given her visceral pleasure. To shock the woman that had no rules, that loved to shock others.

Finally, Edi drew a quick breath in.

"Sky . . ." Her voice was a whisper. "Oh, Sky, what have you done?" Then she stepped around the table and embraced Sky. She buried her face in

Sky's hair and exhaled a quivering breath. Almost as if she was on the verge of crying, though Sky knew better.

"I thought . . ." Sky pulled back. The last week slammed into her in one quick force of memory and almost knocked the wind out of her. She took in a desperate breath, the kind you take after having been underwater for too long. "I thought you were dead."

"I know, I know—I am supposed to be," Edi whispered and pulled Sky close to her again, and this time Sky let her hold her. Her whole body felt like fighting, but also like completely giving in to her mother's tight embrace. Her petite frame, all muscle, now clinging to Sky. "It was so hard, I've been in so much pain, thinking of you . . . it was so hard to leave you, Sky. So much harder than I thought . . ."

Edi, never the queen of foresight. She pulled away from Sky but kept Sky's elbows cupped in her hands, and Sky saw her face up close in the sliver of light coming from the window. She'd aged in those two weeks. She looked thinner, and the skin on her face was etched with new wrinkles. Sky imagined that she also wore the last week on her own face. Edi ran her hands from Sky's elbows to her hands and clasped them together as she pulled her to the window, to the flattened and worn meditation cushions where she'd been sitting.

"What the fuck is going on, Edi? Why are you here?" Sky pulled her hands out of her mother's grip and folded her arms. Edi sat down and motioned for Sky to do the same. But she wanted answers before she sat.

"Do you know your purse was left in your house like you'd been grabbed or something, and there was some bloodstain up in my room, by my window, which was open, by the way."

"What? Jesus, they told me they would stage it like something might have happened to me but that seems a little dramatic."

"What? Who told you? Who is they?" Sky threw up her hands.

"Sssshh, we shouldn't talk too loud. There's always someone close by here, though no one else is in this house. We haven't got a lot of time. I'm supposed to vet you and take you to Jake. We've got fifteen minutes at most. And sit down."

"Well." Sky sat but moved her own cushion a little away from Edi so she could turn and face her head on. "You better start talking."

Edi nodded and bit her lower lip. It was the look she gave when she knew she'd done something wrong. She'd given the same look to Sky both when she told Sky she had adopted a dog the year before and when a week later she told Sky she'd taken it back to the shelter because of her severe allergy to dogs.

"It's hard to know where to begin . . . Please." Edi motioned for Sky to scoot a little closer, her voice low.

"I met Marguerite, so I know I was born here. But that's about all I know." Sky stayed put.

"You met Marguerite? Jesus, I haven't even been gone that long . . . what did she tell you?" Edi scooted her own cushion, a faded burgundy, to Sky.

"Mom, Edi, just tell me what's going on—if we don't have much time, you owe me an explanation first."

Edi nodded and bit her lip again, looking down at her hands. She pulled her cushion forward again so that her knees were almost touching Sky's. "I joined the Ashram when I was nineteen. I was here five years. You were born here, and I left when you were two. I left because it became clear to me that Jake was, well, a predator. I should have seen it earlier. But the sex just seemed a part of the beautiful life and community we were creating, at first. But then he wanted younger and younger girls, and he started to . . . Well, then I got pregnant. And it was a girl, you. It changed the way I saw things, being a mother. And Jake turned on me. I had been his goddess, before, his number one favorite. But after, he acted like I was filthy. It was humiliating. He still does it—that woman who brought you in, you should see the way he treats her now. Even after he picked her up at seventeen, doted on her, kept her in his bed for a full year. I know because it wasn't long after you were born."

Her mother sucked her bottom lip in and looked away before taking a sharp breath in and meeting Sky's eyes again. "I left and never looked back. Except to get Deb, Deb was here too, so she can tell you more stories . . ."

"I know, she told me." Sky watched her mother's face twist.

"Good lord, I really haven't been gone that long. I thought it would take years for this shit to come out . . ." Edi sucked her breath in.

"Keep talking—is Jake my father?" Sky felt that hardness within her again, even though much of her wanted to soften around her mother, around her relief that Edi was alive.

Edi looked up suddenly. Her face seemed to go visibly white. Outside somewhere they could hear a couple of women laughing, a child squealing. Sky watched her mother look again at her hands, saw them shaking. She reached forward and took one.

"I'm a big girl, Mom . . ."

"Sky, you have to get out of here. It's not safe here. If Jake was your father, then maybe it would be safe, but . . . Oh god, oh god," Edi's face tightened, and her green eyes wet and began to shine in the light from the window. She leaned her face just inches away from Sky's.

"Why did you come here?" she whispered, and her hands again cupped Sky's elbows.

Sky had almost never seen her mother cry. She opened her mouth and closed it. "I was looking for you. And if you were gone, I was looking for . . . for him, too, I guess."

"Jake?"

"My father."

Edi drew a sharp breath in, "He's gone, sweetheart, I'm so sorry. I'm sorry I never told you. It was all for your safety, good lord, there's so much to explain. I'll tell you what I can and then"—Edi sat up straight suddenly—"Where the hell's Orion?"

"Ryan? You . . ."

"Yes, he can explain it all to you. He's one of us, of them, of . . . he was born here too, Sky."

Outside, they heard a child laugh, and they both started before they turned back and stared at one another.

"Brother," Sky said the word to no one, to the air around Edi. She no longer felt like she was in her body.

Her body was back in her car sitting outside of her work, dreading going inside. Last Thursday morning. Before Ned touched her. When her body belonged fully to her.

Edi tightened her grip a little on Sky's elbows. "No, Sky, not your brother."

Sky looked at her mother, wishing they both could melt away from this place. This place they had come to, come from. Be back at her mother's house. The window closed. The chair upright. She closed her eyes for a moment to picture it.

"Not your brother. But he was here when you were younger, knows this place in and out. Knows all of the ugly truths, and when I'm gone, you go to him . . ."

"Gone?"

Edi's chin quivered and she brought a fist to her mouth. "I didn't want to have to say goodbye. I wasn't supposed to, even."

"Mom. Mother. Edi, you aren't making sense. Why don't you come home with me? Why did you come back if it's not safe?"

"Sky, listen to me." Edi moved her hands to Sky's shoulders and leaned in to speak into her ear. Her mother's breath hot on her cheek in a way that reminded her of stifled sick nights, Edi singing to her fever.

"It won't be long before someone comes through that door to take us to Jake. You need to tell him that you came to visit me, that you knew I'd be here because I could never stop talking about this place. That you had to see it, but—Sky, listen, this is important—tell him too that you have to return home soon. That your boyfriend is expecting you. That should keep him at bay." Edi's breath caught and Sky realized she was still trying not to cry. "And then tonight, you'll sleep in my yurt, and if he doesn't allow it and this is the last time we get to talk then you have to promise me you'll get out. Tonight. Follow the road to the fork and then take the middle one . . ."

"Back to Ryan?" Sky pulled from Edi's grip. Saw a tear on Edi's cheek.

"Yes, yes! Is he here?"

"He kidnapped me." She folded her arms; she could feel the coconut oil greasing her palms.

"What?"

"He told me he was a cop. He was supposed to be helping me . . ." Sky trailed off, suddenly overwhelmed with shame. She'd been so stupid to believe him. A brief flash of Ned's hands on her. Her face reddened.

"He *is* helping you; you have to let him explain. Tell him he has to or I'm out and there's no deal." Edi grasped Sky's folded arms, her fingers inching them apart.

"What deal? What are you going to do?"

Edi leaned again into Sky's ear. "I'm going to destroy him." She pulled back then and wiped her nose and cheek, and nodded, looking Sky straight in the eye. "I'm going to destroy Jake."

Sky watched her mother's face for a moment, waiting for her to continue. But her mother just nodded resolutely again, and Sky saw something there she hadn't seen before. It was a determination, which fit Edi's personality, but with it something new. Sky opened her mouth to speak when three distinct knocks came at the door. One. Two. Three.

Edi looked at Sky, still nodding. "Okay?" she whispered.

Sky hesitated and nodded slowly back as light flooded the room and a new young woman appeared. Beautiful, dark-haired, blue-eyed. Sky wasn't sure if her mind was playing tricks on her, but she would swear this woman could be Ryan's younger sister. Or perhaps it was that everyone there, since the flicker of the child she'd seen in the oaks, had looked somehow familiar to her.

"He's ready." The woman spoke with pride, and as she turned and Edi motioned that they were to follow, she watched how the woman seemed to glide rather than walk. Liz would certainly mock this woman. Liz. Another pain. The Phil situation, another question her mother might not have time to answer. Her breath hurt to draw at this point.

As they followed the woman out into the lurid sun, this time right into the clearing, Sky could feel eyes on her. She could see visions of figures in white in her periphery, moving in and out. She wondered if she should feel afraid. But she couldn't summon fear, exactly. She felt like she was in a play she was watching. Or perhaps one that she was performing. But one where she could definitely yell "Cut" at any moment and be returned to her apartment. But she didn't think Edi could get out so easily, and if she felt fear it was for her. *Her. Mother.*

They walked a short distance to the big house. Clean and modern looking, triangular. With big windows on the upper floor, looking down at the whole Ashram.

Before the house was a landscaped area, filled with succulents and other drought tolerant plants. The door was the same heavy oak and by the time they knocked, one, two, three, Sky was sure that if she turned she'd see the entire village standing behind her, staring in silence.

After the three knocks, the young woman reached for the doorknob with confidence. Her cheery demeanor added a layer of uncanniness to her mother's fear of this place. Her insistence that Sky get out.

They stepped into a room filled with light. The entire back side of the house was made of windows, an A-frame triangulating up to the ceiling. There were wood floors throughout, with rugs and pillows strewn about the great room in front of the windows. A few knotted afghan blankets. A white cat with one black paw lay on a large faded purple velvet cushion near the window, regarding them with faint interest.

Her mother's hand found her own briefly as the woman turned and ushered them past this room, down a hall, to another elegant wood room. This one with bookcases lining the walls, and another large window looking out the same direction as the other. Her mother gave a brief squeeze and then dropped Sky's hand as they came into the room fully, where Sky saw a man standing by the window. He had straight posture, long hair up in bun, and a bright white tunic. When the young woman closed the door behind them, he turned around.

༄

When Sky was in sixth grade, her school hired a new gym teacher. He was young and good-looking in a clean-cut way and immediately became the talk of the girl's bathroom. But the boys loved him too. He could do backflips, and showed them tricks with a quarter he kept in his pocket and could spin on the back of his hand. A rumor went around that he was dating their pretty math teacher. Everyone loved him. Except Sky. She was wary. Her mother was always bringing nice-looking people home, and sometimes they were good, sometimes not.

Mr. Shane, that was his name, seemed to sense her reserve so he gave Sky space. But then one day in gym class after he'd made everyone start stations with different exercises, he yelled across the searingly bright gymnasium. Yelled her name. The girls all looked at her with the kind of raging jealousy that only prepubescence can conjure, and she blushed. She tossed an orange rubber ball to another girl, wiped her hands on her shorts, and jogged over to where Shane sat on the metal bleachers. He had his arms crossed and was smiling at her.

"What?"

"Sit down for a sec."

Sky sat on the bench next to him. He turned to her and grinned, a perfect set of teeth flashed like a card up his sleeve. "You don't like me, but I think you should give me a chance."

Sky's face burned; she hadn't meant to be that obvious.

"Really, I'm not a bad guy. Look at me." He turned his body fully toward her, and she looked into his face. It was relaxed, clear. And his eyes. Their sea green was flecked with yellow and the light in them reminded her of something wild. He had tan skin and deep dimples when he smiled. He was staring intently into her own eyes and suddenly her embarrassment faded.

It was hard to explain what happened in that moment, and Sky thought about it often afterward, and then occasionally even years later, because two weeks after he stared into her eyes, he was gone. Overnight. No one knew why, and the adults wouldn't say if they knew. Their pretty math teacher took a week off and then came back different, quieter.

But during this moment in the gym Sky saw the way this man could eat you alive. The way you would let him. A kind of animal dominance, a magic spell. When she saw it, she looked away, and then without meaning to, immediately back again. He was extraordinarily attractive. As soon as she thought that he smiled, like he'd read her mind.

"So, we good?" he'd asked and put his hand on Sky's back. She nodded slowly. "Okay, go play." So she got up.

"Oh, and Sky, it's good to be hard to impress. You're smart that way, I can tell."

She walked back to her friends, who wanted to hear every word. She didn't say anything to them, just that he was checking on her. To which they cooed, he's so sweet, he must like you. She felt their smoldering jealousy again and dared glance back at Shane. He was watching her. As if to make sure she had a crush on him now, too. She might, she realized. She liked that he'd noticed her hesitation, admired it even.

Later when she would think of him, she would remember the intensity of his gaze. When she became an adult, and thought back on it, really thought on it, and then later tried to explain him to a college roommate, it became clearer that there might have been something off. The way he disappeared so quickly. Didn't last more than a month. In the dark of their dorm room one night her roommate had said, "Probably a predator. Or a con man. Your poor math teacher."

But still, Sky wanted to whisper across the stale dark, I've never met anyone else like *that*. We don't have a name for that, that kind of draw. There's no word quite right, at least not in English. It's not charm, but something more instinctual. She'd felt laid bare by that gaze and wasn't sure she hadn't liked it.

Now Jake turned around and Sky recognized instantly what it had taken her weeks to see in Shane. His golden-brown hair had only a few strands of gray. His face was square and his cheekbones high. His skin olive and for the most part, besides some smile lines, smooth. His eyes were crystalized pools of luminescent blue. There was no doubt who Ryan's father was. Though Jake's eyes were even bluer, and he stared right into Sky, holding her gaze. Again, he seemed to possess, like Shane, a language of utter dominance. As if there were some stray code of animal DNA within all of us, priming us for submission to this kind of presence. She wished, briefly, that this was her father she was meeting and then immediately corrected her thought. Tried to ground herself. She tried to hear Ryan's voice: *Jake Bridger is a dangerous man.*

He seemed to sense both her acceptance and resistance as if he had orchestrated them both and smiled, stepping forward.

"So you've brought me a gift, Edi?"

"Jake. No."

"The prodigal daughter returns home and then brings another daughter home." Jake stepped forward and reached his hand out to Sky. When she didn't move, he placed his smooth palm against her cheek. "Hello, Sky."

Sky opened her mouth to speak but closed it. Of course, Edi and Sky standing next to each other were an open book to read, their resemblance unmistakable.

Jake came closer and embraced her. Sky didn't have to look at her mother; she could feel her cringing. Sky willed herself to feel nothing and tried to imagine her body like a piece of wood, but it was hard not to want to soften when his smell hit her face.

It was a sweet, rich smell, like vanilla and fresh cut wood, but it was the familiarity that made her mind lose all words, all barriers. She almost gasped aloud.

Funny, how the body remembers where it has been, who has held it. Its point of origin an olfactory horizon within, always recognizable in its simplicity.

"She won't stay, Jake." Edi's voice wavered slightly, as Jake pulled away and held Sky in front of him.

"She certainly turned out how we planned." Jake's eyes wandered her body and Sky for the first time felt the way in which he was not her father.

"You planned."

"Relax, Edi, this is a joyous occasion. A reunion. Sky's just like Persephone, a daughter back from the underworld. Spring has come!" Jake gestured for them all to sit on the sheepskin rugs that lay like a calico pattern in front of the window. "Do either of you need anything?" He poured a tall glass of water from a pitcher on one bookcase and handed it to Sky.

She took it gratefully, wondering how it was somehow cold.

"I want you to be comfortable," he said, "both of you. I trust you've been treated well so far."

Sky sipped and nodded.

"The Greeks had a great tradition. Xenia. It was a sacred ritual to welcome guests to their islands. They would bathe the guest, anoint them in oil, and have them to feast and after that, and only after all that, they would turn to the guest and expect his name, his story.

"They did this in case the guest was a god, or goddess, in disguise. We believe God is within all of us, a white light within, so we do this to recognize the light within all who come here. No matter their intentions." At this last word Sky looked up at Jake, and he smiled. "But I am afraid we didn't have you to feast yet. Perhaps later. Water will have to suffice for now."

Jake paused and sat in a low leather chair above Sky and Edi. Sky wondered how many women had sat around him, heads on his lap, him stroking their hair. Her picturing this made her suddenly raw with the realization that she had an urge to move closer to him. There was *something* about him.

But no, she couldn't want that. She was hungry, tired. She wanted to turn back to her mother. To repeat what Ryan had said to her: *Jake Bridger is . . .*

Jake cleared his throat and opened his hands toward Sky. She understood it was her turn to tell her story. She remembered what her mother had said. But any lie, she felt, would be easily detected by Jake. So she picked her words carefully.

"I came here looking for Edi."

"And you have found her."

"Yes, I have found her."

"Will you try to take her back with you?"

Sky looked at Edi, who was looking out the window, as if the conversation was too much for her to bear. As if her face might reveal what she had said to Sky just moments before, *I am going to destroy him.*

"No," Sky said. "I wasn't sure, but now I think no." Jake raised his eyebrows as if he didn't believe her. "She left me, she left everything, so she must really want to be here. I just"—Sky suddenly felt her voice succumb to the emotional toil of the past week—"I just wanted to make sure she was okay."

"And now you think she is? Okay?"

Sky turned again to her mother, who had pulled herself together and was looking back at her with a sad smile. She reached over and grabbed Sky's hand. Edi, back to playing a role. Good girl, Edi, Sky thought.

"Yes, I do."

Jake nodded and looked at Sky again, leaning forward on his knees. "Well, Sky, I'm glad you think so." He said this in a low voice, almost a growl.

Sky's heart tightened and she wondered what he knew. His eyes met hers again and she held his gaze. She could see the way he could be frightening.

But then he laughed, and the shadow of menace was gone almost as quickly as it had come. His attractiveness almost pulsated from his smile.

"Oh, Edi, Edi. What have you done?"

Edi looked up and watched Jake carefully. Sky's own body remained taut.

"You know, Sky, we have another welcoming ritual . . ." Jake had said her name but was looking at Edi. Looking at her like he wanted to hurt her. Or test her.

"No, Jake, she's not here to become one of us. She came to check on me."

"But it'd be a pity not to show her the circle, it's what we are all about here." Jake looked at Sky and licked his lips. "And it's her destiny, after all, what she was made for . . ." Jake stood and took a step forward but just as quickly Edi was on her feet, between Jake and Sky.

Sky suddenly remembered the box of condoms. A few square packages laid out like a stack of coasters. Hospitality.

Sky stood and said, "I also came because I thought you were my father." This did the trick. The two came apart and Jake's head tilted curiously at her. "I wanted to meet you."

"No, Sky." Jake sat back down and leaned back, his body completely relaxed while Edi backed up, but stayed standing. Sky was struck with the sudden thought that she'd rarely seen her mother so protective. So serious, even. A wave of ache went through her, how she'd longed for this as a child. Someone standing up for her, standing between her and her fear instead of pushing her toward it. "No, I have lots of children. But you are not one of them."

He stopped and looked at Edi, but Sky didn't dare turn around to see her face as well, to read what was between them.

"No, I had too many by the time you came along. We knew I'd need children not mine, women not related to me, down the line, so we made you."

Her destiny. To be Jake's what? Concubine? Child bride? In his harem? She thought of Deb's face. *Things had taken a turn.* Hadn't she said that?

Sky held Jake's gaze. The pools. Saw briefly the version of the past, the split screen where she knew this man as father figure and lover. Where she hated and loved him. Where she knew little else.

Edi had spared her so much, and she wanted to turn and embrace her, to say *I understand now, let's go home.* But she could feel the way Edi's determination rooted her here, tied her to Jake so much so she'd abandoned Sky. Roger. Deb.

No, Sky could never compete with Jake. It was so clear in this moment: this was an old story between them and Sky wouldn't win this time around. The strength of tension that vibrated between the two of them was stronger than anything she'd seen in her mother. It even seemed to make Edi's voice hoarse when she spoke.

"There was more to it than that," Edi said, and Sky turned to her mother's face and saw a flash of pleading in her green eyes, as if to say *Please don't believe that.* Then just as quickly, she put her mask back on (*Picture a bowl of sugar*), smiled, and turned back to Jake. "But that was the main idea, I guess."

"So"—Jake shifted in his chair—"while you are here . . ."

Sky didn't want him to finish his sentence or change the subject. She wanted to hear what Edi couldn't say. "Is my father here?"

Jake's face darkened a little. Was it that he didn't like being interrupted or the mention of her father?

Edi stepped forward and pulled Sky down to sitting again. "Sky, sweetheart." Edi took her hands up and pulled them into her lap. She spoke softly to them. "I'm sorry to tell you this. He's gone. He died when you were a baby."

"Here, he was here?" Sky looked around the room uselessly. She'd missed him by over twenty-five years.

"Yes."

"And he died here? How?" Sky looked at Jake, but Edi put her hand on Sky's cheek and pulled her in for a hug. Her mouth buried deep within Sky's still damp hair, her mother whispered, "I loved him."

Sky felt the words in her ear as a hot wind of hurt and of anger. Why had her mother waited until they couldn't speak to speak of him? Why had she lived with the fantasy of a father instead of the ghost of one? Why hadn't she known anything? Even to know that her parents had loved each other would have meant so much.

Jake chuckled at their embrace, and Edi pulled away. Sky repeated her question. "How did he die?"

"It was an accident. Or was it a suicide?" Jake was watching Edi and Sky could see his power. His charm, but also his unchecked cruelty. "It's been so long, I don't remember." Edi stared at Jake and didn't break his gaze. "Oh, that's right, an accident. Terrible."

Sky waited for one of them to continue but they stood staring at each other, as if each daring each other, goading each other, toward some truth.

"We had mountain lions then. Still do, sometimes," Jake said. "One became particularly bad. Came into the camp nightly. Ate a cat or two. Ate a goat we were keeping. We were afraid it would take a child next. They've done that before, in other places, you know? I had to protect us, so I bought a gun. We began to set a watch, waiting through the night for the lion. Who knows what your father was doing out that night . . ." Jake stopped himself. The cruel smile with which he had begun the story had faded and Sky could see a flash of something else. Regret? Fatigue? Or had he decided to put on a mask of grief for Sky's benefit?

"I am sorry. Especially if you came all this way looking for a father." His eyes met hers and Sky realized she believed his sympathy was genuine.

Sky nodded and felt Edi grab her hand, squeeze it. Jake stood and stepped toward the window and spoke out into the oaks, his arms folded behind his back. "There are many ways to comfort yourself here, and I suggest you stay for a few days at least."

Edi looked at Sky, so she murmured, "Thank you."

"Of course, you can't stay with Edi. She's still reacclimating and while we are happy to have you, we don't want you to confuse her."

"But Jake . . ." Edi stood now.

"No, Edi, remember? I know what's best. You said it yourself when you begged me to let you come back here." Edi closed her mouth. "So you'll take her to Rain. She's expecting her."

Sky wanted to get out of that room. She stood, realizing she hadn't fully exhaled since Jake had first turned around. She wanted to ask her mother questions, she wanted to plan how to get them both back home. All the curiosity she'd had about where she'd come from had now drained from her body. She felt like she already knew enough, maybe too much. That the other details that would come might be even harder to take in.

"Thank you, Jake," she said, hoping to begin the goodbye process.

"You're welcome, Sky, I'll see you again before you leave. I always show my guests a more personal welcome."

Sky wasn't sure whether this was a promise or a threat. Edi took her hand to lead her out. The two took a step toward the door.

"Oh, there is one more thing." Jake turned his body back toward them.

Sky and Edi waited.

"How did you get here?"

Ryan. The house. The hill. The running.

"I mean," Jake continued, "I heard you just appeared in the woods. Like a ghost." He laughed.

Sky thought of the child. Had he seen her run? From which direction she came? She felt a visceral danger here. Edi's lie. Whoever Ryan was. They were depending on her now for their safety, but they hadn't told her anything that would help her help them.

Sky cleared her throat. "I had a friend drive me down on her way to a meeting at a winery in Carmel Valley. She was late so I had her drop me off at the road."

Jake waited, smiling slightly as if he already knew she was lying.

"I took the wrong road and cut through the woods once I saw the Ashram from above."

"And this friend, will she be back for you? I need to know who is coming . . ."

"No, I told her I'd be a few days. I thought that someone here could give me a ride to the bus station." Sky could feel the weakness of her own lie. It didn't make sense. And the fact she had no phone on her, or purse, nothing, made it even less plausible. But she held Jake's gaze. It was one thing she'd improved at since meeting Mr. Shane, holding a gaze. Not looking away. Roger had had staring contests with her when they first met and when she'd won he'd always said, "Good girl."

Roger, Sky thought, if only he was here. If only he would take her mother and her away from this. Or Liz. Someone whose life was not entangled with Jake's.

Jake looked to Edi. "Take her now. And Sky, I'll see you tonight." A sly smile curved onto his lips as he again watched Edi for a reaction to this. Sky wasn't sure what he had planned, wasn't sure if she wanted to find out.

Edi led her out, back past the large room and the huge window where two young women sat now, one braiding the other's hair, and back out into the bright sun.

Sky let her breath out and turned to her mother, but just as she did the two women appeared on either side of them. Or at least Sky thought it was the two women they'd just passed inside. But she hadn't heard them rise and walk out behind them, so perhaps not.

"Come, Sky, I'm Rain." A black-haired girl a couple of years younger than Sky looped her arm through Sky's. "I am going to show you where we put guests."

"But I wanted to talk to my mother . . ."

Edi was being pulled the other direction, her arm looped by another smiling woman. An older woman, Sky saw now, about Edi's age.

"Later, maybe, but for now Jake wants you given a rest. Come now, sweet child."

Sky cringed—there was something not right about this woman in her midtwenties calling Sky a child. She remembered what Ryan had said about some children that had never been allowed to leave. Her world, her memory, her imagination confined to what she could see around her. Not knowing the ocean was a short distance away. The city not much further. An entire civilization waiting for her to discover it. The earth, Sky wanted to whisper to her, is round.

But instead she turned to glance one more time at Edi whose face was visibly anguished. Sky thought she'd never seen her mother look so tired.

"I love you," she said, just loud enough for Sky to hear.

"I'll see you later, I'll see you . . ." But Edi had turned to walk with the other woman. So she stopped and said, "Mom," louder. She wanted everyone to know they were mother and daughter. She wouldn't use "Edi" here.

Edi turned around and nodded. "I'll see you later."

Sky sighed, imagining the moment when Edi would have to explain everything, fill in the massive blank that had underlined Sky's whole life. Edi owed her this, but knowing Edi, she'd somehow get out of it.

Rain took her across the hot village. Fewer were out now that the heat of the day had crested. The dirt was almost too warm for bare feet, and she resisted the urge to quicken her steps. The smell of California sagebrush thickened the air. Sky could hear a child laughing somewhere, and someone was hammering something. But other than that, it was quiet.

It was as if, Sky thought, she'd gone back in time. It was miraculous that she'd been born here, that children survived, though she was sure some didn't. Mothers lost too, probably.

And fathers. *An accident?*

Rain turned her cheery face to Sky. "If you have any questions, let me know. I'm taking you to where you will stay and then I'll bring you to evening meditation, and then dinner."

Sky suddenly turned to her. Could the whole day have passed? Ryan at her house this morning. Waking up in the car ride. Driving. Running. Being found, bathed, oiled. Brought to Edi. Brought to Jake. The sun was slant in the sky. The heat of four or five o'clock. She wished she could get out of that canyon. Back to the ocean. Some place cool, where she could breathe and repeat Jake's words to herself in privacy. Her *destiny*. An *accident, or suicide?*

Rain, Sky realized, was talking. Giving her a tour of sorts. "Everyone helps around here. We have a garden down valley where we grow most of our produce. We all cook, and clean, and build, and do anything else that needs doing. Sometimes members go to work a few weeks at a time to bring in other money for us all. This is really the best way to live." Sky watched Rain; she seemed so sure of herself, as if doubt had never crossed her mind. "And no one hurts anyone else here."

Sky thought of the Grouchy woman's face, her rough touch. She wasn't so sure of that. But she offered this young woman a small smile. "How long have you lived here?"

"I was born here. Jake's my father. My mother died when I was little. But I have lots of mothers here, so it's okay."

So Rain was safe from Jake's attentions. Presumably. Safe in a way Sky wouldn't have been, or wasn't.

"Jake is a little like Zeus, don't you think? I've been reading a lot of Homer lately."

Sky was surprised and raised her eyebrows. She waited for her to go on. If Jake was Zeus, did this young woman think she was gray-eyed Athena?

"He looks just like the pictures in the book I have."

"Are you allowed to leave, if you wanted to?" Sky asked.

Rain looked at her, a little perplexed. "Why would I want to? It's dangerous out there. I mean, that's why you are here, right? Because something bad happened out there?"

Sky opened her mouth, but slowly closed it again. Her mother had gone missing, she'd been sexually assaulted at work, she'd been tricked by a man, lied to by her best friend, and then kidnapped. Again, right now she wasn't the best advertisement for the real world.

"It's okay," Rain said kindly, dropping her arm but still staying close enough to her body to touch it. "You don't have to tell me. You should hear some of the things I've heard from women who join us. What's happened to them, who's hurt them—you wouldn't believe it." Rain seemed for a moment overcome with emotion and Sky thought she might cry. "It's just so hard to imagine people treating each other like that. We don't have any of that here."

"What about accidents?" Sky couldn't help herself.

"Accidents? What do you mean?"

"Like people getting hurt, or dying . . ."

"Oh, a few years ago, a boy drowned in the river. It was terrible."

"That's all?"

"This is . . . I don't know why you'd want to know. My mother's death was with another child. The one younger than me. They both died when he was trying to come out."

"I'm sorry."

"It's okay. Their light has joined the great light now. The light all around us. I can feel their heat even now." She touched her own arm gently and smiled.

They had stopped walking and now Rain took Sky's arm again and led her to a small yurt. They walked up two dusty wooden steps and swung open saloon-style doors. As they entered, Sky saw a tattered old carpet square cut and stringy at the edges that covered most of the floor. The place smelled of musty leaves. Along the circular walls were pallets covered with mattresses underneath fabric banners with Hindu figures on them. On each mattress was some kind of folded blanket. One had been made up with a pillow, faded sheets, and a light blue blanket.

"Here's where you will sleep." Rain pointed to the made bed. "If you want to lie down for a few minutes that would be good. I'll be right outside." Rain gestured for her to sit, before turning to the door and going outside to sit.

Sky sat down and looked at her dusty feet. She wondered how they kept the yurt so clean. It must be swept daily. She thought of the children in white, the little blue-eyed army, working away. She wondered if her mother was under similar surveillance, and where she might be. She wondered what Ryan was doing, what his plan had entailed now that she had gone AWOL. Now that she knew he was trustworthy. Or at least by Edi's standards.

She laid her head back and barely let herself acknowledge that she had a headache—too much tension and heat. She rolled on her side, her face on her arm, the smell of coconut there, and tried to focus on the fact that she was safe. At least relatively. At least right now.

Sky remembered Jake calling her Persephone. She knew a lot about Greek mythology, because Edi knew a lot about Greek mythology, and now she realized why that was. So she knew what Jake meant when he had called her this; it was one of her favorite stories to hear Edi tell.

Hades negotiates with Zeus to take Persephone as his bride and takes her to the underworld. No one bothers to tell her mother, Demeter, who looks everywhere for her. Demeter, a goddess of vegetation and harvest, forgets all else but her missing daughter. The crops shrivel. So Zeus makes Hades return Persephone to earth to end the famine.

However, while in the underworld, Persephone ate one pomegranate seed.

So she is forever bound to the underworld by this act and must return one season a year.

Why, Sky had always wondered, had eating one small seed been such a damning act? Why had her mother not found all these tales painful to tell, if they came from this place?

After about twenty long minutes, Rain—whose perfectly still back Sky had been watching through the half doors, wondering if she would guard her the whole day—stood up. "All right," she said, turning toward Sky, "it's time."

Sky followed Rain into the heart of the commune. Everyone—men, women, children—was walking toward the big house she'd been in earlier. Off the back of it was a large stone patio covered with a wooden pitched roof that was oversized. It would stay shaded or dry no matter the weather. The patio was sandstone, crudely laid, but time had worn down the cement grout and created an even, smooth surface. She briefly imagined telling someone there that she was an expert in such things, thought about turning to Rain as they walked in, but she stopped herself. How irrelevant that would be, perhaps Rain would even laugh that such a job existed. She was sure the narcissistic impulse to name her profession was something to do with this place, the need to define herself for the group around her now as other. As *not* them. Even as she looked in this moment, wearing white and walking with them, exactly like one of them. Born *and* bred.

There were maybe forty people on the patio, each standing a couple of feet apart. They'd spaced themselves quite perfectly, and Sky wondered how they'd come to choreograph this. Had their formation evolved naturally over time, or had it taken a director? Someone like Grouchy, who stood at the front to herd people into place. Sky felt a pang as she looked at Grouchy's back and remembered what her mother had said. A seventeen-year-old version of this woman had been picked up off the street, enjoyed by Jake, then discarded. And then had stayed here for decades as someone's used goods.

The group was silent and Sky stood alone at the back. Rain had left her side to go to a spot up front. There was no space for Sky where she wouldn't disrupt their perfect rows. So she remained in the back, behind a row of children, scanning the figures before her. The backs of all of these people. Motionless, quiet, waiting. Finally, she spotted Edi. Front and center. *Mother.* How did Edi, after being gone so long, wield power here? Why was it her to whom they brought her when she arrived? Edi seemed to sense Sky and braved a quick glance behind her.

Their eyes met briefly. Long enough for Sky to know Edi was not in control of this gathering. She'd be powerless to protect her daughter here.

Sky felt a brief puff of insolence. She was sick of being protected if it meant being lied to.

Then the door to the large house, at the front of the patio, opened and Jake walked out to his audience. The feeling of excitement was palpable; there was a collective exhale, a herd smile that Sky felt and saw around her. She half-expected the group to burst into applause. She noticed that even the children, the ones closest to her, were riveted to attention. Did they think of him as a god? A father or grandfather? How many *had* he fathered? *Zeus*, Rain had said.

Even though the group was quiet, Jake opened his arms as if to embrace them all and then pushed his palms down in little hushing motions.

"My beauties." He clasped his hands together now. "Look at you, look at the joy in this sacred space." There was a wave of scattered giggles. "Are we not the luckiest people in the world?"

"Hear, hear," a man's voice called from not too far from Sky, followed by a murmur of affirmation throughout the group.

Jake smiled even bigger. He looked genuinely happy, Sky thought. As did the people around her.

But then he caught her eye and his smile faded. "I heard today that a man has confessed in suburban Florida to kidnapping a child on her way home from school, abusing her for three days, and then burying her alive in trash bags in a dumpster not a block from her home." He said this as if talking to her at first, and then turned to the others.

Sky shifted with discomfort; she had heard a sentence or two of this story on her car radio a couple of weeks ago. The rest of the crowd was shaking their heads; one woman in the middle of the crowd began to cry quietly.

"This is how dark it is out there," Jake said, "where people don't take care of their own. Where they can't take care of their own. Mothers that work two jobs can't pick up their nine-year-olds and walk them home from school."

Sky was struck by the truth of this statement. This was Jake's trick, she knew by now; there was no arguing with him. There was no saying the world was safe in the face of a story like that. There was no arguing that society *wasn't* sick if things like that were happening.

She felt suddenly very tired. She fought the urge to sit down.

"But enough about there. Let's focus on what we can control ourselves. The light within us, salvaged from the darkness of the ego."

The group seemed to stand straighter. Everyone's feet placed in mountain stance. Hip-width apart. Without thinking, Sky imitated them. She did plenty of yoga. Edi was her mother, after all.

"Perhaps we can make enough light to surround that girl's mother. To spread outwards. Breathe in."

The group raised their hands to their abdomens, placing them stacked underneath their sternums and took a giant inhale. One of the children looked back at Sky. It was a little girl with freckles who was missing a front tooth. She seemed especially interested in Sky's presence. She looked at Sky's hands and nodded. Sky placed her hands on her abdomen and the little freckled girl turned back around, satisfied. It struck Sky that she'd been this same type of girl in school, always wanting everyone to follow the rules. Uncomfortable with the kid who couldn't keep his papers on his desk or stay in line. She had hated even minimal representations of chaos.

"Breathe out, hold. Now, breathe in. Deeply, deeply now. As you breathe in the light, allow the darkness of selfhood, and all negative thoughts, to escape you with your next exhale."

Sky took a breath in. This really wasn't too different than certain yoga classes she'd taken. She watched her mother's shoulders through the group, moving up and down with her breath. She felt a twinge of something, maybe competition, and she decided she'd do this exercise in earnest. Looking around her, she mimicked others' forms and tempos.

As if he'd sensed her shift toward effort, Jake walked through the group toward her. Hands behind his back, softly repeating. *Breathe in. Breathe out.* The tempo was such now, Sky realized, that it was almost oxygen-depriving.

When he reached her, he smiled gently, still talking to the group, *Breathe in, breathe out.* He looked at her as if asking permission and she nodded as he placed his hand over her hands, and when she inhaled, he softly pushed her hands back toward her spine, forcing her to take in even more air. He stayed with her for several breaths. His smell once again like a pull on her, making her lean toward him when she inhaled, rooting out her past like some animal. As he walked away, she continued to breathe, the breaths taking up her whole body, and she wondered who he really was.

The heat of the day was crowning, the sun in its western slant, and the sounds of the breaths were joined by a hawk screeching somewhere above.

The group continued to breathe standing for several minutes, Sky couldn't be sure how long. It took more and more focus and whenever she slowed for a minute, Jake seemed to sense it and turn toward her from wherever he was and her breath would resume. After what must have been at least twenty minutes, but could have been longer, Jake said, "And now be seated."

The Ashram seemed to have been waiting for this and they collectively sank to the floor in one smooth motion, but still breathing. The noise of their ins and outs not unlike the motion of waves. Sky kept it up, but it was surprising how exhausting it was. She also felt the need to laugh, like everything she normally held in was at the point of releasing. Just as she thought this, she heard a few laughs throughout the group, one woman on the far end of the patio seemed to be laughing hard. Or perhaps she was crying. Sky couldn't tell from where she sat. The noise built until it seemed most people were laughing, or releasing a shaky breath, or sigh, like one that had been held for a long time.

She'd lost track of Jake and suddenly he was behind her, whispering at her ear, "Let it go, it's okay, it's okay." He startled her a little and it came out, one loud laugh, almost too loud. But no one turned around, not even her mother. She felt grateful for the privacy.

"Keep breathing," said Jake, "and keep releasing."

She turned to him and nodded. She was going to try what her mother had given everything up for, what had seduced her. But it was hard. So hard. Without holding her breath, it was as if there was no place for the tension of the past several days to hide. She let out a few more laughs but felt that if she let any more of it go, it would all go, and she would cry for a half hour.

As if reading her mind, Jake said, "That's what this space is for—there's plenty of time." She nodded again and felt, to her horror, her chin start to quiver. Another woman let out a loud sob a few rows ahead of her. Again, no one reacted.

Sky breathed in again and felt the heat build up in her jaw, the burning in her ears, and then Jake touched her.

It was only a light touch on the shoulder, but it seemed as if Sky's whole body had become a button, pushable, and at his touch her shoulders collapsed into shaking. She bent her head to her chest and let her body heave. It was a silent sobbing, but she put hands over her face and let it come. Or let it out. She was not, she knew, in control.

And maybe that's what Edi had been trying to tell her with that sad glance backward right before mediation started. That Sky would not only see the source of Edi's shame and terror in the Ashram, but also the source of her peace. Sky, Edi must have known, was about to understand the seduction of this place, its light now a golden hue around them more like firelight than sunlight, its purifying effect undeniable.

Jake's hand stayed on her shoulder, but she was hardly cognizant of that, or of anything else around her.

She just let it out. Everything. All the events of the past weeks, of the past years even, and she didn't name them as they went. She just felt them go.

The ball within her body that had been tightly wound was unraveling now, and she had absolutely no control over it.

It was coming undone.

She was coming undone. She laid her head on Jake's shoulder. Let him stroke her hair.

She, Sky, of all people, for all the ways she was not her mother, was coming undone in this place that felt like both dream and memory. Was, in fact, probably both.

The light had changed again by the time she stopped. The sun had dropped further down in the sky, a relative coolness felt near, and several people and all the children were now lying on the stone patio. A few were still crying quietly but most were just breathing calmly, eyes closed. Presumably deep in meditation. Jake sat not far from her, cradling a woman's head in his lap. She stared ahead like an exhausted child, her face puffy from crying and Sky lay down on her side and looked at her; she was not much older than her and Sky felt like she was looking into a strange mirror. She felt completely empty, a sense of catharsis she hadn't felt for a long time. Perhaps not since that night with her mother when she learned of the rape, when the two had cried together. The feeling was one of incredible lightness, and Sky lay on the cold stone wondering if she'd misinterpreted the *light within* as a literal brightness when in fact it was meant as a metaphorical weightlessness.

Right in front of her she began to hear a soft, rhythmic sound: a child snoring. His face was turned toward her, mouth open, and a little drool gathering on the stone below him. It was the boy from the woods, Sky thought, though she couldn't be sure. Her eyes followed his small body down to his knee, where the cut had scabbed over. Yes, same boy. She imagined they weren't supposed to sleep, and the freckled girl's sharp glance at him when she too heard the small sound confirmed it. Soon his snores grew louder, and Sky felt Jake shift toward them. He walked to the child and looked at him with that curious look. Sky drew a breath in as she realized that she could perfectly picture Jake kicking this child. So thin was the edge of his power, his benevolence.

He looked up then and met her eyes.

Then he crouched down and, still keeping Sky's gaze, stroked the boy's hair gently. She closed her eyes. Felt perhaps the image she'd seen a moment ago, the fantasy of violence, as her own perversity, her *own darkness*, as Jake would say.

She briefly imagined herself trying to explain this place to someone and realized it would be impossible.

For a moment, she wondered if this is why Edi had never tried.

Jake then, in one motion, picked the boy up and took him to the front row. Again Sky drew her breath in, not sure why she was sensing the potential for danger. What if he dropped his limp body on the stone patio to wake him? Cracking his head open?

But Sky again grew hot with her own mistrust when Jake stooped down and placed the sleeping boy in someone's arms. Not just someone. Edi. Edi who reached up and took him. His body too large to be cradled but small enough that she could hold him in her lap, his head against her chest. Still asleep. Imagine sleeping through that, thought Sky. She'd never slept that soundly in her life. Even as a child. Even in Edi's arms.

At this action the group seemed to have awoken from their collective dream, a few whispered endearments, and there was another scattering of soft giggles.

Now that all eyes were back on him, Jake put his fingers to his lips and gestured to the sleeping boy. Then he silently palmed his hands together and bowed the traditional gesture of namaste, which Sky recognized from yoga, and then gave the group a releasing wave before he himself turned back toward his house.

Sky stood with the others and made a step toward her mother, who was the only one still sitting, the boy in her lap like he was an anchor. She had so much she wanted to tell her mother, but really, she just wanted to hug her. Let everything else go. Remember that night, that night you told me what happened to you, she wanted to say.

But before she could take more than two steps, Rain approached her open-armed and scooped her in for a hug. "Isn't it amazing?" She smiled, and then ran her hands down Sky's arms to her wrists, which she clasped. It was an action both tender and firm. She let go of one wrist and then pulled Sky. "Come, you," she said, "time to get you back to your castle."

"But I wanted to talk to . . ."

"Not now, not now. Jake says back with you." Rain gave two swinging tugs on her arm, like they were children. Sky knew there was no arguing, and she let Rain lead her away from the patio, but not before she turned to look once more at her mother still sitting as still as stone, so as not to wake the child, but looking over her shoulder at Sky. Her expression like something from an oil painting: an abstract sadness couched in beauty, wavering with the thickness of the light.

As they walked among others through the commune, Sky could feel eyes on her, as if the group wanted affirmation from this stranger. Rain led her to the door of the yurt.

"Stay here and I'll go get your meal. It may take a bit, as I'll have to wait in line and get both our plates at once."

"Could I come?" Sky wanted to see if she could find her mother again.

"No, we don't let guests socialize among everyone just right at first. You'd be *overstimulated*." Sky could hear the way she'd borrowed this last word from someone else. "Jake will *acclimate* you first. I'm sure he'll visit you tonight."

Sky sat down on the made bed. She tucked her hands under her legs. She felt like she was at some alternate-reality version of summer camp.

Rain watched for a moment, and then sat on the floor in front of her and looked into her eyes. Sky wondered if she was trying to pull the same powerful affect her father had. To see if the magic was genetic. Sky looked at her and smiled gently. It wasn't.

"Thank you," Sky said, hoping that Rain would leave and she could gather her thoughts. Come up with a plan.

"Thank you," Rain replied, smiling.

The light in the yurt came from a dirty bubble of a skylight at the top of the round ceiling; its circle of evening sun landed on the carpet just behind Rain.

Rain rose to her knees then and leaned forward, letting her forehead press into Sky's knee. Sky was confused by this touch but resisted the urge to draw back. She could suddenly hear Liz laughing, if she could see her. Clad in white, in a yurt decorated with dyed banners of Hindu gods and goddesses, with a woman pressing her forehead into her knee.

Sky sighed and put a hand briefly on Rain's thick warm rug of hair. Rain looked up and smiled. "Would you tell me your name now?"

So that's what she wanted. What she'd been waiting for. *Xenia.*

"Sky."

Rain tilted her head curiously before a slow smile spread across her face. "I thought you looked familiar." She stood up and put her palm against Sky's cheek, bowing over her like a nun.

"Welcome home, sister." And with that she turned and walked out of the yurt, swishing through the saloon-like doors with her head high, as if Sky's unwitting return confirmed that she knew all in the world, and all in the world was right. *Right as rain.*

Sky must have waited for almost an hour. She laid her head back on the pillow and closed her eyes but didn't sleep. Her mind played over the scenes of the last week. Sitting at Marguerite's table. Throwing her phone across her bedroom. Liz driving her up to Roger's. Her mother's house. Deb's embrace. Everything with Ryan. Ryan. How taken she'd been with Ryan. Her mother had said he was from here. Maybe Rain didn't have Jake's charm, but Ryan sure might.

Her father. Just the word, *father*, made her gasp a little inwardly in a way it never had before. She'd fantasized for years about finding him, the friendship they would have had. And all this time he'd been gone. Edi not realizing that even that one detail was a gift she'd denied her daughter. She resisted the urge to clench her teeth at this.

And she was also relieved that Jake was not her father. That she didn't have to know him as an origin.

These two emotions, learning of her father's loss and the grief and anger coupled with this relief not to be *of Jake*, felt like a large body of water within her, lapping at the edges of her heart. A horizon she'd turn her attention to when she could. And then she'd learn again to keep her head above the surface knowing what she now knew.

She heard a small rustling and turned on her side. She opened her eyes, and before her in the fading light stood a young boy.

Scrawny and long-haired; his white shorts had long ceased to be white. He looked at her with big blue eyes and smiled. Not the same boy she'd seen earlier but could have been.

She didn't know why, but she smiled back.

"You are pretty," he said, and gave a little bow. She laughed. The children here were otherworldly.

"Thank you." She sat up on the pallet and this brought her eye to eye with him. He couldn't have been older than eight.

"I have a message from Mother for you. She wanted me to tell you to be sure to look for Orion in the stars tonight. She said it's best to see him not too long after dark. Oh, and I'm supposed to give you this . . ."

He leaned over and kissed her cheek. Then he grinned wildly at her; she could see he was missing an eye tooth. He was just the kind of little scrapper that Edi would befriend and send to deliver her message.

"Thank you."

He bowed lightly again, and she bowed her head back. Then he was gone as quickly and silently as he'd come, though this time Sky watched him as he ran out.

Orion. Edi had said he'd have the answers, but it still panged her to go back to him without Edi.

Was she really just supposed to leave Edi to "destroy" Jake? What was Edi planning to do?

She wanted to stay longer, talk to her mother more, but she also knew she should leave before Jake came tonight. She didn't want to find out how he welcomed young women to his sect. She didn't want to be alone with only herself to stop him, she didn't trust herself against his pull. Didn't trust him. Yes, part of her wanted out of this place as quickly as possible, and yet something tugged at her to stay. It reminded Sky of jumping in icy cold water—she felt the need to escape but couldn't help but wonder how it would feel to get acclimated there.

Rain came in as the sky turned the color of flesh with a plate of food and a glass of water. The dinner was a kale lentil salad that lacked much flavor but that tasted good to Sky in her hunger, which she felt intensely as soon as she took the first bite. There was also a chunk of homemade wheat bread that was dense and grainy. Rain sat on the floor and watched her eat, with that content-as-ever look on her face. Sky was too hungry to care.

When she'd almost finished, Rain cleared her throat.

"Are you married?"

"No." Sky shook her head. It seemed an odd question. "Are you?"

"No, not yet. I have a few partners, but I'd like to pick just one soon. I want a child."

"Are you allowed to do that?"

"Yes, we can do whatever we want. Well, as long as Jake thinks it wise. He's sort of our guiding force. Our compass." Once again Sky could hear the way this woman was using phrases she'd heard before. *Guiding force, compass.*

The sun was definitely down now.

Sky wondered if she should ask this woman questions, learn more about the Ashram, but she also was eager for her to leave. Edi had said to go not long after dark. She supposed while everyone was washing up, before anyone thought to check on her. To watch over her.

Pretty, the small boy had said. That sweet boy. What would happen to him? What would his life be like?

"How many men are here?" Sky asked Rain.

"Oh, not as many men as women, but enough. We do have to do some sharing. And they have to get along with Jake and have, you know, a compatible male ego, otherwise they don't last."

Sky nodded. Rain waited for more questions. Sky took the last few bites of her food, and the room grew darker. Rain got up and lit a gas lantern that Sky hadn't noticed sitting on the floor between her pallet and another one.

"There," she said, setting it on the floor next to Sky's feet.

Sky watched the flame for a moment. "I thought . . . I thought there'd be more light here."

"What do you mean? This cult celebrates light, and lightness within, in every possible way. Did you not see, at the meditation . . ." Rain's face showed real concern before Sky interrupted her.

"No, no, I meant literal light. Like lights on in buildings, lots of them."

Rain titled her head at Sky curiously.

"I heard that . . . somewhere." Sky looked down at the plate. She thought of her mother's house, lit up from top to bottom like a paper lantern.

Rain relaxed a little. "That's an older model of the Ashram. We change with the times, and now we celebrate environmentalism. But when I was a child, yes, every building was lit up at night. I used to walk the path through the buildings at night and pretend I was a tiny fairy walking through a forest of stars."

Rain smiled a little at the distant memory. Sky wondered what else had changed, or whether there were any changes Rain didn't like. And would she know how to dislike anything? Was there space for that?

Sky nodded her head and raised her plate. "Thank you," she said.

"You are welcome."

Sky put the plate down on the floor and yawned. Rain took the hint.

"I'll leave you to rest a little." Rain got up. "Enjoy your night." Something about the way she said *enjoy* made Sky want to cringe.

"Good night," she managed. And with that Rain took the plate, leaving the half full glass of water for her, and walked out into the new darkness.

Sky lay down after Rain had left. She'd wait a half hour for complete dark, and then she'd try to go outside and see if a getaway was possible.

After a few minutes she blew the lantern out. Better to see if anyone was close enough that that would get their attention.

She lay in the dark, the moonlight coming in the round window at the top of the yurt. She could hear a small owl starting up nearby. And a warm wind had started to blow. The leaves became audible with it, and Sky could feel it tunneling through the half doors of the yurt. She wondered briefly what would happen if she didn't leave. If she faced Jake. If she refused him. If he simply wanted to talk to her. To work his infamous charm on her. She wondered if it would work; she remembered that first piercing glance. He had been intending to goad Edi throughout their conversation, but she wondered what would have happened if she'd only seen his charismatic side, the intelligent one. The tenderness she'd seen at meditation. She wondered how she would feel right now. She already knew that it would be naive to assume that she, or anyone else for that matter, would be immune to the powers of someone like Jake. Had already felt his charm. But also his cruelty.

And if he wanted to hurt Edi, was it because she had hurt him? The history between them had been palpable. Edi was *Mother* here, a name she'd heard too many people use now. Why? Was she the original counterpart to Jake's father figure? Did she have more responsibility in starting the Ashram than anyone had told her?

And if she stayed, would Ryan come for her? Liz? And when she left, what would happen to Edi? Would she be forced to answer for Sky's departure? Punished? Exiled?

She felt like she was trying to paint a picture from a photograph, but that she could only see a tiny fraction of the photograph. Everyone else had tried to protect her from it, but now they needed her to fill in all the blanks correctly in order to keep them safe. Part of her wanted to rebel and say no. To stay just to see her mother's face tomorrow, both in defiance but also as an act of loyalty. *I won't leave you.*

But more than anything she wanted answers, and if Ryan was where she would get them, then that's where she'd go. She could always come back, of that she was certain. Jake had wanted her, she could tell that much. And felt she was his. A far-flung seed come home to sprout.

A coyote yelped somewhere up the canyon, and Sky took this as a cue.

She sat up.

Waited.

Listened. Leaves in the oaks still crinkling in the wind. She moved both feet to the floor. She wondered vaguely where her shoes were. Her jeans, sweater. Presumably across the commune. She stood up and again waited. The floor was quiet as she walked across it, but she stopped every couple of steps, again listening for any noise outside. The doors made no sound as she swung one side open and looked out. The half-moon was up, and she could define shadows. There were a few lights on toward the main village, lighting the pathways, and many lights on still within the small houses and yurts. Someone laughed and it echoed the way human noise does in the wild.

She stood on the stoop and waited, letting her eyes adjust. She'd half expected to find some child or woman waiting outside, or leaning against a nearby tree, on guard, but she saw no one. She could see the dark outline of the ridge above, the one that Ryan had driven her halfway up, where the house was. She again wondered if they knew there was a house there—they must.

The oaks before her looked like dark beings, with gnarled arms opened up and flaring like the many-armed Hindu goddess in the yurt. She wished she had a flashlight. And shoes. But she took a deep breath and slowly took a step forward.

She ran right into him as he stepped in front of her.

Right into his chest.

How had she not seen him? Had he been standing off to her side the whole time? In the shadow of the yurt?

"Hello, Sky." Jake's voice was quiet and clear, almost childish. The hint of malice with which he'd spoke when Edi was there was completely gone. He took her arms in his hands, still just inches away from her and she felt for the first time how big he was. Tall, with large hands, a wide chest. Again, she thought of Ryan and felt a small heart tug. Ryan growing up here, how she'd misjudged him. She pictured him as one of those children from the meditation, trained to stay still, to journey inward. She wondered if he'd ever fallen asleep, too. If he'd seen Jake's tender side as she had, or if that had only been a performance for her benefit.

Jake turned her body gently and led her back into the yurt, to the edge of the pallet she'd been sleeping on. She wanted to feel fear, but she didn't. Jake squatted and relit the kerosene lamp. As it glowed his eyes shone immediately, and Sky thought about this one genetic quirk. Surely the intensity of their color, their otherworldliness, had helped Jake build what he'd built and had helped him define so many lives, including her own. And certainly her mother's.

Her mother. It was exhausting to think about all her mother had been through. Her mother, somewhere close, imagining her daughter escaping into the woods, barefoot in the moonlight, like a child in a fairy tale. Not knowing she'd run right into the wolf.

Jake sat down cross-legged in front of her, his tunic loose around his legs, sinewed with muscle. He was very fit, thin. A lot of people in Marin would kill to look like the men and women here. Sky herself ran, ate well, and still didn't have the kind of physiques she'd seen here. Maybe it was the yoga; she only went a couple of times a month.

"Do you have questions for me, Sky?" Again, his voice was so placid she briefly felt a temptation to let her guard down. She could smell him again, and in the familiarity of his scent she could almost see herself breaking down, telling him everything she'd been through the past weeks. His eyes took her in fully, as if his whole body was ready to listen to her.

She closed her own eyes, to break from his gaze, and to think of a question that wouldn't hurt to ask.

"Do I have any brothers and sisters here? Like children of my father?"

Jake shook his head. "You were his first and only."

Sky nodded. She couldn't ask about her mother, or Ryan, or Deb.

"What was he like?" She felt a twinge of pride. Not only did she want to know, but she also knew this went well with her story, that she'd come looking for her father.

Jake laughed, and perhaps there was an echo of bitterness to it, but Sky couldn't quite tell. Maybe it was jealousy. "He was tall. Taller than me if you can believe it. Soft-spoken. Quiet. Maybe a little shy." Jake looked away from her briefly. "It was a long time ago . . ."

Sky leaned forward and Jake's body ever so slightly mimicked hers so that the two were closer, like children telling secrets. Jake seemed encouraged by this.

"He was supposed to report to the military, in Monterey. He'd been drafted or something. It was the '70s, and this area saw a lot of draft dodgers. We saw our share, too. Usually they came and went within a few days, but your father, he stayed."

He'd met Edi, Sky thought, even though Jake didn't say that.

"And less than a year later, you were born." Jake reached forward and picked a hair off the edge of Sky's white tunic. Long. One of hers. Or her mother's. Or Sunshine's. Or, Sky realized, anyone here. "How old are you now?"

"Twenty-eight."

"Ah . . . your Saturn return. No wonder you are here."

Her mother had said the same thing on her twenty-eighth birthday, told her she was in for some heavy cosmic shit as she shoved a red velvet cupcake in her mouth.

"Looking for your father . . . and your mother." Jake put his hand on her knee, but she didn't flinch. "I'm glad your mother is here, Sky—I need her. *We* need her." Jake looked from her to the lamp, its glow shadowed his face. "Thank you for sharing her with us."

Sky nodded, unable to say anything back. What would he say if he knew everything? What would he do?

"It must have been difficult for you." Jake slid his hand from her knee down her calf to her foot, pulling it into his lap. He cradled her foot in his large palm like it was simply *his*. Like it was no longer a part of her body. He spoke to her foot—"It must have been difficult for you, growing up without a father"—before he raised his eyes again to her.

Sky nodded again, realizing she was practically holding her breath as she watched him run his thumb lightly into the arch of her foot. Normally she hated people touching her feet, and something that gentle would make her jerk her foot away, but again, she watched. Detached.

"Or did you?" he asked.

She looked up and met his eyes, confused for a moment.

"Did you have a father? A stepfather?"

Sky took a breath in, his thumb on her foot made her scalp tingle. What would Edi have told him? Did it matter?

"No, I didn't have one. It was just E—*Mother* and I."

"Edi, you call her." He brought his fingertips just under her toes. "She told me." He traced his nails along the side of her foot, up her calf. She shivered. "She also told me you weren't that close, that you hated her . . ." Sky could feel him watching her, but she kept her eyes on his hands. Trying to distance herself from the oddness of his touch. The odd *pleasure* of his touch. It wasn't something she wanted, but why did she have to keep telling herself that?

And *hated her*? Sky ignored the urge to cringe at the complicated truth of it.

"So, I was surprised you came," Jake said, his voice climbing to a certain pitch, but he seemed to catch himself and bring himself back down. "Delighted, of course, though."

"I didn't know where she was." Sky remembered Edi's instructions, faintly though. Her brain seemed foggy, and she felt a little drunk. She wondered if she'd eaten something, she glanced at the glass of water.

Or was it just this place? She wondered vaguely what time it was. How late it was getting.

Still, she managed, "But I thought she must be here. She's talked a lot about it . . ."

"She missed us?" Jake reached out and took up her other foot, scooting forward so his head was at her knees. She felt suddenly her own nakedness, her bare skin under thin cotton.

Sky drew another breath in as he ran his thumb along her left arch now. Again, she felt she should stop him, but again she didn't.

She felt like any resolve she'd had earlier was melting and all that was left was ambivalence. And an awakening desire. She looked up and met those primal eyes again, the perfect symmetry of his face.

This was her destiny, wasn't it? The part of her that had been missing all these years? The part that Edi had tried to drag out of her. Abandonment, sensuality, spontaneity.

Well, here it was finally: an almost perverse and inarticulable desire for a man who might have been her father. But wasn't.

The entire time it had been here, right where she'd left it. *Desire*.

Sky remembered to answer. "Yes, she did. She missed it." Her voice came out as a breathy whisper and she thought in passing of her mother's pleas for her to leave. Was it because her mother didn't want to share this? Because she didn't want Sky to have the same happiness she once had? Didn't want her to compete for Jake's attention? All those times Edi had flirted with her boyfriends, all the times she'd wanted to be the only sexual draw in the room. Sky not even trying to contend.

Jake nodded. "And how about you? Did you ever dream of coming here?" He placed her left foot in his lap with the other, before moving them both to either side of his knees. An action that left her own knees open, his face almost touching them now.

Sky felt the sudden flood of pheromones, a salty wetness in her mouth, the way she knew Jake expected her to feel. She looked at the lamp quickly, as if hoping it would bring her back into her body, or rather, her mind. *He is not a good man,* she thought, or tried to think. He and her mother . . . she tried briefly to think of the myth that told the story of a daughter's lust for her father. It was one her mother had told her, she must have learned it from Jake, Sky realized now. What had happened in that story? It was Adonis' mother who tricked her own father into being with her, she conceived Adonis, and then turned into a myrrh tree to escape his revenge.

Though Jake wasn't her father. But being a tree sounded like a relief right then.

Jake sensed her distraction, it seemed, but didn't seem phased by it. "What are you thinking about, Sky?"

"A myth."

Jake's face lit up. "I love myths," he said, and Sky thought, *I know.* Why had she never wondered how her mother knew so many? It was like she had a BA in Classics.

Jake leaned forward then and kissed the rough skin of her knee, just below the edge of the tunic. It was a dry, chaste kiss. "Which myth?"

Sky shook her head. "I can't remember." She didn't want to say—the story would be a confession.

Jake watched her closely and when she didn't say more, he said, "I mentioned the circle earlier. You must have noticed all of our round buildings?"

Sky nodded as Jake absentmindedly again stroked the arch of her left foot with his thumb.

"I studied Greek—mythology, classics, astrology, you name it. I was particularly drawn to the sun's path through the stars and the way the Greeks used it for divination. 'The zodiac' is what we call it. Did you know that 'zodiac' is Greek for 'circle of animals'?"

Sky shook her head. Watched his thumb make its own orbit on her bare skin.

"We are all just animals, moving in a circle around each other, around the sun. The Greeks knew that. I'm a Leo. Lion. Your mother, Sagittarius. The sign of prophets. Both animal and archer. What is her mark? Have you ever wondered?" Jake's thumb on her foot held still and Sky thought for a moment he looked amused. "To me it seems we are forever chasing each other."

Sky cleared her throat. "So the yurts . . ."

"There are no corners in the sky. You of all people should know that." His eyes twinkled up at her. She wanted to look away but didn't. His thumb started stroking her foot again, moving up to her heel. His mouth moving close to the skin of her thigh as he spoke.

"Sky, we are just like our animal signs. The stars align or don't align and push us together and pull us apart, over and over again. Our desire and its circular nature is both our only true will, and our only path to true presence—that's the circle. For those ready to give into their desire, their animal nature, to be in their body. Fully."

She thought of the image of her mother, the huntress. An archer. With a mark now, she knew. The image gave her a renewed sense of grounding, and she felt she had to take advantage of it. "Jake, I'm feeling . . ." She trailed off. She wanted back into her own mind. A brighter light on. She wanted not to do something she would regret.

Jake seemed to know he was losing her. He got up on his knees so that he was eye level with her, and she didn't finish what she'd started to say.

He reached forward with one hand, and she drew back ever so slightly. He looked curiously at her, and then tucked her hair behind her ear on one side, drawing his fingers down her jawline to her chin, which he cupped gently, staring at her with those eyes. She could smell him again and was afraid to breathe in, as if his scent would enter her and give him the final permission he needed.

"Sky." He spoke softly. "I was teasing your mother earlier. But nobody does anything here that they don't *want* to do. You can leave anytime." He brought his face closer to her and it hit her then, that smell. Both innate and sensual. "It's important to me that you know that."

Their faces close, Sky saw little yellow flecks radiating from the blue of his pupils. He was twenty-some years older than her. She opened her mouth to say she understood but found herself unable to speak. She was waiting, she realized, for him to kiss her.

And then, she thought, *I'll run*. And as if that thought had broken a spell, Jake rocked back onto his feet and in one motion swung to standing.

"I should let you sleep, Sky. I'm just so glad you are here."

Sky's face glowed with some new heat. She nodded, pushing the tunic back over her knees.

"Let's spend some time together tomorrow, okay?" Jake leaned forward and kissed her forehead, keeping his face close to hers for a second too long. Just the space Sky needed to know she hadn't imagined those last few moments. He thought his power over her was total. It might have been. Had his own prodigal son not been waiting for her atop a dark ridge. Greek myth indeed. The thing about circles, she thought, is they have no end.

"Good night."

"Good night," Sky managed. Her mouth was dry, and her voice sounded croaked, ugly. But Jake didn't seem to notice as he glided out the door into the night.

As soon as he was gone, Sky lay back on her bed and curled up. She thought she heard his footsteps fade outside but to be sure she reached over and turned the key on the lamp so that she could hide in darkness. Hot tears ran down her cheeks, even though she didn't think that she was crying so much as just leaking.

The longer she lay there, the more she felt like a fool. She knew she was supposed to feel like a goddess, that that was Jake's game, but she understood now how he could manipulate. She put her face into the coarse thin pillow and let out a shaky exhale. Her mother had been trying to teach her to see this her whole life. The difference between a man that *wants* you, and a man who just wants power over you.

The spring of her senior year of high school, she worked at a local ice cream store. There was a boy who worked with her, Dylan, a fellow senior, who was everything she hated. He was a jock, a football star at her school. He made vulgar jokes and objectified every female customer as soon as she walked out the door. Either he commented on how "she definitely should not be eating ice cream," or he said something like, "I feel like we'd be doing a public service if we just gave that one some fat-free yogurt instead of cookie dough." Or, the worst, he'd speculate on how someone he deemed "hot" would be in bed. Or what he'd like to really put in her mouth besides mint chocolate chip.

Dylan was, without a doubt, vile. But he was also very, very good-looking. Broad shouldered, square-jawed, with big brown eyes and a mop of chocolate curls. So, when he tried to kiss her one night when they were closing, she let him.

But by the next shift they worked together, when he pulled her into the back freezer to kiss her again, she had come to her senses.

He shrugged like he didn't care but then one day—when they were the only ones in the shop—he tried again to kiss her and when she pushed him away, he'd slammed his fist into the ice cream case and left the store, leaving her to close on her own.

The next week, she was walking home from school, and he pulled up beside her in his pickup and apologized. Then he begged her to go for a drive with him. She told him no—what she should have told him when he'd first tried to kiss her.

So he called her a bitch, gunned his engine. The next day at school she realized he'd started a rumor that they'd slept together. That she was "easy." Within two weeks, four new boys asked her out, each one deepening her humiliation. She was sure the kiss she had allowed had opened this door, and it was a regret so raw it hurt her throat.

When, a few weeks later at graduation, they said Dylan's name over the loudspeaker, Sky felt her failure as a space inside her own body.

She was quiet the whole drive home from graduation and declined Edi's offer to take her and Deb out to lunch to celebrate. When they got home, she went to lie down on her bed. Usually Edi left her alone when she was like this, but this time she came up and sat on her bed with her. Edi, Sky remembered now, had thought that Sky was worried about her future, or had just noticed the empty symbolism of a ceremony like that—Edi was never one to want to miss an opportunity to criticize the institution. Sky shook her head and pushed her face into the pillow.

She wanted to get it off her chest, so she told Edi everything. In as little detail as possible. There was a guy, sort of, she knew he wasn't a good guy. Lately he'd become more of an asshole, but he'd always been that so why had she ever let him near her? How could she have been so stupid? Sky didn't cry but hid her hot face again in the pillow. It was painful to articulate all the thoughts that had colonized her mind over the past several days. How they'd rooted down like weeds.

Edi didn't respond right away. She just sat there for a while, and Sky realized she was thinking about what to say.

"You don't have to . . ." She wanted to give her mother an out. To end what had become humiliation. But Edi put her hand on Sky's ankle, as if steadying herself, then she cleared her throat.

"Sky, listen to me. Carefully. It wasn't your fault. Any of it. That guy sounds like a real asshole, and we've all fallen for our share of assholes, trust me. It's part of being a woman. Or probably a person."

Sky turned toward her mother, shifting over onto her side.

"Some men, they want more than just you. More than your body. They want *the you*, the self within you. They want to crumple it like paper." Edi looked down at her own lap as if she'd dropped something there. "And if you let them, they will crush you."

Sky watched her mother's face carefully, but she kept it down, her bony hands now both laid lightly on Sky's legs.

"But the thing is, Sky, no matter what they *do*, you still can't let them have *you*. Ultimately, it's you who decides what they take from you once they've done what they've done. And it's shitty, but you can be a victim, or you can . . ." Edi trailed off and looked out the window. It was open, even though it was unseasonably cool for early June. Not that it ever got that hot in summer.

Sky wanted Edi to say more but she didn't press. She was tired. The two stayed in her room in silence for a while, until Edi left and eventually came back with a full glass of red wine for herself, and a half glass of wine for Sky. "To celebrate," she said, "or forget." Sky sat up in bed, still in her graduation dress, and they'd clinked glasses. Then Edi sat on her bedroom floor, and they talked about what Sky wanted to do before she left for college, what Edi was going to do when she left. "I'll be so sad," Edi had joked, raising her glass. "I'll drink wine alone on the floor of your room every night."

That day, when Edi had talked about "some men," Sky had thought her mother was talking about Phil. Or even the man at the festival they'd ran from years before. The "bad man."

But now she realized her mother might have been talking about Jake, that maybe it had even been him at the festival they'd run from. She remembered her mother covering their faces. Hiding Sky. She sickened a little at the memory.

Jake, the man who just a few moments ago was holding her foot, breathing on her legs. The alpha male with a spell. "Our desire and its circular, inescapable nature is our only true will," Jake had said. Her own desire, she thought again, had always been there, as raw and susceptible as Edi had wanted it to be. Edi, who wanted to both protect her and liberate her. And if she stayed, she might find out if Jake could do the same to her as all the others. The ones she'd be naive to believe herself better than. She inwardly groaned as she heard Jake's voice again in her head then—"the ego is the source of all darkness, of all deception, but especially self-deception."

No, she shouldn't stay. She should leave for Edi, even if she wanted to stay for some long-lost version of herself.

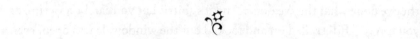

For another hour or more, Sky lay in the dark listening and thinking. She felt like she was a hard tooth in the hot soft mouth of the yurt, of this place. Like she was of the same body, made for the same purpose, but fundamentally different. Losable. She tongued her own teeth, her old habit.

The commune had grown quiet. She heard fewer and fewer human sounds. Voices, laughter, water running in a metal basin somewhere had all faded. It must have been close to midnight. The silence made her thoughts seem larger, made it harder for her to find footing in any action she might take.

Her mind still felt like an MC Escher painting, folding in on itself. She'd have to suppress her perverse curiosity, and even as she knew this, she could half-convince herself that she could stay to learn about herself and her past and her mother, or stay for her mother. But she was afraid of him, Jake. The flashes of malevolence she'd glimpsed when he spoke to Edi.

Though along with fear she felt a longing for her mother that was both very real and unexpected. She would have to leave, she knew that deep down, but it felt a little like pulling off a Band-Aid.

She lay in the dark and once again took deep breaths, trying to remember an exercise Edi had taught her as a child when she needed courage. It was like the exercise to create heat in her body, but in this one, she imagined her body was made of stone, or water. Stone for when she needed strength, resolution, to stand her ground. And water when she needed to be both strong and soft. Flexible yet forceful. These images still came to Sky at the oddest of times, and now she wondered if Edi could have known she'd need something for this moment. Fire, stone, water, sugar—her mother gifting her powers for her own myth.

Her mother.

I help Edi by leaving, she thought. I help by leaving. I help by leaving.

She lay whispering this to herself, trying not to wonder what had happened to her own sense of self since Ned had entered into it, since her life had been upended, since her body had been delivered into this place where all bets of who she was and what she'd do, or not do, were off.

I help by leaving. I leave. I leave, I leave.

When she'd collected herself enough, she rose and without hesitation walked to the door of the yurt and stepped into the night. For the first several feet, she made her way almost on tiptoe from the yurt toward the edge of the commune, expecting to run into Jake, or one of the many figures in white that haunted this oak grove. She imagined them all as actors in a play. A chorus waiting in the wings. A Greek tragedy, she thought, with a silent snort.

Every few steps, as she made her way toward the hill she'd run down earlier, she stopped. Listened. Looked over her shoulder. It was almost disconcerting how quiet it was. The moonlight making the trees into dark figures, the wheat-colored grasses giving the ground a luminous wash, like she was in the negative of a photograph.

The night was warm but still Sky felt a chill through her white tunic; the fabric wafted around her body and seemed to glow in the night. She wondered if she should take it off to better hide herself. As it was, she imagined that she, too, looked like a ghost, moving slowly through the oak trees and cringing every time her foot found a dead leaf that crackled loudly. Cringing, and then pausing. Trying not to think about her bare feet or trip over what she couldn't see. She remembered seeing a few nettle plants earlier and now she placed each step carefully, as if testing water, before bearing her full weight down.

She walked for over an hour.

Not long after the lights and noise of the Ashram were behind her, she crossed the dry creek bed and began to climb. Her eyes were well-adjusted and the moon brighter now, but at times she scrambled up the steep hill using her hands to steady her, to help her know the ground. She grew less worried about noise and found herself whispering to herself at times, "it's okay, it's okay." She tried not to think about the pain in her feet or about getting lost; it seemed inevitable to her that if she went up, she would hit the road that she and Ryan had driven up. Unless she somehow ended up above it, in which case she'd have to wait until dawn to look for the house, the highway. If she reached the ridgetop and could look down the valley, toward the sea, she'd know to stop and wait.

It was a clear night, but Sky didn't stop to see what constellations had risen.

She heard a band of coyotes somewhere in the gulch above the Ashram. Screaming in delight at some fresh kill. She was glad she knew their eerie sounds from nights at Roger's place, glad of the familiarity.

The night sky was now coming through the oaks on the hill above her, a sign that the ridgetop was near, and she sighed. The temperature had dropped significantly and even though she was warm from climbing uphill, she knew she would be cold if she had to stop and wait out the night under some tree. She could sense her feet were bleeding in a few places, that kind of bright-red pain came from her baby toe on one foot, and the inside of her other foot. Once she had fallen forward, and both palms were raw, too. A knee stung. But she wasn't tired. Not at all. She'd keep going, keep going.

And then there it was. An immediate flatness: gravel road. She could feel the sharp and tiny stones immediately in contrast to the dusty brush she'd just walked out of. This had to be it, the middle of the three forks in the road.

Walking up it would lead her to the house, and Ryan, if he was still there. Sky hadn't thought of that question. Would he have waited for her all day there? Or gone elsewhere? He mentioned people to see who would explain things—who were they? Were they in the house? Would they help her?

Her other choice was to walk down and try to get to the highway, but she'd chance running into someone from the Ashram on the main road they shared before the fork. If she made it to the highway, she might be able to flag down a car. But it was well after midnight; she was wearing a dirty white tunic and no underwear, no bra, no shoes. That seemed dangerous too. Anyone could stop. Anyone could pick her up. She didn't think even Edi would hitchhike in the middle of the night half-naked.

Edi had told her to find Ryan. Sky put her fingernails in her mouth and bit for a moment. She hadn't done that in years, but it felt good, biting hard on a part of her she couldn't feel. An owl hooted, and something rustled in the brush on the other side of the road. She should get walking one way or the other.

She stepped out onto the road, wincing at the stones, looking down one more time before sighing and taking a step uphill.

She took a step, then another, moving slow on the sharp rocks.

And then something was upon her.

At first, she thought an animal had pounced out from the other side of the road, a dark flash in her periphery leaping toward her. She'd been trying not to think about the predator of these parts, the mountain lion that Jake had mentioned. They didn't really prey on humans normally, she had thought, but now she instinctively ducked her head, trying to protect her neck.

But it was a human hand on her arm. Human smell. Breath. A human whisper, sssssshhhh, after she audibly yelped. Sssshhh.

She quivered and gasped, trying to back away.

"Sky, ssshhh. It's me, I'm not going to hurt you. You are safe now."

She knew that voice. Ryan.

She stopped and breathed hard, trying not to let escape a half-choked scream.

"Sssshhh, you're safe."

She couldn't catch her breath. He stepped away.

"I'm not going to hurt you."

"You scared me," she said between pants. She bent forward. "Jesus . . ."

Her heart was beating fast. She felt the need to sit down. "What the hell is wrong with you?"

Ryan stepped forward and wrapped his arms around her, cautiously. She let his grip hold her body weight up and sagged into him.

Her mother had said to find him. He had to be safe. Breathe, she told herself, but her whole body still shook.

"Orion," she whispered between breaths, not to him at all. To her mother, to herself, she said it. Her brain connecting dots like stars in all those stupid constellations that had circled around her her whole life, bringing her to this moment.

But still he answered, "I'm here." He pulled her close into a hug, as if they had known each other for years. They had, Sky realized.

"I'm sorry I scared you." He held her like that until her breath calmed. "I'm sorry for everything." Tears ran silently down her cheeks, but she wasn't sure why.

Orion, from the Ashram. Orion, who had so much to answer for. She looked up at him but didn't pull away. She could barely see his face in the dark, but knew it was only inches from hers.

His lips felt warm on hers.

They kissed for a long minute before she pulled away. It was a good kiss, Sky thought, but it was as if she'd just watched it from deep within herself.

Neither of them said anything, Sky just put her head back into his chest and let him put his hand on her head. Then she laughed a little. It sounded bitter and she wasn't sure why it came out that way. She didn't know why she'd let him kiss her either. But at the same time, she knew exactly why. *We are all just animals.* She could still hear Jake's voice.

Herself at this point, she thought, was an abstraction.

"What are you laughing at?" Ryan whispered.

Sky wanted to laugh again and did, just a little. She felt crazy and wanted to laugh more but stopped herself.

"What? Are you okay? What he'd do to you?"

"I don't know, nothing, he did nothing, it's just . . ." Sky pulled away, feeling the cold of the night for the first time. "I mean, I do know . . . I mean, what the fuck is going on? Who are you? And were you just waiting in the bushes for me? How'd you know where I'd be?"

Ryan chuckled; his nervous laugh was back. "Yeah, it's pretty fucked up, the way we got started off." He put his hand on her back and took a step uphill. "But we should get out of this cold, and away, in case anyone starts looking for you."

"Anyone, like Jake?"

"Yeah, like Jake. Though that guy rarely does his own dirty work."

Ryan started to walk, and Sky started too, but slowly—her feet wanting to protect themselves, recoiling at each step. A coyote screamed again, like a woman, down in the gulch and Sky wondered briefly if it *was* a woman screaming. Would Edi suffer her departure? She was about to ask Ryan if they could go get her but before she could, he stopped and squatted down to see her feet.

"Shit, you don't have shoes on. I mean, shit, of course you wouldn't."

Ryan, she thought in the dark, was wearing some kind of black sweat suit.

"And you are probably freezing in that thing. Shit, sorry." He pulled his sweatshirt over his head and handed it to Sky.

She was going to hesitate; it was a little too paternal. Plus, the fog of the day was coming back to her. She remembered the handcuffs he'd put on her. But she was cold, and the sweatshirt was warm with his heat. And they had just kissed. And she would like to feel less naked. She pulled it over her head.

Ryan spoke again, but not to her and Sky realized he'd pulled some kind of walkie-talkie out of his pocket.

"Hey, it's me. I found her."

There was a crackling of static, but Sky didn't hear the response.

A wave of fear struck her like nausea. What if he really did belong to Jake? What if he took her right back there? What would Jake do to her?

"She's fine, we're on the road about a half mile down. Got a problem though, she doesn't have shoes."

Another pause, static but no voices. Sky realized that Ryan must have an earpiece.

"Yeah, can you drive the car down? No headlights, though."

Ryan listened for a moment and then put the radio away.

"Someone's coming. My partner Mike. Be here in a few. Your feet must be in rough shape after that climb."

"It was a lot faster going down there." She folded her arms across her chest instinctively and was glad Ryan couldn't see her face. It was hard to know whether to laugh, or swear, or yell, and she wanted privacy as all those emotions ran through her.

They stood in the silence, in the dark, waiting for the black shape of a car to find them.

When they heard tires on the road, Sky turned to him. "Partner?"

"Yeah, we've been working with SF and Carmel police on this, among others," Ryan answered.

"We?"

"The FBI." Before she could respond, he added, "I'm sorry, Sky," and his voice sounded different. Higher pitched. "I should have told you every-thing this morning. I'll tell you as soon as you are ready, now, when we get back to the house, or in the morning, or whenever. I shouldn't have . . ."

His voice trailed off as they heard the sound of wheels on the loose gravel. They could see red lights glowing from the back of a sedan, but no headlights. Sky stepped to the side of the road, sure the driver, Mike or whoever, wouldn't see them even though he drove at a crawl. Ryan reached out and tapped at the car's hood and it stopped abruptly. He opened the door for Sky, and then climbed into the back seat with her.

The car was warm, and the seats so comfortable Sky almost wanted to softly moan as she sat down. A man's head turned around from the front seat.

"Hey there," he said. "I'm Mike. I work with Ryan."

She nodded.

"Better back up," Ryan said.

"What, you don't want me to go turn around in Bridger's driveway? No shit, thanks."

Ryan didn't say anything. He sat close to Sky, and she didn't move away. She wasn't sure why not. Too tired, maybe. His warmth felt too good.

She realized now the way the cold had permeated her skin, which was wet with sweat from her climb, and now icy to the touch.

They backed up the hill, all the way to the house Sky had barely glanced at before running away. Away to find her mother. There appeared to be no lights on as the car came to a stop in the driveway and they got out. But when Mike opened the large oak door, she saw a well-lit space.

Inside was a beautiful wood room you stepped down into, blackout shades over huge windows, and simple Danish furniture. In the center of the large room was a table covered in papers, and at least a few photographs, all laid out like a map. There was a photo of her mother, from the same era as the picture that Marguerite had given her. But she wasn't pregnant in this one. She was smiling and pretty, stunning, really, neck hooked under the arm of a younger Jake. He was turned toward her, kissing her head, but looking at the camera. They looked like a beautiful couple who knew their beauty better than anyone.

Sky turned to see Mike and Ryan looking at her. Mike was middle-aged, she saw now, and wearing a black sweat suit with an FBI logo on the breast. He had salt and pepper hair, a five o'clock shadow, and his posture was straight and stiff. Mike also seemed to be sizing her up, but Ryan was looking down.

"Your feet."

She looked down and saw that both feet were black, smeared with dirt and blood. One foot had left a trail of blood blots the size of rose petals on the wood floor as she had walked in.

She saw it but didn't care as she looked back at the photograph, surrounded by others, too.

She turned to them again. "What is this place?"

"It's a luxury vacation home," Mike answered. "But right now, it's also our headquarters. Owners are pretty invested in us getting them some new neighbors, so they are happy to oblige."

"Whose headquarters? For what?" Sky turned back to the table. She knew what they would say. All those pictures of Jake.

"We are going to get him, Sky." Ryan stepped next to her. Standing by her side and looking down at the table, he gestured to the photo that had caught her attention. "And your mother is helping us."

Sky woke the next morning wrapped tightly in the sheets she had briefly savored the night before, before falling into a hard and heavy and dreamless sleep. She fought the confines of the bedding and for a moment panicked before she remembered where she was. Remembered what had happened.

Her mother. She'd found her mother. The bathing. Jake. Waiting in the yurt. The boy. The meditation. Jake. Rain. And Jake again. His weird spell. Ryan as predator, Ryan as protector.

Her bones thrummed with all of it. The cuffs, the breathing ceremony, the climb. She felt an acute sense of shame but wasn't sure why. Jake's hands on her feet, his mouth at her thigh; it was as if she had been drunk.

She also felt a sense of anger growing. At her mother, herself, everything, everyone.

She was afraid to move and lay still thinking about what she had read on the internet about cults when she had researched them for hours a few nights before. She'd read that they indoctrinated followers through *isolation*, like not allowing Sky to go to dinner. They also used *deception*, like not allowing Sky, or even other followers, to see the crimes they committed. They made, she'd read, their followers have a distorted view of the outside world—Jake's story about the little girl in Florida as the only story they knew about the world. None of the good. And cults made their people *dependent* on them. None of those people she met, Sky realized, probably even had bank accounts. They probably had nowhere else to go. And here's this leader, this caretaker, this man who is seductive and espouses love for all. No wonder they look away from what they don't want to see. Sky remembered muting the voice inside her own head as Jake touched her. Her own desire to be desired by a man with his power.

She felt nauseous at this memory and let herself escape again, replaying the run up the ridge, and right on cue she felt her wounded feet awaken under the sheets. The pain raw. She remembered Ryan finding her. That kiss. Good lord, she'd have to think about that later. Then coming into this surreal house.

Last night—after she'd stood for a few minutes looking at the table, spread with photographs of her mother, Jake, one of Deb even—Mike had taken charge. He'd taken Sky's arm and led her to the edge of an oval bathtub with little jars of beige bath salts lining the edge. He'd sat her there so she could wash her feet, handing her a small hotel soap wrapped like a present. He'd told her to clean well—Don't want to get infected, he'd said, and she'd heard a slight twang. Maybe from Texas. He'd left her there and come back with a large black T-shirt and a pair of running shorts, both FBI logoed but that looked new.

"You need to sleep, as do we. In the morning, I can debrief you fully." Mike handed her a burgundy towel, dark enough to hide any blood. Ryan appeared in the bathroom door with a first aid kit.

Sky wanted to protest but she realized she could barely see straight. The bright light of the bathroom felt like a drug, she was so tired.

Mike stood up and crossed his arms. "Do I need to put a watch on you, or will you stay here and stay away from the Ashram?"

Sky shook her head.

"Listen, I'm not messing around, I need verbal confirmation from you . . ."

"Mike . . ." Ryan spoke from the doorway, he also looked exhausted.

"It's okay," Sky said. "I'll stay. I promise, I won't run." She caught Ryan's glance in the bathroom mirror. His blue eyes like dabs of paint. A sense of vertigo as she remembered Jake's.

"Good." Mike folded his arms and looked satisfied.

"But will my mother be safe? Will Jake punish her when he finds out I'm gone?"

Mike turned and looked at Ryan briefly, and then turned back to Sky. "He will not."

"But how can you be sure? Should we try to go get her?" Sky pressed the towel around one foot.

"He won't hurt her because he needs her."

Sky looked again in the mirror at Ryan, and he nodded.

"Again, more in the morning, I'll let Agent James show you where you'll sleep, good night."

And he left.

Ryan, then, had sat on the toilet's closed lid, not far from where she sat on the bathtub ledge. She looked up at him and thought briefly of that kiss, and her skin flushed. A brief flash of the Ashram, the sensuality of the place, invaded her mind and she closed her eyes. Jake. She hadn't really wanted him, she *thought* she knew. Or had she? There was something there, in those oaks, that drew her. Maybe she should have stayed at least one night. She'd never quite been daring enough, and Edi had always chided her for this. But Edi was probably glad for once that Sky didn't tempt fate. Maybe she would have if she had known that safety in the form of a luxury home was this close.

Ryan opened the red plastic of the first aid box and took out a roll of gauze and some tape. Sky looked down at her feet in the empty bathtub— only one was still leaking a missive of red down the drain. She picked her foot up, saw a gash open and red like a fish's mouth on the side of the arch. She didn't feel it at all. It was like she was holding someone else's foot in her hand. She thought again of Jake's thumb running along the arch where it was now split open. As if he had willed it.

"Does it hurt?" Ryan asked.

"No," Sky said, realizing her brain wasn't registering the pain it should be, and took the roll from him. She unwrapped it carefully and began wrapping it around her foot. A few layers in she stopped, and let Ryan lean over with dull scissors to cut the gauze, leaving a messy and frayed seam. He then handed her a piece of tape that he'd torn off the roll with his teeth, and she taped it while he pulled the wrap tight.

Then, wordlessly, he'd helped her up and walked her down the hall to an opulent bedroom, with a large white bed in the center of a beautiful wooden alcove. He'd brought the clothes from Mike and placed them on the bed. Then he stood in front of her for a minute. She looked at him and down to the floor. She was too tired to address anything between them. Any attraction.

"I'm sorry, Sky." Ryan's voice almost sounded like it would crack. "It's just, I've known you for so long. I've been wanting you to know me too, for so long, and to make sure you stayed safe. But I went about it the wrong way."

Sky nodded; she didn't want to give him anything just yet. She pulled her hair to one side of her neck; she could still smell the coconut oil from her skin on the ends of it. She sat down on the bed.

"You need sleep," Ryan said, and she could tell it took all he had not to touch her in some way, not to give her another little kiss on the forehead. His restraint was attractive to Sky, but the feeling now was like a distant figure in a crowd, barely discernible through the white noise her brain had become.

She'd fallen back on the pillow, intending to stay awake, but did not remember being able to even for a moment.

Now light streamed through the curtains in bright sharp lines, and as she became more fully awake, a hard ball of anxiety started to grow within her. Her mother. Edi. She had to get her. She had to tell Liz where she was. Deb. A brief flash of work ran through her mind. Jerry. Ned. The blank page of drafting paper with only one right angle drawn on it—the beginning of a fence line as far as she'd gotten when Ned walked into the office almost a week ago. It felt like it had been years.

She sat up slowly, expecting the pounding head she got. She needed water. Briefly, she wished she had a bra and underwear to slip on under the oversized black clothes. She felt like a hospital patient as it was.

When she gathered enough strength, she stood up, dressed, and opened the door. Ryan was visible down the hall in the great room, and he jumped up when he saw her. He'd been waiting for her to wake up, she realized. She limped down the hall.

"What time is it?"

"About eight thirty. Coffee? Mike's on a run."

Sky nodded and made her way to a blue velvet sectional. The room opened to large windows facing west, away from the Ashram, and the blinds were open. The view framed golden hills and clouds and a glimpse of a silver line on the horizon to the west. The ocean. She remembered how she smelled it yesterday in handcuffs.

"Do you have my phone?" Sky asked as Ryan handed her a thick white mug of coffee.

"Yes, I . . ."

"Can I have it?"

"Yes, but I . . ." He pulled it out of his back pocket. It was on its final battery bar. "I did text Liz to tell her where you were. She called about thirty times yesterday. I was worried she was going to come down here . . ."

Sky felt a flush of irritation at Ryan even as she knew he was probably right, she would have come down. That's what she had hung her hope on yesterday when she thought Ryan was kidnapping her. That Liz would come down to the Ashram.

She scrolled through her text messages.

Where are you?

Seriously, call me?

I'm coming over.

Sky, call me. Called Deb. She told me she told you about your mom and Phil and my role in that. I'm sorry. But I'll explain it. Call me.

I'm really worried.

If you don't call or message, I'm calling the police.

And then, Ryan's response to this, pretending to be her: *Something came up. Went to check it out. All is fine. Will call tomorrow.*

Sky put her phone on the coffee table in front of her and rubbed her brow with her fingers. She hadn't touched the coffee yet, but now brought it to her lips.

Ryan had been standing but now took the opposite chair. "I'm sorry, I was trying to protect you and Edi. If Liz had shown up there while you were there. Well, it could have been disastrous."

"Why, exactly, could it have been disastrous? What the hell is going on?" Sky heard the edge in her voice from the other side of her headache.

Ryan looked at her with a blank face, then stood up and walked to the kitchen behind him. She refused to apologize while she heard him, dishes clanking.

He reappeared with a plate, thick and white like the mug. A banana, a bagel with an individual size tub of cream cheese, and a plastic knife. He set it on the table in front of her.

"When you are ready, I'll tell you everything."

Sky put her coffee down. "I'm ready." She folded her arms.

Ryan sat in his chair across from her and looked at the plate of food. He kept his eyes there as he began to speak, his tone even and steady.

"I was born in the Ashram, the first baby. Jake is my father. My mother was a woman named Star, who died when I was a kid. She had a bacterial infection, and Jake refused to let her go to a doctor. Convinced these herbal concoctions he made would cure her. But instead, they killed her. I learned this later of course—I was only five when she died. Around the time she died, your mother, who had always been like a mother to me, had you. I adored you. I held you for long hours while your mother worked or spent time with your father. Your mother let me sleep with her and your family and she watched out for me. And then your father died in what at the time I thought was an accident, when you were still just a baby, and a while after that she took you and left. It was devastating for me, and for a long time I hated Edi for abandoning me. I became angrier and angrier. I hated Jake too, for what had happened to my mother and for Edi leaving. When I was fifteen, all this anger came to a head, and I exploded at him. Went after him. He'd just given one of his mandatory group preaches on peace and love and I just . . . lost it. The next morning, one of the women drove me to the Monterey bus station. She left me with some old clothes and a fifty-dollar bill.

"As if I knew anything about money." Ryan chuckled.

"The next years were pretty dark, but eventually I met a woman who actually cared at a youth homeless shelter in San Francisco. Carol was her name. She helped me study for the GED and enroll in community college. She let me move in with her for a while. After a year of stability, and some college credits, I was able to get into SF State. I went into their psychology program, and then criminology. All this time I started to believe I could actually do something about Jake. Stop him from doing what he was doing."

Ryan stopped and looked up from Sky's plate. "You should eat."

Sky didn't move but just looked at him, waiting.

"It takes a long time to get where you want to be, and after getting a job at the FBI, and doing lots of paperwork, I finally convinced a supervisor to let me investigate Jake Bridger. I didn't reveal my background at the time, which later almost cost me my job, but by the time they found that out, they also knew who Jake was, what he was up to, and knew that they could use me as an asset.

"It's unclear whether I'll still have a job once we arrest him, but I don't care." Ryan sighed. Sky reached forward to pick up her coffee, mostly for the warmth of the mug in her hand.

"We have worked on the case for a few years now. Two years ago, we sent in an agent posing as a new recruit, who is still there, and we have learned a lot. We have evidence of statutory rape, and sexual assault. And our smoking gun has been that we have mounting evidence of Jake's sex-trafficking scheme. But he's very careful, using only his weakest followers as victims; only he and they know the details and the identity of clients. Not even your mother was originally aware that this was the cult's main source of income. So, our new recruit wasn't getting far—it takes years for Jake to trust someone like that. We had hit a wall."

"Whoa, whoa, wait. Sex trafficking?" Sky leaned forward and put her coffee back down on the table.

"Yes, sex-trafficking schemes and cults actually have a lot in common. Isolated, powerless victims, manipulation, groupthink, etc."

Sky shook her head. She wondered briefly whether the agent was a man or woman that she'd seen in the Ashram.

"Super dark stuff. But anyway, Jake, it appears, sends some young women out to work. Most of them are recruits who were already on the street, a few we think are young girls or women born in the cult and groomed for special clients. The rest of the Ashram thinks they are housekeepers or maids for rich folks at their beach houses for the week, but really, they are *very* discreet prostitutes in a sex-trafficking market for the wealthy."

Sky had heard about these schemes in the news at least, the ones for the very rich.

"And to clarify, Jake is in control, but he has very little direct contact with the clients himself. He's smart. It would take someone very close to him to be able to tie him to all of this. Like I said, we had hit a wall.

"But one thing we did learn of importance." Ryan cleared his throat. "Jake, even after more than twenty years, has remained mildly obsessed with your mother. He's even used her as a prophecy. He's told his followers, it seems, for decades now, that your mother, called *Mother* there, will return and lead them to a new level of 'lightness.'

"We wondered how we could use that knowledge. And then about a year ago, the agency became concerned, on what we call 'high alert,' because Jake, when he preached about the future of the cult, began using language like 'shedding earthly forms.' We clearly don't want another Jonestown, so we knew we needed to find someone that Jake would allow in his inner circle so we could get the evidence we needed to make a move against him." Ryan stopped and sighed, looking up for the first time to meet Sky's eyes before clearing his throat again and going on. "It's also why we set up here, to be close.

"Contacting your mother was a risk, for obvious reasons. We didn't know if she might be still in touch with Jake somehow. She wasn't. We also didn't know if her loyalty would extend to him. So we interrogated her. We grilled her. We brought her in, Sky, and we scared the shit out of her."

Ryan's face looked pained.

"I couldn't talk to her at first, in case she recognized me. But I watched the whole interview through the glass. And what we learned was that she hates Jake Bridger almost as much as I do. The agent explained to her the mythos surrounding her at the Ashram. When she learned this, her face just sort of fell. Like she thought she'd gotten out but really, all this time, Jake had still been using her.

"She left FBI headquarters shortly after we told her that, saying she didn't want anything to do with any of this.

"I should have left it maybe, but I'd already risked everything I'd worked for. I couldn't. I went to your mother's house. This was back in December. She was out. I waited on the front porch. When she came home and saw another agent was there, she started cursing at me to go away, but then I told her my name. My full name. Orion James Bridger. She started crying then, with a grocery tote bag still in her hand, but she led me into the house, into your kitchen. We talked that night for hours. The bag of groceries just sitting on the counter. She kept saying how bad she'd felt, how hard it was to leave me there. How the image of me, a child in white standing in the road after she'd kissed me goodbye, haunted her daily."

Sky thought briefly of the boy who'd come to her in her yurt. She put her head in her hands. So, this was another ghost her mother had lived with.

"But, she said, she knew if she took me, his firstborn son, Jake would never rest until she was found. She also told me two things I didn't know. First, that soon after you were born, before she was fully healed, Jake raped her for the first time. When it was over, he said to her, 'I can't wait until that girl of yours is old enough.'" Ryan's voice pinched at this and he paused, avoiding Sky's gaze.

"She told him he was sick, and he said, 'No, I'm not. Why do you think I never let you get pregnant by me? I wouldn't fuck my own child. And you and Mitch made a beautiful girl.'

"Your mother said it was like watching a mask fall off. She saw who he really was. She had seen glimpses, but now she knew. She lay on the floor of his house crying, until your father came to find her. She told him everything. He wanted to confront Jake, but your mother wouldn't let him. He wanted to kill him. Your mother told him to stay with her, but that night she awoke in the yurt and he wasn't there. She was sleeping next to you and me, and Mitch was gone. She was so afraid, she said, but he came back the next morning, his face gray. She knew he'd done something or found something out. But he wouldn't say, he was very quiet. I personally think this was the moment your parents finally began to realize what Jake was doing, the pimping. Over the following months, your mother told me, they quietly began to plan an escape. They had nothing to their name. They needed someone that would help. Your mother contacted Marguerite, wrote her letters.

"But then, when you were about a year old, Jake made Mitch stand watch at night for a mountain lion. She's convinced, your mother, that there was never any lion. That Jake killed a goat to have a reason to get them both out at night, Jake armed. On the third cold night, she woke to the sound of a gunshot and knew. Knew what he'd done. He'd killed your father. He dragged his body into Edi's yurt and told her he was sorry. Jake said it was an accident, that he'd thought Mitch was the lion. He even made a joke, your mother said, about Hercules and the lion. His damn Greek myths, she said.

"I remember that night." Ryan wiped his nose with the back of his hand, even though his eyes were dry.

"Your mother said Jake went into a deep 'mourning' period where he spoke to no one. Except, your mother told me, to her. He came to her one night. I remember that night too. He forced himself on her. Told her he'd kill her if she tried to run away. Edi told me all of this in her kitchen, but this last part she didn't have to. I remembered waking to the sound of her screaming, crying, him over her. I picked you up and took you outside to wait until he left."

"You mean he raped her again, that's what you mean by forced himself on her?" Sky heard the aggression in her voice as if someone else was talking. She knew what Ryan meant. She wasn't sure why she wanted him to say the word "rape" again, why she needed him to acknowledge the more violent terminology. Maybe to distinguish between what Ned had done to her and what Jake had done to her mother.

Ryan nodded and looked down at the floor like he was looking through it. Sky wrapped her own arms around herself. *Edi*, she thought.

"It took her another year and a half to get the courage to leave. And when she did, she couldn't take me, and she couldn't look back."

Ryan's eyes met Sky's, and he swallowed so that Sky could see his Adam's apple move.

"That night, at her house, when she told me all this . . . I forgave her everything. But I didn't tell her that. I told her she could make it up to me by helping me bring him down." He cleared his throat, looked down at his hands. When he looked up again, Sky could see his exhaustion, and she realized he was wearing the same thing as last night. He'd stayed up all night, watching. Keeping her here, she wondered, or protecting her. Or both.

"It took a few more visits, but finally she agreed. She said it was her chance to make things right, to make it up to all the women whose lives he'd ruined, some of whom she'd recruited for him. We had her contact Jake by letter, telling him she was interested in what he was doing now, how the world they'd built together was doing. We coached her on what to say, what would draw out a megalomaniac like him. He asked her if he could come visit her. At first, she didn't want him anywhere near her house, but we told her she had to earn Jake's trust. She was so worried that he'd find you, or that you would find him. She wanted to protect you from all this.

"So he began making visits to her house, always with a few of his most trusted followers. He began encouraging her to come back, to make a new life with them. But he also made it clear that this time, he would be in complete control. He started testing your mother, with little insults. We coached her again, told her that she had to submit entirely in order to get him where we wanted him. I thought she was going to quit on us a few times. Those were long weeks. I watched her struggle and felt terrible, especially after watching her break up with Roger, pick a fight with Deb. We didn't tell her to do those things, but she didn't want to just disappear on them. She told me she wanted to give them an avenue through which to forget her, write her off. But it was taxing, I could tell. But then she would see Jake again, he'd come for a visit, talk about new children and recruits in the Ashram and her desire to destroy him would become again almost visceral for her. Once, after he left her house, she called me and said, 'He's arrogant, thinks he can get away with anything, and there are currently fifteen children living at the Ashram, all of whom are in danger. I'm going to get this son of a bitch, for you and for me.' So your mother was on board except for one thing."

Ryan paused and Sky waited. "You," he finally said, looking at her feet.

Sky barely heard him. Her stomach was knotted. Her poor mother. Edi's childlike behavior, her flashes of anger, her almost aggressive sexuality—it all seemed natural in the context of this horrific story.

"She didn't want to leave you. Hadn't told you anything and didn't want you finding out. But she was also convinced you didn't need her. That you wouldn't look for her long. That you'd figure she'd flaked on you again."

Sky scoffed—this was so typical of Edi. To not really think other people needed her, or loved her, and if she did, to grossly underestimate them.

But as soon as she thought this, she wondered what would have happened if Ned hadn't assaulted her. She would have been busier at work. She wouldn't have made time to go to the police station last Friday, would have left it for this week. Would have given her mother a few more days to turn up. And if Ryan hadn't been there to suggest Marguerite, she wouldn't have talked to her. Would never have known about the cult, would never have become intrigued. The past few days, if she was honest with herself, she'd been looking just as much for her own past, and her father, as she'd been looking for Edi.

But Ryan took her scoff at face value and nodded in agreement. "I know, I didn't believe that either, which was why we were working with the local police in case you reported it.

"We were," Ryan admitted, "keeping an eye on you."

Sky remembered the receptionist and the way she'd paused when she'd heard Edi's name. The way she'd picked up the phone.

"And why I sent you to your grandmother—you needed someone. It was also"—Ryan paused—"why I tried to get you to think she might be gone for good . . ."

Sky's mind flashed to the blood she'd imagined in her mother's house. She felt a flush of anger. "Why the blood? What was that from?"

"It was an old red wine stain, it turns out. Just was in a convenient spot and the color was similar . . . I'm sorry."

Sky suddenly remembered her mother saying that she would drink wine alone on Sky's bedroom floor after she'd left for college. The memory of her mother saying it, and the fact that she may have really done it, was distantly funny to Sky. But she was too distracted to laugh. "Why would you want me to think she was dead?"

"Because, Sky, if you hadn't pursued all this, found her here, she would have been just gone. Who knows for how long."

"What do you mean?" Sky's skin cinched tighter. Ryan leaned forward, she thought he might reach out and touch her knee. She wasn't sure if she would like it if he did.

"She's not coming back, Sky. After she's done here, she'll have to testify and the whole process could take years. She could be in the position to compromise some very powerful people and that's not something they will let go. She's prepared to enter witness relocation, to start a new life. Perhaps permanently, depending on how everything goes. Which reminds me, Mike will have you sign a bunch of confidentiality paperwork."

"No—my mother does a lot of crazy shit, but she wouldn't just leave me like that." Sky shook her head.

Ryan bit his lip. "She would. To protect all those kids from him. To protect you. To end him. To finish what she helped to start. I know that must be hard to hear, but it's true."

Sky found she couldn't swallow. She felt the heat behind her eyes and pressed her fingers into them. She heard Ryan shift from the chair across from her to the couch next to her. Felt his weight as he sat down. She pressed her eyes harder, until she saw slivers of light.

What was worse, she wondered, that she might have thought her mother gone for good, murdered, or that she knew her mother was alive but would willingly let her own daughter suffer by thinking her mother was dead?

She felt such an intense pressure in her jaw she wanted to scream. Ryan's weight next to her also made her want to scream. Not at him, but then again maybe at him, too. But she also wanted him to keep talking;

she wanted to hear it all. Needed to. She took a deep breath in—this calming ritual now ruined, even, by the memory of the meditation in the Ashram. The parts of herself she'd let out in that moment.

She heard Ryan's voice as if from far away.

"But now you are here. Because the one mistake I made was that I didn't think Marguerite would tell you about the cult." Ryan's voice dropped in volume. "But I don't know, maybe I wanted you to know, wanted you to know who I was. Maybe I felt like you deserved to know."

Sky pulled her fingers off her eyes.

"And Sky, your mother didn't just leave. She left a letter in case you didn't accept her 'disappearance.' I have it for you when you are ready."

The light in the window behind Ryan seemed white and unkind. A cloud cover had come, and Sky tried to imagine her mother at the bottom of the hill behind them, listening to Jake, trying to explain where her daughter was this morning. More generally, seducing him to reveal his business, his plans, to speak his own destruction. *A bowl of sugar.* She closed her eyes and she thought of Edi cooing to a man who had raped her. Edi had never been patient, and even as Sky was ripe with anger, she also felt a twinge of admiration for her.

This, she realized, was part of the point. Edi wanting her to be proud—to know she was doing something for someone else, even if it cost her everything. Even if it cost her Sky. Sky, who was really only one chapter of her life.

Ryan stood up and walked to the window. "I might be able to arrange for you to join her in witness relocation, if you want. It's a little riskier, and you'd have to leave everyone, change your career. Make a clean break. But you could be with your mother."

Sky thought about walking away from her life. From the mess with Ned, her bitterness at Liz, and just disappearing. She let out a quaking breath.

They both heard the front door and looked up. Mike walked in from his run, breathing hard. A collar of sweat around the top of his shirt.

"But"—Ryan turned back around to her as if resuming a script for

Mike's benefit—"what we need from you now is to go home and resume life as normal until we arrest Jake. It could be months. We will continue to list your mother as a missing person, and no one can know where she is. Not Deb, not Liz, not Marguerite or Roger. I'll continue to stay in touch with you . . . and give you both real updates and feed you some fake ones for you to tell everyone else."

Mike waved at them and walked into the kitchen. Sky could hear the faucet running.

"This is . . ." Sky lowered her voice. "Ryan, this is crazy. No. No, I can't do this. I can't lie to everyone. I can't leave everyone, I'm not Edi." Sky shook her head and put it again in her hands, she spoke down to the carpet. She felt her whole body start to shake.

"And I can't just go back to work because my boss assaulted me last week—that's why I came into the station when I did, I couldn't go back to work yet. I didn't know . . ." Sky stood up and started to pace, felt heat and salt in the back of her throat, but she ignored the signs of tears like she ignored the gash in her foot.

"Wait, what?" Ryan stood up and took a step toward her, his voice dropping softer, too. "What did he do?"

Sky looked up at him and for the first time since she'd met him, Ryan looked how Sky had felt for days. Blindsided. If it was some other thing that had made him feel this way, she might have enjoyed it. But she was too tired for that.

"He . . . he went after me. I bit him. He tore my shirt . . ." Sky felt these fragments fall from her mouth.

Why was there no language to articulate this? Why did that sense of shame suddenly bloom from within, again?

"Jesus," Ryan said.

But Sky shook her head, she didn't want him making this his own. "Liz helped me talk with my boss's boss, and the next step is to file an official complaint through the Department of Fair Employment, or to make a police report and file charges, I just haven't had the . . ." Sky's voice started to waver again. "It felt like my fault, like I had done something to encourage him, at first. But he keeps calling in the middle of the night . . . I don't know what's going to happen. But I can't go back while he still works there."

She hadn't known this last part for sure until she said it. Her mother might be able to blackmail Phil, to entrap Jake, but she wanted nothing to do with Ned, not even their names on the same police report. She felt her weakness like a small stone nestled under her heart, a discomfort that she felt she'd have to live with always.

"Jesus, Sky, why didn't you, I mean, you thought I was a police officer, why didn't you tell me? Who is this guy? What's his name?"

"I wanted to keep my mind on finding my mother." Sky sighed. And, she thought, now she had learned firsthand what Edi had always tried to tell her: how hard it was to actually *say it aloud* when someone took your agency away, violated you. "His name is Ned."

Ryan had started pacing now, and she could see he was angry. After everything he'd done to try to protect Sky, this situation was out of his control and now she could see his sleepless night fraying his nerves.

"Ryan, it's okay. I'll figure it out. Liz will help me."

Ryan stopped and looked at her like she was a stranger. Finally, he nodded.

"You should eat that breakfast." He pointed to her plate. "I'll drive you back to the city soon—we can't have you gone any longer. You'll have to tell Liz you tried but couldn't find the Ashram. Or couldn't get in the gate. You can't tell her you saw your mother."

Sky nodded. Nothing could surprise her at this point. And she wanted to go home. So, she picked up the bagel, tearing a chunk off. Willing herself to take a bite. It tasted like cotton in her already chalky mouth.

ॐ

The drive back was quiet. Sky wanted to ask if she and Ryan would see each other outside of the reports he'd mentioned earlier. They had a lot to talk about, she thought. But as the drive continued in silence, she wondered if maybe they didn't. She wondered if she had dreamt that kiss, if it would ever happen again. Wondered how she would pretend things were normal, except that her mother was "missing."

As they neared the city, Sky said aloud something that she'd been thinking all day. "I wonder why Jake remained obsessed with my mother."

Ryan looked over at her and let out a gentle laugh. "You don't know?"

Sky shook her head.

"Your mother—and you too, I should say—both have a certain quality to you." Ryan reached over and flipped down the visor in front of her to reveal the little mirror there, smudged with a fingerprint that Sky briefly wondered was her mother's, even though that wouldn't make any sense. Beside the fingerprint, she saw her face, tired.

"I don't know if you can see it," Ryan said, almost bemused, "But I think most people that meet you two would go out of their way to help you. To make you smile. To get you what you want. Something about you both—let's just say you both could start your own cult, any day."

Sky saw immediately that this was true of Edi, how many times had strangers offered to carry a bag, open a door? How many odd jobs had Edi landed by meeting someone at the grocery store? But was it true of Sky? She wasn't so sure.

"I also think," Ryan added, "that her leaving wounded him deeply, that it was like a crack in his power, or maybe just like a bad breakup. I don't think he ever got over his jealousy of your father. I don't think he ever got over *her*."

Sky met her mother's eyes in her own face one more time, then flipped the visor up.

When he dropped her off, she felt like someone had turned her over like a purse and dumped everything out.

"Let me walk you up." Ryan shut off the car.

"No." Sky thought again of that kiss. Jake's hand on her leg. How confused she was. She didn't even want to know what she was and wasn't capable of right now. "I mean, I'm okay."

"Okay. But I'll call you tonight. Don't forget to charge your phone." Sky nodded and put one foot out of the car. He handed her her keys. He must have grabbed them from her kitchen counter yesterday. He smiled at her, a soft smile, and Sky realized what a more relaxed person he seemed now that he'd told her everything. She'd thought him so nervous at first.

Ryan put his hand on her arm. "Wait." He looked at her with his blue, blue eyes and for a moment she did want him to come in. To make her forget everything. But he reached across into the glove box and pulled out a thick envelope with her name on it. Her mother's handwriting.

"Here. I didn't read it."

Sky nodded and took the letter, about to step out.

"Wait, also . . ." Ryan reached into his pocket and pulled out a little brown envelope that was stamped EVIDENCE in faded red ink. He squeezed the edges so it opened and poured her mother's zodiac necklace into his palm. "She left it behind for you, hanging on your softball trophy. I'm sorry I let you think it was left behind by accident. At that point I was . . . fumbling." She took the necklace from his palm, feeling its chain as a grittiness in her fingers. *A circle of animals.*

"I'm sorry," he said, "for a lot of things."

She nodded and stepped out of the car into the cold fog. She didn't look back on her way into the building.

When she got up the stairs and unlocked the door, she didn't feel like the same person who'd last been in her apartment, not at all.

Once inside, she pulled the necklace from her pocket and studied it.

She remembered again learning each sign with fascination as a child. Disappointed she was a ram. She always wanted to be the water bearer, Aquarius. As a teenager, she grew tired of her mother's constant references to astrology and people's signs. Now she looked at the necklace and thought of her mother wearing it all these years. Her mother's own belief then, not just Jake's, that we are pushed and pulled apart by planets, stars, the sun. That our destiny is predetermined. She snorted as she thought of the planets swinging back around, pushing Edi back to the Ashram, pulling her from Sky. Chasing each other, Jake had said.

But for Edi, Sky thought, it wasn't Jake that pulled her back. From what Ryan had said, she had never been able to completely leave the Ashram behind and wouldn't be able to until she made things right.

Edi's circle was one of redemption.

It did explain her choice and, knowing Edi, Sky realized, she would fully believe she'd meet her daughter again sometime. Just as she believed Phil had to be punished, just as Sky and Jake had met again, just as she had met her grandmother. Her mother would believe that all circles loop back, completing themselves differently every time.

She sighed and sat down on her sofa, the necklace still in her palm, where now in the window light she could see that the silver was duller, slightly worn where Sagittarius and Capricorn met. She wondered whether her mother had a habit of fingering her own birth sign, or Sky's. Perhaps both.

She drew a breath in and put it around her neck. She wondered if she, like her mother, would touch it several times a day for the rest of her life. Wear that same spot down.

Then she put the envelope on the kitchen table, where its whiteness seemed to glow. It was the kind of object whose presence would haunt her until she read it, but she couldn't go there yet. She couldn't even look at it, this sign of her mother's abandonment. Even if it was for a good cause. Even if Sky was, technically, an adult.

Maybe later. Right now she just needed to sit still. To gaze at the horizon of grief that awaited her.

In the story of Cassiopeia that her mother told her that night at Earth-Fest, Cassiopeia had been bragging about her daughter Andromeda's beauty, she'd said that she was more beautiful than the sea nymphs. This boasting angered Poseidon, who ravaged the land with water. To appease him, King Cepheus tied Andromeda to a rock near the shore so that she'd drown when the high tide came in. But Orion, or Hercules, saved her and wed her.

Cassiopeia was punished by the gods, then, who hung her in the sky upside down for eternity. And what had happened to the king, she and her mother had wondered that night at EarthFest, the band playing in the background, pot smoke clouding the air. Did he go unpunished?

Years later, Sky had been trying to tell a boyfriend the same story during a campout and he told her she'd gotten it all wrong. That it was Cassiopeia who had been jealous of her daughter's beauty. In her jealousy, she'd tied Andromeda to a rock to drown. But along came Perseus, not Orion or Hercules, to save her, just in time.

Sky had laughed—at the time she thought of course her mother would get it wrong. But in either version, the gist was the same. The mother makes a mistake, the daughter is tied to a rock to await her death, but then is saved, and the mother is punished for all eternity.

It's just whether the mother did it out of spite for her daughter, or pride. Or a kind of careless, reckless love.

In her mother's version, it was pride.

And it turned out, when Sky had looked it up later, that her mother's version was mostly right. Except about Orion. It was Perseus who saved Andromeda.

She wondered now if her mother had made that mistake on purpose, letting the myth be a code for the world that she must have known would someday return for her, the tide she knew would eventually come in.

Hours later, it was dark, and Sky sat on her couch. She'd been too mentally exhausted to move, to shower. She had thought that she'd call Liz and tell her everything. She could trust her; she was good at keeping secrets. Even Edi's, apparently, and she needed a friend in this. But she'd been too numb to do anything. She wanted to go to bed, even though it was only seven o'clock, but first she had to do one thing.

She chewed her lip and her phone buzzed to let her know it was charged.

As she had sat and replayed the past two days in her head, replayed Jake's hand on her foot, his breath, his smell, replayed her own collapse at group meditation, Sunshine and Rain, and the look of fear and determination in her mother's eyes—she saw it all spinning to one resolution. To one thing she *could* do. And she had to do it now, while she was in this state of utter exhaustion. She was afraid if she ate dinner or went to sleep, she'd lose the moment and wake from the dream in which she felt she could do it.

She got up from the couch where she'd sat after coming in the door, still in Ryan's black clothes, still dressed as someone else, and she got her phone off the carpeted floor under the picture window, where she had plugged it in along the wall.

She unplugged the phone and went through her contacts. She hit the call button and turned and stood, feet hip-width apart, facing the window where through the drifting fog she could see the sky turning to a whitish pink, like the bony fade of a seashell.

He answered after one ring.

"Sky, thank god you called, I've been really wanting to talk to you." Ned's voice was hurried, a little desperate. "I think we just had a really big misunderstanding . . ."

"No. Ned, I didn't call you so you could explain. I called so you could listen. So let me talk or I'm hanging up, is that clear?"

Sky listened to her own voice; it was a lower pitch than usual. She felt a cathartic calm and she briefly envisioned all the women in her life. All the stupid ways they had suffered.

Edi.

Liz.

Marguerite.

Deb.

But mostly it was this new version of Edi she was channeling in this moment. *I'm going to destroy him,* she'd said. She remembered years ago, the argument in her mother's kitchen about progress. She remembered Edi's insistence that the patriarchy could only be dismantled in small, personal victories.

Sky felt her body calcify, like petrified wood. As if all the layers of her own past, her mother's past, the anger and frustration and shame and fear and love, too, had finally hardened her to what Edi had always wanted her to be when she needed to be: stone.

So she would do this for her, but for all of them, too.

"You *assaulted* me. You attempted to *rape* me. I know this. You know this. And I will press charges against you. Unless you quit." Sky heard each word enunciated clearly despite the terror she felt she was hiding behind every syllable.

"Come on, Sky, this is . . ."

"No." She pictured herself at seventeen, saying no to Dylan the first time. She pictured telling Jake that he couldn't have her, or her mother.

She saw clearly again the pearly buttons that Ned ripped from her shirt, littering the office floor.

"No," she repeated, to herself, her apartment, as much as to Ned. "No. If you don't quit within the next twenty-four hours, I will make a statement to the police. Lorenzo saw the way my shirt was torn. He will be a witness. My phone records show your drunken calls at 2:00 a.m. We'll destroy you in court."

"You fucking . . ." Sky could hear all the words he said next. She'd heard them all before, on other job sites, from a dozen different encounters with men.

She almost wanted to laugh. As if these words could hurt her.

Use protection, her broken mother had yelled, drunk. *A bad man,* she'd said, waking Sky. *We're safe now,* she'd whispered, driving through the night. The police officer sent to investigate Phil's rape kept asking her mother *what she was wearing,* Marguerite had said. *He forced himself on her,* Ryan had said, how she'd made Ryan say "rape." How he told her, *I carried you outside.*

This last image, Ryan as a child cradling her infant self and carrying her away from the scene of her mother's rape, erased all fear, all hesitation that lingered in her nerves.

Fuck this.

"So it's your call." She spoke over him for the first time ever. Then swallowed. "Call Jerry and tell him you quit within the next twenty-four hours, or have the whole world know what kind of man you are."

And with that she hung up before he could say anything else, before she could undermine herself. She held the phone to her chin for a moment, and while she still stood resolutely, her wounded feet rooting her into her floor, her hands were shaking.

She gently put the phone back on the floor, then looked at it, picked it back up, and switched it to silent. She didn't want to know if he called her back. Not tonight. She tucked her shaking hands into her armpits and went back to the couch.

As she sat, she realized she was fighting back a twitch in her face.

It was, unbelievably, an urge to smile.

She pictured herself having a daughter one day. Whispering to a curly-headed preteen to *Picture a bowl of sugar.*

Lick your finger and put it in the bowl.

Realize it's salt.

And whatever wound he makes in you, rub that salt into it until you scream yourself out of your silence. You are stone, water, fire. Salt.

But not sugar.

The next day, in the first moments of waking, Sky remembered nothing. Her body felt light, and she relished the dream she'd been having. She and her mother were on a beach. They were doing nothing in the dream but "R&R," as Edi liked to say. Listening to waves, lying in the warm sun. It was a happy dream, though Sky had had a perpetual tugging feeling that she had forgotten to do something. But happy still the same.

Only then did Sky fully wake, feel the pain in her feet, and remember. Everything. Her mother, gone to some higher purpose. Rewriting her past. She'd never thought of Edi as a maternal figure, a mothering type. But at the Ashram she was "Mother." Working to protect future children, sacrificing everything, even Sky.

Sky sat up on her elbows and sighed. Her mother was adequate in cults and myth, she thought, but disappointing in suburbia. She wondered what kind of mother she'd have been if they'd stayed in the Ashram. *If they'd stayed.* It was such a heavy thought that Sky had avoided it for the past two days, but now she let herself imagine an Edi with no pressures to conform. A life with Deb as a constant presence. A father figure. She would have felt safe, she thought. Even though she would not have been.

And it's not as if they had escaped entirely. Sky could see now that the world of the Ashram had always been with them—a shadow Sky had felt but just hadn't been able to see, or even imagine. She rolled over and sat up. The sun was starting to edge into her bedroom, a sharp line of light on the floor like it was already trying to cut the day in half.

A before, and an after.

The before, when Sky knew nothing. Persephone, Jake had called her.

Jake had it wrong, she thought now. It turned out Sky was Demeter, and always had been. It was she who spent the last week *looking* for her mother. Her mother the one who'd eaten the bloody seeds Jake offered her so many years ago, forever tying her to that world.

Sky dipped a scraped toe into the white line of sunlight, as if she could disrupt it.

She remembered once when she complained to Liz about something her mother had done. Some slightly inappropriate comment her mother had made to one of Sky's boyfriends. Edi, the being bathed in sexuality. Liz had listened in sympathy, but then she'd said, "You know, I used to think my mom was abusive for spanking me with a wooden spatula. Maybe she was. But then one day, when I was older, she told me how her own mother used to heat up metal baby spoons on the stove, and then press the backs of them into her buttocks. She showed me the scars. After that, I looked at what she'd done with the wooden spatula as resistance, as limitation, as revision, as mercy. As love even."

Sky had listened and nodded, imagining the white-hot pain of those spoons. But now as she stood up for the day, she realized Liz had been trying to get her to understand her own mother. She'd probably known then that Edi was blackmailing Phil, the legacy of the rape, and was trying to get Sky to see *that* as the context for Edi's flirting with Sky's boyfriend. To understand Edi's need to control the men in the room. Safety.

Bowl of sugar.

Sky sighed, blowing air out her chapped lips. So many things to rethink, revisit with this new filter. She walked to the living room and picked up her phone. No calls from Ned, thank goodness. She wished she could call her mother.

She walked back into her bedroom, sat down on her bed, and stared blankly at the digital face of her clock.

Eight a.m. Friday. Just over a week ago, Ned had assaulted her. She hadn't even met Ryan. Hadn't known about the Ashram. Thought she'd never know her grandmother, or her father. She closed the phone and held it to her lips, wondering what the hell she'd do now. Wondering what Ned would do. If she'd made a giant mistake in calling him. *Threatening* him.

Then, as if by some magic, her phone buzzed in her hand.

Jerry.

"Hello." Her voice sounded hoarse.

"Sky, are you okay?" Jerry was kind, but always urgent, always wanting the other person to say something simple like *I'm doing fine.*

This familiarity felt comforting to Sky, so she compiled. Remembering as she did Ryan's plea to her to act normal. Normal like her-mother-was-missing normal.

"I'm okay."

"Good, listen, I know you got a lot going on. But could you come in for a bit today? The reason I'm even asking . . . Well, Ned up and quit. Called late last night. Said he needed to move on. I was surprised—he's not one to stand down and last week he told me you were lying, but Lorenzo backed you up and so I knew it was him that was lying. Threatened to sue me if I fired him. True colors, I guess. And then last night, he calls and quits. But I didn't ask questions—honestly, I was relieved, Sky. But I wanted to call and tell you that." Jerry paused. "And I wanted to say that I'm sorry about what happened and hope it means you'll come back full-time no problem, whenever you are ready. But in the meantime, a couple of clients are on my ass . . . like I said, I know you have a lot going on . . ."

"I'll come in." Sky's voice had cleared. The thought of showering, stopping for her coffee, parking at the office, drawing plans, with no Ned at all, suddenly made her giddy. Just a moment of lightness, the weightlessness of routine, of pretending everything was normal. Maybe she could do that. And maybe she deserved to do that for a day, she thought, as she hung up the phone.

Today, she'd park at her work, and get out of her car right away. Give Lorenzo a hug and get started at the drawing table.

Tonight, she'd tell Liz everything.

And then before bed she'd call Ryan, tell him she'd gone back to work. Tell him that it was okay. They'd check in with each other daily, she knew. They had a well of a relationship to excavate.

Then this weekend, she would call Marguerite, tell her she knew nothing, but suggest they see each other soon, that she wanted to get to know her. She'd tell herself her silence protected Marguerite, and her mother.

And when she was ready, she'd tell Ryan that she'd keep her life, not leave it for any protection program. She'd keep it and think of it always as a gift from her mother. Keep it now that she had the things she'd been waiting for her whole life: her grandmother, a father's name, and a man who'd known her long enough to be a brother.

And she'd save her mother's letter for when she really needed it. When she missed her mother so badly it felt like a flu, because she knew those days would come. Then she'd open the letter, and the photo from her mother's dresser—the one of her mother as a girl with her own father—would fall out.

She'd read the letter and try to understand how this abandonment was the best thing her mother could do. That this grand finale act was what she owed them all. Her chance to redeem herself, to do *one thing right*. To be what was happening to someone, not the someone who things happened to.

Even if it meant that Edi herself would hang upside down forever, lonely in the sky.

The line of sun on Sky's floor was thick now, still sharp, bright.

She sighed. Maybe every daughter feels at one point that her mother is a constellation, an abstraction, she thought. Maybe all mothers ask enormous things of all daughters. Maybe that is another circle, the way mothering goes both ways.

She fingered the zodiac necklace, straightening it after sleep. At least now she knew her place in their circle, their story, she thought. At least her mother hung in the sky not as a punishment but as a sign that Edi had once loved her so deeply, so fiercely, that she'd disappeared.

And with that thought, Sky stood up and stepped right over the sunlight slicing open the floor, and into her after.

Acknowledgments

Deep gratitude is owed to Madison Smartt Bell for his insightful edits and his dedication and enthusiasm for this book from the get-go. Thank you to early readers Robin Yeatman and Lara Ehrlich. Thank you to Kate Gale three times over, and the whole Red Hen Press team, I feel so lucky to be working with such an incredible crew of kind, patient, and smart people. Thank you to Therese Lawless for helping me understand Sky's options, and to her and Jim Sturdevant for hosting us on a research trip. Thank you to Joe Wenderoth, for hosting us in Sonoma County: a memorable location that made it into the book. Thank you to my mom and Aunt Valli for many, many trips to Carmel: it became a natural setting to add.

Thank you as always to my mentors, Melanie Rae Thon, Lance Olsen, and Scott Black. Thank you to Julia Borcherts, and Kaye Publicity, for the continued support.

Thank you to my friends who continually show up at my readings, ask good questions, and remind me that I am so lucky to be a part of an amazing community. Thanks to my family, as always, for their support. In this case, especially my parents, for driving my daughter and me around San Francisco to do research, watching my kids so I could write, and their careful line edits. Thank you to my two amazing children, Ninah and Emile, who are inspiring in their own dedication to creative practice.

Thank you to m, for years of everything.

Biographical Note

Sadie Hoagland is the author of *Strange Children* (Red Hen Press) and *American Grief in Four Stages* (West Virginia University Press), which earned a starred review from *Kirkus Reviews*. Her work has been featured in the *Daily Beast, Salon, Electric Literature, Mid-American Review, Foreword Reviews, Necessary Fiction, Largehearted Boy, South Dakota Review, Passages North, Five Points,* the *Fabulist,* the *South Carolina Review, Writer's Digest, Women Writers, Women's Books,* and elsewhere. She has a PhD in Fiction from the University of Utah and is the recipient of several fellowships. You can visit her online at sadiehoagland. com. She lives with her family in Salt Lake City, Utah.